Andre

Although Andrew was born in the small East Yorkshire town of Goole he has lived in Birmingham for the past 25 years. Having spent most of his working life in the automotive industry he finally picked up the pen when he was approaching his fiftieth birthday… perhaps a subliminal bucket list item of sorts. Other than writing he shares his main interests of live music and walking with his partner, Dee.

Dee Matthews

Dee hails from the Midlands, living near Lichfield for the majority of her life. She works on the early morning shift in a Birmingham casino, leaving the afternoons and evenings free for spending time with family, listening to music, walking, and of course writing. Her other interests include travelling, sewing, and attempting to learn the flute.

Also available by
Andrew Clark & Dee Matthews

The Time Store

Andrew Clark & Dee Matthews

PHELIX

To Paul

Hope you enjoy —

All the best

Andy Clark
&
Dee Matthews.

CLOCK FACE

CLOCK FACE PUBLISHING

Loynells Road, Birmingham B45 9NR
Published by Clock Face 2016

First Published in Great Britain
In 2016 by CLOCK FACE
Copyright © Clark/Matthews 2016
Andrew Clark and Devaney Matthews have asserted their rights
under the Copyright, Design and Patents Act 1988
to be identified as the authors of this work.

A CIP catalogue record for this book
is available from the British Library.

ISBN: 978-0-9930744-2-4

Typeset in 10 / 13 Palatino by CLOCK FACE.

Printed and bound by Short Run Press Limited, Exeter.
Cover Design by Bespokebookcovers.com

For Ronald and Riley.

Acknowledgements.

To Elisabeth Glenister and Freda Matthews, once again, thank you for your input and assistance.

We're also grateful to Mark Trinder, Andy Gough and Chad Harris for their valuable suggestions.

Finally, we'd like to say thank you to all those who bought and read The Time Store. Your support, comments and reviews have encouraged us to continue with our writing.

CHAPTER 1

First Time
Flamsteed Way, London
Sunday 7th September, 1913

Seventeen-year-old Oliver Bradbeer wasn't one for taking risks, far from it, he quite enjoyed his life. If getting hurt wasn't part of his plan, getting killed was certainly to be avoided – no matter what.

During his school years, especially after hitting adolescence, he'd steer clear of playing football wherever possible, and when pushed into a game of cricket by the teachers, he'd be out fielding on the boundary, away from the action. Oliver was far happier to be sitting alone in the corner of Greenwich Park, immersing himself in the world of *Weary Willie and Tired Tim,* his favourite Chips cartoon strip. Either that or, especially if the weather turned, he'd be following his passion and delving into some history books in the local library. He didn't want to be part of any rough and tumble, not even when urged on by his younger cousin, Isaac.

Of course, it wasn't too long before he was tarnished with various monikers; 'sissy', 'sweetie', and more recently 'dilly boy' – whatever that meant. But name-calling was the least of his worries, it was the stones that were quite often pelted in

9

tandem with the verbal insults that hurt the most.

"Who threw it, Ollie?" his mother Jane had asked, as she carefully patted away the now dried blood which had trickled down her son's face.

There was no answer this time – he had, once before. His reward for telling – a good thumping off Bully Bainbridge when he'd found out Oliver had snitched on him. So instead he'd bite his lip, cry for comfort and lock himself away in his father's office.

Oliver knew that both his father, Edward Bradbeer, and his uncle, Philip, had a gift. He knew that they, by using their 'special' bracelets and fancy rings, could travel in time – go places and see things others could only imagine. But he also knew that there were times when his dad would encounter danger, or stare into the face of death.

"Does it not scare you, Father?"

"No, Ollie... No." Edward turned off his desk light, and replaced a fine-tipped graver back into its stand, then using a blood red velvet cloth wiped clean the bracelet he'd just finished. "True time is much scarier – for it's here that we age and it's here that we die."

"So you – we – can't die when we time travel?"

"Not while you're wearing this." Edward passed his son the bracelet. "Now put it on and let's go."

Oliver stared, mesmerised, as the bracelet in his hand shimmered with a faint ethereal white aura. He sensed a warm glow deep within his own inner core as the bracelet's life force sought out its partner – Oliver's signet ring – the one he'd received two days ago on his seventeenth birthday.

Hundreds of times, he'd asked the same question about dying during time travel. Each time his father had assured him that the bracelet, upon sensing no life pulse, would take him to somewhere for rejuvenation – which as far as Oliver was concerned was a magical place up in the north of England, near Harrogate.

Following his father's instructions Oliver placed the bracelet on his left wrist and attempted to fasten the clasp.

"Here, let me help you with that," said Jane, as she entered the office. "They can be a bit fiddly until you're used to them."

"Thanks, Mum."

"There, now off you go. I've laid out some clothes in the Costume Room for you to wear."

Jane waited for Oliver to close the door behind him. "Are you sure about this?" She sighed. "1940… for his first time trip? I mean... Well, you know what I mean."

"I know. But this was his choice… and he'll be fine. I'm going with him." Edward held Jane's hand and tried to reassure his wife.

"Choice? His choice, you say?" Jane turned away. "Why don't you take him to Canada or New Zealand? Anywhere where there isn't a bloody war going on will do. Anywhere other than London."

"It'll do him good. And anyway he'll get to see planes. You know how he's fascinated with flight?"

"German planes – dropping fucking bombs. I'm sure he'll like that!"

11

"JANE," snapped Edward. "There's no need for that language. Oliver chose 1940 – that's where we're going – final."

Jane, feeling defeated, slammed the door on her way out of the office, composed herself and entered the Costume Room.

"You ready?" she asked, looking at her son.

Oliver was wearing a dark blue, short-sleeved shirt with frayed collars, a navy pullover, a pair of grey, knee length shorts, grey socks with a black stripe around the top and a pair of heavily scuffed, once black shoes – all of which had a musty smell. He looked, smiled and nodded a 'yes' to his mother, as he put on a brown coat. It was a bit long in the sleeve for him, almost covering his hands, but at least it stopped just above his knees.

"What's in there?" Oliver pointed to a buff-coloured box which, other than a flat cap, was the only thing remaining on the table of the items his mother had laid out for him.

"A mask. A gas mask – but don't worry, you won't need it."

"Why? Why a gas mask? If I don't need it… then why am I taking it?" Oliver looked concerned. He was scared enough as it was, the thought of his body being ripped apart molecule by molecule and then zapped (as his Uncle Philip would say) in the blink of an eye, twenty-seven years into the future was bad enough – but now he had a gas mask to worry him.

"You have to blend in when you time travel, everyone carries a mask in 1940," replied Jane. She picked up the box and hung it over her son's shoulder. "There… You look the part now. Shall we?"

Oliver looked wistfully up at a centurion's helmet on one of the Costume Room's many shelves, but it was too late to change his mind now – that wouldn't go down well with his father. Giving his mother a brave smile, Oliver picked up his cap and placed it resolutely on his head.

Holding a large green canvas duffle bag, Edward, standing in front of an old wooden door which had an intricate carving of a crest in the upper panel, was waiting for his son to join him. Oliver had been through the door on many occasions with his father and even taken the short fifteen minute walk along the tunnel to the Round Room, from where the Bradbeer family time travelled, but he'd never opened the door before.

"Right. First you need to place your thumb on the pad." Edward pointed to a biometric pad above a door lock, a security device which wouldn't exist for another eighty years outside of Number Five Flamsteed Way. "And then…"

"Yes, Father. I know. I've watched you a thousand times." Oliver, for once feeling confident, rolled back his coat sleeve and placed his right hand upon the carving. "Tempus… Tempus… TEMPUS."

The carved crest immediately lit up with an incandescent light. In the middle there was a crescent moon which was itself in the centre of a clock face, but one with no hands, just numerals. There was an outer circle divided into twelve. Within each segment there were words carved in Latin, the months. Then a final circle divided into four, each quarter having a word inscribed, the seasons – ver, aestas, autumnus, hiems. Oliver gazed momentarily into the shimmering crest. He'd made it change – not his father, and not his uncle… he had, he'd been

13

the one who'd brought it to life. For once Oliver felt strong. Oliver felt powerful.

Then the moons. "Callisto, Hyperion, Rhea, Oberon, Nereid, Ophelia, Sinope." Oliver called them out in turn and as he did so each of the moons brightly shone a different colour of the spectrum. "CHRONOS." The door opened.

As the door closed behind them, father and son stood in the pitch black tunnel. Edward reached into his trench coat pocket and pulled out a torch, not one which ran on dry-cell batteries with a carbon-filament bulb, but a rechargeable LED torch. A torch which could also be brought back to life via good old-fashioned solar power, a torch which he'd bought recently from a car boot sale in late 1990's Croydon.

"Here, carry this," said Edward, giving Oliver the torch. "Let's go."

"Father, have you ever been to 1940 before?" asked Oliver, as they set off walking along the tunnel.

"Yes, once. But not to London. So this is a first for both of us."

"Oh." Oliver pondered on his next question. "Will we be coming here? To Flamsteed Way?"

"No. I thought we'd go north of the river, start off around Shoreditch and then head into the city."

"Will we be gone long? I mean, sometimes you tell me that you've spent a year somewhere – but only seem to be gone for a few hours."

"How long do you want to go for?" Edward asked.

"Don't know really. Hadn't thought."

14

The two Bradbeers didn't say anything for the next ten minutes, the only sounds that could be heard were their own footsteps as they rebounded in echo from the passageway walls and Edward's slight grunt as he shifted the duffle bag he was carrying from one shoulder to the other.

Edward knew that he was about to take his son to London, to The Blitz, to World War II. Of course it was dangerous, that's what he and Jane had been arguing over – but Edward thought that it was about time Oliver grew up and faced his future. He'd had enough of his son shying away from life and burying his head in comic books; a little adventure would do him the world of good.

They continued to walk along the dark, arched limestone passageway and Oliver, deep in gas mask related thought, bounced the torch beam off the walls and onto the gold-coloured line which was inlaid within the terracotta and ochre floor tiles. He pressed down on the switch, flicking the torchlight through its various modes. On – Flash – Constant – Random – Off. If only he could be allowed to take this into Mr Midwinter's science class at school. It would be gold stars and top marks all round, thought Oliver.

"How are you feeling?" Edward disturbed his son's pondering.

"Excited, worried, scared... butterflies," replied Oliver, leaving the torch on constant. "I really don't know what to expect."

"That's understandable. I was pretty much the same when your grandfather took me on my first time trip."

Edward, although not one for showing any tactile emotion, couldn't help himself from giving his son a reassuring shoulder hug. And with that, Oliver, for one brief moment, allowed himself to stop thinking about the contents of the box he was carrying.

"I was just about to come looking for the two of you, thought you might have got lost." A tall man stood up from a brown leather winged armchair and approached Edward and Oliver.

"Uncle Philip," smiled Oliver. "Are you coming with us?"

"No, Ollie. No, I'm not."

"Aw. Go on, Uncle. Please."

Philip gave Oliver a hearty slap on the back, almost causing his cap to dislodge. "Perhaps next time, hey. Your first time trip is special and should be shared with your father. I know I can't wait to take Isaac when he turns seventeen."

Philip and his son Isaac had lived together at The Time Store for the past thirteen years; actually Isaac had never lived anywhere else – and, other than a six month stint living in Cape Town, neither had Philip. Isaac's mother had died during childbirth and for the most Isaac considered Jane to be his mother, a role she happily assumed.

There was an age difference of only a couple of years between Edward and Philip, yet at times it seemed as though there could've been a couple of centuries. Edward, the family man, preferred structure, balance, rules and order – a product of Victorian times if ever there was one. Philip, on the other hand, was a more flamboyant character who loved colour, adventure, spontaneity and a variety of women in his life. He'd have loved to have taken his nephew to sixties London for his first trip – bright lights, music and mini-skirts would be far better than barrage balloons and bombs.

As the three Bradbeers entered the Round Room, the passageway's limestone construction was replaced by a wall of marble on which was sculpted an ornate frieze. Various people from times long past, planets and hourglasses were carved into the polished stone which, apart from the entrance, decorated the entire circumference of the room. The high domed ceiling was painted with a night sky, filled with heavenly constellations, not too dissimilar to a celestial dot-to-dot of stars. It was supported by four scalloped arches which met at the sculpted, round central keystone.

The Round Room had a familiar carving engraved in its entire red granite floor; it was a larger version of the design which appeared on the door Oliver had opened with the Tempus ritual, only this time the moon wasn't in the centre of the clock face. Continuing through the centre of the room, the floor carving and the clock face, as though purposely splitting them all in two, was the gold line which ran down the middle of the passageway; the Prime Meridian.

"Give my regards to Lillian when you see her. And tell Albert he owes me a couple of pints of stout for these," said Philip, handing to his brother a small parcel wrapped in brown paper and tied with string.

"Will do... What have we got here?" asked Edward, shaking the package. "Coffee?"

"Yes... and some chocolate. You know how much Lil

17

adores her chocolate."

Lillian Croll was the licensee of the Kings Arms on Hoxton Street, Shoreditch. Built in the early nineteenth century, the Kings Arms could offer short term accommodation and had been favoured by the Bradbeer family as one of their places of arrival for North London time trips. For the price of a few bars of chocolate and some ground coffee, Edward and Oliver would have a roof over their heads for their first night away.

"Shall we?" instructed Edward as he indicated that Oliver should stand upon the meridian. "It's time."

Oliver tentatively walked to the centre of the Round Room, turned around and placed his left foot to the west of the gold line and his right foot to the east.

"Good luck," shouted Philip, as he tried to reassure his nephew that all would be okay.

Panic, increased heart-rate, clammy hands and a feeling of light-headedness were the least of Oliver's worries – the unknown was far more frightening right now.

"On three," called Edward. "One – Two – Three!"

Philip watched as both father and son disappeared, then turned and made his way back down the tunnel for breakfast.

CHAPTER 2

Ginger Beer

Saturday 7th September, 1940

"Where are we?" whispered Oliver, relieved to find himself still in one piece.

"Well, with a bit of luck, London… 1940," replied Edward. "Lunchtime."

Wherever they were it was dark, not pitch black though. The sunlight was seeping through the small gaps between the door and its frame, and once their eyes had become accustomed to their new surroundings, it was just enough for them to be able see one another.

Oliver could hear the sound of men calling out beyond the door, accompanied by heavy movement – clanging, bashing and knocking. From the noises and shouts they seemed to be guiding something into position.

"Steady… Steady. Over to you a bit… OKAY."

A thunderous roar followed, causing the floor to vibrate. Oliver's heart thumped wildly as he clutched his father's hand. A slow, almost tortured, moaning sound came next – then a loud clatter – and then another sound, this time a squeal. In the background, behind the creaks and bangs, Oliver heard the clip-clopping of horses' hooves, loudly at first... but then disappearing off into the distance until the last clop faded.

"Let's go, shall we?" said Edward, as he raised the sneck on the door latch.

Edward and Oliver Bradbeer stepped out of the small brick-built outhouse into a sunny, warmish, September afternoon. In the distance a brewer's dray was making its way down the narrow road to fill another needy cellar.

The Kings Arms, with its dark wooden exterior and numerous windows, stood on a busy corner of Hoxton Street. It was one of many pubs within the area which enjoyed regular patronage from the locals – or it had done until war broke out a year ago. Most of the young men who hadn't already signed up to serve King and country were living with the constant threat of conscription, so it wasn't surprising when Edward pushed open the front door to find the pub half empty.

"Well, well, well... And look who we have here. If it isn't Ted Bradbeer."

"Albert," replied Edward, nodding his head as he approached the bar. "It's been... how long?"

"Too blinking long, Ted Bradbeer. Too blinking long."

Albert Croll, a tall man in his early forties who'd been changing his cellar coat for his bar apron when Edward and Oliver entered, walked up and shook Edward by the hand.

"Is that it? Is that all you've got?" laughed Edward, dropping his bag to the floor.

"Of course not," beamed Albert, as he wrapped both arms around his old friend.

To Oliver's surprise the two men embraced and back-slapped each other for a good minute, muttering – 'it's good to see you' – 'how long has it been?' – and other such pleasantries. Oliver could hardly believe his eyes… was this really his father? My God, he'd rarely seen him hold his mother's hand, let alone hug her. And in public? Never.

"And who do we have here?" asked Albert, turning his attention to Oliver.

"This is Ollie… my brother's lad," replied Edward, quickly giving Oliver a *'shut up'* glare before he had time to remonstrate. "Just brought him down for a couple of days."

"Well, I'm pleased you have. Come on, let's get you both a drink, shall we? Lil should be back soon, she'll be over the moon when she sees you."

"She out shopping?"

"No… She's just taken over the licence at the Admiral."

"Bloody hell, two pubs. Bet they take some looking after?"

"Three – she's took on the Queen Vic as well," replied Albert, shaking his head in disbelief at his own words. "Mind you, if it weren't for our Maurice we wouldn't manage."

Albert was referring to his older brother Maurice Croll whose agreement to help with the day to day running of the three pubs was the only reason that they'd – she'd – agreed to take on the third.

"Now, what can I get you?"

"Just a cup of tea please, Albert. Bit too early for me. Ollie?"

"Er…"

"How about a ginger beer?" suggested Albert.

"Yes," smiled Oliver. "Yes, please," suddenly remembering his manners.

21

"Tell you what, make that two if you don't mind."

Albert opened up two bottles of ginger beer for the Bradbeers and pulled himself a pint of stout.

"You doing your bit?" asked Albert, almost in a whisper as he led his two guests to a table by the window.

"Come now, Albert. You should know better than that. Loose lips – sinking ships and what have you," replied Edward, quite loudly.

Albert nodded in appreciation, he knew Edward would tell him any news from The North once the pub was completely empty. Edward, on the other hand, didn't want to say too much in front of Oliver, not just yet.

"Well, things have taken a turn for the worse down here… ever since Giles's got hit. I mean, you'd have thought that him up there wouldn't let Jerry hit one of his own," said Albert, as he was about to take a drink.

"Mm. Seems nothing is sacred in these dark days. Not even churches."

"Still… It's another thing to add to all that invasion gossip."

"In…vasion," stuttered Oliver as he spluttered a mouthful of ginger beer across the table.

"Yes, that's all we tend to talk about nowadays," said Albert, as he wiped the table clean with a cloth. "Ever since they closed Brighton beach in July. We'd planned the pub's August bank holiday there, you know. But… well, I mean…with a beach full of barbed wire and mines, it hardly makes for a relaxing day out. Does it?"

"No. Suppose not," replied Edward, trying to sound

sympathetic.

Oliver could feel the palms of his hands becoming sticky, and a chill was running through his flesh. In the space of an hour not only had he been given a gas mask to carry and been disowned by his father – *brother's lad indeed* – he was now sitting at a table with a complete stranger listening to 'invasion', 'barbed wire', and 'mines'… what he'd give now to be back home in Greenwich Park getting a thumping off Bully Bainbridge.

The two men sat and chatted – innocuous subjects – the pub – the pubs – and the North. For the most Oliver sat and listened – seen, but not heard – he was good at that, he'd had plenty of practice. It was only when the last customers left the Kings Arms and Albert bolted the door securely behind them that the real talk could begin.

"Well?" asked Albert, returning to the table with a bottle of whisky and two small glasses. "What's the latest?"

As far as Albert was aware, Edward worked for the Royal Air Force in some hush-hush job in North Yorkshire. He knew, as did all the country, that the RAF were in the thick of things – fighting the Luftwaffe night and day in what Churchill had already called the Battle of Britain. He also knew that the German bombers were relentlessly pounding the country's airfields and infrastructure, although they'd recently turned their attention to London – and that's why Albert was being news hungry.

"Ever heard of a man called Sweeny?" Edward asked. "Charles Sweeny?"

"S-w-e-e-n-y." Albert dragged the name out aloud, giving

his brain time to engage. "American socialite… plays golf?"

"That's the fellow."

"Didn't he marry…? Er…"

"Whigham. Margaret Whigham." Edward finished Albert's sentence for him.

"Yes… that's her. Very beautiful," smiled Albert, tipping a wink. "What about him?"

"I'm up at Church Fenton. Sweeny is bringing a load of American pilots over, and my God do we need them?!" Edward knocked back a shot of whisky and poured himself another. "Our lads barely get any sleep what with the round the clock sorties they're having to fly."

"God bless 'em." Albert raised his glass in a toast.

"So this Sweeny, along with some others, is funding what we're calling the Eagle Squadron."

"Seems we'll need all the help we can get."

Oliver's attention had flitted between his father and Albert as though watching a game of conversational ping-pong. He hadn't got a clue what either man was talking about, but after what he'd heard already today – he thought that was probably best. It wasn't long though before he became unsettled and fidgety.

"Oliver! Sit still lad," snapped Edward.

"Sorry, Dah… Uncle. I'm tired. All this travelling has made me sleepy." Oliver stretched and feigned a yawn.

"Here… let me show you to your room. The lad can have a little lie down before Lil gets back." Albert stood up from the table and beckoned the Bradbeers to follow.

He led them behind the bar and into the pub's sparsely-filled stockroom. Wooden brewery crates with an assortment of brown-bottled stouts and ales stood two and at best three high against the wall. In the good old days these would have been stacked five, perhaps six high, and two deep. From the stockroom Albert showed them into a hallway, again some crates were stacked up, this time against the side of the staircase, filled with empty bottles waiting to be returned.

A picture rail ran around the walls of the hallway, about eighteen inches from the ceiling. Hanging directly opposite the doorway through which they'd just walked, there was a large photographic portrait of a man wearing a naval uniform. Judging by the medals and gold braid around his arms, Oliver guessed he was an admiral of some sort.

"Who's that?" he asked, standing directly in front of the picture.

"Don't you recognise your own King? King George." Albert looked bemused.

Oliver turned to his father. "But... but where's his beard?"

"Come now, Ollie. You've had George the Fifth on the brain ever since school," interrupted Edward, ushering his son away from the picture and up the staircase. "Is it the room to the right, Albert?"

"Yes, that's it. You might want to close the window. I opened it earlier to let in some air."

"Okay, will do."

Oliver, eager for some breathing space, went upstairs ahead of his father, turned to his right, and entered a fairly large room. Along one wall, separated by a large and imposing tiled fireplace, stood two freshly made beds, both with a folded hand towel placed on top of the eiderdown. On the opposite wall, to complete the furnishings, stood a small wooden wardrobe with a mirror inset into the front, and a chest of drawers, on top of which was a mantel clock positioned in the middle of an embroidered table runner.

A large four-paned sash window, giving a view to the rear of the pub, was open by about six inches. Long cream-coloured curtains, heavily lined with black material, hung at either side of the window.

Moments later, Edward closed the door gently behind him and grabbed Oliver swiftly by the left wrist, dragging at his bracelet as he did. Oliver turned to see his father with an index finger pressed tightly against his own lips. Edward released the grip on his son's wrist and pointed to the door.

"It's a nice room isn't it, Ollie?" called out Edward, urgently rolling his hands to prompt a reply.

"Yes… Yes it is. Can I have the bed by the window please, Uncle?"

"Of course you can. Of course you can." Edward reached into his bag and took out a note pad. "Here are your pyjamas. Why don't you put them under your pillow?"

"Thank you, Uncle," replied Oliver with a mischievous smirk.

Edward wrote on the pad and handed it to Oliver.

Think Albert's followed us up.
Don't ask questions – I'll explain later.

"Now why don't you see if you can get some rest for an

26

hour?" said Edward, replacing the pad in his bag. He closed the window and pulled the curtains together. "I'm going to have a walk down to the Admiral. See if I can surprise Lil."

"B… But… Will you be gone long?" Oliver hadn't expected that. He'd felt a slight relief when the bedroom door had clicked closed. Yes, he was still in 1940, but he was with his father, in a normal-looking room, and it felt safe. The thought of being left alone in a strange place – a strange time – was the last thing he needed.

"No. An hour, perhaps two at the most. You'll be fine. Just stay in the room until I get back," replied Edward, opening the door.

"I've got some water for you." Albert, as predicted, was positioned on the landing by the door. He was holding a large flower-patterned jug which he carried over to the chest of drawers. "There. You'll be able to freshen up now."

"Ex-cell-ent. Thank you," replied Edward, dragging out the 'excellent' with a barely hidden sarcastic tone.

"Did I hear you say you were heading off to the Admiral? Only I've got a couple of crates to take up, could do with a hand carrying one. If you don't mind, that is?"

"No… not at all."

As the two men left the room and the door closed, Oliver felt drained. His mouth dried as a sense of dread swept through him. Although London was his city, the place of his birth… where he'd lived all his life… standing alone, in the guest room of the Kings Arms… it suddenly felt quite alien to him.

CHAPTER 3

Troubled Skies

Oliver had cried, indeed sobbed, more out of abandonment and uncertainty than out of fear. He'd lain on the bed mulling over his thoughts from that afternoon, trying to meld together the words he'd heard – invasion, barbed wire, American pilots – and then coming back to *my brother's lad*. At some point though, he'd finally managed to shiver himself to sleep and find some peace away from his mind's turmoil.

It was just after four o'clock when Oliver was woken by an annoying howl, at first listen he thought it was a steam train with its whistle echoing on the wind as its warning blasts bounced along the walls of a nearby dank tunnel. But as his consciousness and senses returned, the hollow drone became more akin to the wails of an incessant screaming banshee.

Hidden at first behind the caterwaul rose a distant ferocious rumble. From the darkened bedroom it sounded as though a thunderous storm was brewing overhead, one so intense it was causing the window panes to vibrate with fear within their frames.

Oliver edged open the curtains – not by much – just enough for him to marry sight to sounds. People on the street below were scurrying here and there in an urgent yet somewhat dignified panic as the omnipresent shrill exhorted them along. He looked to the sky expecting to see a venom of dark angry clouds readying to unleash their wrath on the streets below... he wasn't prepared at all for what was actually happening up there.

The cloudless sky was brimming with a hive of man-made activity. Oliver could see at least twenty – or more – large airship-like silver balloons tethered to steel cables, firmly anchored to... well, firmly anchored to wherever... he couldn't tell. High above the balloons the sky was peppered with hundreds of flying machines. Some, the faster ones, were small, and pirouetted around the sky with an unnerving grace... but the others were large, massive, humongous flying machines... and each and every one of those was cascading small black objects down, onto the city below... they streamed towards the ground like armies of ants marching... only to be followed by more and more distant rumbling.

An explosion burst out between the flying machines, then another and another. Someone, somewhere was trying to blast the airborne monstrosities to oblivion... to blow them to smithereens. Pillars of thick black smoke rose up on the distant horizon; from the direction, Oliver guessed it was the East End.

The wailing continued as the machines flew, the explosions burst, the balloons floated, the windows vibrated, the smoke billowed and the people – the few that remained – scurried. All the sounds layered themselves one by one into a cacophony of terror.

As a tight fear gripped him, Oliver screamed out. He ran

for the door and for the safety of his father's strong, yet comforting arms. Stumbling down the stairs Oliver, continually shouting out, searched the pub's rooms one by one. But no one answered, there was no one there. Oliver was alone, and as the demonic drone of the siren teased at his conscience a foreboding chill took over from within.

He ran for the pub door, the one in the bar, where he and his father had entered, but it was well and truly bolted shut and no amount of shaking and screaming was ever going to open it.

In the cellar of the Admiral Keppel, Edward was helping Albert and Lillian Croll to pull up a few crates to sit on.

"Sounds like he's hitting the docks," said Lil, staring at the cellar's ceiling and trying to place some direction to the far off rumbling of the exploding bombs.

"Difficult to tell with that racket going on up there," remarked Albert. "Not a very nice way to welcome you back to London though. Eh, Ted?"

"No… No, not at all," replied Edward, giving a nonchalant shrug, his mind clearly elsewhere.

"Bet you're worried sick about that young nephew of yours? If he's got any sense he'll be in the cellar drinking all our beer," said Albert, trying to make light of the situation.

"What?" Lillian was taken aback, she hadn't been made aware that Edward had someone with him… let alone a child. "Where is he? Where did you leave the poor boy?"

"Sleeping. He was asleep. Come on, Lil. How was I to know Goering would be…?"

Albert stopped talking, he knew when to close his mouth.

He'd seen the look on his wife's face countless times; that, along with her fiery red hair, was a scornful concoction he'd rather not anger.

"I know he'll be safe," nodded Edward calmly. "But he'll be scared out of his skin."

Although he couldn't reveal to Albert and Lillian that Shoreditch wouldn't get bombed that night and that The King's Arms pub wouldn't get hit at all during the war, he had no choice but to sit tight in the cellar and wait until the all clear sounded. Mind you, he thought, if he'd told Lil that the pub would eventually become a Nigerian restaurant, she'd probably have blown it up herself, even if it did serve up an amazing beef suya.

He was more concerned about Oliver being left alone, becoming frightened with no one to turn to. Perhaps, Edward bit his lip and acknowledged to himself, he'd made a mistake in leaving him. With hindsight, he perhaps should have prepared Oliver a little better.

After about two hours, and to the relief of everyone, the air-raid sirens started up again. Not the dual rise and fall 'warning', but this time the continuous single 'all clear' tone. People streamed out onto Hoxton Street from their hidey holes and shelters to assess the damage. It was plain to see that a gratefulness shone on the faces of many when they realised that their homes and their neighbourhood were safe. But their expressions of cheer and gratitude immediately turned to grief as they became aware of the wall of dense black smoke flecked with burnt orange that was rising high above the buildings to the east and south-east. An eerie shadow on London's skyline.

31

With Albert not too far behind, Edward sprinted the hundred yards or so to the King's Arms in what seemed like a matter of seconds. He rattled at the pub's doors, not expecting them to open, it was more for an indication that someone was there. Albert ran past and quickly unlocked the side door to the pub.

"OLIVER... OLLIE!" shouted Edward as he ran upstairs to the bedroom.

As Albert checked the bar and rooms downstairs he could hear Edward shouting out Oliver's name. At first it was a repeated call of urgency but as he went from room to room with no answer the shouts turned to calls of despair, each one becoming more fragile than the last.

"Where's the boy? Is he okay?" asked Lil, entering the bar. "Have you found him?"

Albert didn't answer. Shaking his head he dropped his stare to the floor.

"Where's Ted?"

"Up... " replied Albert, shifting his gaze. But before he could complete his word Lil was already halfway up the stairs.

"I told him to stay in the room but he must have panicked. Got scared and panicked," said Edward weakly, as Lil rushed into the bedroom.

Edward was standing by the window, twisting at his ring. There was a small gap between the curtains where Oliver had parted them. Lillian tentatively approached him and lightly touched the drapes to one side, allowing them both to look out at the devastation which had befallen London. She gently placed a hand on Edward's shoulder.

"Go and find him," she said, firming her grip. "Go and find him."

From the window Lil watched as Edward, shouting out Oliver's name, ran along Hoxton Street in search of the lad she believed was his nephew. When Edward had become obscured by the buildings she pulled the blackout curtains tightly closed and headed off back down to her husband.

CHAPTER 4

Red Sky at Night

It was hardly the fault of Linus Yale, Jnr., an American mechanical engineer who was best known for his inventions of locks (especially the cylinder lock in the 1800s), that Oliver was able to leave the King's Arms with relative ease. Mind you, if the door had been fitted with a good old-fashioned Wolverhampton-made Chubb lock, then he (unless he had mind to climb out of a window) would have still been in the pub when his father and the Crolls returned from the Admiral Keppel.

After the air-raid siren had stopped its frightening dual-toned wailing, Oliver, under the impression that it was now safe out there, returned to the bedroom, put on his extra-long coat and tucked his trousers into his boots. He deliberately avoided picking up the box containing the gas mask, ran downstairs and exited from the side door of the pub. Hoxton Street was deserted, nothing moved, nothing stirred... the siren's warning had done its job. The Luftwaffe was there.

Had Oliver turned right down Hoxton Street things would have been somewhat different that day. Less than a minute's walk and he'd have been on the doorstep of the Admiral, a few bangs and well-timed shouts and he'd have been sitting in the cellar along with his 'Uncle' and the Crolls enjoying cheese sandwiches and Lillian's homemade pickled onions. As it was he turned left, a haphazard decision if ever there was one.

The close proximity of the buildings meant that Oliver couldn't see much directly overhead. An occasional fighter, black cross boldly displayed on each wing, swooped downwards and then climbed back to its escort duties. And then a cluster of bombers came into view. Against the backdrop of the distant thunderous rumble he heard them, grinding their way across the city, raining their incendiary payload onto the streets below.

Oliver paced down the road, watching in awe. As the planes flew and the bombs fell he felt frightened and yet fascinated, scared and yet spellbound. Oliver, oblivious to his route through the strange wartime streets, had turned right down Whitmore Road and was now heading north. The tightness of the Victorian red-brick houses channelled the fossil-fuelled roars from the engines high above, until it became an ear-deafening vortex of sound.

As he ran, his eyes flitted from left to right in search of the tavern's sign, and the security of his father. It was the panic which carried him forward, the fear was his motivation. He hardly noticed the slight incline of the road's surface underfoot as the buildings beside him disappeared and the skyline opened up.

Oliver was standing on Whitmore Bridge. Below him the Regent's Canal with its well-worn, horse-trodden towpath idled its way eastwards towards the Thames. In the distance, just

beyond the next bridge, stood a gasworks. Behind that…
London burned.

About every two minutes he could see a wave of German
bombers lumbering their way over, their motors grating with an
angry pulsation. In contrast, Willy Messerschmitt's Bf109s
danced through the thermals with precision guidance… that
was until the Hurricanes from Northolt came and dowsed their
party. Oliver, a horror in his heart, stood agog – fixated by the
theatre of war laid out before him.

"Oi, you! Get yer sen under bridge. Daft 'ed."

With a tilt of his head the scene changed. Below him on the
towpath, a heavy horse and its weather-beaten Tyke-born
boatman, both seemingly unfazed by the carnage behind,
guided their empty vessel towards the Grand Union.

"Tha'll soon get it blown off if one of them Jerry planes
claps eyes on yer."

To his right there was an opening in the wall and some
brick steps which led to the towpath below. Oliver made his
way down to join the boatman, to the relative protection
provided by the bridge.

"Is that a Shire?" asked Oliver. Although he'd seen plenty,
he'd never been this close to a work horse before.

"Nah, lad. Phelix… he's a Clydesdale."

"Oh!" Oliver had heard of the Suffolk and Shire, but that
was where his knowledge of heavy horses stopped. "Is it alright
to stroke him? I mean, if you don't mind that is…"

"Aye, go on. He won't bite."

Oliver tentatively approached the huge bay-coloured
animal and ran his hand down the horse's neck. "Hello, Felix,"

whispered Oliver.

"Make sure you call him Phelix... with a P and a H." The boatman emphasised the letters as though talking to a child. "Not a bloomin' F... he don't like it, sayin' his name all wrong."

"Phelix?"

"Aye. There wur three horses born on t'farm that year. Phoenix and Phoebe came first... and then Leon came up with Phelix."

"Leon?" asked Oliver. "Is he the farmer?"

"No, lad. Local vet. If he'd 'ave been born a year earlier it would've been Ezra. Goliath for next year. As it 'appens what we 'ave 'ere is my best mate, Phelix." The boatman smiled, proud to have Phelix as his best friend.

Whilst London's brickwork got battered in the background, Oliver and the boatman – who'd introduced himself as Thomas George, son of a master builder from Pontefract – sheltered under Whitmore Bridge with Phelix.

Throughout the explosions and anti-aircraft fire they talked, mainly about the war and Germany's invasion of Europe, but then occasionally they'd discuss Greenwich, Pontefract and life on the canal bank. Oliver declined the chance to share a cigarette but both he and Phelix jumped at the offer of an apple to crunch on. Every so often they'd be able to feel the faint vibrations through the ground where they were sitting and witness the mayhem through the ripples on the Regent's murky water.

When the last of the Nazi bombers had been chased away Oliver watched as Thomas, wanting to make the most of the remaining daylight, led Phelix off into the distance. Their empty barge followed along, gliding through the water effortlessly, as it was towed towards the Grand Union. Although Oliver had only known them for a short while, he envied their simple lifestyle. He was going to miss them.

The sky was quieter. No engines, no booms and bangs, no cackles and crump noises. The ting-a-ling urgency of ambulance bells could be heard faintly drifting in the distance as they headed blindly to whatever awaited. The black pillars of smoke had turned into dense clouds, with their acrid burning smell carrying for miles on the light breeze.

Edward Bradbeer, in search of his son, was running along Hoxton Street at quite a pace. At the junction where Oliver had inadvertently turned right, Edward turned left and headed along Gopsall Street. Cliques of local residents were now outdoors, exchanging thoughts and opinions on the Jerry bombings, and what Churchill should be doing to stop them. One woman, with a well-worn brush in hand and pail to her left, scrubbed relentlessly at the steps leading up to her door, as though – after a bombing raid – it was a perfectly normal thing to do.

He stopped outside Gopsall Street School and peered over the wall. "Oliver... Ollie," called Edward, hoping that his son would emerge from one of the building's brick-red crannies. He called again, louder this time, but still no one came.

He entered Dorchester Street and looked around. The architecture wasn't the same here. These houses were third rate, thrown up in the latter part of the last century to house the hundreds of migrant workers the canal had brought to the area.

A chill ran through Edward's body. He'd been here before, on another time trip, quite recently in fact, but things were different – or would be different.

He stopped… should he knock on their doors? Tell them to move…? Insist that they did? Would they listen?

'Oh! Hello, I've been to the future… Your house is going to be bombed very soon. And yours. That's right, yours. In a couple of years a German V2 rocket bomb will turn it to rubble.'

Sod it, he thought as he started running and shouting again, that would hardly preserve true time. He turned right at the end of Dorchester Street and headed up North Road towards the canal.

Edward wanted his son to *grow up*, but the last thing he'd intended was to scare him. Yes, he should have told Oliver about the war, about the Crolls… at the very least he should have told him they would both have to play a part.

Edward had thought about twisting his ring… going home, back to 1913… scribing a new bracelet and watching where Oliver had gone… saving the day. Only problem with that was he'd have to live forever with Jane's 'I told you so' rebuke. So time travel, until all else failed, wasn't an option.

From the canal bridge Edward looked south-west. He could see a burly, gravel-featured boatman positioning his barge in Stuart's Lock. There was a reddish-brown horse resting on the towpath. Probably a Clydesdale, thought Edward, judging by its extensive feathering.

When the boatman noticed Edward he tugged at his forelock, more of a 'hello' than a gesture of respect. Had Edward given them the time, he too would have learned that Phelix, with a P and a H, liked to munch on rosy-red apples and that Thomas was a dab hand with a trowel... and more importantly, he'd have discovered the whereabouts of his son.

Edward moved to the other side of the bridge. At first he looked upwards. There were still a couple of Northolt's Hurricanes patrolling overhead, their engines purring rhythmically. In the distance London's shattered docklands smouldered and burned. Death and destruction had been wrought by the might of the Luftwaffe, but Edward knew that the East End's morale was barely grazed.

He looked down at the canal. A fish, possibly a barbell... but more likely a carp... disturbed the gossamer film of the surface water leaving a momentary pattern of concentric circles behind in its wake. Edward's eyes followed the canal's towpath as it stretched out before him. Nothing at all to be seen there, but then it did dogleg quite a bit to the right as it swept away into the distance.

As the afternoon faded into evening Oliver, sitting under the arch of Whitmore Bridge, allowed time to idle away. By turning his head a little to the left his peripheral vision didn't capture the dense black smoke. By tilting it down slightly he couldn't see the barrage balloon tethered to the roof of Brunswick Street Swimming Baths. Perfect... no signs of war. Perfect... no signs of 1940.

What with festering away and inwardly cursing everyone and everything, except his new friends Thomas and Phelix, it had taken Oliver well over an hour to walk what a man in a hurry could have easily managed in a quarter of that time.

His thoughts focused on his father. Why did he leave him alone… in *that* pub? And where was he now? Having another whisky with *that* Albert no doubt. Oliver pursed his lips and clenched his teeth. The feeling of parental abandonment grated at him.

But then what was it Thomas had said? 'I'm sure he'll be out lookin' for thee, lad' and 'Poor bloke'll be worried to death about thee'… Oliver smiled. The thought of his father running around the streets, searching for him, gave some sadistic comfort. The thought of his father being worried to death about him, gave some devilish warmth.

As he walked along the path towards Haggerston, every so often he'd stop to skim a flat stone across the water. "One – Bastard. Two – I hate him. Three – I wish he was dead. Four –" Nothing… the stone had sunk. He switched hands and skimmed the next stone with his left… five bounces this time. That's better, he thought… and then tried again with his right hand.

He played out a childlike competition, left hand versus right hand… in a best of five. Germany was his left, but then he knew that if he applied himself… the right hand of England would win… and it did. Oliver shouted out his inner hatred for his father along with every duck and drake he made… and then… when the competition was over, he skipped – boyishly – along the towpath singing aloud a rhyme his mother had taught him long ago.

> "A duck and a drake,
> And a halfpenny cake,

With a penny to pay the old baker.
A hop and a scotch
Is another notch,
Slitherum, slatherum, take her."

It was the thought of his mother being worried about him that finally made him jump to his senses. Oliver needed to leave his towpath sanctuary and return to the streets above. He needed to get back to reality, albeit a future one – and unfortunately, back to his father.

Darkness had only just descended when the siren's wail returned. Oliver, about to take the steps back to Whitmore Street, recoiled upon hearing the warning tones. On the road above he could detect the sound of people, not many though, as they cried, shouted, panicked and scurried along to their safe havens. Oliver's only retreat was to seek refuge once again under the span of the bridge.

Minutes after the renewed screaming of the sirens, the growling German onslaught returned. Not only could Oliver hear, but he could also feel the explosive booms of the heavy bombs as they ripped apart London's bricks and mortar. They weren't too far away.

Wave after wave after wave of German bombers pounded the living daylights out of Britain's capital. Oliver was magnetised… transfixed… into watching, as the chaos unfolded before him.

The sky was lit up far, far better than any homage to November's Guy and it was far, far more terrifying than any paltry gunpowder-propelled rocket could ever make it.

In the dark of the night, searchlight beams criss-crossed pathways as they sought out their enemy. In the spotlights' glare, Oliver caught a silhouetted glimpse of two German bombers as they released their havoc down upon London's finest.

The anti-aircraft gun crews streaked the night sky with tracer and then blasted their retaliatory shells towards the heavens in a valiant attempt to reduce the Luftwaffe's numbers. Oliver knew if the gunner's aim was true, a thunderclap fire-flash would bring an airborne machine crashing down upon Britannia's terra firma.

The sky was ablaze with a palette of vibrant colours. Vermilion flames flicked, as their zinc yellow tips danced and darted with a Venetian red glaze. The barrage balloons reflected the bonfires below as their silver surfaces shimmered with a magenta glow. But to Oliver, hiding from the bombers' sights, everything was one colour… everything was orange. Burnt orange, bright orange, brilliant orange… London glowed with a deadly orange.

The night was passing slowly. Seconds merged into seconds… it was as though they tried to hold back the passing of time, as though time itself was dragging out the torture.

Suddenly there was a deafening blast, an explosion much closer than any of the others. Oliver stepped out from under the protective arch of the bridge.

A ball of flames wider than the midday sun rose high into the nocturnal darkness leaving nothing but the twisted steel of the nearby gasworks behind as it soared. In one brief moment a bomb, or perhaps an unlucky Nazi He111 had brought the war to within a whisker of where Oliver was standing.

Another explosion, another crash-crack-boom... more flames, more heat, more carnage. Through his teenage eyes Oliver witnessed oblivion. The horror scenes playing in Oliver's mind were echoed through the orange-peel reflections in the canal water. He needed to escape. He needed to go home... and he knew how easy it was to do so.

Oliver held out his right hand and twisted his platinum signet ring so the hourglass motif was palm side. He then rolled up his extra-long coat sleeve to reveal... nothing. In a rushed panic Oliver stripped off the coat and tugged the navy jersey over his head. Nothing. His left wrist... his left forearm was bare. Nothing. His bracelet had gone, Oliver Bradbeer had lost his time travel bracelet. He knew that without the protection of that damn stupid bracelet... years away from home... he could do the one thing his father said could never happen... he knew that he could die.

"Think, Oliver. Think," he growled at himself whilst turning his pullover inside out.

"Slitherum...." He wrenched at the sleeve.

"Slatherum..." He pulled at the neck.

"Take her..." He threw the pullover down in frustration... no bracelet.

As he ran back towards Haggerston, he could feel the increasingly intense heat from the burning gasworks. Had the bracelet come off when he'd been stone skimming? Flown from his wrist as Germany's valiant left-handed ducks and drakes effort failed. Oliver didn't give a monkey's about the pandemonium overhead, he'd been gifted a new-found courage, his survival was all that mattered now.

As the bombers droned and the bombs blasted, Oliver – now down on all-fours – searched every square inch of the towpath for his bracelet. As he dragged his knees across the hoof-indented path he could feel the heat on his right cheek coming from the tormented gasworks.

When, at last, Oliver finally gave up his search... he was broken. His bravado, his courage and his adrenalin had been spent... there was nothing left... except tears.

The blaze behind was dying down, perhaps it was being contained by the silent heroes and their snake-like water-filled hoses... Oliver didn't care. He walked very slowly back to the bridge... eyes left... eyes right... eyes left... eyes right. No bracelet.

As he neared the bridge and the heat relented Oliver felt a chill. He put on his pullover and scanned the towpath towards Stuart's Lock... but there was nothing. He replayed his time with Thomas and Phelix over in his mind. Had Thomas picked anything up? Had he turned his back? Had he tried to hide something? No. No. And no!

Sitting under the bridge he cocooned himself in the long brown coat his mother had given him to wear. Through his tears he managed to block out the deadly sounds of war from entering his mind, and eventually found some solace in his sleep.

The Luftwaffe's attack on London that night was unrelenting... hour after hour it continued. Thousands, perhaps tens of thousands of incendiary bombs rained down as Germany's two step attack on the capital turned the night red. Hitler's Blitzkrieg had begun.

It was just before 6am when Albert Croll, quite by chance, stumbled across the sleeping Oliver. Albert was returning via the towpath to the King's Arms for an agreed check in when, under the bridge, he'd seen the bundle move. At first he'd assumed it was someone seeking refuge... a local, or perhaps a barge hand. If whoever it was hadn't moved Albert would have just left them to their sleep... as it was he decided to ask if they'd seen any waifs and strays.

"He's upstairs. Lil's with him. Getting some food in the poor lad," said Albert as Edward entered the pub.

"Where was he? Where did you find him?" Edward's words, for the first time in hours, were devoid of anxiety. "Is he alright?"

"He's fine." Albert put an arm out across the hallway. "Leave him be for a few minutes... He's had a rough night, let him settle."

Over a glass of whisky Albert explained how he'd found Oliver huddled under the bridge, not more than five minutes away from the pub. He neglected, however, to mention that, in his ramblings, Oliver had referred to Edward as 'his dad' and insisted he had to get back home to '1913'. These could keep, for now.

But a few minutes later Lillian Croll joined the two men in the bar, poured herself a shot of whisky and let out a huge sigh.

"How is he?" asked Edward, worried about the concern clearly shown on Lil's face.

Lil slugged back the whisky, turned to Edward and slowly shook her head. "I don't know where you come from Edward

Bradbeer... or what it is you do."

"Lillian," interrupted Albert fiercely.

"Just go up there and take that boy... your son... back to wherever it is you're from."

Edward didn't argue. Without a word he stood up.

From within the bar Albert and Lillian Croll could hear the stairs creak out as Edward slowly ascended them one at a time, then the sound of the bedroom door as it opened... and then closed. They sat there in silence for five, maybe ten minutes... not a sound could be heard. No one moved.

The Crolls stood at the top of the stairs... outside their guest room. They listened for any sign of life coming from the other side of the two-inch-thick wooden door... but there was none. Lil lightly tapped on the door and gently opened it.

Lying on the bed was a cardboard box containing the regulation ministry issued gas mask. The Bradbeers had disappeared.

CHAPTER 5

Pack up your Troubles
Sunday 14th September, 1913

Oliver, eyes tightly closed, stayed under the covers until he'd heard the heavy front door close. Slowly he climbed out of bed, crept over to his bedroom window and tentatively moved the curtain to one side. Down on the pavement of Flamsteed Way he could clearly see his mother and father, Edward and Jane Bradbeer, along with his uncle and cousin, Philip and Isaac, all dressed in their Sunday best, and all heading off for morning mass at St. Alfege's.

It had been a week since he and his father had returned from war-torn London. A nightmare filled week. His tormented screams had his mother rushing to his bedroom several times in recent days. She'd find him cowering in the corner wrapped in the same long brown coat that he'd worn when he'd travelled to 1940… the one that had kept him hidden and safe from Hitler's inferno.

It might have seemed that it was the experience of war that bothered Oliver, that the Blitz was the root cause of his fractured sleep. But it wasn't. During a period of comforting, his mother had in all innocence rebuked his father's decision to take Oliver back to World War Two.

Two, two... two? If that was two... then when the hell was one? Through constantly, childishly, pestering his mother Oliver had finally learned that World War One – The Great War – was less than a year away. His life, his true time life, was less than a year away from being destroyed. No amount of star-spangled, moonlight-infused girlie jewellery could keep him safe in true time. But then it hadn't done him any fucking good in, as Philip called it, false time either.

"But what would I do?" he'd asked his mother.

Jane had answered, but not truthfully. She knew that her son would turn eighteen just after the war started. She knew that he'd have to go and fight... she knew that he'd have to stand tall in the trenches of Europe, on the battle field of Ypres... or worse The Somme.

"Well... we'll have to wait and see," was all she'd answer, smiling.

"And if I don't want to go... what will happen then? I mean... I mean they can't make me... can they?"

Jane had explained that the choices would be to fight, to possibly become a conscientious stretcher bearer in France, or to go to jail as a coward – the latter would bring so much disgrace on the family that it wasn't an option to consider.

Oliver was having none of it. He'd decided that he wasn't going to be staying around to fight someone else's war. Who was he kidding? Fight – Oliver Bradbeer fight? Like that was ever going to happen. And so it was that behind the crocodile tears, for that's what (unbeknown to his mother) they'd become during the last couple of days, he planned his escape.

With the coast clear Oliver, still dressed in his cotton pyjamas, grabbed his khaki coloured backpack and scuttled as quickly as he could down the several flights of stairs to his father's office.

Once inside he dropped his backpack to the floor, switched on the desk light and then took a dormant travel bracelet from a box on top of the teak bookcase. Upon his touch the bracelet radiated with its familiar ethereal lilywhite aura, it'd come to life.

Oliver removed a leather sand-filled pad out of the top right hand drawer of the desk and placed the bracelet on it. From his breast pocket he took out and unfolded a piece of paper which had a series of both numbers and Roman numerals scrawled across it. He sat down in his father's chair and from the small stand next to the desk light selected a palm-held scriber.

Although he'd never scribed a bracelet before he'd watched both his father and uncle countless times... he knew the scribing didn't have to be neat, just so long as it was clear. One by one, Oliver very carefully copied, onto the bracelet, the numbers and numerals Isaac had written on the paper. (Isaac's Latin was far better than Oliver's.) Several times he had to stop mid-character to dry his clammy palm – the last thing he wanted was for the scriber to slip and him ending up arriving in the middle of the Thames.

When he'd finished he cleaned off the bracelet and returned both the leather pad and the scriber to their homes. He picked up the bracelet and the piece of paper, repositioned his father's chair and turned off the desk light.

Next to the teak bookcase stood an old sideboard on which Oliver's father kept an assortment of soldering tools as well as his trusty Teclu burner. The sideboard (less tools) had originally stood in the front drawing room but when his father wanted more space for the clock collection it had needed to come downstairs.

It had three deep drawers in the centre and a cupboard to each side, all of which had decorative thistle-patterned handles. Oliver, sitting cross-legged on the floor, pulled open the third drawer, the bottom one.

Inside the drawer, packed away like a purpose-built block puzzle, were an assortment of boxes in different shapes, sizes and colours. As he removed them one by one Oliver made a mental note as to how he'd need to replace them. Finally there was only one remaining, the one which interested him.

He took it out – it was an oak box about three inches deep, with a small circular emblem in the middle. He remembered his father having been given it by a customer as a mark of appreciation for a time travel trip. As far as he could remember, his father didn't actually want the gift... but refusal would have been discourteous... and so he accepted it. Oliver guessed that it had never been taken from the drawer since that day.

He flipped the small brass catch to one side and then carefully opened up the lid. His eyes widened, it was exactly as he remembered it – gunmetal grey with a nicely polished wooden handle. The Webley British Bulldog pocket revolver.

Removing the revolver from the box, Oliver held it in his right hand and slipped his finger through the trigger guard. It didn't feel as heavy as he expected – about a pound or so, he guessed – and easy to carry. Perfect.

Also inside the box was a compartment with a small green and red cardboard box set into it.

KYNOCH .442 REVOLVER CARTRIDGES

It was an unopened box of fifty lead bullets. At first Oliver was only going to take a few, perhaps twenty or so. But what the hell... if his father ever saw that the gun was missing, then what difference were a few bullets going to make, he thought... and so Oliver removed the unopened cardboard box and quickly stashed both the bullets and revolver into his backpack.

After returning the oak box to the back of the drawer, he then carefully positioned the other boxes in their correct locations, closed the drawer and then legged it back up to his room.

For the next seven days Oliver, where possible, avoided talking to anyone. Using a combination of coughs and splutters timed perfectly with the odd moan and groan he'd convinced his mother to let him have one more week off school. His father nearly raised the roof when he found out – cursing at the top of his voice – using some words that Oliver had never heard before... not even on the school playing field.

Homework was the compromise. However, Oliver didn't mind. He'd happily study political history at home in preference to school, especially with so much planning to do.

When the house was quiet Oliver would pack, unpack and then repack his bag, ticking off and then adding things to his 'list of essentials' with each repack.

Stashed away at the bottom were the main essentials – the things that once packed, stayed packed. These included a change of clothes – hard-wearing denims, shirt and pullover – plus two extra pairs of pants and socks (one thick winter pair) and a spare vest.

Wrapped tightly in one of the winter socks – 45 of the Kynoch .442 bullets. The other five were already loaded into the Webley Bulldog. Oliver, as part of his convalescing homework had read a few journals and studied some of the schematics printed in various encyclopaedias to learn how to load – and fire – the revolver. Although… he'd not yet pulled the trigger.

Other essentials already packed included a couple of firecrackers, some Maxwell House instant coffee granules, which his uncle had recently brought over from America, and some wine gums (Oliver's favourite sweets). Although not packed yet, Oliver reminded himself that he needed to leave space for both the torch and the revolver.

Things unpacked and left to one side just in case the final repack left some bag room were comics, soap, bath towel, drink flask, two boxes of matches and a hairbrush.

When Oliver did the final repack most things fitted – eventually. Although the soap and hairbrush made way for a block of milk chocolate and a small box of sugar cubes… to cater for his sweet tooth. He also squeezed in a small paper bag with some tablets in – the ones his mother would pack when they went away on holiday – just in case, he thought.

The atmosphere within the walls of Flamsteed Way during that week had become even more brittle, it was as though a dark cloud loomed overhead… ready to erupt any second. Father and son had never been more distant with each other. Edward had tried to talk to Oliver, tried to reason with him. But each time he did, Oliver turned away, and threw his words back at him, finishing what had been a one-sided conversation with, "You left me… alone. Didn't you?"

Not only was the father/son rift starting to have an effect on the day to day running of The Time Store – clients being cancelled and sales being lost – it was starting to cause tension between Edward and Jane.

It was after watching his family once again leave Flamsteed Way for Sunday mass that Oliver made his move. He jumped out of bed – dressed – put on his travel bracelet – picked up his backpack – and headed for the Round Room, via the kitchen… after all he'd need a couple of slices of toast before he set off.

It had been the seventeenth Sunday after Trinity and the mass at St. Alfege's hadn't been one of Reverend Frederick Tackley's best. Other than *Abide with Me* there'd been no uplifting hymns to sing along to, no upbeat sermon to help cleanse the soul and very little heating within the church walls.

Being prominent members of the borough's community the Bradbeers attended church every Sunday. Edward, not one for having the family name dragged through the gutter gossip, insisted – although there were many times when he'd wished he hadn't – that when possible they all should attend mass.

"No Oliver again? Is he still unwell?" asked Reverend Tackley, as he thanked the Bradbeers for attending the service and for their generous weekly offering.

"Yes... he's still under the weather," replied Jane. "Coughing and sniffling all over the place."

"Perhaps I should drop by? Maybe with some books from Sunday School," offered Reverend Tackley.

"That would be lovely. I'm sure he'd really appreciate that wouldn't he, Edward?"

"Well yes, indeed. He'll be over the moon. Cheer him up no end. But what about your elderly parishioners?" asked Edward. "I'd not rest if you passed on any Bradbeer ailment to someone who was on the... shall we say... frail side."

Edward shook Reverend Tackley by the hand and ushered the family along the pathway.

"Yes... perhaps not a good idea then," said the priest as the Bradbeers moved away. He would have chased the matter a little more if it hadn't been for Charles Lowveld, another generous parishioner, who'd been waiting patiently for a word or two.

"You'll have to apologise, my dear brother. To Ollie. And make it up to him in some way," suggested Philip, taking Isaac's hand whilst they walked across Church Road.

"Apologise? Me... apologise?" Edward shook his head in disbelief at his brother's words. "None of this would've happened if he'd have stayed in the room like I told him."

"None of it would've happened if you'd have listened to me in the first place," scowled Jane.

The rest of the walk home was completed in silence and it was only when he was standing at the foot of the six stone steps leading up to the front door that Edward finally bowed down to the pressure both his wife and brother were putting on him.

Edward reluctantly agreed to apologise to Oliver for taking him forward in time to the Second World War and leaving him. He agreed, again reluctantly, with Philip's suggestion to take Oliver into the next century for a visit to something called a Comic Con… and then to something called a theme park.

Philip, deciding it would be best to let Oliver have some time alone with his parents – or vice versa – took Isaac back to the park, and allowed him to play on the swings… a treat he'd never had on a Sunday before.

Edward, with a half-hearted apology to deliver, entered The Time Store and went in search of his son. Bedrooms, bathrooms, kitchen, lounge… Nothing, no Oliver. Globe Room, Costume Room, office, workshop, sales room, rest room, guest room… Nothing, no Oliver.

Jane suggested tetchily that Oliver might be at the park… at play on the swings or roundabouts, so Edward walked the short journey to Greenwich Park expecting, hoping, to see Oliver with Philip and Isaac. But although his brother and nephew were there, Oliver wasn't. They hadn't seen him.

Edward, along with Philip and Isaac, returned back to Flamsteed Way. Now he was beginning to panic, and with their help he set about methodically scouring the entire house from the attic to the basement. It was a more detailed and extensive hunt than the one Edward had undertaken half an hour earlier. Then, he was looking for Oliver, expecting to find him somewhere. Now, he had to acknowledge that, for the second time in under a month, his son could well be missing. They searched under the beds, in the wardrobes, in the pantry, behind the clepsydrae, between the costume rails, behind curtains, under desks… even the coal house. But still no Oliver.

After quickly engraving a couple of bracelets, Edward and Philip, with Jane not too far behind, ran to the Round Room and time travelled three hours into the past.

Edward's arrival point had been the bench at the end of Flamsteed Way. From there he witnessed the comings and goings to and from Number Five. He shrank down slightly as he watched himself, Jane – who was holding Isaac's hand – and Philip leave for church. Stephen Collins delivering the Sunday newspaper had been the only visitor to the door that morning.

Once Edward had seen the family return – Jane and himself discussing his 'apology' on the doorstep – Philip taking Isaac to the park – himself running to the park to look for Oliver – then returning with Philip and Isaac, he knew that Oliver hadn't left the house… at least not through the front door.

Philip's arrival point had been the Round Room. He was to watch it for the next three hours. Thankfully, it wasn't long before there was movement.

"Ah, Ollie… there you are."

"Uncle Philip! B… But why aren't you at church? At mass?" Oliver was surprised, shocked. He'd watched through the bedroom window as Philip, Isaac, and his mother and father had left for church. So he certainly hadn't figured that his uncle would be sitting just outside the Round Room in the armchair.

"I am," replied Philip, now standing. "Probably half way through *Abide with Me* by now."

"Oh?… Oh! I suppose you're going to stop me? Make me

stay?" Oliver felt deflated – two weeks of planning, scuppered at the last minute – so near, yet so far.

"I don't know. I might… depends why you're leaving… where you're going," replied Philip. "Here, sit down and tell me. Have my chair."

Oliver, removing his backpack, begrudgingly sat down in the brown leather winged armchair and prepared himself for a barrage of questions. None came – not straight away.

"I see you've packed well." Philip picked up the backpack and felt the weight. "Bit on the heavy side… I'm guessing that you're not planning on coming back for a while."

"I'm never coming back," Oliver spouted.

"Never?" replied Philip calmly. "Never is a very long time – longer than everything – longer than life itself. Are you sure you're never coming back?"

"Yes, I'm sure. He doesn't want me…"

"Doesn't want you? Is that what this is all about?" Philip spoke louder. He didn't shout though, he wanted to convey some authority without causing upset. "Your father's been running around the park for the last hour looking for you. The swings, the slides… he's searched everywhere."

"Swings… slides…? Shows how well he knows me doesn't it? That's half the problem… he still thinks I'm a bloody child, doesn't he? I've not been on the swings for the last two years!"

"So you're running away forever because your father still thinks you play on the swings?"

Oliver dropped his head and averted his eyes, he was too embarrassed to look at his uncle. "No."

"No. I guess not." Philip's tone now relaxed to reveal a

degree of empathy. "So what's it about then, Ollie? Why are you running? Why are you planning on leaving?"

Tears were welling up in his eyes but Oliver bit his lip and tried to compose himself. He knew deep down that he had to face up to life – the type of everyday life you came across unexpectedly. At times he'd been quite good at that... digging deep and finding some courage... when he needed it. But there were certain things you could do to remove risk – things such as not playing sports at school – things such as avoiding the park at the weekend when Bainbridge and his flock would be there – things such as avoiding wars.

"I'm scared." He looked up at Philip. "I'm scared of the planes – the bombs – the flames – of dying."

Philip lowered his head. He didn't know what to say. He couldn't tell his nephew that all would be okay, that he'd be fine. Because he didn't know if he would be. "Your mother's worried about you... upset."

"I asked her if I could live through the war out of true time. You know... with a bracelet." Oliver sighed. "So I couldn't get killed."

"You can't do that, Ollie. You'd still need to live your life in true time. If you went away for four years... well that's... that's just..."

"Two to three days... Just two to three fucking days," growled Oliver angrily. "And then I'd have to come back... and live through it all anyway."

"But that's life, Ollie. Sometimes we get dealt a good hand – with loads of fun and adventure – excitement and joy. And sometimes..." Philip hesitated and gathered his thoughts...

about being a husband... being a family... about Isaac's mother... "Well, sometimes – good or bad – we have to live with the cards we're dealt each day."

Oliver looked at his uncle... he knew that his words were from the heart. They were words that meant something... words that stirred the memories Philip lived with every day – every minute – of his life.

"And... and if you go, if you walk out..." Philip knelt before his nephew, took his left hand and pulled back his coat sleeve to reveal the shimmering travel bracelet. "One day you'll have to return... no matter when that is. You'll have to return here. This will bring you back... on your very last breath out of true time... you'll be zapped to Tec-Spa and then brought back here... back to this room – the bane of the Bradbeers – to start all over again. Is that what you want, Ollie? Is it?"

"No." Oliver shook his head, and looked down at his bracelet. A chink of a thought came to him. "But if I go away and live life, I just might one day... one day gain the courage to return and see the war through."

Philip stood up and took stock of the situation. If he dragged Oliver kicking and screaming back to the house... then he'd lose. Lose the trust of his nephew, who one day would eventually find a way to escape. If he let him go...? Then, yes – hopefully – one day Oliver would find his strength and return as a man. A man his father would be proud of. Which if all went to plan would at most take a couple of true time days.

"Which year are you heading for?" Philip helped Oliver out of the chair and handed him his backpack.

"1946... after the second war."

"Mm." Philip nodded his approval. "And your plan? You do have a plan don't you?"

"Yes, of course... I'm going to look for Phelix."

Once Oliver had vanished Philip sat back down in his chair and waited patiently until he could hear voices in the tunnel. Voices he knew belonged to himself, Edward and Jane. Once they came closer, he walked to the centre of the Round Room, twisted his ring and time travelled three minutes into the future... his true time.

Edward, himself having returned only seconds before, saw Philip arrive. "Any news?" he asked.

"I'm afraid not, dear brother. Nothing," Philip lied. "And you?"

Edward despondently shook his head and then turned to give comfort to his crying wife.

CHAPTER 6

Bulldog Bite

Oliver's plan, albeit vague, was to travel forwards in time to Greenwich and the summer of 1946, then make his way over to Shoreditch. He would drop in and see the Crolls, thank Mrs Croll for her hospitality – maybe get a free night's lodgings thrown in – and then take to the canal towpath, and head north. With a bit of luck, at some point along the way, he'd bump into Thomas... and Phelix of course.

With right hand clenched to left wrist and eyes firmly closed, Oliver allowed his senses to absorb the surroundings.

There was a bitter smell permeating the air, both unpleasant and offensive – Oliver didn't like it. With the smell came a taste – that too was vile. A light, refreshing breeze touched his face and, although gentle, Oliver couldn't tell if this was carrying the stench towards him – or helping take it away. Close by, his arrival had disturbed the local wildlife, he could hear the rustle of birds in the bushes and trees, the chattering of crickets and a slight scurrying here and there. Further afield sounds carried on the night air – bangs and clangs and other such noises – all of which Oliver found strangely comforting.

He took his hand off the travel bracelet and covered its

ethereal glow with his extra-long coat sleeve, and then took stock of his surroundings. In 1913, Flamsteed Way was an uneven cobbled road. Not smooth to walk across by any means, but at least with the slight camber it was ideal for draining off the rainwater. The ground here, where he'd arrived, wasn't as hard as he'd expected… it was quite soft, indeed very soft, compared to what he was used to.

There was no street lighting to be seen, not even a flicker. Surely the streetlamp outside Dr Evans' house should've been lit by now, Oliver thought.

From his backpack he pulled out a torch. It was the solar LED one his father had brought from the future, the one Oliver had used to light up the tunnel on his first time trip.

There wasn't anything at all familiar about what he could see in the torchlight… no houses, no railings, no streetlights… no nothing. Just trees… trees and bushes. Had the future really changed Flamsteed Way that much? Oliver couldn't help but think that perhaps one of Nazi Germany's bombs had changed what he was used to. He turned off the torch, replaced it in his backpack and headed carefully downhill into what he believed was the general direction of the river.

He'd only walked a few paces, perhaps twenty yards or so, when he noticed some familiarity. Over to his left, nicely silhouetted against the moonlit backdrop, standing proudly overlooking the Thames, Christopher Wren's domes – The Naval College. Thank the Lord, thought Oliver, not knowing whether to be thankful for not messing up completely, or for getting something right – pretty much the same really.

He started running across the Romney Road, towards the

college. Something wasn't right though. The road… it should be smooth… well smoother. Certainly not cobbled.

"Ow! Shit." Oliver screamed as he reeled backwards and crashed to the floor. He'd hit something, ran into something. A bollard… who the hell put a bollard there? He dragged himself up off the floor. There was a dull throbbing pain in his left leg – he'd have a whacking big bruise there by the morning – just what he needed.

This road, the main road, was different. There was no Macadam surface… just cobbles. There was no Purbeck stone footpath… there was no footpath at all. There was however, as Oliver had just found out, a row of bollards which seemed to indicate which part of the road was for vehicles and which part was for pedestrians.

Standing by the black railings of the college, he looked over towards the park. The Queen's House… that was there… where it should be. So was the Royal Hospital School, and in the distance, he could just about make out the outline of the observatory up on the hill. Everything looked so familiar – and yet so strange.

There was a noise. Someone – something was approaching. Oliver crouched down, trying as best he could to obscure himself behind one of the bollards. He could feel the throbbing intensify as his leg muscles stretched, and he grimaced through the pain.

The noise – a heavy rumble together with a mix of creaks and groans – was nearing, becoming louder and louder. It was as though the rumbling was shaking a frenzied fear into everything it touched.

And then it passed. A horse-drawn carriage – four horses – rattled its way along the street stones. Oliver had seen one like that in a motion picture film, at the Century Cinema in Woolwich... Cripes!! What was a Wild West stagecoach doing in Greenwich?

It was at this point that Oliver considered that he might not be where he wanted to be. Yes, all the evidence pointed to him being in Greenwich. But when? Certainly not 1946 as he'd planned.

He could hear voices approaching... men's voices. Oliver headed into the college grounds and tucked himself behind two of the limestone support pillars of the Queen Mary Court building.

The men were dressed in long dark unbuttoned greatcoats, stockings and flouncy waistcoats. One wore a tricorn hat, the other a bicorn naval hat. They both carried square boxed lanterns.

"Did you hear a noise, Henry?" asked one of the men, holding his lantern higher.

Oliver's heart started to race. Had they seen him? Had he ducked down too late? He could hear the sound of their footsteps on the gravel path as they drew closer to his hiding place.

"No... but then it's hard to hear anything with you talking all the time," laughed Henry.

"I'm sure I heard something. Someone's there. Hiding in the shadows."

The men were at most three feet away from Oliver. He could feel himself becoming cold, almost shivering in panic.

What would they do if they found him? How would he explain his clothes? The torch? The wine gums? His dad's gun? Did they have guns? Were guns invented then? Whenever then was. One of them was sure to walk between the pillars, to find him. Should he get up and run?

Oliver inched his left hand towards his right. Running wasn't an option. Disappearing was, though. He was about to twist his ring when two figures, highlighted by the moonlight, walked from out of the courtyard and crossed towards King William Court.

"Scullery maids, Joshua Wells. That's what you've heard, nothing more than scullery maids. Come on. Sooner we've finished our rounds, sooner we can get back to the Ship."

With the tension subsiding and a feeling of warmth returning back to him, Oliver relaxed. He gave it a good minute or two before moving, enough time to be certain that the two men had put some distance between them and him. Before setting off again, he took his father's revolver out of his backpack and slipped it into his right hand coat pocket – better to be safe than sorry, he thought.

Keeping himself tight against the row of pillars, Oliver slowly made his way towards the chapel, skipped down the fourteen steps as quickly as he could – which, given the throbbing pain in his leg, wasn't very fast at all – then he turned right and headed for the East Gate. He had no problem getting through the gate – it wasn't there. The black iron railings were in place, and the gatehouses, but the gate obviously hadn't been erected yet.

He turned from what he knew as Park Row into a narrow

road. The houses were small, thin looking and close-knit. Oliver didn't recognise them – perhaps if they'd built them a bit straighter they might have lasted a tad longer, he thought.

"Stop, Annie Fletcher. Hold still, will you," barked a voice.

"Shit," mumbled Oliver, recognising that the voice belonged to one of the men from before. The one he'd heard called Joshua Wells.

There was a young woman struggling to free herself from the grip of one of the men. The other was standing there holding both lanterns and shouting out orders on how best to hold her firm.

The woman was defiantly hurling abuse at them, cursing them and their families with various types of barbaric diseases, some of which Oliver had never heard of before.

"We've been told to lock you up, Annie. You've been thieving again. Haven't you?"

"Thieving… I ain't no thief," spat Annie. "Who says I've been thieving? Who…? You tell me, Henry Payne… Who…?"

"Constable Firth. We've been told that you've got his pocket watch."

"Why that dirty lying bastard," screamed Annie. "How dare he call me a thief. Do you know… does his wife know what I did for that watch? I earned that watch. Wait till I tell her. And your wife, Henry Payne. Just you wait until your precious Eleanor knows where you go on a Sunday whilst she's at church."

There was a loud thwack. Henry had put down both lanterns and slapped Annie hard across the face, sending her reeling to the ground.

67

"Joshua, I think you'd better leave us be," growled Henry. "Go home, will you. If anyone asks, tell them you've not seen me."

"But..." Joshua protested.

"Go. Go now. I'm not having that dirty little harlot threaten me. Take your lantern and go."

From a darkened corner Oliver watched as Annie Fletcher pleaded for her life. Pleaded for Joshua Wells not to go – begged him to stay. But he didn't. Instead Joshua did as he was asked... did as he was ordered, he picked up his lantern and walked away.

From Oliver's hiding place he could see that Annie Fletcher was a slim, quite probably under-nourished girl no older than twenty. She had blonde hair – although it was in need of a good wash – and even though Oliver as yet didn't appreciate the opposite sex, to him... there was something about her which he found compelling.

Oliver was now faced with a choice... one he'd rather not have. Stay out of sight and let the girl die? Or do something about it? Who was he kidding? Oliver Bradbeer do something about it? Help someone? Never. Not if it meant that he put himself at risk. Let her die for Christ's sake, then let him – Henry Payne – leave. All Oliver needed to do for the next minute or two was to close his eyes and block out the sounds... easy.

"Trollop," shouted Payne as he lashed out at Annie with his fist.

But then... Oliver did have his dad's gun. Perhaps he could use that to chase Henry off... make him leave... scare him. It might work. But then again... it might not.

"Dirty whore." Payne was kneeling over Annie, clutching at her hair... as though he was about to pound her head viciously into the ground.

Or light a firecracker. That could work. The noise would hopefully frighten Henry away, make him run off into the night.

"Scabby little fuck thief. I'm gonna slit you open and be done with you."

Oliver peeked again. From under his greatcoat Henry pulled out a knife. Oliver gasped, then panicked. What if Henry had heard?

Oliver, his body trembling, his mind racing, watched as Henry dragged back at Annie's hair until she had no choice but to offer up her throat to the shiny blade.

"No," screamed Oliver. "No, Henry Payne. NO!"

Payne was startled, he'd not expected anyone to witness his intentions. Standing, he concealed his knife within the folds of his coat and then moved away, leaving Annie quivering on the ground. "And who are you to be interfering with a parish constable's duties? Be gone now."

"Be gone, shall I? And let you take her... put your blade to her throat... murder her?" Oliver felt weak. His mouth had suddenly dried. Was it really him standing there?

"Show yourself. Step away from the wall. Come into the light," countered Payne as he walked, lantern outstretched, towards Oliver.

But Oliver Bradbeer stood firm, running was no longer an option – not that he'd get very far given his aching leg – and neither was disappearing – Annie Fletcher would still die if he returned home. So what was the point? He had to trust the bracelet. If he got killed then surely on his last breath he'd be whisked off to Tec-Spa – that's what both father and uncle had told him – why should he doubt that? Why should he doubt his Uncle Philip? If he got caught, then he could use the bracelet... go home... and be back in bed before the St. Alfege's congregation hit the last verse of Lyte's rousing hymn.

Payne once again pulled out the knife. His killer glint, reflecting from the light of the lantern, shone in his eyes. An evil shadow revealed the weathered creases that the passing of time had etched upon his face.

"Don't come any closer," insisted Oliver. His hand was shaking as he pulled the revolver from his pocket, lifted it and pointed the barrel towards Henry Payne's chest. To anyone watching they'd have thought that Oliver was either very brave... or very stupid. But he was neither. Oliver was very scared.

"I don't know what you're holding there," said Payne. "But it certainly ain't no musket... and if it ain't no musket there's no way you're gonna stop me."

"You're right, this isn't a musket... this is a Bulldog."

"Bulldog?" laughed Payne as he made a grab for the gun.

"Oh, fuck it," said Oliver, as he closed his eyes, turned his head and squeezed the trigger. "In life, in death, O Lord, abide with me."

There was a loud bang as the gun discharged one of its .442 calibre bullets. The unexpected recoil sent Oliver sprawling backwards into the darkened corner from where he'd been watching.

He lay there – motionless – half expecting Henry Payne,

70

knife at the ready, to be standing over him, sneering at him before making his steel-fisted lunge. But Henry didn't come... there was no bone-handled dagger aimed at Bradbeer flesh that night. Not now.

Oliver hauled himself to his feet, picked up the Webley Bulldog and slid it back into his pocket. He staggered over to Annie Fletcher. As he passed the fallen Payne, Oliver kicked the knife away – just in case, he thought.

"Are you alright?" asked Oliver, as he cradled Annie's head within his arms. "Annie, are you okay? Are you okay, Annie?"

She groaned a faint, agonised response. Oliver removed his backpack, unbuckled it and took out the metal drinking flask, unscrewed the lid and carefully poured a few trickles of water into Annie's mouth. He switched on the torch and pointed it over towards Henry Payne's lifeless body. Good, he's still dead, thought Oliver. He pointed the beam into Annie's face, she turned her head and squinted against the bright light.

"Can you sit up?" asked Oliver. He didn't really give Annie much choice as he manoeuvred her into an upright position.

"Is he...? Is Henry...?" Annie couldn't get her words out.

"Dead? Well, yes. I hope so," said Oliver, standing up and looking at the now ex parish constable. "I don't think he'll be bothering you again."

"What are you doing?"

"Looking for something." Oliver, shining the torch up and down the body, moved the folds of material in Payne's greatcoat from one side to another, then rolled him over.

"What? What is it you're looking for?"

"This here... a bullet hole," replied Oliver. He'd already seen the entry wound – and now, thankfully, the bullet's exit wound.

"A what?" asked Annie, standing.

"Um," Oliver went into thinking mode. Did they have bullets back in the olden days? Did muskets have bullets? He picked up Payne's knife and walked over to the small ramshackle house. "It doesn't matter... not now anyway. Who lives here?"

"Me... I do."

That didn't surprise Oliver. It seemed that the constables must have been on their way to Annie's house when they'd nearly bumped into him. Thankfully – or perhaps not for Henry Payne (deceased) – she was obviously at home when they'd knocked the door.

He shone the torch beam back and forth over the wooden door until he found what he was looking for. He took the knife and dug the bullet out from its resting place in the slanting door frame.

"We need to get him off the street," said Oliver, opening the door to Annie's house. "Give me a hand."

"You can't take him in there," protested Annie, panicking. "What if they come after him? And they will. Firth and his men, this'll be the first place they'll look. Joshua Wells will bring them here... he knows Henry was here. Doesn't he?"

"Perhaps." Oliver picked up his things, packed them away back in his bag and threw it into Annie's house. "So let's get him inside, and then..."

"And then what?" interrupted Annie, bending to pick up Payne's lantern and hat.

"Then we'll sort out Joshua Wells."

CHAPTER 7

The Disposal of Henry Payne

He stared over at the body of Henry Payne slumped against the wall of Annie Fletcher's small kitchen area. Had he really done that? Killed a man? Oliver Bradbeer – Olive Rottenale, the school sissy baby (as Bully Bainbridge would often call him) – had actually fired a gun... a real one... and killed a man... taken a life. Oliver smiled, he'd thought that once the adrenalin rush had worn off he'd come back down to earth with a bang, but he hadn't. The feeling he had, the feeling of *winning*, felt good, it felt different... he felt good. Had one squeeze of the trigger changed him that much? Christ, even his leg felt good.

"He can't stay here. We need to get rid of him tonight," said Annie, rifling through Henry's pockets. She pulled out a tatty leather pouch which contained a few small well-worn coins and a silver brooch.

"And where exactly does one dump a body around here?" asked Oliver, sarcastically. "Any suggestions?"

"I dunno... the creek, the river," replied Annie, as she counted the coins back into the pouch.

"Deptford Creek? That's too far away... we'd get seen. The Thames sounds good though."

"Bah! Hardly enough to pay a month's rent," she said,

throwing the pouch onto the dresser.

"Do you have a barrow or something? A cart?"

"No… but I know where we can get one." Annie held the brooch up to an oil lamp… turned it and twisted it one way, then another. "Mm. Might get a few shillings for this down at the docks."

She placed the brooch inside the drawer of the dresser, took a black woollen shawl from a coat peg, and wrapped it around her shoulders. "I shouldn't be too long. Old Man Mayne has a cart... I'm sure he'll lend it me for a favour."

"Favour?"

"Don't ask. With Old Mayne, it isn't very pleasant," said Annie as she closed the door behind her.

For the second time in less than a month Oliver found himself alone in a strange house, in a strange time. But now, unlike before, he really felt as though he could be brave.

Annie's home was as small and meagre on the inside as it was on the outside. The downstairs was just one room – only a little bit bigger than Oliver's own bedroom. There was a large soot-black open fireplace which had a small fire almost dying out at the base. Oliver jabbed at it a few times with a heavy knurled poker – sparking it briefly back to life. To one side of the fireplace hung two black metal cooking pots and a small pan. On the other, bricked into the wall, with an ill-fitting iron door, was an oven.

Then there was the large dresser. Oliver opened the drawer. Knives, forks, the brooch, a pocket watch – probably Constable Firth's – a few needles and some different coloured sewing threads, spoons, and a crucifix, the small type usually found nailed to a wall. He picked up the crucifix and closed his eyes. "Hold Thou Thy cross before my closing eyes," he sang, and then mused at the thought of whether God knew that Oliver Bradbeer was a time traveller. Probably not, he decided, as he replaced the cross.

The upper part of the dresser had some pewter plates and a few drinking cups neatly arranged in a triangular display. There was also a small wooden bowl on the dresser, filled with crushed lavender, its fragrance trying to mask the odour of decaying human waste. Next to the dresser was a small window which looked to the rear of the property – unfortunately, it was too dark outside for Oliver to make any sense of what he could see.

A flight of rickety wooden stairs in the corner led to the first floor – Annie's bedroom, he guessed – Oliver knew better than to enter a ladies chamber without permission. Under the stairs, against the wall, was a large chest decorated with ornate carvings. Oliver lifted the lid and to his surprise found it empty.

In the centre of the room was the table at which he was sitting – large, quite sturdy and well-made. In the middle was a plate on which was some bread, a few apples and a carving knife. A large jug filled with water – Oliver assumed drinking water – and a bowl were the only other two things on the table.

Oliver flinched when he caught sight of a large brown rat scurrying from behind the dresser, across the floor, and then disappearing through a small gap between the stairs and the wall.

Apart from Oliver, his backpack and possibly the rat that left only two other things in the room… the bench he was sitting on… and the dead guy on the floor.

Oliver sighed. Dead guy on the floor, indeed. He still couldn't believe it, believe what he'd done. Of course he'd acted on impulse, not because he was brave or courageous, that just wasn't him. Then there was the aftermath of it all – how he'd got them all inside, found the bullet. Oliver was surprised he'd not just run away, or collapsed into a heap and cried. But now needed to focus, he needed a drink.

He took the small pan, half filled it with water from the jug and then rested the pan within the dying embers of the fire. From his backpack he took out the small neatly wrapped packet of 20th century instant coffee, tapped about a spoonful into the cup and replaced the packet into his bag.

He wondered when in time he actually was, where he had ended up. He assumed, looking at Henry's attire, that it had to be the 1700s. Oliver pulled his coat sleeve back to check the bracelet. He felt a relief when he saw the shimmering platinum links, thank God it was still there – thank God he'd not lost it this time. He checked the date he'd inscribed onto the oval disc – the one he copied – MDCCXLVI.

M. That's a thousand, he thought. D, five hundred… six, seven, fifty, less the ten, and then plus six. Seventeen-forty-six. "Shit… HOW? That fucking Isaac," cursed Oliver. "There's him telling me that his Latin is better than mine!"

In the next few minutes he decided that although he'd looked forward to a life on the canal towpath with Thomas and Phelix, he was quite enjoying the thought of being from the future. Knowing things that would happen, as time ticked by, gave Oliver the feeling of being powerful – after all he'd wielded

20th century firepower against 18th century steel… and won.

Boiling water from the pan fizzled onto the fire and snapped Oliver out of his world-dominating daydream. He filled his cup, replaced the pan, sat back down and enjoyed the thought that no one in Europe had ever drunk a cup of coffee before. Oliver Bradbeer had just changed history… the world would never be the same. He laughed.

His laugh was just trailing off when Annie returned. "Something smells good."

"Do you know what it is?" asked Oliver, smugly.

"No, but it has a rich, almost dark smell… quite similar to the aroma in the city's coffee houses, I'd say," answered Annie.

"Do you go into the city much?" asked Oliver.

"Only to pick up work," laughed Annie.

"What is it you do?" Oliver was curious.

"I'm a seamstress… amongst other things. Anyway, the drink? Certainly reminds me of the city. What is it?" asked Annie.

"Oh… just a blend of ground French herbs. It's a common drink where I'm from." Oliver now felt somewhat deflated, his world-conquering coffee drinking achievement had just been blown out of the window.

"And where is that exactly? I mean… where are you from?" Annie picked up the cup, nosed at it a little and then drank some.

"I'm from the north… Pontefract. Have you heard of Pontefract?"

"I've heard say of it. People… I mean scholars really… they talk about it once having the mightiest of castles. Stronger than

78

any around. Is that true?"

"Erm…" Oliver didn't have the foggiest. His knowledge of castles wasn't that brilliant. Windsor, Warwick, Dover and Leeds were all that sprung to mind. And why anyone would want to call a castle Leeds Castle when it was nowhere near Yorkshire was beyond him. And so he embellished what little he knew. "Yes, that's true. It was by far a wondrous and magnificent building, with amazing walls and towers – mighty enough to hold back any fire-breathing dragon, my fair maiden."

"Dragons… away with you." They both laughed.

"How was the drink, by the way?"

"Certainly smells and tastes like coffee." Annie took another sip. "What do you call it?"

"Instant. It's from House de Maxwell. Did you get the cart?" Oliver thought it was time to move on.

"Yes. But Mayne needs it back by first light."

"And the favour?"

"Favour?" Annie looked puzzled.

"Yes, favour. You said you'd have to do Old Mayne a favour."

"Oh, yes… he wasn't up for it," she laughed.

Oliver was lost.

After a great deal of tipping, pushing, pulling and lifting, it had taken them the best part of fifteen minutes to get Henry Payne's body onto the cart. Oliver's earlier adrenalin strength had completely faded away and now Henry appeared a lot heavier. They covered him with a shabby-looking blanket and set off down East Lane towards the Thames.

Thankfully for Oliver and Annie, East Lane wasn't cobbled. This meant that not only was the cart easier to push... but they'd also not wake half of Greenwich in the process.

Their plan, which they'd discussed between the body-lifting grunts and groans was... Dispose of one Henry Payne (deceased) in the Thames. They were hoping that with a bit of luck the tide would take him before anyone started asking questions.

Next... Find Joshua Wells. Lure him somewhere and 'do him in'. (Details to be discussed once Henry had been disposed of.)

Last... Return cart to Old Man Mayne. Head back to Annie's... then sleep.

"What about disposing of Joshua's body?" interrupted Annie during the drawing up of the plan. "Surely we should do that before returning the cart."

Oliver agreed and slotted into the plan... Dispose of one Joshua Wells (soon to be deceased) in the Thames before the return of the cart.

As they turned left into what Oliver knew as Crane Street, Annie noticed a couple of scholars staggering their way drunk-blind towards Norfolk College.

"Hello, boys," she said, linking arms in the centre of both men. In one split second she'd turned both them and their attention away from Oliver. "How would you two fine gents like to take advantage of a sweet maiden tonight? Only a shilling a piece."

"Oh... Annie Fletcher. If only I had the strength," said one.

"And only if I had the shilling," said the other, laughing.

Annie dallied along with the gents, kissing them as she went... but only until Oliver had made good ground. Then she bade them a good night and caught up with the cart.

"So what do they get for a shilling then?" asked Oliver, in complete innocence.

"Me... Me, of course," replied Annie.

"You?" Oliver stopped pushing the cart. "What do you mean? You?"

"Surely to God? Have you ever? I mean... have you ever had the pleasure of a woman?" Annie had a childish grin on her face... almost wanting to tease an answer from Oliver. "Well, have you?"

Oliver remained silent. He felt he should be able to answer. Of course he now knew she was talking about 'it'. Friends, if that's what they could be called, at his school talked about doing 'it' all the time, especially with Joan Cartwright from Woolwich. Give her a bag of liquorice and Joan Cartwright would let anyone touch her – down there – with their fingers... but only until she counted to twenty.

Although Oliver had never had the courage to approach Joan with such an offer, he often wondered what it would be like to touch a real girl – down there.

"No," he finally replied.

"Then, when you're ready, you can have it for free," said Annie, much in the same way as a fruit seller would casually gift an apple to a child.

With the Thames to their right they walked silently along the riverside path in front of what Oliver called the Royal Naval

College and what Annie called the Royal Hospital. It was all very quiet, as though the buildings themselves were deep in slumber. River waves could be heard lapping on the lower steps as they approached the Hospital Stairs. Their plan… dump Henry Payne into the Thames from the stairs, tip him from the cart… and then look for Joshua.

But it wasn't that easy. It would've been if the stairs led straight down to the water – but they didn't. Instead they ran alongside the stone embankment, turned 180 degrees and then dropped down to the river. The silhouettes of several moored pleasure boats were highlighted by the moon as they bobbed about aimlessly on the incoming flood tide.

"We either try and throw him over the railings… or tip him down the stairs, roll him around the bendy bit… and then bounce him down the last bit… and then off he floats. Goodbye, Henry Payne. What do you think?"

"Over the railings," replied Annie.

"Good. I was hoping you'd say that."

Oliver butted the cart up to the waist-high railings, at most he'd have to ply the body about twelve inches – simple.

Simple… that was until Oliver removed the blanket and found out what happens to the human body in that period between actual death and rigor mortis setting in. The period where the muscles relax to the point of releasing any built-up waste.

"Oh! For fuck's sake. That's all I need. Why me?" said Oliver, grossed out by the sight of Henry covered in his own faeces. Turning away, Annie couldn't help but smirk. More at Oliver's reaction than at Henry's corpse.

Oliver turned the cart around, so that it was now sideways on to the railings. He grabbed Henry by the shoulders. "Come on. You get his legs."

To Oliver's surprise they managed to get the body over the railings without too much effort and without putting their hands into anything messy. The cart did smell a little and was now in need of a good clean... but that would have to wait.

"Goodbye and good riddance to you, Henry Payne," said Oliver, turning away.

CHAPTER 8

Hold on Tight

The killing of Henry Payne in any modern civilised court would certainly have been viewed as self-defence... and, given the circumstances, any right-minded jury would have had no option but to have found Oliver Bradbeer 'not guilty' of murder. But...

"Yes, sir. I'm from the future. I've travelled back in time... No, sir. Of course I didn't mean to come here. I made a mistake and should have ended up just after the Second World War. Yes, sir. It's called a torch. It gets its power from the sunlight, then stores it in there... and then lights up for the night." Not guilty of murder – but life imprisonment for insanity. What a choice.

There was another alternative. Turn his back on Annie Fletcher and... now that was the question... and do what exactly? Anyhow, Annie had promised him 'it'... so for now it was worth him staying around.

"So where does Joshua live?" asked Oliver, temporarily abandoning the cart in the King Charles courtyard.

"He rents a room at the tavern," replied Annie.

"Where?"

"Right there... Ship Tavern," said Annie, who was

pointing at a brick and timber building standing on stilt-like piles which were driven into the riverbed.

The only thing that Oliver recognised about the tavern before him was the name. To him, the Ship was a large three-storey Victorian Palladian-style building, with bay-windowed balconies and a roof terrace. One famed for its ballroom and fine dining, chandeliers and whitebait. One which, on first glance, should've been a good hundred yards or so further down the shoreline.

In order to shake off his disorientation, Oliver turned his attention to the yet to be built foot tunnel. "Wouldn't it be wonderful? I mean, could you imagine, how much life around here would be different if only you could walk to the other side of the river?"

"Eh," replied Annie, wondering what the hell her new-found friend was going on about.

"Imagine a tunnel… under the river. Oh… I don't know… Perhaps starting from there," Oliver pointed to where he knew, one day, the Greenwich Foot Tunnel entry would be. "And then coming out… over yonder. Can you imagine it?"

"No, not really. That would be stupid. Digging under water, indeed. You've been drinking too many of those French herbs if you ask me. Anyway… why would anyone want to go over there? We've got more than enough fields over this side."

Oliver laughed.

The Ship was all closed up for the night, and other than occasional faint flickers of candlelight coming from some first and second floor rooms, Oliver and Annie couldn't see a thing.

"Do you know which room is his?"

"That one," replied Annie, pointing to a first floor window at the side of the building.

"Are you sure?"

"I should be," she laughed. "I've been in it often enough."

"Okay... as long as you're sure." Oliver bent down, picked up a small stone and threw it at the window.

"What are you doing?" asked Annie.

"Well, once we get him to the window... You tell him you need him, tell him something's wrong with Henry." At least that bit's true, thought Oliver. "Then when he's down, I'll sort him... then we dump him in the Thames with his mate."

"Sort him? How?" Annie looked concerned. Joshua was by no means as big as Henry... but he was still far bigger than her new friend.

"Leave that to me," replied Oliver, slipping his hand into his coat pocket and caressing the Bulldog.

Touching the gun's cold metal gave him strength. Earlier, when he pulled the trigger on Henry Payne, it felt good. The sensation as he squeezed it back within the curl of his finger warmed him – took away the nerves – removed the doubt. He wanted that feeling to remain within, not fade away with the passing of time.

"Well, as long as you know what you're doing." Annie bent over to pick up a stone.

"Mm. Well, I'm not too sure about that."

Annie threw the stone up at Joshua's window. Any harder and she'd have put the glass through. Seconds later, Oliver jumped away, hiding in the moonlight shadows as the bedroom window was pushed upwards and Joshua Wells appeared, looking understandably disgruntled.

"Who's there?"

Annie waved her arms, beckoning him to come down.

"Who is it?" Joshua growled.

But Annie didn't answer. Although Oliver had told her what to say, she didn't reply. Joshua would recognise her voice – she didn't want that. She didn't want him shouting her name out. Not in the middle of the night – not when she was about to lure him to his death.

"Help. I need your help," shouted Oliver, in a high-pitched voice. "It's Henry… come quickly."

Oliver and Annie watched as Joshua rattled his bedroom window back down, then waited patiently for a sign that he was coming – there was nothing. Thankfully though, a few minutes later Oliver spotted the light from a candle flame flickering in the room.

Oliver moved away. Annie watched as he disappeared into the night. Shivering from the cold river breeze she stood by the large door at the front of the tavern and waited nervously for Joshua to come down. It wasn't long before she could hear the scraping of the huge bolts being drawn back, and then the door creaked open.

"This better be good, Annie Fletcher," said Joshua, closing the door behind him. He looked surprised to see Annie again that night, in fact he probably hadn't expected to ever see her again – alive. He held his lantern up to Annie's face. "What's happened?"

"Henry… It's Henry." Annie's voice echoed with feigned panic, as she led Joshua along the riverside path towards the

Hospital Stairs. "When you left he dragged me to the river."

"River ... Why the hell was he dragging you there?"

"He was screaming at me. Shouting at me." Annie stopped. "He was going to kill me... throw me into the river."

"Where is he, Annie? Where's Henry?" Joshua was concerned.

"Down there," answered Annie, pointing to the stairs. "We... I mean he... He tried to push me down. Down the stairs." She sobbed.

Joshua stood by the railing, the one over which Oliver and Annie had unceremoniously dumped Henry's body little more than twenty minutes ago. There had been enough time since then for the flood tide to rise up to cover a couple more of the stone steps, but unfortunately it hadn't risen enough to carry away the body.

Joshua raised his lantern; from its light they could make out a figure below. Other than from the movement of the river's current-driven waves the figure didn't stir. He could see the row boats rocking from side to side, groaning as they touched one another. Other than the sounds from the river the night was quiet.

"What happened?" he asked.

"We struggled. I grabbed the rails," stuttered Annie. She looked for her friend... the stranger... but she couldn't see him. Had he left her alone? Abandoned her?

Joshua moved to the top of the stairs. "And?"

"Well, I had to fight back, didn't I...? I mean there was no way I was just going to let him..." She paused, gathered her thoughts and then continued. "Then he slipped."

"Slipped?" Joshua crouched down and felt the surface of the steps. They were dry.

"To the bottom. He fell to the bottom… I waited. You know? To see if he moved." Annie dropped her head. "But he didn't."

Joshua scuffed the sole of his right shoe across the top step, and then the next. Nothing… his grip was perfect. He walked cautiously down a couple more, holding out his lantern before him as he went.

Annie scanned the river walk footpath. Where was he? Her friend? Now was the time to strike – to get Joshua – to kill him.

Joshua repeated his shoe-scuff process. Okay, the grip wasn't as sure as the top steps, but it was still good enough to walk up and down the steps safely. He turned the 180 degrees, and was now four steps from the water.

The figure before him lopped about in the murky river. Joshua needed to grab hold of it, drag it up at least two steps. He knew he had to be quick, it wouldn't be long before the tide swept away the body. He gripped onto one of the folds within Henry's greatcoat, and pulled.

The body twisted. It had been prevented from floating off by one of the mooring lines, but now Joshua had jolted it free.

"Annie, come here and hold this," shouted Joshua, as he raised his lantern again.

"I ain't coming down there," she protested vehemently.

"Just to the midpoint," shouted Joshua. "Just come halfway… Hold the lantern."

His command, the urgency in his voice surrounding the demand, was overbearing… Annie reluctantly obeyed. Keep a tight grasp on the railing, she edged her way down towards Joshua. Her mind was twisted with confusion. She was torn between the suspicion that she'd been betrayed, and the inevitability of fulfilling Joshua's demand. She was ragged with notions of deceit and abandonment.

She knew she should run – escape. But Joshua would hunt her down. She'd not be safe. If she helped him – helped him retrieve the body – then he'd see the hole which had been torn into Henry's flesh. Either way Joshua would know that his friend, Henry Payne, had been killed.

"Get here, and hold this," instructed Joshua, handing Annie the lantern.

Annie, her knuckles icy white, held the black iron rail with her left hand. Whilst ever there was a breath remaining within her… there was no way she was ever going to let go. With her right hand she accepted the lantern – but then dropped it.

"You stupid bitch," yelled Joshua, letting go of Henry's body. Both body and lantern slipped into the rising water.

He grabbed Annie's right hand. She screamed out into the night, hoping that someone would hear her, that someone would intervene. But no one came… she was all alone.

Joshua wrenched her away from the railing, pulled back his fist and then swung.

There was a thunderous crack, then another.

Joshua Wells, arms splayed, fell back against the wall. He could feel a burning sensation within his chest, as though something was scorching him alive. His vision blurred, fogged. He slid downwards. Water… he could feel water touching his stockings… touching his knees.

A hazed figure in the shimmering moonlight… a man. In one of the boats. He was calling out Annie's name.

Slumping forwards, Joshua hit the river, the freezing water upon his face was the last thing he felt. Both death and the Thames had taken him.

CHAPTER 9

Private Investigations

It had been a week since Henry Payne and Joshua Wells had died – been killed. Their bodies had been washed up downstream. Henry's body was discovered the following day, face down on the Erith mudflats. Joshua had made it a little further along the Thames – his body had been found two days ago, entangled among one of the supports of the Greenhithe wharf.

Tittle-tattle gossip swept through South London like wildfire. Their deaths were being discussed in coffee houses, inns, taverns and churches by all. Robbery – plain and simple robbery had been the motive. It had to have been, neither man's body carried money. Whoever had done this was probably out at sea now, a merchantman – at least that's what the rumourmongers were saying.

Parish Constable William Firth wasn't paying any attention to the bar room hearsay, for fear of losing any more good men he'd doubled up on patrols. Someone might still be out there for all he knew.

Firth had interviewed the regulars of the Ship Tavern, and although many had seen Joshua arrive on the night in question, no one had seen him go back out again. Joseph Stafford, the

Ship's landlord, had reported that one of his scullery maids had found the front door unbolted during the early hours. But no one knew why. Eventually the two scholars who'd staggered along the waterfront had been questioned – one of them remembered bumping into Annie Fletcher that night.

Although he'd knocked, Constable Firth, accompanied by two of his deputies, didn't wait to be invited into Annie's house. He didn't even open the door using the handle. One swift kick and the door, now swinging on its hinges, opened with ease.

"What the fuck," screamed Annie, startled by her visitors.

"Put down the knife, Annie," commanded Firth, wielding a musket. "On the table. NOW."

Annie, who'd been skinning a rabbit, did as she was ordered, and slowly placed the knife down on the table.

"Not come for your usual then, William?" said Annie, taunting the constable.

Firth ushered his two deputies to wait outside, closed the door behind them and then back-handed Annie across the face. Her head reeled to the side, she'd make no more sarcastic innuendos about his liaisons with her.

"No? Then what is it you're after?" asked Annie, her face smarting from the slap.

"The night Henry Payne and Joshua Wells disappeared. You were seen out… on the waterfront."

"I work the waterfront… you of all people know that," she protested.

"Come on, Annie. You can do better than that. Both you and I know that they came to see you… Tick fucking tock, bring back any memories?"

"They came here, you know they did. For your frigging watch."

"And?"

"I gave it them. Worthless piece of shit it was anyway."

"Is that it? They came here and you just handed over the watch?" Firth, moving closer to Annie, knew that she wouldn't give anything up too easily, at least not without a fight. He grabbed her by the hair, twisted it round in his hand and pulled her face towards his. "You sure you're not lying, Annie Fletcher?"

"No, look," screamed Annie. Holding up her arm, she showed Firth the bruising on her wrist. "Wells did that to me. Told me he'd break my fucking arm if I didn't hand over the watch."

"And then they left?" The bruise on Annie's wrist was in line with what Firth was expecting. He released his grip – for now he figured she was telling the truth.

"No." Annie dropped her head. "Then... then they… the pair of them…"

"Don't tell me. They treated you like the dirty little whore that you are?"

Before Annie could answer, Firth's attention was drawn to noises coming from upstairs – creaking floorboards.

"Annie? Is there someone there?" Oliver, fastening up some buttons on the loose fitting shirt Annie had acquired for him, came down the stairs.

"And who do we have here?" asked Firth, once again assuming the role of law-abiding, rule-enforcing parish constable.

"A friend, *Constable* Firth," replied Annie, quickly. "You know… a friend?"

Firth knew what Annie was implying, she had to earn a living somehow. "I've not seen you in these parts before, sir. Are you new to the area… or just passing through?"

"Erm… new to the area," chose Oliver. "I'm looking for work."

"Work?"

"Yes. I travelled down yesterday, from Pontefract… From the north… Yorkshire, do you know it?"

"I'm well aware of where Pontefract is," Firth snapped. "Why are you here? I mean, staying here… at Fletcher's?"

"She's cheap."

"Well, we know that don't we?" laughed Firth. "Yes, sir. We certainly know that."

"I didn't mean…" Oliver was about to protest, but Firth was laughing so loud that it didn't matter.

"And so what do you do? For work?"

"Clocks… I clean clocks. And repair."

"Clocks?"

"Yes… mainly churches. But clocks, watches, pocket watches… those types of things."

"Mm," replied Firth, sceptically shaking his head. "Well, I'm not too sure we have the need for many… clock cleaners. Builders, carpenters… yes. People who clean clocks…? Well, what do I know?"

"It's the big thing in up in York," boasted Oliver.

Firth had heard enough. Annie didn't have his watch, the

bruise on her arm told him that. Yes, there were witnesses who'd seen her out, on the streets. However, there were witnesses who'd have seen her out most nights, plying for trade.

"Well, I'll leave you alone. Let you get back to your rabbit," said Firth, about to open the door. He stopped, and turned. "If I come across anyone who needs a clock cleaner... not saying I will, but just in case... who should they ask for?"

"Phelix."

"Felix...?" replied Firth.

"Yes... Phelix..." Oliver hesitated slightly. "Phelix Bainbridge."

CHAPTER 10

The Bells of St. Clements
April, 1747

For seven months now, Phelix had been cursing the day Firth had asked him his name. He was pleased to be using the name Phelix, although he was getting tired of telling people it was with a P and a H, to the point of now 'letting them off' if they didn't say it right. Truth be told he couldn't tell the difference. He'd even started thinking and feeling as though he *was* a Phelix. He felt proud to *be* Phelix.

Unfortunately, the surname 'Bainbridge' had just jumped into his head at the time. One moment of indecision, one brief hesitation, and he was stuck with it. Bully Bainbridge, bane of his school life – and now Phelix had himself become a fucking Bainbridge.

Oliver Bradbeer was now just a tiresome irritant who occasionally nagged in Phelix's head, sticking his two-penn'orth in when it wasn't needed.

He was still living with Annie Fletcher. They actually made a good team – worked well together – shopping, cooking, cleaning, robbing people. They often targeted wealthy travellers, men who would pass through from the city.

Phelix used his Bulldog (or Northern Musket, as he'd told Annie it was called) to help lighten the load of their victims. Although they stuck mainly to money, that and whatever they could offload the same day down at the docks, Phelix did have a soft spot for acquiring a nice pair of shoes – the more ridiculous they looked – the better.

He'd become a bit of a regular at both the Feathers and the Ship, and also a bit of a novelty, especially amongst the scholars and surgeons. He'd started by overhearing conversations – eavesdropping – and then he'd jump in with his theories and ideas. Now they'd invite him to their bench or table for 'Phelix's opinion' – and they'd listen.

Of course history, especially English history, was by far his favourite subject at school. So he'd been right about Archibald Hamilton becoming Governor of the hospital, he'd also been right about Lord Lovat getting arrested on Loch Morar a couple of weeks ago. Phelix nearly blurted out that a spectator stand would collapse at Lovat's beheading, and that twenty people would die... but he stopped himself just in time.

At home... as that's what he now called it... Annie and Phelix shared the bed – not together though. He slept whilst Annie was out 'earning a shilling' and she'd sleep whilst Phelix was out 'clock cleaning'.

They had come close to doing 'it' a month or so ago. Annie had it all organised, she'd decided... that was 'the night'... the night when Phelix would enjoy both the scent and the flesh of a woman. The passion was building and Annie was quite impressed by what she could feel under Phelix's trousers – but then it was too late, for Phelix... the moment was over.

In the last few weeks though, Annie had been feeling under the weather, certainly not herself. She was developing a fever, sore throat and headaches, and she was also losing weight rapidly. A reddish-pink rash developed on her wrists and hands. Eventually, after a lot of nagging, Annie showed Phelix the flat, broad, whitish, wart-like lesions which covered her genitals – they were spreading. Phelix was worried – Annie knew exactly what it was – she had syphilis.

"I bet it was that fucking priest," ranted Annie. "He was a right filthy bastard."

"Priest?" Phelix was confused.

"Yes... that French fucker, Roger de bastard Strang. I knew there was something wrong with him when I saw it," she sighed. "But he paid well... and bought dinner... So I just..."

"Just what?"

"It doesn't matter," croaked Annie, pleased that she never took Roger in her mouth. "It doesn't matter."

But it did to Phelix. He had friends who worked at the hospital, maybe they could help. He ran down to the Ship Tavern in search of advice.

The Ship was one of those taverns with a multitude of uses. For the residents of Greenwich and surrounding areas it was a local. For some – those who rented a room – it was home – or the best place that they could call home. For travellers – it was a place to lay their head for the night – or perhaps a place for a hearty meal. To Joseph Stafford, the Ship's innkeeper, it was purely business – and a very good one at that. He'd recently told Phelix that after another couple of years' hard slog he could sell up, pack up and move north. Maybe Scarborough or Whitby, it didn't really matter so long as there was water and ships, he didn't care.

"Ale?" asked Joseph, seeing Phelix enter the bar. "I've opened a fresh one this morning."

Since arriving in the 1740s and having a severe bout of diarrhoea, Phelix refused to drink anything else except ale and coffee, and even the water for the coffee now had to be distilled. Thankfully he'd paid attention in at least one science class at school and knew how to condense steam.

"Yes please, Joseph," replied Phelix, throwing a penny on the bar.

"Put it away, will you. I've already told you… first one's always on the house."

"You sure, Joe?"

"Of course… Thanks to you and those ibr… ibru…"

"Ibuprofen."

"Yes… those. Thanks to those my knee has never felt so good," smiled Joseph, handing over a jug of ale. "Now… how do you say it again?"

"Eyeb-you-pro-fen," replied Phelix, slowly.

"Well, Phelix. The next time you're up there… in Nottingham… you can tell that Mister Boots from me… he's onto something there with these things."

"Will do," said Phelix.

Ibuprofen was one of his mother's favourite medicines, although he didn't quite know which decade she'd bought them in. Phelix, jug of ale in hand, nodded in appreciation of his free drink, and then walked over to one of the bay windows where two people were seated.

"Ah. There you are, Phelix," called out a large, colourfully-dressed man, who stood up to welcome Phelix to the table. "I want you to meet a very good friend of mine. Phelix, this is James Lind."

Lind, a young man in his early thirties who wore a long grey coat, flouncy shirt and gold embroidered waistcoat, stood up and offered out his hand to Phelix. "Pleased to meet you. Do join us," said Lind in a smooth Scottish accent.

The man who'd introduced James Lind to Phelix was Archibald Hamilton, Member of Parliament for Dartmouth and, as predicted by Phelix, the Governor of the Royal Hospital Greenwich.

"Archie," replied Phelix, sitting. "It's good to see you too. Have they finished building that hospital of yours yet?"

"They tell me they have, Phelix. But perhaps we'll never know," laughed Hamilton.

"I need your help… Please," asked Phelix, not wanting to waste time. "Only… it's Annie."

"Annie?" questioned Hamilton, not knowing who she was.

"Yes. Annie Fletcher. I live with her. I mean…" Phelix sounded flustered. "I mean… I don't 'live' with her… but I share her house. She's a seamstress. Not a very good one, if you know what I mean."

"What's wrong with her?" asked Lind, showing concern.

Phelix leaned in closer. "Syphilis. Least that's what she called it. She's got these things… On her body… And down

101

there," he whispered. "Look like warts... only bigger."

"Certainly sounds venereal," commented Lind. "Are you sure she's a seamstress?"

"Can you help?" Phelix sounded hopeful.

"I'm sure he can," boasted Hamilton, confidently. "Can't you, James?"

"Archie, if only I could. But the *Salisbury*... the Channel Fleet. We sail tomorrow – on the tide – I must be getting back." Lind sounded genuinely upset that he couldn't help. He called for Joseph to bring over some paper, and scribed a letter. "Take this to Lock Hospital... Do you know it?"

"No," replied Phelix, accepting the letter.

"It's near Hyde Park. Give it to Bromfield – he's a friend of mine. They'll hopefully be able to treat her."

"Hopefully," said Archie.

"Yes... they use salts... and white mercury. Works well in some." Lind dropped his head. "Not so well in others, I'm afraid."

"And if she doesn't... I mean, if this Bromfield can't help?" Phelix stood up to leave, his face was full of dread.

"Nothing that bad." Lind assured him. "In most cases the rashes should clear in a couple of months. Now I too really must be going – I have some scurvy trials to prepare for."

"Scurvy?" asked Phelix, moving a chair to one side to allow Lind to pass.

"Yes. More trials, I'm afraid." He sighed, and shook both Archie and Phelix by the hand. "Biscay this time. My money is on the cider – hopefully that will work."

"Nah," smiled Phelix, walking away from the table with Lind. "Just give them a couple of oranges and a lemon each day... that'll do the trick."

The Ship Tavern, Greenwich c 1860
Illustration from Cassell's History of England (special edition, A W Cowan)

CHAPTER 11

Mirror, Mirror on the Wall
Tuesday 9th May, 1747

Having syphilis had a serious impact on Annie's money earning potential. This meant Phelix had now become the breadwinner, the sole provider, which in turn kept Constable Firth and his deputies busy fishing bodies from the Thames.

Together with advising isolation of the patient, the physician at the Lock Hospital had prescribed a mercury treatment for Annie. Even though they'd carried out his instructions to the letter, after three weeks things – the lesions – became worse, not better. Annie's face, arms, legs, chest and back were covered in them.

"I'm going out for a while." Phelix gave Annie a reassuring smile as he handed her a cup of hot coffee. "I won't be long."

"Phelix," she croaked from her sick bed. "Your clothes. You're wearing your…"

"Yes. Don't worry." Phelix was wearing his 'Oliver' clothes again. He'd not worn them since the night they'd met. "I promise… I'll be back soon."

Once downstairs, Phelix went over to the large wooden chest which he was now using to store his belongings. He lifted the lid and took out the Bulldog. There were two rounds remaining in the cylinder – that meant three more deaths which Firth had to investigate.

Phelix opened the box of Kynoch's, reloaded the cylinder, counted the remaining bullets – thirty-six – and then replaced the box back inside the chest.

He'd used nine since he'd arrived in the 18th century. Payne and Wells – they'd both got one apiece. After that, there was the first man Phelix and Annie had robbed together. He was a big man, it took two bullets to bring him down. Next, a good few months later, was the French priest – Roger de Strang – he also took two. Phelix had ridden the stagecoach with him to Dover. Strang squealed like a pig when the first lead bullet ripped through his trousers and removed his syphilitic member. For the second shot Phelix aimed between de Strang's eyes. It would've been a perfect shot had it not been for the potholed road... instead it tore a hole in the priest's throat.

Then there were the three he'd shot in the last week. The first had been a complete waste of time. The man – whoever he was – hadn't been lying when he said he had no money. So much effort for nothing.

The second – a trader of some sorts from the city. Phelix had politely advised him not to be so flash with his money in the Feathers. "You never know who's watching," said Phelix. But the man just told him to fuck off and mind his own business. Big mistake.

The last bullet had been two days ago. Phelix could've sworn that someone had been following him back from the Ship. Lurking in the shadows, concealed by the dark, watching his every move – he'd not liked it.

Phelix had crossed through the open space of the hospital grounds, trying to draw out his stalker, trying to catch a glimpse of his pursuer. He'd tucked himself in between two of the large support pillars of the King William Court, and then crawled – hidden by the wall – back towards the Painted Hall.

Two men had entered the grounds. Large men – wielding large clubs. Phelix had recognised them. They'd been hanging around outside the Ship. He knew what they were, what they did – there was no way he was going to be impressed. Not that night – not ever – war wasn't his thing. He'd come here to avoid it – the last thing he wanted was to be pressed into it.

The men had split up. One had walked towards the road, the other towards the court. Phelix, avoiding being caught in the moonlight, had made his way back towards the river. A slight detour and he was soon home.

But there'd been a third member of the press gang standing by the Hospital Stairs. It was this one who'd taken the bullet. It was this one that had ended up floating in the Thames.

Making a mental note that he might at some point need to buy more bullets, Phelix closed the lid of his chest, slipped the Bulldog into his pocket, picked up his backpack and stepped away from the chest. He turned his signet ring palm side, rolled up his left sleeve and touched his bracelet. Two seconds later he was back in 1913, standing in the Round Room.

Both the Round Room and the passageway were empty. He'd been gone over eight months. Phelix didn't know how long that had been in true time… but he'd guessed maybe three, perhaps four hours.

He was taking a risk. If anyone came down the tunnel now – he'd be found. Forced to live in the 20th century – forced to live through the war – forced to leave Annie.

But why was the life of one scabby whore so important, anyway? She'd have already been dead for over a hundred years. She'd have definitely become worm food by now. Oliver's voice nagged in Phelix's head.

Encircled by the total darkness, and finger-feeling his way along the wall, Phelix made his way down the pitch black tunnel to the entrance door. He sank to the floor. He had a long wait ahead of him. It would be at least twelve hours before he could chance entering The Time Store.

Totally exhausted from the week's events, Phelix slept and then slept some more. He feasted on two hard boiled eggs and three wine gums, all washed down with sips of water from his metal flask. It was his need for the toilet which finally broke the wait. Rather than having to go through the tempus ritual when he needed to get back into the passageway, Phelix placed a small wedge into the jamb of the door to prevent it from closing.

According to the clock in the rest room, he'd slept longer than he'd thought – it was now the early hours of Monday morning.

Phelix crept silently upstairs, to the apartment. He could hear voices – Oliver's parents. Hers was filled with tears, sadness. His was mixed – wrought with anger – but mellow with concern. It was almost as if they were talking about a different person, one from long ago.

Hearing his mother's voice for the first time in eight

months made Phelix weep. He would love to have walked in – surprised them – hugged her – and then left again; but it wasn't going to happen. Phelix took a deep breath, shrugged off the moment, and entered his father's library.

He scanned the shelves, looking for a medical book, hoping to find a more modern remedy for syphilis, and he did… find a book. 'Female's MEDICAL GUIDE: Contains a Description of the Causes, Symptoms and Cure of DISEASES PECULIAR to FEMALES.' Page 25… Syphilis. Phelix scanned to the cure. Leeches, white mercury and salt tablets. Not good enough, there had to be something else.

At the bottom of one of the shelves, sandwiched between some infrequently opened leather-bound books, was his mother's medicine tin. He opened the lid. Inside was a white paper bag, the one he'd taken the ibuprofen from. Printed on the bag was a blue oval, with 'Boots' printed across it, and inside was a receipt. Boots the Chemist, Cutty Sark Shopping Centre, Church Street, Greenwich. The tablet box had a 'Best Before' date embossed into one end. 10/2013.

Of course he knew what a Boots was, they'd recently taken over William Day's Drug shop in Woolwich. His mother complained that their prices would rise – but they didn't. Phelix replaced the tin and headed back downstairs. If he was going to find a treatment for Annie, a cure, then he'd have to go into the future. October 2013 was as good a place as any to start.

Once downstairs he entered his father's office, removed the travel bracelet from his wrist, fastened it securely around his left ankle for safe keeping and tucked his trousers into his boots. He then inscribed two new bracelets, the first with October 20th 2013 and the second with May 9th 1747. After returning the scriber, Phelix made his way to the Costume Room.

He turned on the light and stood in front of the big mirror in the corner, Phelix was shocked. He looked different. Gone was the child – the adolescent – who wouldn't say boo to a goose. In the reflection, especially in his eyes, Phelix saw something – the one thing which he thought he'd never see. Confidence. He smiled and the reflection smiled back. He pulled the Bulldog out of his pocket, twirled it around in his hand and swiftly pointed it at the mirror. So that's what they'd seen, he thought – before they died – he was satisfied.

He moved over to a drawer, one in which his father kept money. The drawer was full of neatly stacked and indexed envelopes. Phelix pulled out the one marked '£ Sterling – 2010', opened it and took out £200 – all in nice crisp £10 notes. He replaced the envelope, closed the drawer and headed for the Round Room.

As he made his way down the passageway he could see the glow from the celestial ceiling shimmering in the distance. It was the same incandescent light, the same aura which the travel bracelets gave off. He walked with purpose. One more time trip, find what he needed – a cure – and then back to Annie. Back to the life he felt comfortable with, where he now belonged.

He straddled the meridian, and thought about the future, it weighed heavy on him. The nineteen-forties had been bad enough; explosions, bombs... war. Was he ready for twenty-thirteen? The unexpected? Only one way to find out. Phelix, closing his eyes tightly, put hand to bracelet... and disappeared.

CHAPTER 12

Big Issues
Sunday 20th October, 2013

"Fucking hell," Phelix growled. He was standing nearly knee-deep in water – cold water. "Who the fuck put a pond here?"

It was just after midday and Phelix was standing in the middle of the boating pond through which, quite by chance, the Prime Meridian ran. Although it was a Sunday and the park was busy, thankfully, other than a five year old girl who was being dragged to the observatory for an afternoon of enlightenment, no one saw Oliver Bradbeer – a.k.a. Phelix Bainbridge – appear in 2013.

After hauling himself out of the pond, he headed over to the play area and sat on a bench overlooking the swings. He took off his boots and emptied out the water.

Lots of children were playing in the park, pretty much the same as in his day. He laughed – his day! Christ, that was only a mere hundred years ago. Except there were some differences; different play things – much brighter and more of them.

Phelix saw something – someone. He stared – he couldn't help it. He'd never seen a black child before, and there was one, a girl – just feet away from him. Playing with the other kids – as though it was normal? Was it? How the hell did he know? Shit, he thought. She saw him and smiled at him. Not knowing what to do, feeling uneasy, Phelix smiled back, then turned quickly away.

He noticed there was a memorial plaque neatly embedded into the top rail of the bench. Inscribed on the brass plate was: "In Loving Memory of HELEN BRADBEER – Always Let the Children Play."

Oliver began to nag – he wanted answers. *Who was she? When did she die? Was she a Bradbeer, or had she married a Bradbeer?* But Phelix didn't care – the fewer the better, he thought. Then he had an idea – a brainwave. Inspired by Helen Bradbeer, he suddenly had a plan to change the past – and the future – for every Bradbeer. Surprisingly, Oliver agreed.

Phelix replaced his boots, not forgetting to tuck in his trousers. He picked up his backpack and then, with an evil laugh, skipped past the bandstand and out of the park.

Less than ten seconds later, Phelix was back in Greenwich Park, sitting against the railings, eyes closed and head in hands – trembling.

Three feet away, on the other side of the railings, was the 21st century, and as yet Phelix wasn't ready for it.

"Motor car," he mumbled. "It must have been a motor car."

Phelix heard the sounds of another as it drove by, brakes squealing as it slowed down for a speed bump, and then accelerating towards the junction, only to squeal out again as it came to a halt.

He could hear people talking as they walked past, general chit-chat about general things. Were they oblivious to him? Surely not – he was almost at their feet – surely they must have seen him? They had, he realised... but they ignored him and carried along, minding their own business.

Standing up again, Phelix opened his eyes. Taking a deep breath, he walked out of the park and tried to comprehend his surroundings.

In reality, from what he could see, nothing much had changed in a hundred years. The neat row of three-storey houses across the road were the same, although some now had bright yellow doors – others green, blue or red. The gardens were the same, well-kept and cared for. Phelix noticed that each house had a tall, olive green 'thing' standing almost like a sentry at the front gate. Some had numbers on, house numbers – they all had lids and wheels. One thing he did notice though – given all the chimney pots, not one had any smoke coming out – how strange.

In front of the houses, neatly lined up along the road – more motor cars. Amazing, he thought. "Freelander, Ford, Cit... Cit reo." Phelix gave up. A small van pulled up outside a house. Phelix heard strange, loud music. He watched – fixated by the sounds – could there really be a whole orchestra... and singers in that small carriage? The music stopped and a man carrying a large red padded bag got out.

In fear of another car coming, Phelix ran across the road to the parked van. He peered through the front screen – nothing. The side windows – again nothing. He went to the rear windows.

"Oi." The man had returned. "What the fuck do you think you're doing?"

"The... the... musicians... in your motor carriage. Where

do they sit?"

"Eh? What the hell are you on about?"

"You have music players in your..." Phelix read the writing on the side of the van. "Giorgio's Pizza carriage?"

The delivery driver had heard enough. With the music blasting out once again, he left Phelix to choke on the exhaust fumes.

Phelix, with one hand tightly clenching the Bulldog, continued walking. The railings of the park were now replaced with the familiar high brick wall. Of course, some of the trees on the other side were far taller than he remembered.

He passed the Wakelin house with the collection of wild flowers flourishing in the garden. The house was still shabby, still in need of a good coat of paint – surprising considering that old man Wakelin worked in a paint shop. It wasn't long before Phelix reached the doorway of the Plume of Feathers.

He'd sat outside and had many a lemonade there, on the bench, in his younger years. Mr Lawrence, the landlord back then, would keep him topped up, whilst his father and uncle mixed with the locals. More recently, albeit in the 18th century, when the pub was known simply as the Feathers, he'd sat and had several jugs with Stephen Whitall – several too many on some occasions. The sign above the door now declared Susan Rose as the current licensee. Was there time for a quick one? Perhaps once he'd done what he needed to.

He turned right down Feathers Place, he was now less than a minute away from what was his home. Two men were coming towards him, they'd walked out of Flamsteed Way, talking loudly – laughing – they were in good cheer. Phelix dipped his

113

head and wondered if they were related to him in any way. Perhaps they were... He remembered his plan, the scheme he'd come up with whilst sitting on Helen Bradbeer's bench – he laughed.

Phelix stood on the corner of Flamsteed Way. Other than a different road surface, the passing of time hadn't changed it one bit. He was drawn to the wooden bench, under the tree, at the end of the road. From there he could look at Number Five and see all the comings and goings.

He pondered on what he'd do if he saw anyone. Run up and shoot them? *Bang... You're dead*. Introduce himself? *Oh... Hello. You don't know me... But I'm Oliver Bradbeer. Yes... That's right... the coward who ran away from the war.* He suddenly preferred the 'shoot them' option.

It didn't really matter. No one came – no one left.

He headed back onto Feathers Place and continued his walk into Greenwich. KEEP CLEAR, KEEP CLEAR, KEEP CLEAR was sprawled, in large white letters, across the narrow road, and NO PARKING signs were pinned high up on the walls. Phelix thought the area had become very restrictive. The buildings before him were bland, non-descript, devoid of Victorian or Georgian character. If this was progress – forget it, he thought.

He ran towards Park Row, to familiarity.

He needed to check – to confirm to himself – what had altered with the passing of time. Phelix politely stopped an elderly lady who was walking past. "Excuse me. That building over there, what is it?"

"That's the Naval College," she replied, helpfully. "Or at

least it used to be."

"Used to be?"

"They call it the Old Royal Naval College now," she answered, whilst walking away. "If you have time, you should go and see it."

Phelix, his heartbeat bounding and imagination racing, reached the Romney Road. Motor vehicles of every shape, size and colour were everywhere. Big red buses, some crammed with standing room only, some idling without a fare on board. Vans, trucks, cars, motorbikes – the likes of which Phelix couldn't ever have imagined – were in front of him. All of them stationary, not moving an inch. He couldn't help but think how much simpler and quicker the stagecoach was. His mind flitted back to the night he arrived in 1746, the night he met Annie.

He ran across the road and entered the college grounds through the East Gate. 1746, 1913, 2013 – on the outside nothing had changed, Phelix felt at ease.

He joined the parade of tourists sauntering between the grand designs of Wren and Hawksmoor, maybe in years to come he could be a guide here. He smirked. *This is where I killed a member of His Majesty's Press Gang. And over there… that's where I hid from the constables in 1746.* Perhaps not – no one would believe him.

As the tourists climbed the steps leading to the chapel, Phelix cut across Grand Square and headed towards the river. He eased down his pace and stared out, dumbfounded with disbelief, across the river towards the East End docklands.

In 1747 it was full of tall mast sailing ships, heading for the Americas or Africa, naval men o'war armed and ready to set sail to fight the Spanish for some pieces of eight. In 1913 it was bustling with clippers, serving the oriental tea routes, steamships and liners, tugboats and coal carriers; the workhorses of the Thames. Phelix remembered the nightmare of 1940, remembered how the docklands burned. The pillars of smoke, the flames, the orange – the Germans.

Now he saw buildings, tall monstrous buildings which filled the horizon. Infrastructure had replaced industry, skyscrapers had replaced ships, and bricks had replaced boats. The London that Phelix knew was no longer there, it had changed beyond all recognition. For better? For worse? The only thing that Phelix could be sure of was that London smelled far better in the future.

Deciding to save himself from any further 21st century trauma, he headed back to the comfort of the King Charles Court. He liked what he knew, what hadn't changed. But it didn't last. A minute later he was standing at the West Gate.

"What the fuck!?" The buildings across the river had been bad enough, but this was worse – far worse.

Some pub-hating bastard had knocked the Ship Tavern down. In its place, not only had they dug a whacking big hole in the ground, but they'd put an old clipper in it. The Cutty Sark.

"Turn your back and don't look – it isn't real," muttered Phelix. He couldn't see why so much fuss was being made over an old tea ship. Hadn't they seen one before? He walked on in disgust.

"*Big Issue*, sir?"

"What is?" Phelix, on his way to Greenwich Market, encountered what seemed to be a street seller.

"*Big Issue*, sir?" The magazine was thrust towards him. "Would you like to buy a copy of the *Big Issue*?"

"Don't you think I've got enough?" asked Phelix.

"Eh?" The magazine was pulled back.

"Issues! I mean. Someone has knocked my favourite pub down. The woman I live with has syphilis. I'm one-hundred and seventeen years old. I've killed God knows how many people... and I've never had sex... Now how many BIG fucking ISSUES do I need?" ranted Phelix, as he stormed off towards the market.

CHAPTER 13

Shopping for Annie
Sunday 20th October, 2013

Phelix's plan was to change the timeline – for every Bradbeer. Appropriately, it had come to him whilst he was sitting on Helen Bradbeer's bench in Greenwich Park. He couldn't wait to get back to the 18th century and set the wheels in motion, 'turn the cogs' as his uncle Philip would say. But first he had a little shopping to do.

He turned right down Turnpin Lane, a narrow alleyway which ran along the back of Greenwich Market. Goddards was still there, on the corner, selling pies and mash, as it was in his – Oliver's – childhood. The smell made Phelix feel hungry, the rumble from his stomach reminded him that he hadn't eaten for a few hours.

The surface of Turnpin Lane was lined with both square and rectangular stone slabs, precision laid; jigsaw-like. A row of bricks, three wide, ran perfectly down the centre, a border at some point in time, possibly to settle property disputes.

The buildings on either side were very close together. Some, back in the day, had been homes, others contained traders selling live and dead meat, fish, eggs, butter, poultry, fruit and vegetables, one even sold bicycles. Nothing much had changed, although most of them now were coffee shops or cafes, or traded trinkets and beads. There was one sign which seemed to jump out at Phelix. Rosemary Copperpot – Alternative Medicines. Excellent, he thought, pushing open the door.

"Good afternoon. Can I help you?" asked the assistant, who was warming her hands on a mug of hot freshly-made herbal tea.

"Erm…" Phelix looked around. To his right was a large cabinet. Rows of bottles stood neatly lined up, almost to attention, awaiting orders to advance. He didn't read their labels. There was a poster covering the wall behind the counter. A naked woman lying down. Her skin was lightly tanned, her body well-toned, shapely. Stretching his neck, he peered over the counter for a closer look. "Are they needles?"

"That's acupuncture, sir," she replied, dismissively.

"What does that do?"

"Well, it's a very effective treatment for ailments such as pain, allergies, migraines."

"Pain? You stick needles into someone's body and it cures their pain?" Phelix shook his head in disbelief, he was a tad confused.

The assistant didn't answer. Instead she smiled dutifully and then returned to sipping her tea.

"I'm trying to find a medicine… for a friend."

"For what condition, sir?" she asked, looking as though she now sensed a sale.

"Syphilis."

119

Thankfully, the impact of the dropped mug didn't shatter the glass sales counter. Nor was the point of sale terminal drowned in herbal tea.

"Only, she has these lesions – all over her body. They look awful," continued Phelix, retrieving the mug from the floor.

The red-faced assistant stood speechless.

"Another friend… well, more a friend of a friend, referred her to the Lock Hospital. I don't know if you know it… Specialises in venereal diseases." There was a sink in the corner of the shop, by the side of it there was a large roll of paper towelling. Phelix took three pieces.

"Thank you," said the assistant as she watched Phelix wipe down the counter. "You're being serious, aren't you? I mean, you're not taking the piss are you?"

"Taking it where? Does she need to have a urine sample… a specimen?"

"No. No, I mean, your friend. She really has…"

"Syphilis! Yes," interrupted Phelix. "She caught it off a French priest… Although at the time it didn't matter, he paid well apparently."

"Paid well?"

"Yes. My friend, Annie, she's a prostitute. Not a very good one though. But he paid her two shillings."

"Two shillings? But that's…"

"Yes… Twice her normal rate," boasted Phelix. "Anyway. Once her skin went funny we went to see the doctor, at the Lock. He gave her white mercury and salt tablets. Bit mediæval if you ask me… I'm not sure how I can help her."

"This is for real, isn't it?"

"Yes, of course. My friend. She's ill. What would you recommend?"

"Um, er. Let's have a look," said the assistant, having accepted that she wasn't being wound up. She tapped away on the computer. "Mmm…"

"Mmm? What?"

"Mercurius… Merc Cor… Arsenic Album."

"So mercury and arsenic then?" sighed Phelix, sensing his journey into the future was in vain.

"Afraid so. But if I was you…"

"Yes?"

"I'd get some proper medicine. Something from the doctor, on prescription."

The Rosemary Copperpot sales assistant directed Phelix to the pharmacy on Church Street, suggesting they were more likely to be of help.

There was a bookstore just before the chemist. Thinking that forewarned is forearmed, Phelix detoured into the store.

A few feet inside the door, in the centre of the shop, was the checkout. "Excuse me!"

"Yes. Can I help you?" There was a young petite woman serving. Darcy, according to her name badge.

"I'm looking for a book on diseases and cures."

"Any particular disease?" asked Darcy, trying to be helpful.

"Syphilis," answered Phelix. "I need to know if there's a cure other than mercury."

"Have you tried looking at the internet?"

"No," replied Phelix. "Which shelf is it on?"

"If you'd like to follow me, I'll show you where our science and medicine books are," Darcy said, as another assistant joined her behind the counter.

Darcy led Phelix up a flight of stairs to another sales floor, and then pointed him in the right direction. Unfortunately, he had to pass the history section before hitting the medical books.

Thirty minutes later, clutching four books, Phelix returned to the ground floor checkout. He'd chosen: *Print Culture, Crime and Justice in 18th-century London - History of Crime, Deviance and Punishment. Albion Ascendant: English History 1660-1815. The Great War – 1914 ~ 1918.* Plus, *Classic Album Covers of the 1970s.* None of these contained any modern cure for syphilis.

"Did you find what you were looking for?" asked Darcy, ringing up the sale.

"No… I gave up. I'll ask next door," replied Phelix, handing over £60 for the books.

Darcy took Phelix's money and handed him his change and books. "Just give me a minute. I'll look it up for you on the net."

"Net?"

"The internet…" replied Darcy, thumbing at her smartphone. "There you go, penicillin. They'll keep it next door… But you'll need a prescription."

Phelix thanked Darcy for her help and then left the bookstore. He'd remembered something – bullets. Where could he buy those from? He turned to ask Darcy, but she was in full flow with another customer. Never mind.

He entered the chemist. In contrast to the dark surrounds of the bookstore this shop was far brighter, much better lit, and busier. Phelix made his way to the pharmacy counter at the rear.

"Can I help you?"

"Yes. Erm... Could I speak to someone, please? The pharmacist? It's about a disease," said Phelix, following Darcy's instructions.

A tall, dark man – not black, but certainly darker than white – stepped out from behind the counter. Phelix, although he'd never seen anyone from the Indian sub-continent, guessed he was from that region. "Can I help you?"

"I need six ounces of your finest penicillin, please," replied Phelix, pleased that the pharmacist spoke English.

"Do you have a prescription? From your doctor?"

"No... but then it's not for me. It's for a friend," answered Phelix. "She's got syphilis. The internet has told me that penicillin will cure it."

"Yes. But she needs to have it prescribed by her doctor."

"But, we went to the doctor's."

"And?" asked the pharmacist, aware that other customers were also wanting his services.

"They gave her white mercury... and salt tablets. But they haven't worked," replied Phelix, downheartedly. "The hospital also gave her a bucket of leeches... But well... I mean... could you sit there for hours on end with leeches all over you?"

The pharmacist had moved on. He hadn't the time for nutters, he had sales targets to meet.

"Excuse me!" shouted Phelix. "I thought you were serving

me."

"I'm sorry, sir. But without a prescription there's nothing I can do for you. Nothing at all. Now is there anything else I can help you with?"

Phelix accepted defeat. He'd have to work out how to get a prescription. He was about to leave when he remembered something. He removed his hand from his coat pocket.

"Oh... I need bullets for this," he said, pointing the Bulldog revolver at the pharmacist. "Now can you help?"

The shop immediately filled with frantic panic and ear-piercing screams. One woman, in her desperate bid to flee the store, knocked Phelix. The gun fired, and three bottles of adult chesty-cough linctus hit the floor. Thirty-five seconds later Phelix left the chemist with two plastic carrier bags crammed with penicillin tablets. Now for some food, he thought.

The street outside was pretty much deserted, the gunshot had seen to that. However, there were some people who went about their Sunday afternoon as if everything in Greenwich was as it should be. They were oblivious to the fact that the person exiting the chemist shop had, seconds earlier, brandished a gun and killed three bottles of Benylin.

Phelix turned into the Cutty Sark Shopping Centre. He'd seen quite a few people leaving the centre carrying or eating food with a big fancy 'M' on the packaging.

"Can I take your order, please?" asked Nolan, who was proudly sporting a name badge with three gold stars.

"I'm hungry. What fayre do you suggest?"

"Fair?"

"Food. What is good? Healthy? Nutritious?"

124

Nolan's attention was redirected as he was drawn to the sounds of the sirens and commotion outside. "What's happened?" he asked Phelix.

"Where?"

"Outside. Something big must have happened by the sounds of things."

"Possibly. Now could I have two of those, please?" asked Phelix, pointing to a picture of a Big Mac. "And some of those fried sticks."

"Is that two meal deals?"

"Erm… Yes. With some shaken banana milk."

One of the restaurant staff, who'd been outside, came rushing behind the counter, eager to share the news with her colleagues. "There's been an armed robbery. One of the shops, not too sure which. Police are everywhere out there."

"Won't have been Waterstones," laughed Nolan, bagging up Phelix's meals. "Who'd wanna nick a book?"

Phelix wasn't paying any attention to what was being said. He was too busy reading the menu behind the counter. He'd seen something which he thought was bound to cheer Annie up.

"And can I have a Happy Meal, please? One with nuggets of chicken, small fried sticks, bag of fruit and a carton of milk," asked Phelix, reciting from the menu.

He walked out of the restaurant, and into the shopping centre. Police were swarming everywhere, some armed, others not.

Perhaps it was just luck that the police didn't stop and search Phelix. Or maybe, at that point, they'd not been given a clear description of who they were looking for.

But a man, laden down with several bags of shopping in one hand, carrying a tray of drinks and two bags of food in the other, and also clutching a Happy Meal box between his teeth was hardly a priority to be stopped.

Phelix made his way along Church Street, turned down St. Alfege's Passage and entered the quiet little park. After dining on a Big Mac and two boxes of fries, all washed down with a banana milkshake, he reorganised his bags, turned his signet ring and, via a quick stop in the Round Room of 1913 for a change of bracelets, he finally returned back to 1747. Home, as he now liked to call it.

CHAPTER 14

A Little too Far
Greenwich – September, 1747

Within two weeks Annie was cured and back to her normal self again… with one exception. Phelix insisted that her days of French priests, parish constables and anyone else who had a few odd coins to spend were over.

Within three weeks of Annie being cured, a queue had formed outside her house. It seemed that every pox-ridden whore and politician in London had heard about her wondrous recovery. Whatever she'd been taking – they wanted some of it.

Phelix, of course, took advantage of the demand, selling his thirty-day syphilis remedy to the needy for a decent profit. Every day, they would turn up, pay for their daily dose of 'Bainbridge's Penny-Shilling' as it was called, and then leave. From day fifteen, once they'd been cured, Phelix substituted the penicillin for a powder mix of salt and mercury.

They even drew some attention from the Lock Hospital, which resulted in Archie Hamilton bringing some surgeons to visit. But in the end the medical men were more concerned as to why leeches weren't being used as part of the remedy. Bloodletting was an important part of any cure, they insisted. Phelix laughed this off, and questioned the quality of the Welsh leeches they used up at the Lock.

After three months it didn't really matter, the cupboard had run dry. With no tablets left to grind down, Annie and Phelix shut up shop. Still, they'd made a tidy sum, more than enough for Phelix to put the cogs in motion for his plan.

Annie cringed, she couldn't look. She turned away so that she couldn't see the hammer as it fell. If he missed – hit her hand – it would smash it to smithereens.

"Hold it straight. God damn you, woman," cursed Phelix. He swung.

There was a loud crack as the heavy iron hammer hit its intended target… a wooden stake.

"Morning, Phelix… Annie," called out Constable Firth, as he waded through the long grass towards them. "What are you folks up to at this early hour?"

"Morning, William," replied Phelix, taking another swing at the stake, pounding it further into the ground.

"Constable," smiled Annie, burning her eyes into Firth's forehead. "Not seen you for a while, *have we*?"

"No… no." He inclined his head towards Annie. That was going to cost her. He smirked, then looked at Phelix. "What are you doing? With all these stakes?"

"Ever heard of enclosure? Land enclosure?"

"Well, yes… But…"

"This here is common land… No one has the rights. No one's ever claimed it." Phelix stopped swinging the hammer and pulled out a rough map of the local land holdings. "And as you can see… no one tends it, grazes animals on it or uses it for hay.

And as it's not enclosed, well…"

"Can you do that? Just claim it for yourself?" Firth was out of his depth.

"Come now, William. Surely you of all people should be aware that the enclosure of manorial common land was authorised under the Statute of Westminster in 1285."

"Was it? Erm… I mean, yes. Yes, it was. 1285, that's right." Firth didn't have the foggiest.

"And have you never heard of the Inclosure Act of 1773?" Phelix mumbled the year. "No…? Well, give it time. You will."

"But why this scrap of land? It ain't fit for anything," answered Firth, shaking his head. "Probably why no one enclosed it in the first place."

"Shall we just say it reminds me of where I grew up. Now… if you'll excuse me. I have a fence to erect." Phelix once again swung the hammer down.

With Annie's grudging help it took him three days, and ten blisters to enclose *his* land. He'd figured that this was time enough for the locals to vent their moans, and also for any landowner with a legitimate vested interest in the enclosure to step forward. As it was – no one bothered.

Phelix's plan had taken shape. He thought that if the land wasn't available to build on, then there'd be no Flamsteed Way. No Flamsteed Way – no Bradbeers – the very thought made Phelix laugh out loud.

By the time October had arrived the purse was once again empty, and the food cupboard was bare. According to Phelix's books a harsh winter lay ahead, preparation for that was also needed. So once again out came the Bulldog – which Phelix didn't mind, he sort of missed it. And off came the knickers – which Annie didn't mind, saved her having to lie to Phelix about where she'd been half the nights.

"Can't you just get some more penny-shilling?" demanded Annie, for the umpteenth time.

She wasn't too keen on the idea of having to drag more dead bodies around Greenwich. Plus, trade for the local girls had only just recently recovered following Phelix's last shooting rampage. It wasn't right, all those poor hard working women, with hungry mouths to feed, having to resort to *serving* and *cleaning* just to make ends meet.

Although he'd enjoyed having the money, Phelix hadn't relished the attention which the penicillin trade brought to the door. It would only have been a matter of time before they would've been hauled off somewhere to answer questions.

"No," snapped Phelix, polishing his revolver. "No more penny-shilling. I'm not going to go through this again. No – no – and NO."

"What about that fucking enclosure? Can't you sell that?" Annie snapped back.

"No. Now shut the fuck up, will you!" shouted Phelix. He'd had enough. She really needed to shut up.

"Well, you had to go and waste half the bloody money we'd earned on a fence. And for what? So no one could steal three bushes and a sodding tree?"

God, would she ever be quiet? Clenching his Bulldog tightly, Phelix lashed out at Annie, then lashed out again, again, again. It was only when she'd fallen to the floor and crawled into the corner, that he stopped the beating.

Phelix was standing over her. Annie could feel a faint trickle on the side of her face; she reached to her cheek. Blood. A throbbing, pounding pain inside her head took hold, it wouldn't go, wouldn't ease, not for a while anyway.

Annie stared into the barrel of his Northern Musket, stared into his narrowed eyes and for one brief moment stared into the face of death.

"Why did you push me? Why didn't you stop? Why couldn't you just be quiet?" Phelix spoke softly, almost in a calming whisper. Slowly he shook his head. "This is your fault, Annie. If only…"

Her fear subsided as she watched him walk away, then she felt relief as he picked up his backpack and the door closed behind him. Annie dropped her head into her hands and cried. Cried tears of guilt. Perhaps he was right – perhaps it *was* her fault – perhaps she had pushed him a little too far.

CHAPTER 15

Old Ben Abbott
12th May, 2012

In the middle of his enclosure, situated between two large common dogwood bushes, was a small mound of earth. Phelix, when he needed to be alone, needed time to think, would sit on the mound and just let time frizzle by at whatever rate it wanted. Now, after Annie's thumping, was such a time.

He knew he'd done wrong lashing out at her the way he had, she didn't deserve it. After all, she'd only been telling the truth, voicing her concerns and – although she did go on a bit – he hadn't listened. His answer to her worries about food, about the forthcoming winter, was to repeatedly hit her – it seemed that now he needed to make amends for his actions.

The Oliver within him suggested a nice piece of jewellery – women liked jewellery. Phelix allowed Oliver's buried memories to surface as he remembered how much his mother's face would light up when his father gave her fancy trinkets on her birthday.

Phelix suddenly felt a shudder run through him, the thought of his mother made him feel alone – he felt lost. Staring out at the land before him he could imagine where, in years to come, the steps leading up to the front door of Flamsteed Way would be. He remembered the time, a good few years ago, when he and his mother had returned from Freeman Hardy's with a much needed pair of new school shoes. He'd not been allowed to wear them on his way home – just in case he haphazardly scuffed the shiny leather – and so he'd sat down on the third step, put them on, and then ran inside to show his father.

And what of him now? Gone was the scrawny pigeon-chested boy, the innocent child who needed his mother's help to tie his laces. In his place was a man, overflowing with confidence, strength and character – someone who his mother would be proud of. And gone was the coward, the boy who at times was even afraid of his own shadow. But in his place – a thug, a bully, a rogue – a murderer. What would his poor mother think of her little boy now?

She'd be disgusted…. That's what she'd be, disgus…

"Shut up, Oliver. When I want your opinion, I'll ask for it," snapped Phelix.

Pushing Oliver out of his thoughts, Phelix removed his travel bracelet from his ankle, fastened it around his left wrist and using his signet ring returned to his own true time.

Leaving the Round Room he decided against using the torch to light up the tunnel. He couldn't quite work out how long he'd been gone in true time. Was it the morning? Would anyone – his uncle, his father – be travelling off somewhere, perhaps to look for him? The last thing he wanted to do was alert anyone to his presence.

As it was, he was able to sneak into the office, scribe a

bracelet which would take him into the 21st century and then make it back to the Round Room unseen.

Once again, Phelix's arrival point was in Greenwich Park, though thankfully this time it wasn't in the middle of the boating pond. He'd scribed the bracelet for an arrival time of 5pm; however, judging by the lack of people meandering about, it had to be a lot earlier.

Looks like you fucked up there, laughed Oliver, who'd awakened in Phelix's head.

"Yes, like you could have done any better," growled Phelix.

Silenced, Oliver didn't reply.

Phelix decided against visiting Greenwich Town and headed across the park towards Blackheath. He passed a wizened, weather-beaten old man sound asleep on one of the benches near the observatory. The man was wrapped tightly in several layers of shabby clothes, topped off with a crumpled blanket, all of which served to fight off the morning's chill. Phelix stood momentarily and watched for signs of life, and then moved on when he saw the man turn slightly.

Pulling up his coat collar to stave off the cold, Phelix walked on. A few benches further down there was another tramp, by the sounds of his toad-like snores he was deep in slumber. At his side there was a four-wheeled trolley, a cart of some description, crammed with bags stuffed with oddments of everything, empty cans, some large sheets of cardboard and a metal plate. Phelix paused, then continued walking – past the Wolfe statue, past the Royal Observatory and out towards

134

Blackheath Avenue.

The avenue had changed considerably since Phelix's day. Instead of a picturesque road lined with oak trees, Blackheath Avenue had become a wide open area with lots of white lines painted everywhere. Phelix soon realised that these were marked out for people to leave their automobiles.

He followed the footpath to the left of the parking area. A small iron fence chaperoned visitors away from the park's lush, undulating acres towards the Pavilion Tea House. Phelix picked up a large canine-mauled stick from the ground and with a spritely step skipped along the pathway dinging and pinging the stick along the fence's parallel bars as he went. His childish game didn't last long though, as the line of the fence was soon broken by an ornamental arch. Phelix, dropping the stick back to the ground, walked through.

Before him stood Sir Henry Tanner's Pavilion Tea House, a two-storey octagonal building in what Phelix knew as the rustic style. It had been built in 1906 when Oliver was nearly ten. Now not quite how it originally looked though, thought Phelix – the open veranda running round at ground floor level and the balustrade that ran round above the veranda had been removed. Phelix glanced upwards and saw the dovecote topped with its weather vane, showing Nelson looking through his telescope. That was the same, he remembered.

With his father – *Oliver's father* – being friends with Sir Henry he'd often be dragged up to visit the site during the pavilion's construction. Then when it eventually opened its Georgian-styled doors to the public, the family were among the first in the area to be served with The Pavilion Tea House's finest afternoon tea. Phelix smiled, and although it belonged to Oliver, he liked that memory.

"Spare some change for a drink, please."

"Sorry? Change?" replied Phelix, snapping out of his scone and strawberry jam daydream.

It was one of the men from the park benches. Judging by the lack of trolley – the first bench, thought Phelix. The man's blanket was wrapped around him, tied in a knot around his neck, almost cape-like, but dragging along the ground. He was somewhat smaller than Phelix imagined, although at some point in his life, probably before he developed his stoop, the man possibly stood taller.

"A few coins, enough for a cuppa-tea, please," replied the man, sheepishly.

Phelix looked into the man's eyes and saw sadness – years of sadness. Nights, winters, decades – perhaps a lifetime of sleeping under the stars – had ingrained the definition of sadness upon this man's face. Yet maybe time had been kind enough to etch a means of survival, for it was this very sadness which compelled Phelix to dig deep into his pocket and...

"Tell you what," said Phelix, holding out a few crumpled banknotes. "Walk with me for a while – be my guide for an hour or two and these are yours."

"G – Guide?" stuttered the man, whose stare was almost burning a hole into the notes.

"Yes. You know… answer a few questions and what have you." Phelix took one of the notes and stuffed it into the man's coat pocket. "You can have that one on account."

"What sort of questions?" The man looked frightened, his

weather-worn skin tightened as worry took a hold. "What if... I mean...what if I don't know the answer?"

"Well, that will be two of us then," laughed Phelix. "Shall we start with an easy one? What's your name?"

"Ben... Old Ben... Old Ben Abbott," replied the man, spurting out as much information as he could.

"Right, Ben. I'm Phelix..." There was a slight pause. Phelix slid his right hand into his coat pocket and cupped the Bulldog into his palm – it felt cold. His index finger eased its way through the trigger guard and then gently caressed the firing mechanism. "Phelix Bradbeer."

What? Oliver was outraged. Phelix ignored him.

"Phelix." Ben, outstretching his hand for Phelix to shake, didn't show any recognition of the name Bradbeer.

Phelix, who was hoping (and worrying) that the name might prompt a conversation, released the Bulldog from his palm, removed his hand from his pocket and accepted Ben's handshake; and with that the two men moved on.

After a few moments, Ben slowed his pace and took out a large polythene bag which had been crammed into his pocket. From around his neck he unknotted the blanket and stuffed it into the bag. As the two men walked slowly along Blackheath Avenue, Ben stopped at a waste bin, removed the black liner, stuffed his blanket into the bottom of the bin and then replaced the liner. Smart idea, thought Phelix, wondering how many other things were concealed in London's bins.

The park was starting to come to life. With over-indulgent calories to shed, the first of the morning's joggers had now taken to pounding the pathways. Early morning risers filtered

137

through the open gateways – dogs tugging at their leads, sticks to chase and balls to catch.

"What day is it?" asked Phelix, offhandedly.

"Saturday, I think," replied Ben. "Not too sure really, it's been a long time since it mattered."

Phelix had many, many questions to ask, most of which Ben could easily answer.

"What's that?"

"A parking meter. Surely you've seen one of those before?" replied Ben, who'd wandered off to pee behind a tree.

"Erm, no. What does it do?" asked Phelix, watching a path-pounder run by. "What's she got in her ears?"

"People – car drivers – have to pay to park their cars… that machine gives out the tickets," answered Ben, buttoning his flies and looking at the jogger. "Earphones – you know – for listening to music."

Phelix's knowledge of music was limited to hymns at St. Alfege's, concertos with mother in the West End, the odd sea shanty with Annie down at The Ship… and the barbaric noise he'd heard from the pizza charabanc the last time he visited the future – none of which he'd like to listen to whilst running. Still, perhaps one day he might give these 'ear contraptions' a go.

"What's the circle in the middle of the road for?" asked Phelix, who'd decided against asking where the music came from.

"Where did you say you're from?"

"I didn't." Phelix's response was curt. "The circle?"

"It's a roundabout…"

"A what?"

"It's for traffic. Whoever gets there first goes first."

Phelix stood in the centre of the mini roundabout, stretched out his arms and twirled around until he felt lightheaded and dizzy. "But what happens if two cars get here at the same time?" he asked, walking uneasily back to where Ben was waiting.

"The one on the right gets to go first."

"Oh," replied Phelix, nodding slightly. He wasn't too sure he understood, but as he was now eager to move on he accepted Ben's explanation.

The parking spaces around them slowly filled as the two men continued down Blackheath Avenue towards the park's gates. On their right they passed the Greenwich Park cricket pitch – Phelix's mind conjured up a summery image of leather screaming out as it cracked against linseed-fed willow and headed for an arm-raising six. Of course his memories were Oliver's and those were of spectator rather than participant.

"Have you got one?" asked Phelix, shaking *wimp* related thoughts from his mind. "An automobile?"

"A car? Yes… Got two. Keep them up at my house." Ben's reply, although croaky, was quite animated.

"Where's that? Your house?"

"I was being sarcastic," tutted Ben.

"I'm sorry…" Phelix, his cheeks reddening, felt embarrassed. "Have you ever had one?"

"Long time ago. Before…"

"Before what."

"It doesn't matter," sighed Ben.

The two men walked between a pair of tall brick pillars, both capped with limestone ornamentation and each topped off with a plain square lantern – they'd exited the park. Before them, in the distance, they could see the spire belonging to All Saints Church in Blackheath.

"Tell you what," said Phelix, who'd noticed that Ben's pace was slowing. "Let's sit down for a few minutes. You tell me about yourself and I'll tell you a bit about myself."

Ben, who was grateful for the rest, agreed.

Over the next few minutes Phelix learned that Ben, although he looked older, was (at Ben's best guess) in his mid-fifties. He'd been living rough, out on the streets, under the stars, ever since he'd 'lost it all' after some Black Monday back in the late eighties. None of what Ben was telling him made any sense to Phelix, but he did recognise loneliness, failure and the feeling of not being understood.

"Would you ever like to have it back?" asked Phelix. "Normality… your house… your car… your life?"

Ben snorted a funny kind of laugh, his pupils widened as his eyes lit up at the thought of 'normality'. But then the spark fizzed away as the thought of 'bills', 'commitment' and 'responsibility' filled his head with dread.

"Yeah." Ben's face cracked a smile. "But perhaps somewhere out in the country would be nice. Somewhere quiet, eh? Now what about you? What's your story?"

Phelix pondered for a moment on where to start. Should he tell the truth? What difference would it make – Ben wouldn't believe him, and if he did, what good would it do him? No one would believe one of society's lowlifes – *time travellers indeed.*

140

"Well, I was born in Greenwich. Not far from here actually. Only I was born... in the last century."

"Yeah... me too," laughed Ben.

"Mm!" Phelix acknowledged he'd got that wrong and corrected himself. "I mean, I was born in ninety-six. Eighteen ninety-six."

"Yeah, right." Ben gave Phelix a contemptuous look and stood up. "Let's get you to Blackheath."

"Sit back down, please Ben." Phelix spoke softly. "Let me explain... or at least try to."

Phelix told Ben everything. Everything except the trouble he'd had with his father, everything except his real name being Oliver, everything except the killings and the robberies.

They argued, or at least Ben did, over the possibilities and impossibilities of time travel. Of course, he didn't believe Phelix one iota, but as there was still the opportunity, the dangled carrot of money, Ben went along with whatever Phelix was telling him.

"When the day is over... and it's time for me to return... I'll show you," said Phelix, calmly standing up. "Let's go, shall we?"

The two of them continued their walk along the white fine-stone footpath which cleaved its way through the heathland towards Blackheath itself, Ben trying to explain how traffic lights worked, and then having to explain what *'it's hardly rocket science'* meant. In the end, Ben gave up. "I'll show you when we get to another set of lights, okay?"

Their conversation shifted to the view on the horizon behind them, Canary Wharf. Phelix painted a picture of industrious dockland life, tall ships, clippers, and schooners – the hustle and bustle, be it Georgian, Victorian or Edwardian. Ben brought Phelix up to date with how the modern-day docks had functioned. He explained how cheap oriental imports, the severing of old colonial ties in favour of new European trade, along with air freight (another complex subject for Phelix) had all contributed to the downfall of London's docks. Ben then related how, phoenix-like, London's new Docklands area had risen from the ashes of the old – urban regeneration at its best.

The time was just after seven according to the clock on Ferrey's All Saints Church which now stood before them. It was a quaint little church, built on land donated by the Earl of Dartmouth and, Phelix explained, consecrated by the Bishop of London in 1858.

"How do you know all this?" asked Ben.

"Local history – used to be a bit of a passion of mine," replied Phelix, feeling relieved that he'd not forgotten some of what Oliver had learned.

The buildings in and around Blackheath Village mainly pre-dated the 1900s – most were three storeys high and symmetrically uniform in their Victorian red-brick construction. Other than the bright and bold fascias above the shop fronts and the 20th century street furnishings nothing much had changed in Blackheath since Phelix's (Oliver's) last visit here with his mother a few, true time, weeks ago.

Although there were plenty of commuters milling around and rushing here and there, Blackheath, with its numerous pubs, cafés, restaurants, hair-salons and estate agents, had yet to come to life. Fashion boutiques with their sparsely dressed shop fronts offered garments at prices which would have kept a Victorian family fed for a year – a Georgian family for a lifetime. Ben tried to explain about the cost of living in London – house prices, rents, rates and what have you.

"Yes, I understand all that," Phelix countered. "But this is Blackheath. You know – the place where they buried the dead."

"Dead?"

"Black Death… the Plague." Phelix explained that, for centuries, Blackheath had been associated with the 1665 Plague and the Black Death of the mid-14th century, and that it was nothing more than one of London's burial pits.

"But that's just urban myth, legend," protested Ben.

"Is it?" said Phelix, looking back in the direction of the heath. "Haven't you ever wondered why they've never developed the heathland? You know, built on it?"

It was a rhetorical question, one which Ben could perhaps, on another day, debate with a tourist or someone else of 'his kind'. As it was, Phelix was feeling hungry, more so now he could smell the teasing aroma of bacon wafting down the high street.

It had taken almost twice as long for Phelix to decide on which sauce, red or brown, to have on his bacon baguette as it had taken him to eat it. In the end, after troughing down one with brown sauce on, he returned to the sandwich store for another, with red. Ben, on the other hand, who'd chosen the no sauce option, was just happy that he didn't have to go rifling through the trash bins in search of discarded morsels to feast on.

It was whilst sandwich scoffing, and much to the annoyance of several passing motorists, that Phelix (who'd just been given a crash course in how a pedestrian crossing worked) found great pleasure in continually pressing the 'STOP' button on a set of traffic lights.

"Is there a jeweller's store in Blackheath?" asked Phelix, who'd now become bored of his traffic control game.

"Think so," replied Ben, finishing off his sandwich. "Blacks... if it hasn't closed down."

The two men meandered along the high street in the general direction of where Ben hoped Blacks jewellery shop would be. Phelix wasn't in any hurry, he still had over an hour to while away before the 9am high street store unbolting ritual commenced. Ben wasn't in any hurry, he still had sixteen hours to idle away before he returned to his park bench slumber.

They passed several clothes shops, none of whose bright display lights managed to entice Phelix into a spot of window shopping. However, something in one window did catch his eye.

"Chinese food... to take away." Phelix shook his head in disbelief. "FREE home delivery... I've seen it all now."

"No, you haven't," tutted Ben, almost silently.

Phelix scanned down the menu and laughed loudly as the thought crossed his mind of some aged, little Chinese man knocking on Annie's door with a pork char siu and fried rice.

Three shops later and they were standing outside Blacks of Blackheath.

"Georgian," declared Phelix, looking at the parade of shops which Blacks stood in, before deciding to re-evaluate his decision. "I think."

"How can you tell either way?" asked Ben, who hadn't got

144

the faintest when it came to construction periods – they were all just buildings to him.

Phelix didn't answer. For once, he wasn't too sure. He knew that in Georgian construction they used yellow bricks – he'd passed enough piles of them walking through Greenwich with Annie to know that.

To the right of the shop there was a large passageway leading to the rear. One time access to the stables, suggested Phelix, who was now making a mental note to visit Blackheath when he returned to the 18th century. In front of the passageway, sandwiched between modern flagstones, was a small stretch of older cobblestones – Phelix liked these.

The shop front itself retained many of the store's features, curved glass windows, tessellated entrance floor and foxed Victorian mirrors above the doorway.

"Probably became a shop in… around…" Phelix touched the front window, flicked the glass with his finger and then placed his right ear against it. "Eighteen-seventy… perhaps sixty. At a guess."

"You can tell that just by flicking the glass?"

"Nope," grinned Phelix. "By reading the signs."

"Signs?"

Ben groaned as Phelix pointed to the neatly tiled entrance floor. Embedded within the mosaic it read, 'Est'd 1860 – H.A. Figg'.

Still having nearly an hour to kill before Blacks opened, the two men continued their walk along Blackheath's now much busier high street.

Other than the posters advertising Awayday-Deals to

145

countryside retreats, Blackheath railway station hadn't changed much since it had been built in the 19th century. The station was a London Brick design, featuring several high arched sash windows and two doorways which led to the lower level platforms. The only thing of note which caught Phelix by surprise was a sign indicating the direction of an 'Automatic 24 hr toilet' – he had so many questions.

Thankfully for Ben, they needed to cross the road and once again Phelix took great pleasure from stopping the traffic using the lights outside the nearby florist's shop. This meant that Ben didn't have to try to explain which part of the toilet process was *'Automatic'*.

Much to the disgruntlement of the management, they whiled away the last hour over a couple of coffees in a rather pretentious café. Phelix had chosen a small table by the window for them to sit at, one which gave him a perfect view of Blacks.

"Do you get much of this?" asked Phelix, commenting on the atmosphere.

"Not really – not my kind of place, if you know what I mean."

They both laughed.

"Well, Ben," said Phelix, fishing into his coat pocket and handing over some crumpled ten pound notes to his new friend. "This is where we say our goodbyes."

"Goodbyes?" replied Ben, tentatively accepting the money.

"Yes, my friend. Looks like they're opening..." Phelix pointed towards the jewellers and sighed. "I'll be able to get what I need and then return to my own time."

Ben looked, almost sympathetically, at Phelix as he stood

146

up – his eyes searching for answers – his mind trying to understand. "You said that you'd show me – prove that you're from…"

"Another time."

Ben raised himself out of his chair, readying himself to leave with Phelix. "Yes."

"I will. Trust me. Before the end of the day, I will," Phelix replied, indicating that Ben should sit back down.

Phelix approached the café's counter.

"Sir?"

"I must be going, but another coffee for my friend please," said Phelix, as he handed over a ten pound note. "Keep the change."

CHAPTER 16

Blacks of Blackheath

A small brass bell rang out as Phelix pushed open the wooden front door to Blacks and stepped inside.

The shop looked as old on the inside as it did on the out. Tired displays of polished silverware cluttered small glass shelves which appeared to have been randomly positioned here and there. Jars of mustard and preserves sporting silver lids nestled between photo frames and serving spoons. None of these would make an ideal *'I'm sorry'* gift for Annie, Phelix thought.

Umpteen necklaces, pendants and brooches sat shining away under the halogen glare from the stainless steel spotlights which were suspended from the high ceiling.

Trays of rings filled one of the glass topped display cabinets. Diamonds sat with cubit, rubies sat with amethyst – there was no rhyme nor reason to how they were presented, as they were offered for sale at anything between pocket money and pay cheque prices.

Tankards, trophies and tags were perched on the shelves behind the counters along with signs offering a *'Free Engraving Service'* with every purchase. Other signs touted *'Watch batteries fitted – while you wait'*, *'Watch straps fitted – from £7.00'* and

'Jewellery Repairs – Free Quotes'.

"Morning."

"Morning," replied Phelix, placing his right hand into his coat pocket and cupping the Bulldog revolver in his palm. He'd been greeted by a smartly dressed middle-aged man who was placing a couple of trays filled with higher-end merchandise into a more befitting cabinet.

"Can I help you at all?"

Phelix hesitated, he could feel his index finger caressing the revolver's trigger guard. "I'm looking for a gift – for a friend."

"Lady?"

"Yes," replied Phelix, thinking his answer could've been somewhat debateable by many of the Ship's regulars.

"For what occasion? Birthday?"

"No… No, nothing like that." Phelix, running his thumb over the gun's smooth wooden handle, considered his answer. "It needs to say – sorry."

"Sorry?"

"Yes." Phelix, feeling unnecessarily embarrassed, gripped the Bulldog tightly and slipped his index finger through the trigger guard. "Only…"

"There's no need to explain, sir. Do you have anything in mind? Bracelet, necklace… perhaps?"

"I hadn't really thought."

"Does she – your lady friend – have any pieces which we could complement?"

"Complement?"

"Yes, sir. Complement… match!" explained the jeweller.

Many *pieces*, some fine – others not so, had passed through

149

both Annie and Phelix's hands in the past year or so. With the exception of one – Henry Payne's brooch (which still remained hidden amongst the crucifix, spoons, and needles in the drawer of Annie's dresser) – all of them had been traded for essentials – food, money, alcohol, bribes.

"A brooch perhaps?" The jeweller noticed that Phelix's eyes were drawn to the selection neatly displayed on two velvet cushioned pads. Removing the pads from the display plinth, the jeweller placed them on the glass counter for Phelix to peruse.

"Mm, possibly." Phelix relaxed his grip on the Bulldog.

There were roughly twenty pieces in various sizes and styles displayed on each of the pads, and although flowers and butterflies accounted for the majority of designs, other patterns ranged from a jade turtle to a gold and silver Celtic cross.

The one which caught Phelix's attention was a small, intricate heart – a beautiful brooch which had several different sized rhinestones set into a rose-tinted mount, finished with an arrow flashing through the centre.

"Are they real diamonds?" asked Phelix, pointing to the brooch.

"No, sir. Diamante – set into a u…" The jeweller paused – stuttered, and then hesitantly continued. "Unique mount which contains a touch of Welsh gold."

Phelix had noticed the change in the jeweller's tone, and then realised why. His travel bracelet had slipped down his wrist and was now resting on the back of his hand. It had been the bracelet's luminous lily-white glow which had caught the jeweller's attention.

"Touch?" Phelix lowered his arm, allowing his sleeve to

once again conceal the bracelet.

"Sorry?" replied the jeweller, his mind elsewhere.

"You mentioned a touch of Welsh gold. Is that what gives it the pink colour?"

"Er… er… No. That's copper." The jeweller took in a deep breath and regained his composure. "I have to ask. Do you mind if I take a look? At your bracelet? Only I've…"

"Erm..." Phelix was caught off guard. It was alright showing someone the bracelet – it was the damn questions which followed that he didn't care for. But, as the jeweller was being helpful… "Yeah, sure."

Releasing the gun, Phelix removed his right hand from his pocket and rolled back his left sleeve. His bracelet, radiating with its familiar ethereal aura, shone brightly on his wrist.

"Do you mind?" asked the jeweller, indicating that he'd like to touch it.

Phelix shrugged.

"It's platinum, isn't it?" asked the jeweller, touching one of the links. As he did so the bracelet's halo-like gleam pulsed.

"Yes. I believe so," replied Phelix, drawing his hand away and allowing the glow to return to a constant.

"It's a bit loose though. Ever thought of having a few links removed?" suggested the jeweller. "It's a wonder you haven't lost it."

Phelix's mind raced to its hidden canal-side memory. Oliver, Shoreditch, 1940. Slitherum, slatherum – lost it. "Could you do that?"

The jeweller picked up a telephone from behind the sales counter and pressed one of the numbers on its keypad. "Karen?

Do you mind coming down and watching the shop? I've an alteration to do."

Less than five minutes later Phelix found himself standing in the jeweller's small, cramped workshop at the rear of Blacks.

The chaotic organisation of the store flowed into the workshop. Boxes – both small and large – were piled here and there, crammed under tables and stacked on shelves. Some had lids, most had labels.

Along one of the walls, under a shelf holding ledgers, pamphlets and booklets, there was a small, cushion-topped table. Several pieces of jewellery, mainly rings and watches, were carefully laid out, each with a brown hand-written tag attached. A small sign pinned to the back of the table clearly identified the pieces as *'Repairs and Alterations'*.

Under the window, positioned to make the most of any natural daylight, sat the jeweller's workbench. It was an old wooden table, with a large semi-circular cut-out crafted into it. The surface was covered in leather, padded in some places, worn in others.

Phelix recognised most of the tools which were racked up in various stands – tweezers, reverse action tweezers, scribers, pliers (round nose, snipe nose, half round and flat nose), pincers, screwdrivers, magnifiers, files, mallets – along with bashers and bodgers of every shape and size.

To the right was a borax dish along with a cone, next to this a soldering block, some iron binding wire and a rather fiercely burning melting torch. Phelix watched as the jeweller sat himself down onto a small swivel stool and manoeuvred himself into the cut-out.

"Let's take a look then."

After some dithering, Phelix unfastened the bracelet and handed it over to the jeweller.

"How does it do that? The glow, is it kinetic?"

"Something like that," answered Phelix, who decided that he liked that explanation enough to file it away for use on another day.

"Mm… Not the best clasp I've seen," remarked the jeweller, fastening the two joining links together and then pulling them apart with ease. "Bit Victorian, if you ask me."

"Is there better?"

"Better? Definitely," replied the jeweller, without hesitation. "You can have anything from clip and turn clasp to permanent – your choice really."

"In that case." Phelix, untucked his left trouser leg from his boot and pulled up the material to reveal his second bracelet; the one which would always take him home, the one which would return him to his own true time – September, 1913. "You can start with this one."

It took the jeweller less than five minutes to carefully remove a pair of links and the clasp from the bracelet. Then, after several attempts, he managed to balance it back over Phelix's ankle. With a strip of thick leather to protect the flesh, the jeweller, using a platinum filler wire and years of experience, then carefully laser-welded the bracelet back together.

The jeweller then pointed to the shining bracelet on Phelix's left wrist. "Would you like me to do that one?"

Phelix shook his head. He'd thought about having its clasp altered, but he only needed to use the bracelet to return to the

Round Room – he was hardly going to lose it in the next few minutes. "I'll leave that one, for now."

The jeweller moved away from his bench, and with the aid of a small step ladder, retrieved a brown cardboard box from one of the shelves. He opened the box and sifted through a selection of small bubble-wrapped parcels. He picked one and handed to Phelix. "The brooch. The one you liked."

"Thank you," replied Phelix, who'd almost forgotten why he'd visited the jewellers in the first place. "How much do I owe you?"

"Nothing. It's yours… That's if you don't mind me keeping those?" The jeweller pointed to the links and clasp he'd removed from the bracelet. "And if you come across any more… well, you know where I am."

Phelix nodded in agreement, the few pieces of lifeless platinum were hardly of any use to him.

The jeweller left Phelix with Karen, who dutifully placed the 'I'm sorry' brooch in a more befitting padded gift box.

"Would there be anything else, sir?" she asked, handing Phelix the box.

"No, thank you," he smiled. Phelix turned to leave the store, but then hesitated.

Oliver was talking – shouting at him. *Oh yeah, just walk out. Smart move, Phelix.*

"What?" whispered Phelix.

You can't leave half a sodding bracelet here. Idiot.

"Two frigging links and a clasp! Why do I need them?"

Are you as thick as two short planks, or what? Evidence, future usage, whatever. Think about it, stupid.

"Is everything okay, sir?" asked Karen, looking at him.

Ignoring her, Phelix moved over to a display cabinet to continue his argument with Oliver. He had to admit, Oliver had a point.

Well? asked Oliver.

"Hold on," Phelix hissed. He needed to think. For all their new-fangled lives people here were still scared of guns. Very scared. And… not many people seemed to have them.

Remember that incident in the chemist, Oliver reminded him.

Yes, he hadn't actually shot anyone. Just brandished the gun. Maybe guns weren't allowed in the future, and… he'd got what he wanted. So why not try that again here?

"Okay," he said to Oliver. "You've convinced me."

He felt into his pocket and put his fingers around the Bulldog.

Good idea, encouraged Oliver.

Phelix walked to the jewellery shop door, drew the bolt across and turned its hanging sign to read 'closed'.

He turned to Karen and slowly lifted the Bulldog from his pocket. He didn't even need to point it at her.

"O… Oh God! What do you want?" She was holding onto the counter.

Phelix smirked. It looked as though her legs were buckling, giving way. "There's something I forgot – from your workshop."

It was easy. Karen stood at the counter quivering, and even Mr Black himself had shown no objections. Phelix helped himself to couple of items from Black's workbench, stuffed them into his backpack, and then retrieved the platinum bracelet links and the clasp.

He was now back in 1913, his own true time, and had just entered his father's office.

"Fucking lousy bastard," he ranted, as he swept everything from his father's desk onto the floor with his arm. "Just three – just three fucking bracelets."

He could hardly blame his father – he could hardly blame anyone – he'd been the one who'd taken, used, abused, and yet not returned any of the time travel bracelets. But then again, he didn't realise he had to.

He picked up and replaced the stand of engravers back onto the desk, took out a leather sand-filled pad from the draw and quickly engraved a bracelet – 15.05.2012. "That one's for Ben," Phelix said aloud. A promise is a promise, after all – be it good or bad.

He'd spent a little more time engraving, perfecting and embellishing the bracelet which would take him back to the 17th century, back to his Annie. After a few seconds of deep, thought-related turmoil, he decided that it would be best to give Annie some time to get over the beating he'd given her. But how much time? A day? A week? A month? A year?

Phelix asked Oliver for advice, and between them they'd decided that it was better to be safe than sorry, a woman's scorn and what have you. Four years should do it, he thought, as he fastened the bracelet around his left wrist.

He was just about to leave the office when he noticed, amongst the pile of things which had crashed to the floor, a small framed picture of his mother – Oliver's mother.

Carefully retrieving the photograph, he sat back down in the chair and smiled. For that one brief moment it wasn't Phelix Bainbridge who was holding the picture – Oliver Bradbeer had, in both body and mind, returned.

Happy memories of his mother filled Oliver's head – summer walks, birthday parties, theatre trips, West End shopping along with there-there hugs and unconditional love. It wasn't long before these childhood recollections brought a tear to his cheek. After letting out a deep sigh Oliver replaced the photograph, wiped the tears from his eyes, then stood up and left the office.

His walk along the pitch black passageway towards the Round Room was slow at first, it was as though the younger Oliver within him had surfaced a little stronger than had been intended. Yet the more dominant Phelix took control and very soon the gait became more purposeful.

But what about Mother? Oliver, memories afresh, was nagging, the pace slowed.

"Shut up, will you. I've told you, she'll be fine." Phelix lengthened the stride.

Not if your plan works, she won't be.

"My plan?" Phelix shouted. "It's as much yours as mine… and don't you forget that."

Yes, but I didn't think, did I? I mean… it's bad enough putting an end to Uncle Philip and Isaac… but I can't let you hurt Mother.

"She's not a Bradbeer, you idiot. She only married one."

But…

"And look what she ended up with for her troubles… You."

Me?

Phelix abruptly stopped walking and sat down on the tunnel's tiled floor.

"Look, your mother… our mother, will be fine. She only married a Bradbeer. Which means when I've, when we've, finished… and the plan has worked she'll still be born… still be alive."

But what will happen to her?

"Unfortunately, my dear Oliver, that's something we'll never know."

And Father?

"He won't exist. If the Bradbeers can't buy Flamsteed Way none of them will exist." Phelix laughed.

None of them? None at all?

"Well… some will. Only they won't be the ones that you know. They'll all have met and married someone else."

Who?

"How the fuck do I know? Are you stupid, or what?" Phelix's tone was quite aggressive.

Okay. But when it's over. When we know that your plan has worked, can we just get on with a normal life?

"Yes, of course. Anything else?"

There wasn't. Thankfully, for now, the voice inside Phelix's head had gone. Rising from the floor he continued along the passageway and entered the Round Room.

First, using the bracelet he'd just scribed, Phelix made a quick trip to Tuesday, 15th May 2012 to get some information. This was followed by an even quicker time trip back to Saturday the twelfth.

158

With his promise to Ben now kept, Phelix, pleased to be returning to the 18th century, once again straddled the gold meridian line which divided the ornate circular room into east and west, looked at his travel bracelet and took a deep breath.

The date he'd inscribed on the bracelet read 26.05.1751, the year of the Calendar Act, the year with only 282 days. He wondered whether he'd arrive back in May or July, either way – it didn't really matter, he wasn't going to quibble over a couple of months. Nearly four years would have lapsed since this morning. Annie would be four years older – four years wiser. Phelix hoped that with the passing of time there'd be forgiveness for his actions – for the beating.

"One way to find out." Phelix twisted his signet ring palm side, clasped his bracelet and disappeared, away from the world he loathed.

CHAPTER 17

Room Seven
26th July, the 5th month of 1751

After three hefty kicks, and splinters flying, the door to Annie Fletcher's ramshackle house finally gave way and Phelix, Bulldog in hand, foaming at the mouth with rage, stormed inside. He was after blood – Annie's blood.

A woman, far older than Annie, cowered in the corner by the bottom step, cradling a small crying child in her arms.

"Please," she pleaded. "We have nothing! Nothing at all."

"I know you're in here, come out," shouted Phelix, as he hurriedly brushed past the woman.

As though possessed, he thundered up the rickety wooden staircase and pushed open the bedroom door – nothing. With an unrepentant want for revenge hurtling through his body, and half-expecting to find Annie blenching with fear under the mattress, Phelix threw the bed to the wall. Again – nothing.

"Where the fuck is she?" he demanded, racing back downstairs and confronting the woman. "Where the fuck is she?"

"Who?"

The sobbing child, a boy in fear of his life, moved away as Phelix dragged the woman to her feet. He gripped her tightly around the throat and, pressing her against the wall, raised her from the floor. "Annie fucking Fletcher," he spat out wildly as he cursed.

The woman didn't reply, she couldn't – panic had taken a hold. She was gasping for air, if the light was any better Phelix would have been able to see the colour draining from her as his pincer-like grip cut off her air supply.

Let go of her – she knows nothing.

"Who asked you?"

You can see it in her eyes – she knows nothing. Just let her go.

Phelix let go. The woman, seconds away from passing out, moments away from her date with the gravedigger, dropped to the floor. Roles reversed, the child ran back to comfort her.

Now find her.

"Don't you worry – I will."

Good, then make the whore pay for what she's done. Unusually, and somewhat quite demonic, Oliver's voice laughed out in Phelix's head as he left the house in search of Annie.

He ran along the waterfront towards the Ship, it was as good a place as any to start, given that it was obvious that Annie had moved on in the last four years.

Business in the tavern was as expected for a midsummer night. Loud, incoherent banter filled the left bar as traders, sailors and locals vied to get their rambling points of view across to one another. In the bar to the right, a cacophony of music, stomping and chanting filtered out into the Greenwich night – a magnet for local revellers.

Phelix turned to the left, where both drinkers and diners

straddled the wooden benches. A couple of dogs, landrace collies, grazed between tables on discarded scrappits of sinew and bone. In the confines of the Ship's sooted brick fireplace, flames jumped around like wild firedancers performing for the night-time crowd. Picking up an unguarded jug of ale from a table, Phelix, keeping his head lowered, entered a room just off the bar.

The snuggery, as Phelix knew Charles Dickens would later call it, was a small comfortable room which, unlike the bar, benefitted from cushioned benches and chairs for the Ship's patrons to relax on. Heavy, pleated curtains hung from the two windows, which now thwarted the last light of the day as it tried to enter the room. With only two lanterns, and a near-spent candle struggling to provide any decent light, the room was an ideal setting for an intimate encounter. And, given the Lord Mayor's regular Monday night purge on street prostitution, the snuggery had also become an ideal room for the local harlots to ply their trade.

Phelix scanned the room. Couples – be they man and wife or client and whore – sat, almost huddled together along one of the walls. A lone man, waiting for a lady of the night to enter and sell him her pleasure, sat waiting patiently in one of the armchairs. Two men, doctors from the hospital judging by their appearance, both slightly worse for wear, were sitting in the corner by the window. Sandwiched between them, laughing and joking as though she'd known them forever – Annie Fletcher.

Phelix, concealed in shadows, sat at a bench directly across from them.

What are you waiting for? Uncontrollably, Phelix's hand slid into his coat pocket and gripped the Bulldog. *Do it.*

"Not here, too busy. Wait until they're outside – until she's alone."

Coward. Just give me the gun – I'll do it. Oliver's voice echoed inside Phelix's mind.

"No," shouted Phelix.

"Pardon, sir?" asked the man sitting in the armchair.

"Sorry. I thought one of those bleedin' dogs from next door had followed me in here," replied Phelix, without hesitation.

"Yes, they can be a bit of nuisance. Are you here on business?" asked the man, turning his armchair towards Phelix.

"Erm." Phelix's attention had shifted back to his quarry; Annie was about to go off with the two men and earn her shillings.

"Are you in Greenwich on business? Or pleasure perhaps?"

Phelix picked up his ale and used the jug to hide his face as Annie and the two men walked past. He waited for the snuggery door to close behind them, then stood up.

"Business," he replied, replacing the ale jug onto the table. "Definitely business."

From the snuggery doorway Phelix watched as the two men led Annie through the crowded bar towards the stairs which led up to the bedrooms.

"Wine to our room please, Joseph," shouted one of the men, slapping Annie playfully across her buttocks. "Better make it two bottles, though. This one can out-drink the both of us."

"Straight away, Mister Carter." Joseph Stafford, standing

behind his bar, acknowledged the order and directed one of his serving girls to fulfil it.

Phelix waited on the bottom step until he saw the young, tray carrying wench approach. "I'll take that, if you don't mind," said Phelix, forcefully taking the tray. "Which room?"

"Seven," she hesitantly replied, not knowing whether to protest or not.

"Thanks," smiled Phelix, tossing the girl a silver sixpence.

Rooms five, six and seven at the Ship were reserved for the local working girls to use. Joseph didn't mind his inn being used as a brothel – a bawdy house – as long as the men who frequented the rooms were spending money, Joseph was happy.

Phelix, somewhat cautiously, made his way up the large wooden, carpeted staircase. Although he'd been a regular at the Ship for a few years, he'd never ventured up the stairs, he'd never had need to.

The door to room five was slightly ajar. Tempted by curiosity Phelix touched the door open with his boot and stepped inside. Along one wall were two small, identical, chests of drawers, 'the twins' as one of the Ship's chambermaids would call them. On top of the nearest stood two plain wooden candlestick holders each sporting a partial candle stump. Over the years the wax from the tallow candles had streamed, somewhat larva-like, down into the twists which had been turned into the wood. Between them stood a polished brass candle snuffer and some small wick trimming scissors. The second chest of drawers had a jug of water, a bowl and a couple of towels on top – one neatly folded, the other not so. Standing behind both chests, propped against the panelled wall, were two mirrors – not very practical for vanity, but ideal for reflecting the candlelight.

In the corner, by the window (for obvious reasons) stood a rather shabby-looking and somewhat toxic-smelling commode. In the centre of the room was a large, fabric-draped, four-poster bed with a leather riding crop placed in the centre of an eider bolster.

Phelix knew what the crop was for, and guessed that it had been left by a previous occupant. However, he had no idea why anyone would want to tether a stirrup and chain to each of the bedposts. Bewildered, Phelix left the room.

Even though the raucous noise from downstairs filtered its way onto the first floor, several different sounds were coming from room six. Grunts and groans, shouts and squeals, along with the scraping of furniture across the floor could be heard behind a woman's heightened demands of "Oh my God – Oh my God – DON'T STOP – Oh My GOD – Yes! Yes! YES!" Phelix, shaking his head in disbelief, placed the tray on top of a small occasional table and moved on to room seven.

In comparison to the previous room, seven was quiet. Phelix touched the side of his head against the door and listened for any sounds which he could decipher. He could hear the two men talking, demanding – demanding something from Annie. But what? Then came a hard slap, a sound he was all too familiar with.

Phelix knelt down and peered through the door's keyhole. Although the light wasn't brilliant he could see Annie on the bed, crouched on all fours. One of the men, Carter... the wine orderer... his shadow reflecting onto the wall, was behind her, his hand hitting out at her thighs as he pushed into her. The edge of the keyhole prevented Phelix from seeing the other man; however, he could clearly make out a hand grasping at Annie's hair... forcing her head downwards.

His palm clammy, Phelix turned the door handle and slowly attempted to ease the door open, but it was locked.

"Is that the wine? Leave it outside," shouted one of the men.

"I can't, I'm not allowed to," squawked Phelix, giving his best attempt to sound feminine. With his eye still at the keyhole he watched as one of the men, the one who'd been holding Annie's hair, climbed down from the bed.

Removing the Bulldog revolver from his coat pocket, Phelix picked up the tray and watched the door. Not only could he hear the soft sound of footsteps as they approached, he could feel the slight movement in the floorboards beneath his soles as the man, less than a few feet away, stepped closer.

Phelix's heartbeat intensified. He tensed as he heard the clunks of the lock tumblers as they turned under the weight of the key, then he took a step backwards as the door's handle twitched as it was being gripped on the other side.

He recalled the night that he saved Annie's life. The night that he morphed from child to man – then from man to killer. The night that the Thames took the bodies of Joshua Wells and Henry Payne – the night on which the feeble, weak-minded Oliver Bradbeer became Phelix Bainbridge.

Leave her, she's not worth it.

"You've changed your tune all of a sudden, haven't you?"

Yes... But.... What if you – I mean we – get hurt?

166

"Stop being a bloody coward will you! You either want revenge – or you don't."

Oliver's conscience didn't answer – it was too late.

When he opened the door, Christopher Marlow, junior physician by day, whore tamer by night, didn't get quite what he expected.

Instead of being greeted by the beautiful smile and corset-enhanced cleavage of one of Joseph's finest girls, Marlow was greeted by Phelix Bainbridge's size ten boot striking into his groin.

"What the hell?" shouted Carter, casting Annie to one side and leaping from the bed.

"Phelix?! Oh God. No!" Annie recognised him instantly, but her pleading was all in vain.

Phelix, with the force of his entire bodyweight behind him, had smashed one of the two wine bottles into the side of Marlow's balding head. Crimson droplets of imported French claret blended with Warwickshire blood, and splattered over the cheap Irish bedlinen.

"Just stay there," shouted Phelix, raising the Bulldog at Carter's head. "Just stay there."

Shoot him. Let him have it.

"Shut up, Oliver… Shut up."

"Oliver? Who's Oliver?" Annie stared at the door, as though half-expecting someone else to come barging into the room.

And you can shut that filthy tramp up. Ruining our fucking plan.

Phelix, Bulldog in hand, dropped to his knees. Clutching agonisingly at his temples he screamed. "Leave me alone, Oliver. Just leave me alone."

Although fraught with panic, Carter, sensing the disorientation in his aggressor, ran for the open doorway, and fell, almost blindly, down the stairs to his safety.

"Phelix?" shouted Annie, as she grabbed her clothes off the floor and started edging her way towards the open doorway. "Why?"

But there was no answer. Phelix, oblivious to what was going on around him, and with tears running down his cheeks, rocked slowly on his knees.

Annie, now holding her clothes tightly, changed direction, she gingerly stepped over Marlow's blood-oozing body and approached her one-time friend, the man whose debt she would be forever locked into. "Phelix?"

Again, no answer. However, this time there was a change. Not a change in Phelix's manner, not a change in his stance – but a change in his eyes. Annie could – much worse than the last time – see pure, unadulterated rage in Phelix's eyes. She, like Carter seconds earlier, ran.

It may have been the hasty, candlelight enhanced, movements of Annie getting dressed which brought Phelix out of his trance-like state, or it may have been Oliver's silenced demands fading into the ether. The pulsating throb inside Phelix's head now eased, taking away the piercing pain with it.

With his senses recovering, Phelix surveyed his surroundings. Bedroom – the bed – crumpled covers. The floor – broken glass – Marlow's blood. Annie – she'd been naked and vulnerable – and now she was gone, running scared. And so she should, thought Phelix, his purpose returning.

He could hear shouting, growing louder – nearing. People – one, two? A crowd perhaps – on the stairs. Phelix frantically looked for a way out – there wasn't one. Window? There'd be a drop – too high? Door? Too many people. "Fuck!" The bed? Yes. Phelix moved quickly.

"In there," shouted Carter, directing Joseph Stafford and his mustered hands to the bedroom. Carter himself, having no weapon, lingered behind.

Joseph, raised lantern in his left hand, flintlock musket gripped tightly in his right, stepped over Marlow's lifeless body and cautiously entered the bedroom. "Sh-show yourself," he called out in a nervous stutter – but no one moved. Joseph, edging along the wall, moved to the right of the bed and, his finger teasing at the iron trigger, he used the musket's barrel to push the curtains apart. "Show yourself or we'll..."

"He's under the bed – get him," ordered Carter loudly from the doorway, as he moved aside to allow the four armed men into the room.

Carter was right, the bed had moved, and Joseph had seen it. All five armed men surrounded the large wrought iron bed. Four of the men pointed their muskets, primed and ready to fire at whatever or whoever flinched. The fifth man had a rather outdated harquebus, which, although the firearm deserved to be in an eighteenth century museum, packed a far greater punch than any of those new-fangled muskets.

"This is your last chance... come out now. We will fire,"

169

announced Joseph, looking for agreement in his friends'
expressions.

"One." Joseph had been here before. Usually youngsters
breaking into the cellar, trying to steal, trying to prove
themselves. His grip was sure.

"Two." And yes, Joseph had also been here before – several
times. Quite often it would be fighting drunkards or visiting
sailors, who needed a swift lesson on paying their way. His aim
was true.

"Thr - eeee." There weren't many times he'd had to count
this far before and when he did, calling out 'three' usually
calmed the situation. But Joseph, clenched palm gradually
becoming clammy and hand beginning to shake under the
weight of the musket, somehow knew this time was going to be
different.

"FIRE." It was Carter, standing in the doorway, standing
by the body of his best friend, who'd given the order – shouted
out the command.

As though rehearsed, the five trigger fingers acted
simultaneously and for a split second the semi-darkened room
was aglow as dragon-like sparks danced from their flintlocks.
Each of the guns cracked loudly, resonating in their own unique
way as, in unison with one another, they discharged their
deadly shots into the bed. The volley tore into the mattress,
sending eider feathers violently floating on the wisp of ignited
gunpowder. Spent sulphur permeated the air with a stench of
rotten eggs, a hideous odour which would linger long into the
night.

As Joseph Stafford had entered the bedroom, Annie Fletcher, with a solitary tear rolling down her cheek, had pushed her way through the mass of people who crowded the Ship's staircase and with Christopher Marlow's bitter taste still in her mouth she headed for the door.

She knew Phelix wasn't the nicest of people, but he'd been her friend. He'd been there for her, at first by chance, he'd stepped in when Henry Payne was about to kill her... she owed Phelix more than just friendship, she owed him her life... more tears started to stream as Annie shook the memory away.

Phelix had been there for her, cared for her, nursed her through the syphilis – how she wished that those days could be returned. Those days, once the lesions had cleared, were good. They had money, Phelix's 'penny-shilling' medicine had seen to that, but then it had changed – *he* had changed. It was that fucking enclosure – his so-called 'plan'. It was as though nothing else mattered to him. Annie then remembered the beating, she recalled the pain he'd inflicted upon her. And then he'd gone. She'd figured he couldn't face up to what he'd done. Or he just didn't care. So why had he come back, after so long? What did he want? Perhaps she owed him nothing, she was a fool to think she ever did.

Her pace faltered slightly as she heard the musket shots cry out over the bar room chatter. With a heart-wrenching sigh, Annie regained her composure, wiped the tears away from her face, opened the door and stepped out into the warm night air.

CHAPTER 18

Without Remorse

It had been Constable William Firth who, after discussing the ownership of a certain piece of land with one Septimus Wood, had introduced him to Annie Fletcher.

At the time of introduction, Phelix had been missing for over a year and, as Firth himself had witnessed Annie enclosing the land, she had, by default, become its legitimate owner. Septimus, who intended to build houses on the land, had paid her a fair price. Annie, in turn, had crossed Constable Firth's palm quite generously, and now, two-and-a-half years later, the houses – on Phelix's enclosure – were nearing completion.

Annie had put her windfall to good use. She'd bought herself what she considered to be a beautiful silver pendant, and now lived in a larger, rat-free house on Stockwell Street. It was there, upon leaving the Ship, she headed.

It had been a warm day in Greenwich, a little muggy if anything. The evening streets were unusually quiet. Annie, confused about her feelings for Phelix, walked quickly. Head lowered, she passed a young couple who were either coming from or going to – where, it didn't matter. She turned down Fryers Road and almost collided head on with a barrow boy returning home from a hard day's graft down at the market.

172

From the corner of her eye Annie noticed a fox, slinking between the buildings across the road, slyly braving the urban night as it searched out a scrap or two to feast on.

Barely a minute had passed since Annie's anguished departure from the Ship when she heard a sound; it startled her. It was a sharp, almost painful squeal, which drifted towards her from the darkened shadows on the opposite side of the road – her pace hastened further. The noise followed.

She caught the outline of someone... a man... following her. Annie's heart thumped – she was scared.

The noise changed direction – she stopped. It was in front of her, echoing against the night. Through the warm air, Annie felt an unearthly chill sweep over her body, the discord teased at her mind.

"Where are you going, Annie Fletcher?" The man, silhouetted against the moonlight, called out. His voice... the words... sounded hollow, devoid of feeling.

"Who's there?" Annie shouted out, and as she did so there was a hope that she'd attract some passing attention. But there was no answer, no one came running to save her. He knows my name, she thought. She looked over to the man, but he'd gone. A trick of the light, perhaps? Quick, Annie think – *the Ship* – she needed to get back to the Ship, to the safety of numbers.

"The darkness deepens." It was the voice again.

Turmoil – Annie's mind was in turmoil. The man, he'd been in front of her – twenty feet away – standing there. And now – how could it be? He was behind her – chanting – singing.

Annie took childlike steps towards him, she felt compelled to seek the identity of her tormentor, yet she was fearful of what each step would reveal.

Something was on the floor before her, a glint upon the footpath. Annie stopped and looked down. It was a knife – had it just been placed there? She recognised it – but from where? A distant past? A distant memory? She wanted to pick it up – examine it – but she didn't. What if he attacked her – caught her off guard? She looked up – he was gone.

She turned – nothing – he wasn't behind her. She turned again – nothing – just the knife. All was quiet, no noise, no singing and no man. Her heart rate calmed, her breathing steadied.

"Hello, Annie. Going somewhere?"

She didn't have time to answer. A hand had grabbed her tightly by the hair, pulling at her roots, and she was twisted down to the ground.

She could see the knife… it was at arm's length. Screaming wildly… kicking furiously… she reached out for it.

"You ruined my fucking plan, bitch."

"Phelix? Phelix! How the…?" spluttered Annie, desperately clawing for the blade. She knew he should be dead. She'd seen Joseph Stafford and the others, they'd entered the bedroom. She'd been outside – Phelix hadn't left – he couldn't have – she'd have seen him. Then she'd heard the shots – for fuck's sake, that was two, maybe three minutes ago. She screamed into the empty night as her head impacted the footpath.

Battling the trauma, Annie stretched out her hand. Her fingers brushed at the knife's hilt, she could feel it, she could sense the ingrained ridges which time had worn onto the bone-crafted handle, if only she could hold it.

Phelix was ranting at her, berating her for everything. She didn't want to die... not here... not tonight. Finally, with one last pain induced effort, she grasped the knife. It felt good. Through the pain, she felt good. One chance was all she needed. One lunge and this would be over.

Pushing her feet hard against a wall and using Phelix's own bodyweight Annie managed to twist herself to face him. She could see a burning anger in his eyes, this wasn't her Phelix, this wasn't the man she cared for – wasn't the man she loved.

A fist hit her full in the face, just below her nose, she could feel her teeth cutting into her bottom lip as Phelix drew his hand back for another swing. The second punch didn't land, it brushed past her cheek, as did the third. There wasn't another.

She could feel her petticoat tearing as Phelix grabbed at her, shook her. With the knife clenched knuckle-tight, Annie swung her arm back. This was it, two seconds and it would be over. And then what? And then Firth could fish this bastard out of the Thames, she thought. With one last surge of energy, Annie brought her arm forward towards Phelix's back, but as she did her head once again struck the pavement, only this time harder... much harder.

Annie was a split second too slow, she could feel her arm drop under the weight of the knife, then her palm opened and the knife fell back to the ground. "Why?" she agonisingly whispered, as she faded into unconsciousness.

It was on Joseph Stafford's count of 'two' that Phelix, cramped under the bed, had brought palm to wrist and returned to 20th century safety, back to the Round Room. Hell bent on revenge, and without hesitation, Phelix headed straight back to 1751.

Keeping a safe distance, he'd followed himself to what had been Annie's house and then spied from the shadows as he'd kicked in the door. It had felt weird watching himself, knowing what was going to happen, where he was going to go next. He'd been standing outside, listening to the screaming woman's mercy pleas as they filtered through the thin walls of the house, and it had given him the feeling he craved for, that feeling of power.

Phelix had watched himself enter the Ship, waited until he'd seen Annie leave, followed her onto Fryers Road and then, with the help of a couple of back and forth time trips, he'd pounced.

He dragged the unconscious Annie down one of the narrow alleyways which branched off Fryers Road.

Just get it over with. Kill her. What are you waiting for? Get the gun out and pull the fucking trigger.

Phelix, who'd somewhat calmed down, ignored these bloodthirsty demands. Instead, and much to Oliver's nagging disapproval, he resorted to opening up his backpack and eating the last of the wine gums.

Annie was slumped up against a small pile of bricks which were stacked near the alley wall, and even though the bruising around her left eye looked severe, and there were a few trickles of now dried blood down her cheek, Phelix thought she looked peaceful.

As far as he was concerned his plan was now over. Ruined

by Annie. The house – his childhood home – had been built. The Bradbeers would move in – he in turn would be born – and the cycle would begin again.

It never occurred to Phelix that all he needed to do, to put things right, was go back a couple of years, perhaps four, and make a few changes here and there. Instead, he dreamt up a new plan and decided that, when this was over, to finally head for 1946 and begin his search for Thomas the bargeman plus his namesake Phelix, of course.

With his decision made, Phelix tucked his trousers back into his boots, slung his backpack over his left shoulder, placed the brooch which he'd acquired for Annie in her hand, and stood up.

Is that it then? You're not going to finish her?

"No, Oliver. I'm not," replied Phelix, calmly.

Coward. Give me the fucking gun. I'll do it. Phelix's right hand slipped into his coat pocket.

"No," he shouted, removing his hand.

Do it… she ruined everything. Can't you see?

It could've been the movement of Phelix placing something in her hand, or the harsh shouting she could subconsciously hear, or perhaps a mixture of both, either way Annie had come round.

Every inch of her head was pulsating with a searing agony. Her scalp felt as though it had been stretched beyond belief by the hair twisting, and the area above her left ear throbbed with a dense, biting pain from where her head had hit the footpath. With her tongue she could feel her swollen lip, feel the indents her teeth had made in it and taste the blood. Annie tried to open her eyes, but could only see hazily through her right, and nothing at all through her left – this didn't surprise her given how tight her face felt.

There was a devastating soreness throughout her body, and it felt as though she'd been kicked and punched all over. Although, with her senses slowly returning, and even though she had a jagged corner from one of the bricks digging into her back, Annie decided it was best if she didn't move. The last thing she wanted right now was to give Phelix an excuse to inflict more suffering on her fragile body.

Annie could feel something in her palm; Phelix had put it there – he'd actually been quite gentle – but what was it? What was she holding? Annie risked a look – a brooch – he's given me a fucking brooch, she cursed.

Voices – Annie could hear muffled words, people were talking about something, about her. She listened carefully... tried to focus on the voices, but she could only hear one, Phelix's. Who was this Oliver he was arguing with? She'd heard Phelix call out the name in the Ship. What was he to Phelix? A friend? He'd never talked about a friend – he'd never mentioned the name Oliver before. Who was he?

She heard Phelix shout. "No, Oliver. For the last time, no!"

Maybe this Oliver was standing to her left. Annie was too scared to turn, if only she could see through her left eye, catch sight of him.

She could see Phelix remove something from his pocket. Her heart rate rapidly increased, her body tensed – Phelix was holding his Northern musket. Christ, she'd seen him use it several times, knew what it could do, how well it could kill.

178

Then she heard Oliver's intentions. Annie's legs suddenly felt warm and wet.

"I'll throw the fucking thing away," shouted Phelix, waving the Bulldog in the air.

Why would you do that? Oliver, as usual, was in contradictory mode.

"Because you want me to kill her," snarled Phelix.

But you wanted her dead. You wanted to kill her. Five... ten minutes ago... that was all that was on your mind. And I should know.

"Yes. I know that. You fucking idiot."

Then do it... What are you waiting for? Just do it. Coward.

"Killing her won't change anything, will it?" argued Phelix "I'll still love her."

Having had enough of the squabbling. Phelix knelt down, unbuckled his backpack and slipped the Bulldog down to the bottom.

Annie's breathing was becoming more aggressive, she was scared, frightened for her life. Phelix had turned his back on her, he couldn't see her. Oliver, was he there? It had gone quiet. Annie braved a look to her left. Nothing – there was no one.

"It can stay in there now," said Phelix.

A few seconds passed. Had Oliver left?

"No," Phelix snapped. "Let's just go, get out of here."

Annie was confused. Who was Phelix talking to?

"Kill her if you want then. But I'm having nothing to do with it, Oliver."

It suddenly dawned on Annie that there wasn't a second

person, there wasn't this mysterious Oliver – Phelix was arguing with himself. Two people, two personalities, locked into one body – one mind.

Annie thought about the man who laughed with her, was there for her – cared for her. Then she thought about the man who hit her, punished her – belittled her. It all made sense now.

What if Oliver was the stronger? He wanted her dead, and Phelix had just told him to do it, just told Oliver to kill.

"No, it's staying in there. Use Henry's knife if you're going to do it."

Annie knew she had to move, had to do something – and quick. She could see the knife on the floor, just to the side of Phelix. Shit – was that really Henry Payne's knife? Annie watched as Phelix leaned slowly towards it. Panic seized her, she couldn't run – he'd be too fast for her – he'd catch her. She couldn't fight – he was far too strong for her – the bruises were testimony to that.

Her heart palpitating wildly, Annie dropped her 'new' brooch and grabbed hold of one of the loose bricks from the stack, and then, channelling her last ounce of remaining strength into her legs, she lunged at Phelix's head.

Phelix had just picked up the knife when Annie, brick clenched tightly in her right hand, struck him on the side of his head. Screaming out both in shock and agony, he fell to the ground.

"Why, Phelix? Why?" Annie cried out against the night. She hit out again, although this time not as hard – not as accurate.

"Bastard." She struck for the third time – hitting Phelix's

shoulder.

Fourth time – his arm. Annie sobbed.

There wasn't a fifth. The brick fell to the ground, she hadn't the strength to hold it, let alone swing it. It didn't matter, Phelix was out cold.

Annie, weak at the knees, bereft of energy, slowly pulled herself to her feet. She'd had enough, her body had taken more than enough.

Phelix – Oliver – whoever – lay beaten, bleeding and bricked before her. She'd won.

"You won't be needing this any longer," said Annie, grabbing hold of Phelix's backpack. She took one last look at the man sprawled out in front of her and shook her head. Annie showed no emotion towards him, no feeling – her contemptuous look conveyed a thousand words.

Physically hurt, looking bedraggled, Annie Fletcher turned and staggered out of the alleyway.

Less than two hours later Annie's battered and bruised body was found on the corner of Fryers Road by Parish Constable William Firth. She had been repeatedly slashed and stabbed, in what Firth later described as a crazed, manic attack. Robbery – Firth deduced, as Annie's pendant was missing.

There was no mention of a khaki coloured backpack in Firth's report.

CHAPTER 19

Joyride
21st September, 1913

As the cold water cleansed Annie's blood from his hands, Oliver wept. His tears were filled with remorse and shame – guilt racked at his conscience.

He'd been frustrated with Annie – annoyed, angry. And why not? After all, she'd ruined his plan. But did he really have to take her life, kill her? But surely it hadn't been him, had it? It hadn't been the weak, feeble, cowardly Oliver who'd done the deed. No! It was obviously that bastard bully, Phelix Bainbridge… he'd done it.

With heavy heart, Oliver sighed as he watched the last remaining swirls of crimson-infused water disappear down the plughole.

It was time to say goodbye to the 18th century, he had nothing there any more, no reason to return. Annie would always remain in his heart and in his mind – the whacking great lump on his head would make sure of that. With the water still running, it now felt the right time to say goodbye to Phelix – wash him away – after all, he'd brought nothing but death and destruction into people's lives.

Leaving the rest room as he'd found it, Oliver opened the

182

door to his father's office. He shook his head in self-disgust at the mess, his mind flashing back to Phelix's earlier tantrum. "Oh, God! What have I done?" he cried, as thoughts of self-condemnation ran through his head.

After several minutes of self-berating, Oliver pulled himself together. He needed to have his wits about him – he needed to concentrate. His plan was for the future – 1946. An idyllic canal-side life. One filled with barges, towpaths, horses and apples – one without guns, bullets and death.

"Shit... bullets!?" Oliver grabbed his backpack from the floor and quickly rummaged through it. The Bulldog was there, some of his clothes, a roll of filler wire, a comic, some other odds and sods – even the coffee – but no Kynochs. "Damn...! Annie's trunk."

He reached for the bracelet box, and even though he knew that there'd only be one solitary bracelet in there, he still felt dejected as he looked at it.

1946 vs. 1751. Canal vs. bullets. Running away vs. doing what was right. Oliver knew he couldn't leave the bullets back in time. He had to retrieve them, he had to go back... he had no choice but to return to the 18th century.

Grabbing the bracelet from the box Oliver fastened it to his wrist... It fell off. "Bloody thing!" He fastened it again, this time he made certain that the clasp was secure... he shook his wrist... Once again, the bracelet fell off.

Taking the roll of platinum filler wire, Oliver cut off three short pieces, each about two inches long. Wearing the bracelet, he carefully entwined two of the strips around the clasp; folding, twisting, and threading them into a neat circular ball. Using a pair of snipe nose pliers, Oliver compressed – squashed – the soft platinum ball into an almost circular disc.

Finally he went over to the sideboard and lit his father's Teclu burner, regulated the influx of air by adjusting the screw nut and placed a crude copper-tipped soldering iron in its roaring blue flame. He slid a thick strip of leather between the bracelet and his wrist, then using the soldering iron and the last piece of filler wire, carefully infused the tanglement together. Not perfect by any means – but good enough, he thought, shaking his wrist to confirm that the bracelet was secure.

Oliver had just turned the burner off when he heard voices in the corridor. With his ear pressed to the office door he could hear two men – Edward and Philip Bradbeer, his father and uncle. They were talking about him – talking about a search. He heard a door close – the voices quietened.

Silently, Oliver left the office. His father and uncle were in the rest room, their conversation wasn't civil.

"I don't care what you thought. I still can't believe you lied to me." Oliver heard his father shouting.

There was a muffled, somewhat subdued reply from Philip. Oliver couldn't quite work out what was said, but gathered his uncle was being apologetic.

"And just what the hell am I supposed to tell Jane?" There was a loud noise – a crash. A chair being kicked, the table being overturned, thought Oliver.

He'd heard enough. Oliver removed the small wedge from the passageway door jamb, eased the door open and, in total darkness, made his way along the Prime Meridian towards the Round Room.

Although it would only take him about ten minutes to do, the walk along the pitch black tunnel was a lonely one. In the past he'd used this time to reflect, to think and to plan. Now, with his father's voice lingering in his mind, he was using this time to worry.

Wouldn't it be much easier to go back? Tell his father what he'd done. Surely he'd be able to put everything right – wouldn't he? Oliver, feeling a reassuring warmth inside, turned around and slowly headed back towards the doorway.

But then his father would find out about – the gun – the killings – Annie. Oliver stopped. Could he really admit to his father – his mother – that he was a killer, a murderer?

Decisions… decisions.

Oliver turned rapidly. Was someone there in the dark – standing next to him? His mouth went dry, his heart quickened.

Look at you, scared of your own shadow. Pathetic.

"Phelix? But…"

But what? Phelix's tone was aggressive. *You can't hide from me. You can't hide from yourself.*

Oliver suddenly felt weak. There was a throbbing pain in his head. Pulsating, pounding pressure by his left temple. He reached over to the wall for support, yet crumpled to the ground under the agony of the punishing pain. "Stop it, please," he cried.

If you go back we'll have to go to war, remember? Have to fight. You don't want that, do you? You don't want to get us killed, do you?

The pain intensified. "No," screamed Oliver. "No…"

Good. Then get up. We have to find those bullets… I've a feeling we'll need them.

185

With the pain vanishing almost as quickly as it had arrived, Oliver pulled himself up. Ordinarily he'd have argued with Phelix, countered him, but now wasn't the time. Phelix was still angry, furious about being bricked by Annie. Oliver had to be careful. Phelix was right about one thing though – he didn't want to go to war. He didn't want to get killed.

"Erm, Phelix? Just one more thing."

Yes?

"Which way is it?"

Phelix didn't answer.

Oliver wasn't too sure which direction he was facing, in the last few minutes he'd turned, twisted and tumbled so much it had disorientated him. Still, there were only two choices. If he made the wrong one it wasn't the end of the world – he'd just have to turn round.

Thankfully, for once, he'd made the right choice. He felt a sense of relief when he saw the familiar shimmer of the Round Room in the distance.

"Won't be needing that for a while," he muttered, fastening his backpack up and leaving it against the wall of the Round Room. Stuffing Henry's knife into his boot and the Bulldog into his jacket pocket, Oliver straddled the Prime Meridian.

He now had a revised plan. Head to 1751, find the bullets. Then 2013, stay in the guest room, break into the office, steal a bracelet. Head to 1946, find Thomas. Easy, thought Oliver, as he turned his signet ring palm side, closed his eyes, and clasped the travel bracelet.

He gave it five, perhaps six seconds and then removed his hand from the bracelet. Something was wrong. There were no noises. No crickets, no birds, no banging… no clanging. It didn't feel any warmer, or colder… there was no rain, no breeze. No smells either – nothing pleasant… nothing putrid. Nothing had changed.

Oliver opened his eyes. Yes, he was still in the Round Room… but had he travelled anywhere? Moved in time? No, he can't have, he thought, looking at his backpack against the wall. His eyes dropped to the bracelet, to the engraving. His heart sank. "Fuck!"

He hadn't bloody engraved anything. He'd been too pre-occupied – the clasp, the Teclu burner, the wire. Then there were the voices – his uncle's… his father's.

Complete blithering idiot, said Phelix.

The engravers were in the office, but he couldn't go back there… he couldn't risk it… couldn't risk getting caught. No problem, thought Oliver, dismissing the issue. Just use one of the old bracelets and go back to 1747. Eventually, he'd be back to the day that he left Annie. Feeling the hairs on his arms stand to attention, Oliver shuddered. That was the day that he… Phelix… beat, bashed and belittled the poor woman. Oliver dropped his head in disgust… that was the day he hurt her. It was at that point that Oliver sensed a revelation of sorts – he finally twigged what he needed to do.

Annie did something for him… she made him feel alive… and he loved her for it. Okay, he had a strange way of showing his affection. Beating, stabbing and then killing wasn't the most romantic of actions a young man could do… but that had been Phelix.

It didn't bother Oliver that Annie slept around… business

was business, after all. Plus she earned a damn sight more money whoring herself out than he brought in from clock cleaning. It was time to return to Annie – to make amends.

Oliver knelt down, and searched amongst the detritus that had accumulated in the bottom of his backpack. "Not that one," he muttered, casting aside a bracelet he'd engraved for his first trip into the 21st century.

Had he not been so focused on his rummaging, Oliver might have heard the sound of encroaching footsteps behind him. But as it was…

"Nou."

Oliver, scattering Maxwell House across the floor, suddenly found himself being dragged across the Round Room to the meridian line. With his left arm hoiked behind him and a random knee pressed hard into his face, he lay sprawled along the East/West divide.

"Kry die ring."

Oliver's father had once told him that you could enter the Round Room ten thousand times, and that each and every visit would reveal a hidden secret, a little gem of intricate design. Oliver, cheek squashed hard against ceramic splendour, had never previously noticed the minute turquoise diamante fleck in the surface of the toe-trodden tiles.

"Get off me. LET ME GO!" he screamed out, as he kicked and twisted in an attempt to free himself.

Overpowered by the weight of two, possibly three attackers, Oliver struggled. He could feel someone tugging at his right arm – pulling it out from underneath his chest. They had his wrist – they wanted his ring.

They want the ring – don't let them get it. Phelix's voice rang out in Oliver's mind as he tightly clenched his right hand into a fist. Not to hit, not to punch… if there was any chance of escape then Oliver needed to protect his ring.

"Kry dit. Kry dit fokken ring, sal jy." Oliver could hear the shouts… the commands of the man who was pinning him down. He knew it wasn't English that he could hear, it sounded more German or Dutch.

"Hy sal sy hand oopmaak nie."

"Smash it with the hammer." The one shouting out the orders spoke in English.

Hammer? Phelix sounded shocked.

"Hamer?"

"Yes… Get the fucking hammer and hit it. Break his fucking fingers if you have to."

Don't open your hand. Get the gun… use it.

Oh, and how exactly am I supposed to get that, Oliver thought? Which hand does *he* expect me to use?

"Hold him steady, will you. So I can swing."

Oliver could feel the cold touch of metal on the back of his hand… it moved – only slightly – but it moved. He felt it again – felt the grip on his wrist becoming tighter, and although he couldn't see anyone, Oliver imagined that there was a man, lining up his aim – preparing to swing the hammer down.

Oliver's thoughts darted back to his enclosure – the fence post – Annie's hand. In his mind he could see the force of the hammer – almost hear it – as it crashed down on the post – splinters sent flying. Oliver, feeling his body relax, opened his hand – the man took his ring.

"Got it – now get the bracelet."

As they rolled him over onto his right side, Oliver could see them – two men. The first, the one who was holding him down, looked a little younger than the other, but perhaps it was just an effect of the subdued light, the shadows. They were both wearing black; long black coats, black trousers, black shirts, one even wore a black tie – both wore black spectacles. Neither had hair.

You can get the gun now.

Phelix was right, Oliver could feel the Bulldog digging into his hip. He moved his right hand to his side, but there was too much weight on him – he couldn't get his hand into his pocket.

"It won't come off. He's done something to the clasp." For the first time Oliver could clearly hear their voices – their accents – South African. But why? What did they want him for?

One of the men, the one who'd taken his ring, had a bottle in his hand. He was pouring out some liquid onto a cloth.

Get the fucking gun will you. Use it. It's them or us.

"But I can't shift him. He's too heavy," Oliver grunted.

Then bite him, panicked Phelix.

"Bite him?"

Yes… you act like a fucking girl… you might as well fight like one.

As Oliver sank his teeth into his attacker's forearm an ear-piercing scream filled the Round Room. Along with the bawl there was a shift in bodyweight. Phelix's suggestion had worked. Oliver, hand now in pocket, could feel the Bulldog.

"Fok. Die bliksem my gebyt."

That curse was the last Oliver heard.

190

The pungent smell was the first thing he noticed – then the wetness of the cloth as it was positioned over his mouth and nose. With his teeth almost grinding under the pressure, Oliver clamped his lips firmly closed. Kicking out wildly he held his breath. If only he could pull out the gun – use it.

He needed to breathe. Surely he could just open his mouth for a second, he thought – he'd be quick. Then the gun. Everything felt soft, everything went woozy. The man holding the cloth – he looked funny, thought Oliver, smiling. Then his body fell limp.

"Look at my arm. He's taken a bloody chunk out of it." The man Oliver had bitten rolled up his sleeve to reveal a perfect set of teeth marks.

"Stop complaining, will you." The second man removed the cloth from Oliver's face, poured some more liquid onto it, and then placed it back over his mouth and nose.

"Chloroform?"

"No. You've been reading too many crime books my dear brother. Chloroform isn't any good… it takes ages to work. I prefer Desflurane… much quicker."

The man, the one who Oliver had considered as the younger looking, tried once again to undo the clasp on Oliver's bracelet. "He's joined it – soldered it I think. I'm going to have to break it."

"It won't work again if you do. Can't you roll it over his wrist?"

The disc made it impossible to roll, but the man did try to slide the bracelet down over Oliver's wrist. He was doing quite well – but couldn't move it past Oliver's thumb joint. "His hand's too wide."

The 'older' brother removed his tie, peeled Oliver's coat down over his left shoulder and, using the tie, formed a tourniquet around Oliver's upper left arm. "This should slow his blood flow down. Make it easier to slide the bracelet off."

"You're full of good ideas today."

"Shh! I think someone's coming. Look..." He was right, someone was coming. Distant footsteps blending with distant voices could be heard rebounding from the wall of the passageway. Along with the noises, faint flickering lights could be seen. "Torchlights."

"We'll have to leave him."

"We can't. If we leave him here... we might not make it back."

"Kill him then."

"He's got a bracelet on, stupid. He'll go straight to Tec-Spa... then we'll lose him again. We need to move him."

"Where?"

"1751... Once we have the bracelet we'll put him in the river, I'm sure that copper would love to meet our dear Oliver."

The two black-clad South African brothers hauled the anesthetised Oliver to his feet. With the torchlights closing in on their position in the Round Room, the 'younger' brother twisted his own signet ring palm side and pulled up his left sleeve to reveal a pulsating time travel bracelet. With their arms linked with Oliver's, the three men disappeared, leaving behind only a khaki backpack, a Desflurane-impregnated cloth and a scattering of coffee granules.

CHAPTER 20

Tec-Spa
Some Time in the Future

Oliver had been at Tec-Spa for several weeks; *it was the healing process*, he'd been told. According to the 'freaks' in the white coats both his body and mind had endured *severe trauma*, and both needed time to heal.

He'd arrived in the pool with his arm in tatters. It was the bracelet on his ankle – that had saved him – saved his life. Apparently they'd been expecting him. It was Tec-Spa's surgeon who'd repaired, healed, *bodged* – tidied up his left arm. In a few more days, if all was well, he'd be fitted with a prosthetic limb – how wonderful, he'd been told. Oliver had visions of himself being left with nothing more than a crude metal hook, but apparently, or so he was informed, they didn't use pirate-limbs any longer.

It was one thing being able to see that your arm was missing, but Oliver's brain was having trouble keeping up... especially when he had an itch... or wanted to pick something up. The most basic, everyday tasks had suddenly become complicated... getting dressed... eating... toileting. Oliver had to re-assess his every move.

His surgeon had told him that it was a good sign – his brain

193

communicating with his missing fingers. Told him that something called his neural connections and nerve endings weren't damaged... *God only knows how,* he'd overheard one of the 'freaks' say.

Tec-Spa itself, just as his father had told him, was on a large gated estate, just outside Harrogate. The main building was a Victorian-built, Jacobean-style house, with many chimneys and numerous rectangular windows.

From his bedroom window Oliver had a perfect view of the large sweeping driveway and the huge black entry gates, ideal to see any arrivals or departures. Only thing was, Oliver never saw anyone arrive – and he never saw anyone leave.

Apparently, in the future, the work of the Tec-Spa was commonplace, similar services could be obtained in any of the country's spa towns, so why here – what was so special about Tec-Spa?

Two things. First, it was private – secure. No questions were ever asked, no details were ever taken. Secondly, it had a wing, the East Wing, which was reserved exclusively for the Bradbeer family. Apparently, Oliver was told, a token of appreciation for services once rendered, as well as a down payment for services yet provided... to whom, Oliver wasn't told.

When it wasn't raining, he spent his days wandering around the Tec-Spa's magnificent undulating gardens. The grounds had numerous pathways crossing through the parklands, which led to buttercup meadows, bluebell copses and rolling green fields, all of which were designed to provide the patient with excellent relaxation therapy.

A stream meandered its way through grove, thicket and field… Oliver followed its never-ending flow as the often white-water torrents carved their way through the Yorkshire countryside en route to the River Nidd.

He should have been using this time to attain some peace within his life, but instead Oliver, on his bad days, used it to seethe, sulk and smoulder – on his good days, to ponder, plot and plan. Revenge was his only goal – his priority.

Oliver was forbidden to have contact with any of the other Tec-Spa guests; he was reminded that the slightest of conversations could contaminate time. If only they knew, thought Oliver. It didn't really matter though. Oliver had only met six people during his stay… and they all worked there.

First there were the four *'freaks'* as Oliver had labelled them… his nurses, carers, warders… guards. They each worked an eight hour day, with one always on a rostered day off. They attended to his day to day needs… food, bathing, changing dressings. Not only did they provide Oliver with stimulus from his own time… books, papers, et cetera, they also provided the rules… or at least made Oliver aware of the rules.

Then there was his advisor. Her job was to update Oliver daily on his progress… offer advice on how best to recuperate, on how best to relax. If he had any questions, she'd try – if, under the rules, she was allowed – to answer them. More often than not though, she wasn't. Oliver had taken a shine to her, quite fancied her in fact. He called her his *Joan Cartwright,* after that girl at his school, and wondered how long she'd give him, down there, for a bag of liquorice.

Finally there was *Tired Tim,* his surgeon. Of course his

name wasn't really Tim, and he never really looked tired, but Oliver thought it was only decent to name him as well.

"Morning, Oliver. How are you today?"

"Morning," grunted Oliver, pulling his bedcovers over his face.

It was one of the freaks – breakfast freak. She was raising his window blind, forcing the light of a new day upon him. He had tried to keep them out... lock his door... barricade himself in... but that went against the rules... risk assessments, apparently.

"I've laid out some clean clothes for you... Your shower's running... Breakfast?"

Every day was the same. At 8am precisely, one of the freaks would come in, fresh clothes would be laid out – clean joggers, underwear and a short-sleeved shirt. He was advised not to wear sleeves, it would help him accept his *condition*, help him embrace his stump.

Oliver would have exactly fifteen minutes before she'd return with breakfast. Fifteen minutes to freshen up and get dressed. Of course it didn't matter if he went over the fifteen, he had nothing to hide... they'd all seen him naked. To Oliver being ready on time meant dignity... but more importantly... it meant a hot breakfast. Today, like every other day for the past three weeks... he was ready.

The fifteenth minute ticked by, the door should be opening, but it didn't. Oliver, now feeling slightly peckish, checked the time... it was definitely eight fifteen.

The sixteenth minute went by. Perhaps she'd forgotten something... had to go back.

196

The seventeenth went by. Maybe she'd dropped his breakfast and had to start again.

Eighteenth. She could have tripped... fallen and banged her head. She could be unconscious... blood everywhere.

Nineteenth. Abducted and sold into a life of slavery. Kidnapped by a voodoo witch doctor and fed to a lost tribe of cannibals. Maybe a sacrifice for a sun-worshipping cult ruled by a dead Egyptian Pharaoh. Oliver's imagination was in overdrive.

Twentieth... the door opened, breakfast had arrived.

"You're late."

"You're not my only..." The nurse stopped herself mid-sentence.

"What... you mean there's someone else here? Another Bradbeer?" Oliver was excited.

"I'm not at liberty to say." The nurse spouted the standard textbook reply.

"That means there is, then." Oliver tried baiting her. "Doesn't it?"

The nurse didn't respond. "Your appointment with the advisor has been rescheduled."

"Rescheduled?"

"Yes. Ten o'clock. But don't worry... It's only for today," replied the nurse, leaving the bedroom.

This is it then... what we've been waiting for.

"I know," whispered Oliver. "I wonder who it is. Do you think it could be Dad? Or Uncle Philip?"

It doesn't matter. If it's a Bradbeer they'll have a ring... Get the

197

ring and we can get revenge... Get revenge for whoever did this.

Oliver looked at his left arm, at his stump. Phelix was right, this was it.

At 9.59am, thirty minutes earlier than usual, Oliver stood outside *Joan's,* his advisor's, office door. Her office was situated at one end of a rather lavish hallway. Paintings of gentry who'd long since died hung next to scarlet-jacketed, crop-wielding huntsmen with their hounds nosing out a scent. Tally-ho, indeed.

Along the hallway a chiselled-footed grandmother clock chimed 10am. Oliver's thoughts swiftly left the world of fine art and foxes and returned to his appointment with Joan. He wondered whether it had been rearranged because of the new arrival, or whether it was just coincidence.

"Morning, Oliver. Please, take a seat." His advisor, sitting behind a glass-topped desk, beckoned him to sit.

She was a very attractive lady. Brunette, quite slim, well-tanned and although displaying a little cleavage... smartly dressed. During their conversations Oliver would often try to be humorous with her... but only because he liked the way her cheeks dimpled and her pupils dilated when she smiled.

"Morning, Joan." He'd asked if she didn't mind being called Joan, he'd explained it was far friendlier than Advisor, and she hadn't objected. "I see I've been shunted forwards. Busy day?"

Joan was thumbing through a file with Oliver's name on. She smiled, but didn't answer. Oliver, unable to tell if she was being rude or professional, sat and waited patiently for something to happen. But nothing did.

Joan, having finished reading, eventually broke the silence. "Drink?" she asked, placing the file down and pulling open the top left hand drawer of her desk.

"Er…" said Oliver.

"There's a good enough reason to celebrate today." Joan pulled out a Macallan 1939 malt and two small shot glasses. "I have some good news for you, Oliver. Your prosthesis has arrived."

"It has? My new arm… new hand?" Oliver beamed, that was good news indeed. Definitely worth celebrating, but not with that stuff. He'd tried Joan's whisky before, never this early, though. Anyway, it didn't matter what time it was – morning, afternoon, evening – he didn't like it.

Joan passed Oliver a half-full glass, of one of Scotland's finest single malts. "We've scheduled you in for fitment this evening. If all goes well, you'll be back home tomorrow… Ice?"

He didn't have much choice really, Joan had already tonged a cube of ice into his glass whether he wanted it or not. "Home? Tomorrow?" Oliver picked up the drink.

"Yes," replied Joan, looking over at a door to her left. "We'll return you to your own true time… and at your own true age."

"True time… Do I have to?" Oliver, putting the glass back down, suddenly felt drained. "I mean… do I have to go back home? Couldn't I just…"

"Well, it's either back home… to the Round Room."

"Or?" asked Oliver, picking up the glass and necking its contents in one swig.

"Or back to 1751." Joan looked at a door to her right. "Back to the night you died. But…"

"Yes?" Oliver, his palate burning, coughed.

"Well, with you not having a ring… you'll be stuck there. And…"

"And?" Oliver was clearly agitated. "And, what?"

"Look, Oliver." Joan lifted her glass and swallowed her drink straight down in one gulp. "It would be fair to say you haven't really had much luck in the eighteenth century, have you?"

Oliver groaned, she was right. A tough decision had to be made, an uneasy choice if ever there was one.

"You could go out and get some air, take a walk," suggested Joan. "You don't need to decide until tomorrow, do you?"

"No, I suppose not," replied Oliver, trying his best to sound upbeat.

"Good." Joan stood, a sign that, for her at least, the meeting was over. "Let's get that arm of yours sorted first."

Oliver nodded, she was right… a walk would do him the world of good.

"One more question," asked Oliver, about to open the door. "If you don't mind, that is?"

"Go ahead. Can't promise I'll be able to answer it though."

"Do you like liquorice?"

"Yes. Why?"

Closing the door behind him, Oliver left the office.

CHAPTER 21

War Hero?

Decisions, decisions, decisions, Oliver hated them. The one he now faced was not, by any means, an easy one to make.

Joan had given him two choices. Option one, be returned home, back to Greenwich 1913, back to his father. Option two, go back to 1751, Georgian Greenwich, back to the night he died. But that wasn't the decision Oliver was struggling with… well, not yet.

Oliver, taking Joan's advice, had gone for a walk. He stepped over the rotting timbers of what was once a country stile. Either side of the timbers lay the remnants of a dry stone boundary wall… large flat moss-encrusted stones peppered the fields… some scattered here and there… some in crumbled piles.

At the edge of the field, well out of sight of any prying eyes, stood a small copse of trees. Oliver, now sitting under one of the trees, liked it here… it reminded him of his enclosure… of a time when he was happy.

Well? asked Phelix.

"I don't know."

You could always commit suicide.

"NO… How could you even suggest that?" Oliver

201

shuddered. Bracelet or not, the thought of taking his own life was definitely not an option.

Well, you need to hurry up then. You're running out of time. Leave it any longer and…

"I know… I know… Now can you just shut the hell up and leave me alone, please?"

Oliver knew that the 'freaks' only worked on the Bradbeer wing. 'Breakfast freak' had hinted that she had another client, this meant there was a good chance that somewhere, in one of Tec-Spa's many rooms, there was another Bradbeer. If there was a Bradbeer – then there was a ring. If Oliver was to find the room, find the ring, then, as Phelix had implored, he needed to act now.

At pace Oliver made his way directly back to the house. He entered the East Wing through a wide panelled side door which led into a small vestibule.

"Oliver Bradbeer," he announced, looking up towards a camera mounted in one corner. Seconds later, accompanied by a delicate buzzing sound, a door into the main wing opened. Once inside the hallway, Oliver, walking slowly, headed to his room.

Over the past few weeks he'd not really taken any notice of East Wing's layout, he hadn't needed to. However, things were different now. He knew that the door directly opposite the vestibule was a cloakroom of sorts – he'd used it often enough for boots and waterproofs.

Oliver guessed that to the left of the cloakroom there was some sort of a staffroom. He assumed that he was right, as he'd seen two of the nursing staff enter with high heels and handbags, yet exit wearing flat shoes and white coats. There were several other rooms to the left of the staffroom, none of which he'd ever seen anyone use. At the far end of the wing's ground floor there were three more doors.

The first door was the door to *Tired Tim's* office. The second, via a covered walkway, led to the Tec-Spa's treatment centre and the natural water pools, where Oliver had arrived – where his bracelet had brought him. Behind the third door – the East Wing's stairwell.

Oliver, having taken the stairs to the first floor, opened the door to his room. Exasperated with frustration he collapsed onto the bed.

What's wrong now?

"It's useless… There's too many doors and I haven't got a clue where to start," snapped Oliver. "And… and even if I did…"

Try them all, then.

"Then what? Oh… Hello, I hope you don't mind… Only thing is, I need your ring… Yes, I realise it's your most treasured possession… but really I need it."

Just get changed… we'll worry about the persuasion bit once we've found the damn thing.

Hanging in a vacuum-sealed pack on the left side of the wardrobe were Oliver's clothes – the ones he'd arrived at Tec-Spa wearing – the ones he'd been killed in. Oliver removed the pack and, placing his foot on top to hold it steady, unzipped it.

"Wow." As Oliver pulled back the zipper, a cotton-fresh fragrance sprang out at him. Full marks to the Tec-Spa for their laundry service, he thought.

203

Not only did his shirt feel stretched, his trousers were also a tad too tight… so, top marks were also awarded to the Tec-Spa's kitchen. Oliver, without hesitation, tucked his shirt into his trousers and removed his coat from the pack.

"It's not here," shouted Oliver, shaking his coat.

What isn't?

"The gun… the Bulldog. It's not here." Oliver abandoned his coat on the bed and turned his attention back to the pack.

There were only two items remaining, one which had saved a life – his own. The other which had taken a life – Annie's.

"He was right…" said Oliver, picking up his bracelet, the one which had been fastened to his ankle. "It didn't let me die."

Oliver felt saddened that he hadn't trusted his father back in 1940, back on his first time trip. If he had, things would be different now, life would be different. One thing for sure, he thought – as he struggled to secure the bracelet around his ankle – I'd have two hands.

The last item in the pack was Henry Payne's knife. Oliver let out a deep, anguished sigh as he picked up the blade. Closing his eyes, he could hear Annie's screams resonating in his memory, he could picture her blood-soaked body as it slumped silently to the ground, he could feel the euphoria of his last kill. For once, the sensation he sometimes craved had left a bitter aftertaste.

Come on, will you. You haven't got time to feel sorry for her. Find the God damn ring, will you.

It was thanks to Phelix's timely intervention that Oliver snapped out of his remorse-filled reminiscing, tucked the knife into his boot, and once again focused his attention on what he

204

needed to do.

He stood in the first floor hallway. To his left, before the turn to Joan's office, he counted seven doors. To his right, another three, one of which was the stairwell. If only he had a floor plan – a map of the East Wing.

But, of course! There was one, he remembered... a floor plan... in his room... on the back of the door. One of the *freaks* had pointed it out when he'd first arrived, when she'd explained the 'Fire Evacuation Procedure' to him.

Oliver darted back into his room. There it was, hidden in plain sight, framed on the inside of his door – '*What to do in the case of an emergency*'. He'd seen it countless times, but never paid it any attention. His room was G3 – he could see it on the first floor plan – in bold. There was his evacuation route – marked by green arrows.

Oliver scanned the floor plans. Ground floor: Kitchen. Closet. Toilet. Stairs. G1. Theatre. Office. Spa. Office. CR1. Staffroom – he'd assumed right. Cloaks. First Floor: Toilet. G3 – his room. CR2. Store. Closet. G2. Office. Office. Blank. Blank. Stairs. Oliver, looking for any further 'G' rooms, scanned over the plan again. There were three – his own and two others; the search had narrowed.

G2 was the closest. It was on his floor – just by Joan's office – it had to be the favourite. Closing his door behind him, Oliver quietly sneaked along the corridor.

Using the hilt of Henry's knife, Oliver rapped lightly on the door to G2. No answer. Oliver tapped again, this time not so lightly. Again – no answer.

Oliver, thankful of Tec-Spa's risk assessment policy,

opened the unlocked door and slowly entered G2.

"Good afternoon," Oliver called out, knife clenched tightly behind his back. "Hello."

The room was almost identical to his own. Bed, bedside table, bedside lamp and a wardrobe. Under the window, like in his own room, stood a set of drawers, on top of which was a kettle, some little packets of tea and coffee, three packets of assorted biscuits and some little white containers which Oliver had found fascinating when he'd realised that they contained milk. How he loved the future.

Oliver thought that the room felt void. It had a cold chill about it, an eerie feeling of sorts… an unused emptiness. Oliver, sensing the difference from his own room, walked over to the wardrobe. He assumed if a guest was using this room there'd be a vacuum-sealed bag hanging in the wardrobe – there wasn't.

G1 then. Phelix echoed Oliver's despondency.

"Yep. Looks that way," sighed Oliver, closing the wardrobe door.

Using the evacuation plan on the back of G2's door, Oliver checked his route to G1. It was on the ground floor, past the cloakroom, past the nurse's staffroom – it was the furthest fucking room in East Wing from where he was now, he moaned.

After stuffing the biscuits and milk capsules into his pockets, Oliver hurriedly made his way to the door marked 'stairs'. Having descended to the ground floor in seconds, Oliver cautiously edged open the door leading to the hallway. It was empty.

There were seven doors between him and G1. He walked past *Tired Tim's* office, the room where he'd had no choice but to accept the loss of his left arm. The next door he passed was the one which led to the Tec-Spa's natural springs, to the pool he woke up in, where his life was restored.

Then there was the door to the courtyard and the gardens beyond, the doorway to adventure, as Joan called it. Opposite these, was the cloakroom and then the nurses' staffroom, the door to which was just opening.

"Both of them should be gone this evening. Tomorrow at the latest."

Oliver crept into the cloakroom.

Freaks.

"Think so. Must be their shift change," whispered Oliver.

Bit too early. Are you sure?

"How the heck do I know?"

Oliver listened to the hallway conversation through the keyhole. Nothing exciting – nothing interesting. A few minutes later the talking stopped, only to be replaced by a constant noise, a sound that – at best – could be described as an irritable whine.

He slowly edged open the door. There was a woman in the hallway – someone he'd not seen before. She was dragging the noise – a machine – behind her. In her hand was a large stick which she was pushing across the carpet, a long concertinaed tube connected stick to noise. Oliver, closing the cloakroom door, wished the noise would stop.

What is it? What's she doing?

"I dunno… something to the carpet, I think."

Hey… It could be a Puffing Billy… only smaller… This is the future, after all.

"It doesn't matter what it is," replied Oliver, the noise grating away at him. "She's in our way."

Just get out there and grab her then.

"And do what... Dance?"

No... Drag her in here... hit her.

"Hit her?"

Yes... Hard though... you know... until she passes out.

"Phelix?"

Yes?

"Shut up, will you... You're getting worse than that thing out there."

The noise continued, passing the cloakroom door at one point. As Oliver sat and munched on a packet of bourbon creams, he wondered if it was all worth it. Phantom twinges stirred the nerve endings in his left arm. He couldn't help but think that if he took the ring, he'd have to leave immediately. If he left, then he'd face the rest of his life with just a stump. Yet if he stayed... yes, he'd have to endure the wrath of his father – but at least he'd have a new arm.

After about another ten minutes or so, the noise stopped. Then there were a few bangs and clunks, followed by the sound of a door opening and closing. The hallway fell silent. Oliver, once again, slowly edged open the door... the coast was clear. He quickly made his way to room G1.

Oliver tapped lightly on the door, and then again, this time harder. He turned the door handle until he heard it unlatch from the jamb, took hold of Henry's knife, then using his foot pushed the door open. "Hello?"

Yes! Result.

"Hoorah!" chirped Oliver quietly, noticing that the bedcovers were ruffled.

Along with the untidy bed there were other indicators that he'd found the right room. First, on top of the bedside table there was a used coffee cup along with an empty biscuit wrapper. Then there was how the room felt, unlike G2, this room had a warmness about it, a feeling of life.

Oliver walked over to the wardrobe, took a deep breath, and opened it. Staring at him was a vacuum-sealed bag. In the bottom corner, as though patiently waiting, a familiar object… a platinum travel bracelet. "Thank you, Lord," he mouthed, tilting his head upwards.

Removing the bag from the wardrobe, Oliver placed it on the bed. Using the knife, he pierced the bag and pocketed the bracelet.

"Oliver? Ollie?"

Startled, Oliver's heart jumped, he hadn't quite expected that. Someone was behind him. Someone who knew him.

"Ollie? Is that you?"

Oliver turned towards the voice. Standing outside the en suite, holding a white bath towel around his waist, was a man. He was a tall man, well built, muscles everywhere. His hair was shoulder length, wavy, dark brown, his face had chiselled features… which reminded Oliver of his Uncle Philip. But most importantly, noticed Oliver, the man had – on the fourth finger of his right hand – a ring.

"You don't recognise me, do you?"

Oliver wracked his brain. The voice didn't sound familiar,

209

the man didn't look familiar. Yes, there was a touch of Philip about him, but his uncle was much older. "No," Oliver replied.

The man laughed. "You mean you don't recognise your own cousin?"

"Isaac?" Was this man really his cousin? Philip's son. It couldn't be – the man before him was a good fifteen, perhaps twenty years older than Isaac.

"Surprised, Oliver? Not as much as me. You're supposed to be..." Isaac paused. "I mean, I was at your..."

"Supposed to be what?" interrupted Oliver. "At my what?"

"Dead, Ollie. You're supposed to be dead. You went missing... I was at your memorial."

Dead, coughed Phelix.

"Dead? But how? When...?" Oliver felt shocked... he hadn't expected that.

"Buried on the underground apparently. No one really knows... So, what happened there?" asked Isaac, pointing at Oliver's stump.

Tell him you lost it in the war.

"The war. German cannon fire."

"The war? So you did enlist? Bravo, Oliver... Tell me more... what happened?"

This should be good, laughed Phelix.

"The battle of Aubers Ridge... France," replied Oliver, thankful of his 21st century book purchase.

Oliver told Isaac what had happened. How he'd almost single-handedly defeated the German 6th Army, and how he'd have succeeded had he not stalled to rescue a fallen comrade. An indecision which had cost him his arm – a German shell. How that had ended his war.

"So what happened then?"

"Blandford Camp Hospital… Dorset." Oliver looked down at his arm and smiled.

"But didn't you go to 1946? To avoid the war?"

"Mm." Oliver considered having a go at Isaac, for messing up the Latin numerals, but decided against it. "I was going to… but decided on 1746 instead."

Oliver gleefully recounted some of his 18th century adventures. The one about how he was nearly press-ganged into the navy. How he'd met James Lind and suggested that there could be a fruitful cure for scurvy. Then how he'd fallen in love with the beautiful Anne, a close cousin of the Duke of Grafton.

"Did you stay there long? Marry her?"

"I stayed with her until the end," sighed Oliver. "Until she died in my arms. That's when I came home… signed up."

"Dad was right then," cheered Isaac. "You did find your courage."

Pathetic… to think he believes this bullshit, groaned Phelix.

"So everyone back home thinks I'm dead then? My grave? Where is it?"

"There isn't one."

"Why?"

"You were never found. You never returned… Everyone just presumed…" Isaac sighed. "As you went missing in 1913… that's when we… I mean, your father… assumed you'd died."

211

"So I could be alive then?" questioned Oliver. "Couldn't I?"

"Well yes, I suppose so. But..."

"But what?"

"Well... It's 1931 now... I mean, that would be your true time. Eighteen years have passed. Surely, if you were alive... we'd have known by now."

Oliver had no comeback to that. Perhaps Isaac was right, maybe he had died. "And what of my parents?"

"They moved. North... after the war. To Menston, Yorkshire. Not too far from here, actually. Uncle Edward gave my father the keys to The Time Store, made him promise not to..." Isaac stopped. "He's the custodian now."

"Made him promise what, Isaac? Made him promise what?"

"Oh, nothing... It's just that he made Dad promise not to go around changing the world any longer – no more righting wrongs and what have you. It's all a bit boring really... we're just history watchers these days."

"Because of me?"

"Yes, Oliver. Because of you. Still, I could always change it back," laughed Isaac.

"Back? How?"

"When custodianship passes to me, of course."

Inside, Oliver was seething. Isaac, custodian of The Time Store – never. Isaac, taking what was supposed to be *his* future, *his* birthright – never.

"Isaac... I need your help." Oliver feigned sadness. "I have to return to the 18th century... to my son."

Nice one, commented Phelix.

"You have a son?"

"Yes... Phelix. He's... eight. Well, I mean, he was eight... when his mother died. When I left." Oliver lowered his head. "I need to get back to him... only... only..."

Isaac approached Oliver and touched him lightly on the shoulder. "How can I help, Oliver?"

"They've given me two choices. Go back to where I died... Blandford... or..."

"You died?"

"Yes. The gangrene set in," expressed Oliver, patting his stump. "Then the fever took me."

What did you say that for, stupid? You can't come to Tec-Spa in true time, ranted Phelix.

"Or they can send me back to the day it all began, back to 1913. The day I scribed my true time bracelet."

"I don't understand, Ollie. What can I do?"

"When they shipped me back to England, to the hospital. Someone... I don't know who... took my ring." Oliver held up his right hand and spread his fingers for emphasis. "Isaac... if I'm to return to my son... then I need your ring."

"But, Ollie. I can't... you of all people should know that." Isaac backed away.

"I know... I know. I'll just have to return home then. Still, mother will be happy, having me back. And they won't have to leave, will they? I mean, they won't have to move here... to Yorkshire." Oliver grinned at Isaac. "And you and Uncle

Philip… you won't need to concern yourselves with the custodianship any longer. Will you?"

Isaac, all hesitation gone, took off his ring. "Here, take it. Go to him, Oliver."

Oliver, displaying fake reluctance, accepted the ring and then embraced his cousin the best he could. "Thank you, Isaac… Thank you."

With head lowered, Oliver walked towards the door.

Isaac waved a goodbye. "Good luck, Ollie."

"Thanks."

"Mention me to your son. What was his name?"

"Phelix," replied Oliver. "It's Phelix."

Fucking… idiot.

CHAPTER 22

Unwanted Return

Joan's office looked different in the dark. Oliver hadn't really noticed the water-filled tank on his daily visits nor the funny looking fish darting around their sunken treasure chest. Nor had Oliver seen the numerous certificates and awards, illuminated by the tank's silhouette-like glow, on the wall above.

There was a large bamboo-print blind covering the window behind Joan's empty desk; thankfully, on one of the only days they'd had some sun up in Yorkshire, Oliver had observed Joan as she closed it. Therefore, by the process of elimination, if he did the reverse, then it would open.

One twist, one turn, one tug, one pull, one clatter... and voila! The room was flooded with light. Not quite as expected though, thought Oliver, stepping over the blind, which was now heaped on the floor behind him.

He looked at the two doors leading from Joan's office. The one to his left, if he'd read Joan's mannerisms correctly, would take him home, to 1913, and – if Isaac was right – to his death. The one on his right would take him back to when he'd already died – to that night in 1751, the night he lost his arm. That's the one he wanted.

Get the whisky. The one in her drawer.

No… I don't like it.

I do, protested Phelix.

"Okay… if I must," replied Oliver, shaking his head. "Hang on… How can you like it, if I don't?"

Just get it, will you.

Oliver pulled open the desk drawer and took out the bottle of malt. He was just about to close the drawer and make good his escape, when he noticed his name staring up at him. Oliver Edward Bradbeer. It was his folder – the one Joan had been holding earlier. He could see that, underneath his folder, there was another – Isaac's. Oliver removed them both.

Open Isaac's first.

"Why?" asked Oliver, about to open his own. "Does it matter?"

Don't want any shocks do you?

"Shocks?"

Yes… What if this place knows when you're gonna die, and I mean really die… You wouldn't want to know that, would you?

Phelix had a point. There were lots of things in life Oliver would like to know – but the day of his death wasn't one of them. He placed his file to one side and opened Isaac's.

Name: BRADBEER – Isaac Philip.

D.O.B. 22nd March 1900. Greenwich, London.

Death: 29th June 1979. Juliaca, Peru.

Father: BRADBEER Philip Robert 1874 – 1956

Mother: BRADBEER Charlotte 1875 – 1900

(Nee Morrison)

Custodian: 1934 – 1968

A list of all Isaac's Tec-Spa visits followed. His age at the time... the dates... whether death or for rejuvenation... and treatment cost. For each entry the charge read 'Nil'.

After this list there was another page with a few handwritten notes. "That's interesting."

What is?

"Apparently Isaac meets his grandson, David. They have dinner together."

Didn't think you could do that...

"We can't... Well, we shouldn't. You know, all that true time contamination bullshit. Load of crap if you ask me... Oh My God! No way, fuck!"

What? What is it?

"This page... It lists all of Isaac's misdemeanours. You know, what he's done wrong."

Ha! They'd need more than a fucking page for yours, then!

Oliver didn't respond.

Come on, let's have a look at yours.

"No... Anyway, what do you mean mine? You did most of it."

There was one more page in Isaac's file – a family tree. It showed Isaac in the middle. Below him... three future generations. Above him... three generations of ancestors. Oliver quickly covered the top half with his own file, and then read the names below.

According to the family tree, Isaac had two sons. The eldest – Peter Isaac. The youngest – Matthew Oliver. Peter and his wife Victoria had one son – David. The one who Isaac met for dinner, thought Oliver. David Bradbeer married Helen Lane... they had three children; Jason, Sarah and Daniel.

Helen Bradbeer… That's her from the park, isn't it?

"Park? What the hell are you going on about?"

You know… park bench… Helen Bradbeer… She gave you the idea for the enclosure.

"Oh, yes." The penny dropped. "Her."

Oliver closed Isaac's file and picked up his own.

Slowly. Open it slowly.

Oliver slid Isaac's file inside his own and positioned it to cover the top part – the part with his own death recorded.

There was only one entry in Oliver's Tec-Spa visits. This one.

We know that already. Move to the next sheets… Let's see what they know about you.

Oliver scanned down the first sheet, reading and chuntering as he did so… until… "No way!"

What?

"Remember that night... when they tried to press gang me?"

Don't you mean me?

"Whatever. They weren't from the navy…"

Who were they then?

"Don't know. It just says 'the family'."

Keep looking.

Oliver continued reading, calling out the occasional random date here and there as he did, until eventually he found what he wanted. "Got it. Jason fucking Bradbeer, Flamsteed Way, London. 30th July 1751 – 21st September 1913… He's the bastard who did this," ranted Oliver, waving his stump in the air.

Do you think that's where the gun is? In 1751?

"Stands a chance... it's either there... or in the Round Room."

Or with the fucking South Africans.

"Mmm, possibly," replied Oliver, not liking the thought of losing *his* Bulldog.

The folder... why do you think there are two dates?

"One must be my true time date." Oliver re-opened Isaac's file at his family tree. "There he is – Isaac's great-grandson, Jason the 'axe-man' Bradbeer."

What else does it say? What else happened?

"Nothing – just date, time, where and who," sighed Oliver, who'd been hoping that the file would fill in all of the blanks left in his memory.

Shh...! Someone's outside.

Phelix was right – Oliver could hear voices chatting away in the hallway. It sounded like *Tired Tim* and the woman, the one who'd been dragging the machine across the carpet. Time to go, thought Oliver.

He'd opened the door on the right, hopefully the one which Joan had indicated would take him back to the 18th century. Oliver had half-expected an ornate room, something similar to the Round Room – but perhaps not so grand. What he'd stepped into was no bigger than his old toy cupboard back home – and it was certainly in need of a good lick of paint.

Attached to the wall directly in front of him, about a foot apart, were two large platinum rings – large, as in they were more wrist-sized than finger. The rings were connected by a smooth platinum bar which had an hourglass symbol engraved in the centre.

With the tip of his index finger, Oliver hesitantly touched one of the rings – it glowed. He could feel a sense of relief flow through his body as he watched the familiar ethereal splendour radiate its aura. He touched the other ring – nothing.

Slipping his coat to the floor, Oliver rolled up his left sleeve, took a deep breath and pressed his stump against the second ring. Thank God, he thought, releasing his breath. With the left ring emitting its lily white sheen, Oliver touched the other with his right hand. He then watched as the individual glows from the two rings surged towards each other along the platinum bar. At the precise moment at which the auras fused together in the centre of the hourglass – Oliver disappeared.

With his eyes firmly closed, Oliver lowered his arms. He didn't need to open his eyes, he didn't need any visual confirmation – he knew he was no longer at Tec-Spa.

He could feel the warm night air press upon his cheeks and smell the pungent river fragrance as it wafted in the air around him – worse still, he could taste its bitterness on the back of his throat. Oliver smiled, he liked it here.

CHAPTER 23

The Knowledge

Where are we? asked Phelix.

"The park," replied Oliver. "Can't you see – up there? The observatory."

Oliver was right. Up on the hill, silhouetted against the evening sky – Greenwich's Royal Observatory. However, Wren's 17th century construction wasn't the only thing silhouetted by the night; Oliver could see three people walking down the hill towards him.

Concealing himself behind the trunk of a mighty oak, Oliver listened. They were talking about the dinner they'd just enjoyed with the Astronomer Royal, James Bradley – and about the moon, the stars, and the fabric of time itself.

As they passed his hiding place, Oliver heard one of them – a woman – call out to the others. She used their names – Dan first – apparently he'd suggested that they go to see a house in the final stages of construction – *their* house. The second name she used was Jason – he was talking about a museum display of sorts.

It's them, isn't it?

"Yes." Oliver's blood was boiling. There they were, the very people he was hunting – the ones he held responsible for taking his arm – heading to Flamsteed Way, to see what they insisted on calling *their* house being built.

And?

"That means… it must mean… that my arm… it can't have been taken yet." Oliver felt relieved, he felt that he would be able to stop them.

If only you still had the gun.

"Ah! But I do have the knife," said Oliver, reaching down into his boot.

Don't be so bloody stupid. There are three of them, you know. Three of them against a bloody cripple, some chance you'll stand. And then what? What if they catch you? You'll end up being locked up. No arm – no life – and no future. Is that what you want?

"No, of course not." Oliver knew that Phelix was right. Even though revenge seemed only a few feet away, it wasn't possible. He could perhaps, at best, take one of them out… but the other two…? The odds were stacked against him. Oliver, concealed in the moonlight shadows and skulking in the semi-darkness, continued to follow the Bradbeers.

It was evident that Tec-Spa, in returning him to the place he'd come from, had apparently automatically returned him to a slightly earlier time. Perhaps that's how it worked. After all, what would be the point of sending someone back to face a bullet or perhaps a blade, only to be struck down again – and again.

As he neared the edge of the park, Oliver could clearly hear the sounds of enjoyment, the sounds of high spirits… the sounds from the Plume. Did he really want to follow these fools any further? Did he need to follow them and watch his own arm being hacked off? Or, how about a nice jug of ale instead? He paused momentarily to consider, and then, drawn by the need to know, Oliver continued to follow.

Are you sure you want to watch? Your arm...

"Not really, but..."

Keeping his distance, Oliver carefully trailed the three siblings – hiding in a doorway – sneaking a little further – then back into another doorway, until he watched them turn into Flamsteed Way.

Peering through the iron railings of the corner house, Oliver could see a dishevelled mass slumped in the middle of the road. Given the information he'd read at Tec-Spa, he made an assumption.

"That must be me."

What are they doing?

"They're walking towards me... no, they've stopped. She hasn't though... she's holding my wrist." For a brief second Oliver felt a twinge in his stump.

What's happening? What's she doing?

"She's checking for a pulse... she's shaking her head."

But you're alive... surely they can see that. You've got a bracelet on...

"It's not glowing... they're talking about it."

What are they saying? What are they doing? Can you see the gun?

"SHUT UP... For fuck's sake, shut up! Can't you see, I'm trying to listen?"

Sorry...

"They're looking up now," Oliver hissed. "Oh shit! I think

223

they've heard me... shouting. Oh no... no! He's picking up the axe."

Oliver turned away, he'd seen enough. With the sound of the axe whooshing through the air, and tears in his eyes, he headed for the Plume – it was time for that drink.

Look, I've said I was sorry... Are you going to ignore me all night?

Phelix had irritated, infuriated, annoyed and angered Oliver – he'd well and truly pissed him off.

Don't take it out on me... I told you not to go... I told you not to watch.

Tucking himself away over in the corner, Oliver put down the quart he was drinking, and sighed. Phelix was right – he *had* warned him. Perhaps, thought Oliver, he was taking his anger out on Phelix – blaming him for what was nothing less than his own stupidity.

Oliver was snapped out of his daydream of self-admonishment by the rapping of knuckles on his table. "Is that yours?" It was Stephen Whitall, landlord of the Plume.

"What?" answered Oliver, gruffly. "Is what mine?"

"The ale. Only... there's a man over there." Stephen pointed over to the bar. "He reckons that you've picked up his drink. And truth is, neither me, nor our Charles can remember your custom."

"Surely you must remember me?"

"Phelix...?" There was a look of surprise on Whitall's face. "My God, Phelix. It *is* you."

No... It's not me. If it was me, Whitall... you'd be picking yourself up off the floor by now.

"It's been how long?" asked the landlord, pulling up a bench. "What's happened? Your arm?"

"Press gang grabbed me, didn't they?" Oliver took a swig from the quart. "Three years... three years out at sea. And this..." He held up his stump and sighed. "This is all I've got to show for it."

Oliver, always one for spinning a good yarn, told how he'd lost his arm in a rigging accident. Then – once returned to England – how he'd convalesced down on the coast, down in Winchelsea.

"So what brings you back up here?"

"Annie," replied Oliver, dropping his shoulders. "I heard about Annie Fletcher."

The landlord leaned forwards. "Nasty that was... what happened to Annie, nasty!"

"Do they... do they know who did it?"

"Old Joe up at the Ship, he reckons it was some deranged madman, someone called Oliver. Hearsay has it that he killed a doctor as well... Dr Marlow."

Deranged madman, Phelix laughed. *They've got you right, haven't they?*

"Oliver? Oliver who?"

"That's what they reckon. But no one really knows what happened. By the time Firth had got round to asking questions, Annie had been – well, you know – been killed. Carter, from the hospital, he swore blind that someone had been hiding – under the bed."

"And was there?" asked Oliver. "Was there someone under the bed?"

"No... the room was empty. Firth has Carter locked away for killing Marlow. But I don't think we'll get to know anything more about that... the hospital will want to keep that quiet, you know how funny they are about gossip." Stephen stood up and pointed at the ale jug. "Suppose I'd better go and pour him another one, hadn't I?"

"Thanks," nodded Oliver, acknowledging that the quart before him had indeed belonged to the man standing by the bar.

"You be careful though, Phelix. Rumour has it that this Oliver wasn't the only name Annie shouted out that night."

Finishing off the ale, Oliver walked out into the Plume's yard and relieved himself against the wall.

Probably be best if we don't stay around here. Let's find the Bulldog... and the bullets... and leave.

Phelix was right, admitted Oliver. The sooner they were gone, the better. Unhooking a triangular barn lantern from the side passage wall of the Plume, he headed off in search of the Bulldog.

Flamsteed Way had an eerie quietness about it – a strange, somewhat ghostly chill hung in the air. Oliver, lantern in hand, tentatively approached the spot where earlier he'd seen himself – the dishevelled mass – the spot where he had been unceremoniously dumped.

Holding the lantern close to the ground, Oliver could clearly see – splattered – several traces of his own blood.

There, to the right. Something's shining.

Phelix was right, there was something shining. Oliver, placing the lantern on the road, walked over to where he'd seen the silvery glint, knelt down and picked up the Bulldog.

He gripped the gun in his palm, caressed the smooth metal trigger, and smiled. "Feels good."

Come on. You don't have time for dilly-dallying… we need to find the bullets.

After slipping the Bulldog into his right pocket, Oliver picked up the lantern.

"Hey. I want a word with you."

"What the…" Oliver, reeling backwards, was startled.

A man had entered Flamsteed Way – he started to push and shove Oliver around. "I'll teach you to pinch my fucking beer."

In the swaying lantern light, Oliver could clearly see a look of fury on the man's face. Another push – another shove – Oliver released his grip – the lantern fell to the floor – its flame extinguished.

"And I'll teach you to make me look like a fucking idiot," shouted the man, taking a swing.

Falling backwards, Oliver hit the ground hard. How had he let himself be taken so easily, taken by surprise? Oliver was fuming. The South Africans had jumped him – but he'd been outnumbered then – at least there'd been two of them.

What the hell are you waiting for? Gun… STUPID… use the fucking gun.

"It's not that bloody easy when someone's trying to put their boots through your ribs," snarled Oliver, trying to right himself.

"Whatever you picked up – whatever you stuffed into your scabby pocket – I want it." The man let loose another volley of kicks.

"Take it... you can have it." Oliver, trying to defend himself against the incessant blows, couldn't believe his luck. "Just let me get up and you can have it."

One born every minute, laughed Phelix.

Raising himself to his knees, Oliver placed his hand into his pocket, and cupped the Bulldog. A familiar sound followed, a crack – succeeded by an immediate flash of light.

With the Bulldog's recoil still pulsating through his muscles, Oliver watched as his aggressor fell before him.

He's still alive. Again... shoot him again, demanded Phelix.

"Is this what you wanted?" growled Oliver, waving the Bulldog at the man. "IS IT?"

"P-Please..." begged the man, who was writhing on the ground clutching at his chest.

Shoot him...

Oliver, a fire burning in his inner depths, aimed the Bulldog at the man's head and squeezed the trigger. It clicked.

"FUCKING HELL," screamed Oliver, kicking out in rage.

You'll have to leave him... you need to find those bullets.

"No..." Oliver spotted an axe – one he'd never seen before – one with which he felt an immediate connection. He picked it up.

Gentle moonlight began to peer through a break in the cloud cover, and Oliver, his one hand tightly gripping the haft, raised the axe above his head. The man beneath him squealed out into the empty night as the axe fell, cleaving into his chest. Flesh and muscle tore open.

Feels like hickory, thought Oliver, as he drew out the axe and swung again. Bone cracked.

Perhaps white ash, if it's American. The axe swooshed through the stillness. Ribs splintered and blood splattered.

Or maybe it's English oak.

"Maybe." Oliver laughed out, as he continued to swing, chop and hack at the already mutilated body before him.

With the axe weighing heavy, Oliver, fire now doused, and covered in blood, cast the innocent carpenter's tool aside and knelt by the side of the man he'd just killed.

He hadn't wanted this – another death on his hands. But this had been self-defence – he'd had no choice, had he? Anyway, someone had to pay – someone had *it* coming. The South Africans – Jason 'fucking' Bradbeer – and now sailor boy; enough was enough.

Oliver unbuttoned his shirt pocket and removed a pendant – Annie's pendant. He'd give Firth his *killer* – someone who could carry the blame for Annie's death. Oliver tucked the pendant into one of the dead man's pockets. Then, with the cloud cover returning, he picked up the lantern, and vanished into the dark of the night.

Oliver hadn't vanished too far. He'd just gone down the stone steps leading to Flamsteed Way's basement yard. To his surprise, one of No.5's windows was open. Using a wooden trestle for support, Oliver raised himself up, and climbed through the open window.

Where's this?

"Don't know... kitchen I think," replied Oliver, blindly stumbling around. "I need some light."

Patting around the work benches and tables, Oliver searched for a means to light the lantern – a tinderbox.

Try the fireplace...

Phelix was right – in the corner of the hearth, waiting to strike into action, a small wooden tinderbox. And better still, Oliver realised that the kitchen fire had been left banked.

Once the banked-up ashes had been set aside, it only took him a few seconds to rekindle the hidden embers, throw a few logs onto the flames, and light up his lantern. He'd guessed correctly – he was in the kitchen.

It looked somewhat different from what he was used to – much larger, far more spacious. He needed a point of reference, something he recognised – the door leading to the basement yard would do.

Oliver imagined that he'd just put away his bicycle and was coming in for afternoon tea. To his left was the window he'd climbed through – eventually there'd be two large Belfast sinks and a drainer there. He could picture Cook, knife in hand, topping and tailing a bunch of carrots. 'Have one, Master Oliver. You'll be able to see in the dark.' Lies, obviously.

To the right was the cold store. Oliver recalled the memories of making winter ice bricks and packing them tightly between layers of straw in the room's stone pit. The small room was empty now – even its door hadn't been hung, yet.

Beyond the storeroom were the stairs leading to the

ground floor, and after those there should've been a wall – but there wasn't. Instead, there was another set of stairs.

Walking the line of where he imagined the wall to be, Oliver could see what was – and what would come to be. To his left – the kitchens. To his right – his father's office, and the Costume Room – between these, set into the wall, a large sarsen stone. Oliver held the lantern up to the stone's smooth surface, the flicker of light revealed a familiar shape engraved into the sandstone – an hourglass.

Oliver walked into another room, and although there was an additional opening on the far wall, the room was very familiar to him – it was The Time Store's rest room. Being curious as to what was on the other side of the wall, Oliver walked through the opening.

Once the house was finished, the spot where Oliver was standing would be a gardener's room of sorts. This room led out to what was for the moment a jumbled building site, but what would eventually be part lawn, part allotment.

In the centre of the room was a small wooden table, on top of which was an empty porcelain water jug, two floral patterned wash bowls, and a pile of towels. Filling the jug from a near-full barrel of water, Oliver stripped off his shirt and washed away the splatters of blood which covered him. After drying himself off, Oliver returned to the barrel and dunked his shirt several times to cleanse the blood from its fibres, and then returned to the now roaring fire.

Oliver, who'd been curled up, fast asleep in front of the fire, had been woken by the sound of raised voices. Someone – a worker

231

– a watchman, perhaps – a passer-by, had stumbled across his handiwork, and now it seemed that every man and his dog had gathered on Flamsteed Way.

Even though the sunlight couldn't quite sift through to the basement level, there was more than enough daylight for Oliver to make sense of his surroundings. Buttoning up his semi-dry shirt, he returned to the room he'd washed in, unbolted the rear door, and made his way across the building site down to the Romney Road.

For a Sunday morning, sleepy Greenwich was bustling with life. Mass, markets, and murder – they all had a certain appeal to many. Thankfully for Oliver, no one was interested in the small ramshackle houses just off East Street.

Using the stock of the Bulldog, Oliver rapped on the door to Annie's house, or as it was now, Annie's old house. The woman, the one he'd near-strangled to death, opened the door, and then recoiled backwards with fright.

"No… no, don't be scared," said Oliver, trying to calm down the now hyperventilating woman. "I'm not here to hurt you."

Aren't you?

"Get away… GET AWAY," screamed the woman, throwing a wooden bowl at Oliver.

"Look, I'll sit here," whispered Oliver, sitting himself down on a chair near the fireplace. "I just have a couple of questions to ask, that's all… and then I'll be gone… I promise."

A brief stand-off of silence followed. The woman, a quivering wreck, in fear for her life, was huddled up on the bottom step of the rickety staircase; Oliver, trying his best to relax, warmed himself by the fire.

"I used to live here… with Annie… God bless her soul." Oliver, speaking softly, jabbed at the fire with a knurled iron poker. "I'd look out for her, you know? Make sure she didn't get hurt… make sure she didn't get into trouble… those kind of things."

Replacing the poker in its stand, Oliver turned to face the woman.

"I even cured her… and half of the politicians, priests and prostitutes in London. She had syphilis… they all had syphilis," said Oliver, standing up and walking over to the woman. "And… I had a medicine."

"P-Please, don't hurt me," she sobbed.

"I have a friend… another friend… just like Annie." Oliver sighed. "She needs the medicine… without it she'll die."

"B-But… but I don't have any… any medicine. Why are you asking me?"

"There was a chest… a trunk. Just there," answered Oliver, pointing under the stairs. "I kept the medicine in there… I need to find the trunk."

"We… I mean Annie… She burnt it."

"Burnt it…?" Oliver suddenly felt weak, drained of all energy, devoid of all colour. "W-Where? Why?"

"Out there… out the back. Annie didn't want it anywhere in the house… she couldn't face looking at it. It reminded her too much of you."

"But what about my things? Did she…?"

"Everything… everything got burned," interrupted the

233

woman, who'd sat upright. "I helped her carry it out… helped her set it on fire. We stayed out and watched it burn… We'd have stayed out all night if it wasn't for the…"

"For the what?"

"For the bangs. There were loads of them. I mean, it must have been – the fire that is – it must have been so hot that stones were sent flying everywhere. One nearly hit me… some ended up in the walls."

The Bulldog made a plopping sound as it hit the murky brown water. After a few seconds the small concentric ripples vanished, and the now useless Webley revolver sank to the silted riverbed of the Thames.

That's that then.

"Yep," sighed Oliver, watching the river's waves lap against the Hospital Stairs.

What next?

"We have three choices," replied Oliver. "Stay here… or, we could use Isaac's bracelet and go to 1931."

Or?

"Use the one on my ankle and go home."

1931 it is then.

CHAPTER 24

Cuttin' Cousins
Saturday, November 1ˢᵗ ~ 2014

There'd been little change to Hawksmoor's St. Alfege's in the last century. Any slight alterations that had been made since the day Reverend Frederick Tackley preached from the pulpit, Oliver hadn't noticed.

He wasn't really the church type – if being *dragged* there every Sunday wasn't enough to turn a young lad against religion – being made to attend Sunday school certainly was. Still, the pews offered something which Oliver needed – time alone.

Once back in 1931, Oliver had entered what was now Philip's office, and engraved another bracelet – one which would take him into the future.

He'd travelled to 2014 to seek his revenge. Revenge against Jason Bradbeer – the man who'd taken his arm. Revenge against Daniel… and Sarah… they'd been there. So in Oliver's eyes they were as much to blame as their brother.

He'd toyed with the idea of travelling to their childhoods – exacting his vengeance whilst they walked to school – or played in the park. But then if he did, they wouldn't know why, and that wouldn't do.

235

Oliver shook his head and sighed. "It was never supposed to be like this... I mean... when I left... when I ran away. It was so I could *avoid* bloodshed... But I suppose you know that, don't you?"

Oliver looked up at the altar, and the arched stained-glass window behind. The stunning colours reminded him of life. The blues... they were for the skies... the falling bombs... the Luftwaffe. The greens... they were for the fields... his enclosure... a ruined plan. The whites... the winter's snowfall... the Ship's Irish bedlinen... Marlow's death. And finally, the reds... a nice drop of wine to go with the Plume's pheasant... Annie's blood-soaked body.

He lowered himself to the kneeler pad. "*And*, I saved her life. If it wasn't for me, she'd have died on that first night – the first night we met. And... and with the same knife."

Oliver's eyes dropped to the small cross under the window. It wasn't inlaid with gold nor encrusted with jewels – not at all fancy. But the message was still the same. Christ died on the cross for our sins. Oliver couldn't help but think of his own transgressions.

"So if anything – I gave her life, didn't I?"

What the hell are you rambling about?

"I need to offload – clear my mind."

Atone? You? Hope you're not trying to clear me from your mind again.

Oliver laughed. "Phelix – you're just about the only thing that keeps me sane in this mad world."

A door creaked open – someone had entered. Oliver, changing from kneeling to sitting, could hear footsteps approaching.

"Good afternoon. Don't let me interrupt your penance."

The priest, thought Oliver. "I'm done, but thank you."

Done… You've only just started.

The priest pointed at Oliver's arm. "War wound?"

"Er, yes…" replied Oliver, thinking about the excuse he'd fed to Isaac. "Yes… a stray shell."

You've not even mentioned killing Henry… and Joshua what's his name.

"Wells."

"Wells? Is that in Afghanistan?"

"Excuse me?" Oliver was confused.

"You said Wells. Is that where you lost your arm?" asked the priest.

"Ah…" Oliver twigged. "No, France."

Oh yes… then that French priest – d'Strang. I can't see you admitting to that one in here!

"Could they not save it?"

"Save it?"

Save it?

"Yes – reattach it – microsurgery."

"Can they do that?"

"Well, I'm no expert. But I'm sure if they do it straight away… or soon after… then, yes."

Change of plan. We need to get the arm – commit suicide – back to Tec-Spa. Then revenge.

"Agreed… Although I'm still not convinced about committing suicide."

"Suicide?" The priest was shocked.

"Yes," said Oliver. "But it's okay – it's painless."

Oliver stepped out into the cool November air, how he wished he'd chosen a summer month to travel to – how he wished he'd not left his coat in that closet-sized room at Tec-Spa.

He walked round to the back of the church, the stone cobbled pathways and well-kept gardens were exactly how he remembered. Exiting onto Roan Street, with its boxed glass streetlights and metal rails, Oliver headed for St. Alfege's Passage. The sweet shop at No.16 had gone – its peppermint drop shopfront replaced by a paradise of leaves.

Oliver noticed another building he recognised – a pub. It was being constructed the last time he was down here, or maybe it had just opened – he couldn't remember. It was a tall thin redbrick building, sandwiched between bland modern day housing. The sandstone block above the first-floor window confirmed Oliver's memory – 'The Earl Grey 1913'. The pub still had its original olive green tiled façade – a popular embellishment of Victorian watering holes. He pondered on the fate of his youth – had it all been lost? Had it all disappeared with the engraving of the bracelet?

Rush-hour traffic choked up the roads, and the footpaths were crammed with people, heads down, avoiding any contact as they passed unseen in and out of each other's lives. A disgruntled child moaned about how its world would end if its parent didn't buy it any chocolate. Oliver laughed. Now he understood what his father meant by 'children should be seen, but not heard'.

Using his recently discovered traffic management skills, Oliver crossed the road and headed down Turnpin Lane. The market was drawing to a close. Fascinating, Oliver thought. Boxes were being packed and stacked, crates loaded with plates, trolleys stuffed with dollies, cases bulged with laces, and under the counter fags were hidden away in bags. Not too bad, thought Oliver, wondering if he had the time then maybe he could make another rhyme.

Enough, groaned Phelix.

"Enough of this stuff…?"

With a purpose in his gait, Oliver walked through the hospital grounds. He could see where he'd hidden from the *press gang* – and where he'd stashed Old Man Mayne's barrow. He then passed between the Queen Anne court and the college chapel, recalling the throbbing pain in his leg, the one he'd had after walking into a bollard. Perhaps his youth hadn't been lost – perhaps it had just been spread very thinly over the centuries of time. Oliver liked that explanation – it sounded good.

It was just before six o'clock when he plonked himself down on the bench at the end of Flamsteed Way. The leaves on the trees were all but gone, and the swan-necked streetlights had already turned themselves on. Other than a black cab with its diesel engine idly chugging away outside No.1, Flamsteed Way was, as usual, no matter what the century, quiet.

Oliver didn't have long to wait for any movement, it was bang on six o'clock when the front door to No.5 opened. Oliver could hear the sound of The Time Store's clocks as their chimes filtered through the open door; with synchronised precision they announced the arrival of the new hour.

Four people descended the entrance steps onto the footpath. He was pretty certain about three of them – they had to be Jason, Daniel and Sarah, figured Oliver, recalling the names he'd overheard in Greenwich Park – the ones he'd read in Isaac's Tec-Spa file. He had no idea who was with them, though – who the second woman was. But then, from where he was sitting, he had no idea which of the two women was Sarah.

Go on then – what are you waiting for?

"Their father – David – he's still in there."

How can you tell? The place looks empty to me – no lights on.

"Trust me… Someone's still in there."

Oliver was right to be patient, ten minutes later another man came out of No.5. So that's David, thought Oliver, as he watched his great-nephew pull the door closed – and lock it.

Okay, I'll give you that one.

Once David had turned the corner into Feathers Place, Oliver made his move. He ran over to the house, pushed open the black iron gate and quickly made his way down the steps leading to the basement yard.

To his left there were two wooden doors. In 1913, the first door was the coal house, the second – that was a toilet, for the kitchen staff. Next to these doors, set under the footpath, was an arched recess where he and Isaac kept their bicycles. Along with a few window boxes awaiting a spring replant, an old wooden bench occupied the recess now.

Oliver tried the door to the kitchen – unsurprisingly, it was locked. One by one he tried to push up the three sash windows – they were latched.

Now what?

"Guest room," replied Oliver, without hesitation. "We can get in through the guest room."

Under the steps was an open archway in the wall, one which led to No.3's basement yard and then another archway to No.1's; a service route which linked all the yards – from there he could gain access to the rear of the buildings – the gardens.

As long as Oliver could remember, the family had kept a guest room – a haven of sorts – where any time travelling Bradbeer visiting London could stay. Fastened onto the wall next to the entry door was a coded key box. Thanks to one of his pocket money chores of keeping the room clean, Oliver knew the code, which was ironically 1751, the date of Flamsteed Way's construction.

Of course, the guest room hadn't always been there, Oliver knew that. When the houses were built this was just a back door, one which led into a gardener's room. Oliver had used it after killing the man – the one who'd followed him from the Plume – the one he'd shot and then axed. He'd come in here to wash away the blood.

Pulling the bed into the centre of the room, Oliver, using the handle of a spade he'd found in the garden, tapped against the wall.

What are you doing now? asked Phelix.

"Don't you remember? There should be a doorway, an opening somewhere along here. If only we could… yes! Got it." The tapping noise had changed from a thud to a hollow, shell-like echo.

Oliver kicked against the wall, kicked harder, and then kicked again. He'd been right – several hefty kicks later and Oliver was standing in what used to be the Georgian kitchen, but was now The Time Store's rest room.

241

From the rest room he made his way to the office – his father's office – David's office. Oliver stood at the door. Where its handle should've been there was a modern-day contraption – one he'd not seen before. Oliver tried twisting, pushing, pulling – nothing. There was a pad – Oliver placed his ring on it – nothing. He tried the bracelet – nothing.

Break it off, then.

Oliver ran back to the guest room, grabbed the spade, and returning to the office, used the spade to smash off the lock.

What are you looking for?

"Clues," said Oliver. "Clues."

Oliver spent ten minutes, perhaps fifteen, perhaps twenty… sifting through piles of papers, records and journals. He found an old newspaper – a copy of the General Evening Post. One of its headlines was 'Bloody Greenwich Murders'. Oliver read the article.

The body of seamstress Annie Fletcher had been discovered on the night of Monday 26th of July 1751 off Fryers Road, Greenwich by Parish Constable William Firth. Annie, a well-known local nightwalker, was to have been arrested by Firth as part of the regular Monday night scoop which was run by the authorities in a bid to clean up the streets. Considered a hardened prostitute, Fletcher would have been taken before the mayor and probably ended up in Bridewell Prison or at best the local compter. As it was, when Constable Firth found Annie Fletcher, yards away from the Ship Tavern, she'd been murdered… stabbed and slashed several times.

Oliver read the second report – the one about the man he'd shot and hacked to death. Constable Firth believed this to be a revenge attack for the recent murder of seamstress Annie Fletcher. Oliver laughed... idiot.

By the time he'd finished his search, the office looked as though it had been trashed, nothing remained on the shelves.... nothing remained on the desk. Oliver opened the desk drawer and removed the bracelet logbook. He read out the day's entries. Daniel – Emma Brewer – Ironbridge June 1, 1779. Sarah – Alice Brewer – Ironbridge June 1, 1779. Daniel – Emma Brewer – Worcestershire October 14, 1994. David – Middlesbrough April 5, 1983. Finally another for Sarah – Worcestershire October 14, 1994.

"That's funny..." said Oliver, once again reading the entries out aloud.

What is?

"These tick marks here – everyone has returned – everyone except Sarah."

I thought she left earlier... with the others.

"That must have been these two," said Oliver, pointing to the entries in the book. "Emma and Alice Brewer."

So... this Sarah...?

"Yes, I know," replied Oliver, who was already heading for the Round Room.

Oliver, the motion sensors illuminating his route, had run at speed down the passageway.

What now?

"We wait," panted Oliver, sitting down on his Uncle Philip's armchair.

He didn't have to wait long before a rather wet and tired-looking woman appeared in the Round Room.

Oliver, with the knife gripped tightly behind his back, welcomed the arrival. "Good day to you. You must be Sarah."

"Who the hell are you?" demanded Sarah, obviously somewhat startled.

Oliver took a step towards her. "Don't you know? I think you must recognise me," he snapped.

"Stop playing games," demanded Sarah, taking a step back. "I'll ask you again – who are you?"

"I'm Oliver Bradbeer – and I've come to collect my hand."

"Hand? What the hell are you on about?"

"You know. You were there when your fucking brother chopped it off," screamed Oliver, waving his stump at Sarah.

"Oh shit. *That* hand… it's gone."

"GONE…" growled Oliver. "Where?"

"We incinerated it. Destroyed it."

"WHAT?" screamed Oliver, lunging for Sarah with his knife.

Oliver went berserk. Thrust after thrust he lashed out at her. Cutting at her flesh again and again, he frantically attacked Sarah's left arm until she fell to the floor.

Sarah pleaded with him to stop, but Oliver, with Phelix chanting in his mind, attacked relentlessly.

I fear no foe, with Thee at hand to bless,

Ills have no weight, and tears no bitterness.

"Where is death's sting?"

Someone's coming.

Phelix was right, a not too distant light had come on down the passageway. Oliver lashed out one last time, then disappeared.

244

CHAPTER 25

Recuperation
Friday 5th December, 2014

It had been a wonderful time really, despite the pain and her limited manoeuvrability for the first week or so. Sarah Bradbeer had been recuperating at her grandparents' cottage just outside High Wycombe.

She'd been injured just over a month ago – it wasn't bad enough to attend hospital though, especially given the reason for her injuries and all the potential explanations. Her father had checked her wounds at the scene, then called Jason and Dan, her two brothers. They'd treated the cuts the best they could and took her upstairs to rest in her apartment. It was only the following day, when she'd had a good painkiller-induced sleep and the adrenalin had faded, that Sarah realised she was somewhat worse than she'd originally thought. As well as the lacerations, one of which was fairly deep, she'd sprained her left wrist after falling awkwardly. So it was decided that she would get away from work, and The Time Store, to heal and recover.

Once away from London, her life felt simpler... and lazier... as everything was done for her. Meals were cooked for her, clothes washed, the house kept tidy – she had time to chat with her grandparents. There were no day to day meetings with clients, no time travel, and she had space to relax and think.

The thinking side of things wasn't always good, as however much she tried to avoid it, she knew she had to tackle *that* incident – Oliver in the Round Room – she was still shocked about the entire thing.

He'd been there as she'd returned from her time trip – just standing there – demanding his missing 'hacked off' hand. When she'd told him that it had been incinerated, he'd kicked off, produced a knife and, using his one remaining hand, lunged for her. He went berserk, chanting something about 'death's sting', thrusting and slashing and cutting again and again, attacking her left arm. It seemed as though he didn't want to kill her (she assumed he wouldn't dare to attempt to take the life of one of his own Bradbeer descendants) but he definitely intended to maim her, as *he* had been – cause damage to her, to hurt her. And he'd succeeded – she'd been hurt in more ways than one.

Although her arm had been worse than her family had thought on that first day, it was healing nicely now; only a slight stiffness and pain remained after the initial agony. She assumed there'd be some scarring, given the multiple cuts she'd received. Sarah had come to terms with that, figuring that she was well overdue an injury in the course of time travel. Okay, it didn't technically happen during time travel, but that wasn't really the point. What was more difficult was dealing with the fact that it was Oliver Bradbeer who'd done this to her.

She couldn't stop reliving over and over that brief time with Oliver. He had obviously been in some heightened state of panic, made worse by the realisation that his arm had been destroyed. But even if Oliver had time travelled to a different time – prior to his hand having been incinerated – when they still had it in the freezer compartment – it couldn't have been fixed – surely Oliver should have known that, shouldn't he? It was obvious he'd been to Tec-Spa – his stub had been healed – so it would've been impossible to replace his hand anyway.

Was she even certain that it had been Oliver Bradbeer? Oliver the young man, as opposed to Oliver the teenage boy? Jason had asked her the question the day after the incident. Was it the same Oliver Bradbeer? An older version of the one who'd mysteriously disappeared in 1913? Yes, Sarah was sure. Who else could it have been?

She couldn't fully understand his frenzied panic nor his terse and abrupt disappearance, but it had upset her.

She'd been at Copthorne, her grandparents' cottage, for just over a month now, recovering. They'd all come to see her of course, her dad first of all – he'd spent a couple of days with her – it had given him an excuse to see his parents as well. In fact he'd spent more time with them than with her – she'd caught them deep in conversation a couple of times. About what she didn't know at first, but as her father was leaving he told her that John Brewer was to be taken into the employment of The Time Store, to do general maintenance et cetera, and assist on the more complicated time trips. Although Sarah hadn't met him yet, she'd time travelled with his two daughters a few weeks ago, so she was pleased at this. After all, now John had sorted himself out, he needed a break.

Her older brother Jason was next to visit. He came with stories of his new girlfriend, hoping it would put a smile on his sister's face. All Sarah could do was roll her eyes and remind him of the last one, Melissa, who had strung him along for a good few years, and then abruptly vanished from his life, by virtue of her moving out of her apartment (in the same block as Jason's) and not even bothering to leave a forwarding address. Bloody hell, he's bounced back a bit quick, thought Sarah, especially considering the tearful text he sent last week.

They'd discussed Oliver of course. Sarah remembered the look of shock on her brother's face when he realised it must have been him who'd chopped off Oliver's hand, not knowing at the time that it was an ancestor of theirs, obviously. Jason initially figured Oliver could have been looking for him rather than Sarah, to wreak revenge. However, he also reported that Dad's desk had been found somewhat untidy and that Oliver may have been in the office for some reason. Jason then suggested that her encounter with him could have been quite accidental. They could only conjecture so much though, and they agreed that when she was better they would have to delve deeper, probably by undertaking some explorative time travel expeditions. However, Sarah guessed that Jason would perhaps begin his investigations sooner. Where had Oliver come from? And where had he gone?

A few days later, Dan came with Emma. Naturally, they were concerned, but once they knew she was on the mend, they were too 'loved up' with one another to have any further detailed conversation. They left after a few hours, declining the offer of dinner, saying they had a table booked at Le Manoir aux Quat' Saisons.

Even Alice, Emma's sister, had paid a visit, having checked first that it would be okay. Sarah had said of course, and after all the family stuff and stress about the actual reason why she was there in the first place, she found that she was really looking forward to it. Alice had arrived with a small posy of flowers, hugged Sarah, then pulled back the instant she realised that Sarah was still in some pain. They'd got on well, just the two of them together. Alice was not at all bolshie and abrasive like she had been the last time they'd met, when Alice was so questioning and angry about everything. They'd agreed to meet up again for a drink before Christmas.

For the first couple of weeks Sarah had enjoyed all the visits, but in the end she was relieved to see them go, so she could get back to her peace. She spent time out in the garden, pottering about. It reminded her of her childhood when they used to come out to her grandparents' house more often. She would play games with Jason and Dan in the large and then untamed garden, often squabbling, and afterwards sulking on her own when her brothers became too rowdy.

The tranquil month away from London was coming to an end. Her family had been urging her to return. Sarah Bradbeer, experienced time traveller, who'd swashbuckled her way through many an adventure through the eras, had been floored and flummoxed by one of her own ancestors, and she'd needed a break from her normal life. Now she had to face up to it. It was time to go home.

CHAPTER 26

Heading Home
Friday, December 5th ~ 2014

Sarah, wearing thick black leggings, winter boots with imitation fur around the tops, a vest top, an Amsterdam t-shirt, a thin short-sleeved cardigan, a thicker long-sleeved cardigan, gloves and a warm padded coat, hugged and kissed her grandparents one last time and got in the car. She felt the cold at this time of year, more so now, since she'd been mostly cosseted in the heat of the cottage for the past month.

Although she'd spent time in the garden, it was always with the knowledge that warmth was never too far away. Even the couple of restorative trips into the village were cushioned by the visits to the coffee shop she'd incorporated into her schedule. She'd dropped into the charity shop too, in search of a woolly hat, but had come out with a CD of panpipes music that reminded her of the psychic fair she'd been to a couple of months ago.

Sarah had delayed her departure, having been tempted by the offer of 'just a quick bite to eat' before she went. Gran was not capable of supplying a quick sandwich though – her catering skills extended far beyond that, and Sarah had sat down at the dining table to homemade celery soup, three different types of sandwiches (crusts off – that never happened when she was a child) and a gorgeous trifle for pudding. Sarah was happy to be leaving on her journey back to the reality of The Time Store having consumed a hearty lunch.

Jason had sent her a text that morning, saying she was expected at the regular Friday meeting, and they would be holding it later than usual, at 3pm to give her time to get there. She turned out of the drive just after one. This was slightly later than planned but she figured she still had enough time to take her grandfather's 'scenic route'. Sarah had thought his suggestion was a lovely idea as she'd not been that way for a good few years, so it would be nice. Also she wanted to take it easy and not have to negotiate busy motorways, A-roads and dual carriageways.

Despite her later departure, she calculated that she would arrive at Flamsteed Way well before three, still time to dump her stuff in her apartment and have a cup of tea before the meeting. Then she could relax again for the whole weekend before starting work properly on the Monday.

It didn't hurt too much to drive – she'd had a few practice runs around the village the day before. She'd hired the car for three days, and they'd said she could drop it off anytime on Saturday at the closest hire branch when she returned to Greenwich.

The local roads were more picturesque than the motorway – and hence more meandering – she'd originally thought this would put more strain on her arm, but eventually concluded that at least she could stop for a break anytime she wanted, rather than waiting for a service station.

Sarah had mixed feelings about returning to work. She

251

understood now why her grandparents had moved out here, away from London – she was really going to miss them, and the quiet life. But she was just gone thirty, obviously nowhere near retirement age, not like her father. She smiled to herself – she craved the excitement of the city. As she'd got steadily better, the pull of the hustle and bustle increased. She was ready to return. She wondered what Jason had found out about Oliver so far... that was the bit she was dreading. But for everything else...? She couldn't bloody wait.

The road was clear, and for early December it was a bright day, albeit a little chilly. She was driving, keeping her speed at just below forty, taking in the scenery, miles of hedgerows, trees and open fields, nothing overly awe-inspiring, just pleasant and calming. She assumed the fields were empty of produce now; the farmers implementing their crop rotation over the winter months – if they still did that. She was definitely not the agricultural type at all. Maybe she could go back in time and work on a farm pre-industrial days – see what it was like. She rolled her eyes whilst she was driving. Nah... who was she trying to kid?! She could barely tell one brand of tree from another. Although she did know what an oak looked like. And a sycamore. And there was now a third one she knew as well, after recently going back in time to witness John Brewer's car crashing head-on into that horse chestnut tree. That was about it.

She liked the soothing effect of the general open countryside, and she was enjoying the drive. They used to come this way when they were kids – nearly every week, there and back – to visit their gran and granddad. One or other of their parents would drive and she would read, or think, or fight with her brothers, or beg for just one more sweet. At that age she was not taking much notice of the exact route. After her mother had died, the visits were cut to once a fortnight, as her father had a lot to do back at The Time Store, and they took to going on the motorway to get there quicker. Every alternate week, her grandparents would come to Greenwich.

And then, as Sarah, Dan and Jason had grown older and reached their teenage years, the attraction of grandparents at the weekend had taken a backseat, in favour of friends, boy/girlfriends, going out, hanging around, shopping, drinking, experimenting – definitely for the most part staying well and truly in London.

She hoped Jason's latest – er – conquest would work out well for him. What had he said her name was? Rhiannon? Well, anyone was better than Melissa, who'd never been right for him. She didn't think Melissa had ever been aware of the family's travel abilities, thankfully. Maybe it was better to be like Dan and Emma, who'd met because of a time travel connected reason. Then at least they could be open and honest right from the start, and not have the awkward 'there's something I need to tell you' conversation a couple of years into the relationship. She decided to ask her father what her mother had said when he'd revealed he could travel in time.

She passed through a small village... and then back onto the open road. The traffic seemed heavier all of a sudden. The scenery was different now, more trees at the side of the road, less fields – in fact as she drove a bit further the road dipped down in front of her and she could see a dense wooded area, and she suddenly remembered this from her childhood, as vividly as if it was last week. She drove down the hill, and then round a sharp bend. And… slammed on the brakes, coming to an abrupt, tyre-screeching halt about half a metre behind the car in front.

Sarah's heart was thumping – there was no danger – it was the shock of having to react quickly, the immediate jump away from her relaxed state of mind. What was going on? Had she missed the road signs? Probably. She leaned as far as she could to her right, peering in an attempt to see something. The queue of traffic was too long to reveal any hint of incident ahead.

She hoped it wouldn't be anything serious – she'd been making good time up until now. After five minutes of not moving, she turned up the volume on the CD player. She'd put her recent panpipes acquisition on at a low level at the start of her journey. After a few more minutes, a stream of about seven or eight cars passed by travelling in the opposite direction, and soon after, the line she was in shunted forward a few metres. Traffic lights, she figured. Temporary traffic lights – roadworks…? On a Friday afternoon? Shocking! Wouldn't they have all gone home by now?

The CD, which had been playing its last (long) track, finished and then started again. Another stream of traffic, another slight movement forward. She began a small impatient tapping on the side of the steering wheel, not in time with the music. Surely someone should have got out of their car by now and started to investigate the cause of the problem – they're a patient lot out here, she thought.

But, although time was ticking by, it wouldn't be the end

of the world if she missed a few minutes of the family meeting. She thought about sending Jason a text to warn him that she might be a bit late, but then realised she'd thrown her handbag in the boot with her other luggage.

The music had reduced itself to a soporific mantra of three notes of flute playing, which seemed to be going on for an unnecessarily long time. Sarah opened the glove-box to pick a different CD, then realised that she was not in her own car.

She looked up, and saw a massive low-loader carrying a somewhat large digger on its platform. It was approaching from the same direction as the intermittent trickle of cars. Beware large plant approaching. She giggled as she remembered as a teenager imagining a massive cactus, or yucca or something, approaching. That was before she knew what large/heavy plant really was.

It rumbled past, followed moments later by another line of cars and vans. Work must be finished for the day. But still, the next movement of cars in her direction was not free flowing. She did drive further forward than before though – a good fifty metres, then stopped again. What now? She looked around.

To her left was a driveway, more like a very short farm track by the state of it. On one side of the drive was an overgrown hedge, and on the other, what she supposed had once been a front garden. Then there was the house. As she stared at it, it began to look familiar. She'd seen it before – possibly quite a few times – she had a feeling that she knew it well, but it was not the same as her memories.

She made an impulsive decision, turned the steering wheel to the left, and pulled onto the drive.

CHAPTER 27

Meeting with Apologies

Jason Bradbeer, future custodian of The Time Store buildings and business, was drumming his fingers on the large wooden table in the centre of the rest room, and occasionally flicking rolled up bits of paper at his younger brother, Dan. The current custodian, their father, David, luckily for them, was not in the room.

Jason had arranged the regular Friday family meeting for 3pm rather than the more usual 1pm, to allow Sarah plenty of time to return from their grandparents' house. She was already half an hour late. David had announced that he was off to the toilet and then to make some phone calls, and when Sarah arrived he would bring her downstairs and the meeting could start.

"Want another coffee?" asked Dan, retrieving two bits of paper from the floor and throwing them ineffectually at Jason.

"Yeh, might as well. Dunno where Sarah is." Jason stood up. "I'll make it this time."

"Did you text her?" Dan handed his brother two used cups from the table.

"No reply." Jason placed the cups on the small kitchen worktop which ran along one wall of the rest room, clicked on the kettle to re-boil the water, and added a spoon of coffee to the dregs in each of the cups. "Hope she's okay."

"She'll be fine – probably just talking to Gran and lost track of time."

"She knows she's got this meeting."

"Yes, but a month away from work – no deadlines. Well, you know – she's only just getting back to normal."

Jason returned to the table with the two coffees. "I suppose... but I thought she was eager to get back. I've got an update on the Oliver incident – and there are some other matters we need to discuss as a family – in a structured meeting environment."

"Yeah." Dan barely glanced upwards.

"I've also prepared a business directive. A statement of goals for us, going forward."

"Oh... yeah?"

"Yes. As you know, Dad has agreed for us to branch out a bit – try to solve more serious issues, rather than just acting as a time travel agency."

"Of course, yes." Dan was suddenly attentive, un-slumping himself from his seat. He finally understood what Jason was on about.

"The question is this," continued Jason. "How do we find these so-called serious issues? And how do we choose which ones to take on?"

"How indeed? A very good question, and well asked." David Bradbeer stood at the door to the rest room, a slight smile on his face.

"Any sign of Sarah?" asked Dan.

"No, nothing," replied David. "Have either of you tried to contact her?"

"No reply." Jason reprised his answer.

"Right, I suggest we leave it another ten minutes and then start without her – she'll have to catch up with anything she's missed when she finally arrives. John's upstairs – I was just showing him some of the new timepieces we have in. Does anyone mind if he sits in on the meeting?"

"No, not at all – it'll be good for him to see a professionally run discussion in action." Jason glanced at Dan, expecting him to be smirking sarcastically, but his brother was, unusually for him, looking deadly serious. "Dan…?"

"Okay, yes, no problem." Dan felt suddenly and unexpectedly nervous. "Just gonna text Emma."

John Brewer was Emma's father. Dan was fairly well acquainted with his new girlfriend's dad, having taken him on a botched time trip to see himself in a car crash, and inadvertently allowed him to bring about his younger self's own death, which had the knock-on effect of causing the time travelling John to die as well.

This had meant that Dan was left with no memory whatsoever of the entire incident. The family called it Dan's Anomaly and he had to endure jokes about it for five years until Emma, John's younger daughter, telephoned a psychic radio show to try to make some sense of a changing newspaper headline, in which she thought both parents had died when she was a child. Dan had heard Emma's conversation and realised the time and date of the mysterious changing headline corresponded exactly to the moment he had been found on the floor of the Round Room with an unexplained singed arm and a gap in his memory.

He'd finally managed, after a long and involved ruse at the Mystic Moon Psychic Fair, to contact Emma. They'd gone back in time to the crash scene, saw that time travelling John was about to lock his younger self in the car so he could spend as much time as possible with his dying wife before being pulled out, and realised this would cause him not to be rescued alive. Thanks to Emma's timely intervention her father had been prevented from locking himself in. His other self, that is.

So everything had turned out fine again. Emma and her sister Alice got their father back, their memories of the crash where they lost both parents as young children now had a fresh memory of John having survived.

Unfortunately this new memory then included John having gone off the rails, the kids moving abroad with their auntie and losing touch. But it had all ended happily. John got his daughters back, Emma and Alice got their father back, John got himself a job at The Time Store, and Dan got a girlfriend, who he fancied like mad.

'Ems... your dad's in our meeting... need to make good impression... any hints?'

'xx'

Dan knew full well that any other (rare) visitor to the family meeting and he would normally have the upper hand, feel confident about his position and abilities. But although he'd been through a lot with John, who was now in fact his employee, trainee at that, Dan was, at the moment, feeling like a teenager trying to look good in front of his new girlfriend's dad. Emma was no help. His text alert sounded a few minutes after he'd sent his two texts.

'Just chill x'

David returned to the rest room with John, and the two older men sat down opposite Jason and Dan.

"Right, let's start," said Jason. "Apologies, for Sarah's absence... dunno where she's got to... but welcome, John, to this meeting."

"Thank you," said John, smiling across at Jason and Dan.

"My plan was to start with bringing you all up to date on my recent findings about Oliver Bradbeer, our elusive ancestor, but..."

"I suggest you leave that until we have Sarah here," said David. "She needs to know first-hand about any developments, and you don't want to have to go over it all again. Plus we could do with her input on this one."

"Yes, Dad." Jason was bristling.

"Good, so what's next on the agenda?"

"Well, that would be my new statement of goals for The Time Store," announced Jason. "Going forward."

"Thought time travel was the way backwards," Dan blurted, before realising that he hadn't really planned on being so flippant in front of Emma's father. Not a good start.

"Yes, Jason. Good idea." David, adjusting his cravat, turned to John. "We recently had an episode where we were helping a lady from Middlesbrough come to terms with her son's suicide, years ago, as a teenager. He hanged himself from the loft hatch, after finding out one of his sister's friends had died as a result of taking drugs. Drugs he had been forced to supply. We couldn't prevent his death, obviously, but we found ourselves getting somewhat involved with the situation, and wanting to do something. Something that went against The Time Store's ethic."

"Preserve true time," chanted Dan.

"We went back in time and had the whole Tarelli family arrested – preventing many years of future drug supplies by them. That was a departure from what we usually offer to our time travelling clients. It was Jason who convinced me that we had to do it."

"Yeah," said Jason. "This was the first time the Bradbeers had intervened and exacted retribution like this for about a hundred years."

"Except..." Dan stopped himself abruptly. His dad didn't know about that little trip to the doomed HMS Association a few years back.

David glanced at Dan. "Yes, what we normally provide is trivial in comparison – an enhanced holiday experience, if you like."

"Except your car crash, John," resumed Dan, relieved he'd saved himself from blabbing. "That wasn't trivial." He looked at John for confirmation.

John seemed a tad overwhelmed. He opened his mouth to speak – nothing came out.

"So what is this so-called statement of goals?" asked David.

"Finally..." Jason shuffled his papers, sorting through the sheets until he found what he wanted.

Jason, mainly for John's benefit, explained briefly how The Time Store operated a century ago. He read the notes from Edward Bradbeer's personal journal which referenced Oliver's disappearance and the resulting decision to forbid time travel to be used for anything other than recreational purposes.

He talked, at great length, about the future demands on the business and the need to drive sales. The focus was to be on customer appreciation, customer satisfaction and customer return.

Jason then turned to the World of Timepieces Exhibition and its continued global success. The feedback from the current host city, Madrid, was excellent; The Time Store needed to build on this – education at every level was a key goal. Jason proposed that, in time, this was an area which John could develop.

After a much needed break for coffee, Jason continued. The Time Store, he suggested, should be even more selective – have a more stringent criteria for its travel clients; then, to the annoyance of Dan, spent time outlining this criteria. He proposed a reduction in customer travel trips to six per month. Two each for himself, Sarah and Dan. This in turn would allow them to focus and develop The Time Store as a brand.

He talked about the turmoil of true time. Preserving it had always been their number one priority and yet, by reintroducing the 'old ways', true time had to, at times, be cast aside.

Jason suggested that their retribution beneficiaries should be chosen by 'chance' – and not by any form of advertising. They should watch the news, listen to people, read the papers and then follow the story. They shouldn't be drawn in by grief, loss or hate – but more by what is fundamentally right and what is undeniably wrong.

"This all sounds very impressive," said David, when his son had finally wound up his presentation and sat down.

"Yeah, good work, Jase," said Dan.

"Very business-like," said John quietly.

"And have you found our first case? Who's going to be the first beneficiary of these new goals?" David leaned forward on the table.

"Well…"

"He's been too busy devising it all and typing it up!" Dan threw a stray ball of paper at his brother. Another step towards not impressing John.

"So, have we got any potential clients… of any kind… this week?" asked David.

"I've got two," boasted Dan, finally convinced he'd said something right at last. "Jase…?"

"Yeah," replied Jason. "I've got this guy who wants to travel back to see a motor show."

"Mmm," muttered David. "Hardly awe-inspiring."

CHAPTER 28

Childhood Memories

By the time Sarah had got out of her car, she'd remembered everything about Apple Tree Cottage. It was where all those years ago they would quite often stop to buy home-made jam, honey and cakes on the journey back. The couple who owned the house would sometimes invite them all in for a cup of tea, or lemonade for the kids (home-made of course), and a chat, or a runabout in the garden to 'stretch their legs'.

Mr and Mrs Dorrington were lovely, Sarah recalled. She presumed they owned rather than rented as they kept it so nice, and grew so much stuff. So where were they now? The house was so obviously empty. Not the sort of empty where they'd just nipped to the shops, or even gone on a two week holiday to escape England's bitter winter. But totally empty, dark and devoid of life, cold and unloved.

Sarah used her gloved hand to wipe away the grime of several years from the porch window. There was a large pile of newspapers inside on the floor, in varying degrees of ageing yellow. The weekly news over the years accumulating until some bright spark paperboy realised there was no one home and stopped delivering.

She mooched around the back. The garden was

overgrown, untended. Even for the time of year Sarah could tell that nothing that could possibly be offered for sale had been grown there for a good while. She sat on the wooden garden bench, now dirty and encrusted with a thin layer of moss.

The plant life was taking over, trails of green tendrils trying to claim the cottage as their own, dragging it down to their roots. In years to come the old clay drainage system and indeed the very foundations would be cracked and destroyed by the underground activity of plants – and trees.

The Dorringtons… were they dead? But if so, surely the property would have been sold on and improved, modernised and lived in by now. It seemed such a shame – it was a charming little cottage. Sarah remembered that she'd had some happy family afternoons here, despite the sibling mini-fights. It was the sort of place where she might herself want to retire to in years to come.

She stood up from the bench and walked a few paces down the garden. There'd been an uneven brick path leading through the grass – she could still see glimpses of it beneath her feet as she ploughed through the wilderness to the large vegetable plot. She remembered Jason pulling up a carrot and blaming her – she could still hear her mother's comforting voice, reassuring her she knew it wasn't really Sarah who had done it.

She resolved to ask her father if he knew anything about what had happened with the house when she got back. Shit – better start making tracks, get back to real life, family meetings and time travel again.

She pulled out of the driveway and saw that the last of the workmen were dismantling the temporary traffic lights.

Daylight was starting to fade now, she was well aware that she would be late for the meeting, and she'd had chance to take her phone out and text an explanation, but it had slipped her mind.

The road was clear here now, but the closer she got to home, the more the London traffic slowed her down, so she arrived in Greenwich much later than her intended time. Thankfully her usual resident's parking space was still free. She expertly reversed in, and got out of the car. Home at last.

She looked up at the splendour of the four-storey Georgian building. No.5 Flamsteed Way, the middle house of a residential row of five, displayed no outward evidence of also being a retail establishment.

The main door was closed. It was after five o'clock. She climbed the six stone steps, slightly worn over time, and opened the door with her key.

The vestibule was chilly – she must suggest having some sort of heater in here during the winter months. She entered through the ornately decorated inner door with its mix of clock hands, cogs and Roman numerals etched on the glass, and into the warmth of The Time Store. She decided not to go to her apartment to dump her stuff. Better get down to the rest room, she thought, see if they're all still there.

She was suddenly so happy, so excited to be back. She made her way through the downstairs sales room, following the gold line – the Prime Meridian Line – indicator of zero degrees longitude, the reason The Time Store was in Greenwich.

The rest room was empty. There were four dirty coffee cups on the table. Four…? And a scribbled note.

We've adjourned to the Plume.
Three appointment cards in office.
Can you post them please?
Jase.

CHAPTER 29

The Plume of Feathers

The Plume of Feathers in Park Row, Greenwich, was the Bradbeers' local. Situated a little to the east of the Prime Meridian, just a very short walk from Greenwich Park, The Plume, or The Feathers as it was originally called, had been a drinking house for a few centuries, and hence had been frequented by many generations of Bradbeers.

"Four pints of Doombar please, Kim." Jason Bradbeer stood at the bar.

"Just a coke for me," said John.

"Okay. Make that three pints and a coke please."

"I'll put them on your tab," replied Kim, reaching for a glass and pulling the first pint. "How's Sarah?"

"She's fine, back today… except… she's not back yet. Can we have a glass of red for her though – she'll be in soon – I've just had a text from her. She's at the post office and on her way here."

"No probs," said Kim.

Jason and John carried the drinks over and joined David and Dan who were sitting at their usual tables in the corner by the window.

"Did Sarah say how long she'd be?" asked David.

268

"About ten minutes," replied Jason. "Maybe sooner."

John sipped his coke. "Dan? Are you and Emma doing anything special over the next few days?"

"Well, I'm not seeing her on Monday – she's going to see The Augustines at The Roundhouse with a friend of hers," replied Dan. "So I thought that we might nip to Paris tomorrow or Sunday."

"That'll be nice," said John. "Bit of a rush though?"

"31st March 1889," said Dan, smiling. "The opening of The Eiffel Tower."

"Ah, sweet," mocked Jason.

"Sarah's here," said David, standing up to give his daughter a hug.

"Finally," said Dan. "What kept you?"

"Well, hello to you too." Sarah picked up the glass of red from the table, knowing it was for her, and took a swig. "I was delayed – road works. Actually I stopped to look at…"

"Right, well you're here now," interrupted Jason. "We've held most of the meeting already – I'll tell you about it later. But we left out the Oliver stuff, so are you okay with going over it now?"

"Yeah, I suppose so," said Sarah, sitting down next to her father. "Hi, John. Good to meet you at last. Is Dad keeping you busy?"

"Yes, but it's been great, thank you. How are you feeling?"

"Fine, fine, thanks. Ready to get to work next week."

"Can we get on with it?" said Dan. "I'm starving."

"Let's start with what we know about our mysterious ancestor," said David, looking at Jason.

Jason briefly summarised what they knew from Bradbeer records.

Oliver Bradbeer, son of Edward Bradbeer, their great, great uncle, had disappeared in 1913, aged seventeen. Information was sparse, but the general consensus was that Oliver was buried somewhere in the tunnels that made up the London Underground system. There was an assumption that Oliver had messed up somehow, on a time trip. The purpose of his travel trip and what effect it had on true time was never known, but theories ranged from the Mexican revolution, to the disappearance of the steamship *Calvados* in the Marmara Sea. The mystery surrounding Oliver had led to Edward declaring that The Time Store was forbidden to use time travel for anything other than recreational activities.

"So," concluded Jason. "Oliver cocked up, then. This meant two major changes. One – we became a travel agency – something we now propose to change. And two – with Oliver's disappearance, shortly after the First World War Edward stepped down and custodianship passed on to his brother Philip, our great-great-grandfather."

"But…" faltered John, looking at Sarah. "Is Oliver back…?"

"He made a brief appearance…" Sarah began.

"Yes…" said David. "And it was obviously Oliver who'd ransacked the office that day."

"And kicked shit out of the guest room wall," added Dan.

"He attacked me – in the Round Room – chanting something about death's sting," continued Sarah. "But I've looked that up and all I can find is a reference to a dagger in a stupid game and part of a line from a hymn."

"*Abide with Me*," said John.

"Yes, that's the one. And he was demanding we gave him his hand back. No mention was made in the records of 1913 that Oliver had lost his hand. And…" This was where Sarah couldn't grasp the enormity of the situation. "He looked a good few years older than seventeen."

Jason took up the explanation once more. "When I spoke to Sarah after the Round Room incident, we realised, deduced, that it may very well have been me who chopped off Oliver's hand."

"Hold on… what?" Dan spluttered on his drink. "Why does no one tell me these things?"

"Dad thought we'd be better to wait until we were all together and Sarah was feeling better." Jason had the grace to look sheepish. "And anyway, you were always with Emma."

"Ah… so everyone knows, except me. Fantastic. Typical." Dan paused. "But…?"

"You know when we went to Flamsteed Way in 1751? To see the house being built?"

"Yeah, there was a dead body. I know. You chopped his hand off trying to get our bracelet. But I thought…"

"Well, my initial research indicated that this body was a deckhand from an offloading ship. It was in the papers back then. So we thought – Dad and me – that it was just a random coincidence that had no impact on The Time Store in any way at all."

"Then when I was attacked, we began to have a rethink," said Sarah. "It was definitely Oliver – an older Oliver – in the Round Room. And so all that stuff with the hand? It then became not random at all. But still I don't get it. I saw his arm –"

"What was left of it," said Dan.

"Yeah, what was left of it – perfectly healed – a Tec-Spa intervention if ever there was one. But we had the bracelet. And anyway…" Sarah stopped. "Jase – hang on a minute. This doesn't fit. If it *was* Oliver, which it was – I've checked our photo album – it's definitely him – how could he get to Tec-Spa if he was already dead and we'd nicked his bracelet? Or… why wasn't he already at Tec-Spa before we had chance to nick his bracelet?"

Jason sighed. He had been prepared for this, but it wasn't going to make it any easier. "He wasn't dead."

"What…!?" Four voices in unison.

"I'll tell you over dinner."

Jason had bought some time, but he felt his father's disapproval during the time it took to order food, get more drinks, and wait for the meals to arrive.

He cut into his steak and braced himself. "When I went back on my own to 1751 to investigate, I saw two men arrive – time travel type arrive – South Africans I think from the accent – with this person, body, whatever, in between them. They dropped the body and vanished when they heard us three coming into Flamsteed Way – remember, we'd only gone there on a whim. Then Sarah checked for a pulse and couldn't find one – we realised that he had one of our bracelets on, but when we heard a noise – maybe the builders coming back – I picked up an axe and chopped off his hand –"

"And part of his arm…"

"Yeah, whatever. But it was all rushed, then we came back.

But after we'd all got back to 2009, as I watched – you know, on my own – the South Africans came back – told me it was a good thing we'd got his hand – and bracelet. I found a tourniquet on his arm – that's why we didn't find a pulse. And he looked dead."

"But he wasn't." David glared at his son.

"No… but those South Africans were gonna chop his hand off anyway. They said he was on the verge of death and to let him die."

"Great, but you didn't tell us this bit," said Sarah.

"No. At the time I didn't think it mattered. I told Dad the bit about the South Africans. We couldn't work out who they were. So we just left it. I incinerated the hand, so I didn't bother to check the DNA sample."

"So Oliver was alive?" asked John.

"Yes, but on the *verge* of death," replied Jason.

"He didn't die though, did he?" said Sarah. "He couldn't have done."

"He might have had a second br…" began Dan.

"More drinks anyone?" shouted Kim from the bar.

"Yes please," Jason called. He certainly needed one.

"I'll have a beer this time," said John.

"I can't take any more of this right now," Sarah said. "What else did you discuss at part one of this meeting?"

"Statement of goals," Jason began, glad to change the subject. "We're intending to revert back to the original Time Store ethos and put right some wrongs."

"Even in the light of this *new* Oliver info?" queried Sarah.

"Yes," said Jason. He looked at his father. "Dad?"

"Yes," confirmed David. "More so now, as it seems that this is one of the wrongs we need to put right, eh?"

"We also need to update the newspaper ad to reflect these new changes," continued Jason. "Dan? Could you do that?"

"Yeah," said Dan. "I've got one. 'Need to write some wrongs? Our time travel vigilante service can help.'"

"I'll do it," sighed Sarah.

"Here you are, four pints and a large glass of red," said Kim, placing a drinks tray down on the table in front of Sarah.

"Thanks, Kim," said Sarah. "Right. What else, Jase?"

"We only have three clients next week," replied Jason.

"Anything exciting?" asked Sarah.

"I've got one, which is about cars... nothing too exciting though, just a trip to a seventies motor show. Dan has two, but we might have to drop one – there's a clash of times."

"Can't see why," interrupted Dan, looking at his brother. "Sarah could do one of them now she's back, couldn't she? Maybe the Scottish one."

"Is that okay with you, Sarah?" asked David, joining the conversation. "It's something to do with the Loch Ness monster isn't it, Daniel?"

"Yes," replied Dan, his gaze shifting between father and sister for confirmation. "I can still take Stuart Ramos on his pirate adventure then."

"No problem. Should be fun, I've never been to Loch Ness," said Sarah, readily accepting the client. "Oh. By the way, Dad. I was going to ask this as soon as I got back, but what with everything else, I forgot. It's why I was late. Remember that little cottage we used to stop at when we were kids?"

"Yes... I think so. You mean where we'd get honey and cake?" Seeing Sarah nodding, David continued. "Apple Tree Cottage."

"That's it. Well, I stopped there. There was no one in. I mean, the cottage was empty. Garden overgrown, you know? It was so sad. I just wondered if you knew what happened to the owners."

"The Dorringtons? I don't know," said David. "I didn't realise they'd gone."

"Dead obviously," muttered Dan.

"Maybe," said Sarah. "But it's such a shame about the house. Would anyone mind if I did a bit of investigating?"

"No, not at all," replied David. "Go ahead. Let me know what you find out."

"Okay," said Jason. "So now all we need to do is focus on finding a few clients who need our help, as per our new guidelines. Any ideas? Anyone seen any stories in the news? Or can you think of any past potential clients who we couldn't help, but maybe we can help now?"

"No, not yet," said Sarah.

"I'll have a think," said Dan.

"I thought you'd got one, Jason," said David.

"Er... I've got a suggestion," John said. Everyone was looking at him. "It might take a few days to set up, though."

"Could you elaborate please, John?" asked David.

"I had a friend," said John, nervously. "Dan? You might remember me telling you about him when we first met."

"The man who died?"

"Yes," replied John. "Patrick Kelly."

CHAPTER 30

'X' Marks the Spot
Tuesday, December 9th ~ 2014

It had been fun to begin with. The south coast of Australia, beautiful sunshine, a nice bit of sea fishing in the morning, and a bottle of rum to enjoy whilst watching the evening sunset. However, after three weeks of it, Dan was becoming bored – perhaps pirate hunting wasn't that exciting after all.

Dan had taken the call from Stuart Ramos two, true time, weeks ago – quite by accident. He'd been hanging by the phone most of the morning, half-expecting a call from Emma. Had Dan not darted across the sales floor when the phone finally rang, it would've been Jason who'd have answered, and probably Jason who'd have met with Mr Ramos.

It was their more than brief chat – all about pirates and treasure maps – which compelled Dan to arrange an immediate meeting with Mr Ramos. It also helped that Stuart worked at West India Quay, Canary Wharf, about twenty minutes away.

During their initial meeting, Stuart had recounted his childhood memories. Not the usual ones about holidays, birthdays or a magical shopping adventure, and nothing at all to do with such trivialities as school, or brothers and sisters. No, for Stuart Ramos, his earliest memories in life were all about 'the map'.

From the age of five, perhaps even earlier, Stuart's grandfather would tell him stories about his swashbuckling ancestors, the ones who'd lived in the Golden Age of Piracy, lived and died by the code – the Pirate Code.

His favourite story when he was younger – the one he could listen to over and over again without ever becoming bored – was the one his grandfather called 'The Tale of Sebastian Ramos'.

Sebastian, the last of the Ramos pirates, sailed under the command of the legendary Spanish pirate Benito 'Bloody Sword' Bonito in the early 1800s.

Of course Benito hadn't planned on becoming a pirate, it just happened. "Fate took a hold of him," according to Stuart's grandfather. Allegedly, or so the tale goes, Benito only became a pirate because he couldn't sing – and so Stuart had grown up thinking that there weren't many career opportunities back then. As with most legends though, there were many versions surrounding the life and death of Bloody Sword Bonito.

One such legend tells of his ship being taken by a British man-o'-war after Benito sailed from Port Phillip Bay, his apparent hiding place for the 'Lost Loot of Lima'. His refusal to reveal the whereabouts of the 'booty' earned him the hangman's noose.

Another version ended with Benito putting his pistol to his head and pulling the trigger, in preference to allowing himself to be taken by British pirate hunters.

Yet another legend tells that Benito was betrayed by two British crewmen, the two who'd coincidentally helped him hide the Lost Loot.

Benito had a ruthless streak, a tendency to always get what he wanted, and if he didn't... well then he'd certainly live up to his name of Bloody Sword.

The Catholic Church had amassed a huge treasure trove in Lima, Peru. As the Peruvian War of Independence loomed, the treasure was to be transported to Mexico for safekeeping by Captain William Thompson, commander of the *Mary Dear*.

But Thompson proved to be unable to resist the temptation; with the help of his crew he turned pirate, cut the throats of the guards and priests, threw their bodies overboard and headed for Cocos Island, where he and his men allegedly buried the treasure.

Before he'd had the opportunity to return and collect the treasure, one of his crew, Trevados Diablo, had divulged its hiding place to Benito, who in turn, had claimed the treasure as his own.

On his way back from the meeting, Dan had scoured the internet on his phone, searching for any scraps of information which supported Stuart's story. Most of it was there – the Lima Loot – Benito Bonito – William Thompson and the *Mary Dear* – Cocos Islands – and something about Queenscliff – Wikipedia was an amazing site.

Getting Jason to approve the time trip for Stuart hadn't been a problem. Jase had been most curious, and had asked more questions than anything else about Benito becoming a pirate because he couldn't sing.

Dan and Stuart had set up camp just north of Queenscliff, on the recently named (for them anyway, having gone back to the early 19th century) Swan Island. From their remote vantage point they had the perfect position to watch the arrivals and departures in and out of Port Phillip Bay.

"Anything?"

"No," Dan huffed. "Not a sausage."

It had been the same for the past three weeks – nothing. No merchants – no marauders. No traders – no treasure.

Given the isolated location of the island, Dan had easily persuaded his father to allow him a few home comforts. Nothing exciting though; a cool box – which they had to keep buried, some music – which they had to keep low, and some dominoes – which they found they had to play with over and over again.

It was after God knows how many feasts of flathead and whiting, that Dan, hankering for a nice juicy steak and a couple of cold beers, placed palm to wrist and went on a quick 21st century shopping trip. It was the following evening that Stuart, whilst finishing off one of these beers, spotted the wind-filled jib and foresails rounding the bay's southern peninsular.

"At last," Dan cried out, jubilantly. "Get the fire."

Using his empty plate as a spade, Stuart doused the small camp fire with sand and then joined Dan in watching the majestic warship as it sailed into Port Phillip Bay.

"The *Vanquish*," declared Ramos, excitedly. "It's the *Vanquish*."

Stuart was right, and as they watched Benito 'Bloody Sword' Bonito anchor the old third-rate ship of the line, just

279

inside Port Phillip Bay, the intrepid time travelling pirate hunters sat and swigged the last of the ice-cold Belgian lager.

The tale of Sebastian Ramos started very early the following morning. Apparently, according to Ramos family legend, he hadn't been chosen for the task he was about to undertake for his strength or loyalty – Sebastian had been chosen because he was awake.

Having taken turns to catch some sleep, Dan woke Stuart in time to watch the second of two small rowing boats being lowered into the bay.

"They're laden with the treasure," said Dan, passing Stuart his binoculars.

"The Lima Loot… who'd have ever believed it?"

"Who's in the boats?"

"Benito's in that one… that's Sebastian at the oars." Stuart pointed to the first of the two small boats. "Trevados Diablo is in the other… with a guy called Farrissey."

Again, Stuart was right, Jim Farrissey from England, a wood turner by trade, was at the oars of the other boat. In his quest to piece the tale together, Stuart had traced the Farrissey family tree back to the times of King John and Runnymede.

"They can't be…" Stuart was baffled. "They're heading here. That's…"

"Not what you expected?"

"No, not at all," Stuart. "I thought they'd be heading for Queenscliff. The tale definitely tells of them hiding the treasure, but there are no caves on Swan Island. So what are they gonna do, bury it?"

"Perhaps we should stand up and ask them," Dan laughed. "Come on, we better move further round. Can't have them seeing us."

Disturbing several orange-bellied parrots, Dan and Stuart concealed themselves amongst the coastal scrub, then watched as the four filibusters manoeuvred the loot inland. Whilst Benito and Trevados counted paces and made maps, Jim and Sebastian then took to the shovels.

Then it turned nasty. Diablo and Farrissey, friends of old, turned against Benito – and killed him. Then after drawing him for the gulls to feed on, they turned on each other.

"I never expected that," said Dan, shaking his head in disbelief.

"I did. The tale tells of Diablo and Farrissey fighting to the death, whilst Sebastian seeks refuge from their blades."

"Seeks refuge?"

"Yeah – as in – he runs away."

The fight didn't last long, if Diablo had been blessed with longer arms… then he might have been 'last man standing'. But as it was, Farrissey won the day, and just as he began to feed Diablo his own fingers, Dan and Stuart watched as Sebastian Ramos dragged one of the small rowing boats back into the bay.

Wiping Diablo's blood from his hands, Jim Farrissey headed back for the rowing boats, only to see Sebastian out at sea – rowing one boat, with the second, tethered to the first, following behind.

Dan and Stuart watched as Sebastian abandoned one of the boats on a Queenscliff beach and then returned to the *Vanquish*.

"Come on," said Dan. "Best we head home."

Over a much needed coffee, Dan recounted their big adventure to Jason.

"No wonder Australian legend has it that a Queenscliff cave became the final resting place for the Lima Loot," commented Jason, wishing he'd been there. "What happened to this Farrissey guy?"

"Probably became fish food," replied Stuart. "The tale mentions that the *Vanquish* was indeed taken by a British man-o'-war... but neither Benito's body nor the treasure were ever recovered."

"And the map?" asked Jason, who'd been transfixed by Stuart's story.

"I don't think there is one. Or should I say... I've never seen one."

"But what about the treasure?" persisted Jason.

"From what we can tell the only thing anyone will be finding on Swan Island is lost balls."

"Eh?"

"It's buried under the Queenscliff golf course."

It was later that afternoon, during his second report of the tale, this time to Sarah, that Emma, who'd planned to go Christmas shopping with Dan, arrived in the rest room.

"If I hear one more bloody yo-ho-ho off this idiot I'll scream," said Sarah, opening the rest room door for Emma. "Dan thinks he's Captain friggin' Pugwash all of a sudden."

"Captain who?" Emma laughed as she gave Dan a kiss on his cheek. "I think that's a bit before my time... I see him more as a... Captain Jack Sparrow."

"Jack Great-Tit, if you ask me," said Sarah, laughing in tandem with Emma.

"Arrrrgh! Ye pair of scurvy sea-dogs. Be ye ready to set sail for the Americas?"

"Yes," replied Emma. "You come too, Sarah. You know shopping isn't his thing. We'll take on Herald Square and then Saks… together."

"I wish," replied Sarah, sighing. "I've got a client to see this afternoon."

"Don't forget the watches will you, Dan?" said Jason, as Dan and Emma were leaving the rest room.

"Watches?" asked Emma, getting the feeling that Dan's suggestion to go on a New York shopping trip was more business than pleasure.

Dan didn't reply, he'd been rumbled.

CHAPTER 31

Fragmented Sleep
Thursday 11th December, 2014

On any other day at nearly five in the morning Gary Lockett would've still been tucked up in bed, entwined in his duvet – after all, usually he'd not have to get up for another two hours. But today, forty-nine year old Gary just couldn't settle. He'd spent most of the night drifting in and out of consciousness, far too many things on his mind to be able to get proper sleep.

Since his return home from work on Monday afternoon, his plan – if that's what it was – had started to pick up, started to gain momentum, started to be real. He was now living it, thinking it and, unfortunately for Gary's need for sleep over the past three nights, dreaming it.

He'd lain in bed thinking things over in his mind; questioning what would happen if he was found out... caught red-handed or identified in years to come. His thoughts danced around the events of last night... the park, the trees and the boy, and then – flicked to whether he'd hidden it properly, concealed it well enough... or would it be found?

Finally, after giving up on the idea of any more sleep, Gary dragged himself into the shower and stood beneath the steaming hot spray, cleansing himself of all his yesterdays... all his shame… all his doubt.

Gary hadn't had an easy life. He'd just reached his teenage years when his father had passed away, and life – as his school reports reflected – went from very good to 'could do a lot better, needs to focus his attention'. He'd had to grow up pretty quickly though, being the only *man* in the house. And so life, housework and employment took the place of lessons, homework and exams. A pretty tight swerve in priorities especially for a grieving child who was also battling the life changes which puberty threw at him.

Unlike his two sisters, Gary only really began living his own life a few years back when, upon his mother's death, he was finally released from her shackles and taunts. He'd put up with it, not for her… he didn't give two shits about her, the witch… he'd put up with it because she'd promised him the house if anything ever happened to her. Unfortunately, when she died there was no will and so, under pressure from his sisters, the house – his home – was sold and the money, although they didn't deserve a penny, was split three ways.

Perhaps if he'd been a stronger person, not as weak-willed as he was, then things – his life – could've been very different. But it was too late to wallow in all that now.

After ten minutes under the waking water Gary dressed, not for work though, he wasn't going in today. He'd chosen a patterned shirt and a pair of flared denim jeans to wear, both of which he'd bought from a local charity shop, just for today. The jeans were perfect – not too tight, and easy to remove.

Gary picked up the phone and speed-dialled his work. Time to ring in, he thought. He'd recited his excuse – his lie –

several times over within his mind, he tried to use this as a thought diversion, after all anything was better than thinking about the boy again, or worrying about getting caught, no matter how difficult he found it. If only he'd not used his remaining day's holiday for that wasted dental appointment a few weeks back then he wouldn't have needed to lie. Mind you, if all went well today... who'd care... he certainly wouldn't.

Gary poured himself a cup of coffee, and stared down at three photographs of a young boy, neatly lined up on his kitchen table. One showed the boy, no older than twelve... perhaps thirteen, sporting his new Arsenal kit, and playing football in the park with friends. The second picture, a school drama production. This time the boy was dressed in running whites, he was playing the role of the young Russian in *The Railway Children* and could be seen supported by the Waterbury children following his dramatic accident. The last picture was the boy's school photograph, with him smiling as he proudly showed his new 'prefect' badge to the camera.

He picked up this third photograph and ran his finger gently down the boy's face, as though stroking his flushed cheek. He replaced the picture and picked up a small brown square envelope, similar to the type in which his father used to get his wages from the foundry. Squeezing the sides with his right hand Gary allowed the contents to fall into his left palm – a red and gold school 'prefect' badge. He placed the badge on the school photograph, left the kitchen and entered his sparsely furnished lounge.

Gary grabbed the remote control from its home on the coffee table and turned on the TV in time for the morning's news. He folded away the bed so that it once again became his tattered and frayed sofa, then replaced the cushions which he'd regimentally stacked on the floor last night.

The headline news item was a story about the disappearance of yet another foreign aid worker in the war-torn Middle East – this time Canadian. Gary, neatly folding away his bedding, didn't catch the aid worker's name, but then he didn't care. If they're stupid enough to go out there in the first place, then what do they expect, was his way of looking at it.

It was the second news story, one from closer to home, that caused Gary to stop straightening the cushions. He didn't turn to face the screen, he didn't want to.

- Police and local volunteer search groups will continue their search in and around both Eltham and Woolwich Commons at first light for missing schoolboy Alex Norman. Twelve year old Alex was reported missing by his parents after he failed to return home from Bexleyheath Academy yesterday afternoon. CCTV footage clearly shows Alex, along with school friends, boarding the number 89 bus which usually takes him home from school. Footage then shows Alex leaving the bus several stops earlier than normal at the Red Lion Lane stop on Shooters Hill Road, which borders Eltham Common. Police are eager to trace these four passengers who also alighted the bus at the Red Lion Lane stop, or anyone who was in the area from 3.30pm yesterday afternoon.

- Do the police have any clues or leads as to why Alex left the bus at that point – perhaps from friends?

- No, not at this moment. They've traced the other pupils who were travelling the same route as Alex, but as yet there's been no information given to the media.

Gary had heard enough, wiping tears from his face he turned off the television, finished his coffee, picked up his coat, grabbed some paperwork from the windowsill and stuffed it into his jeans then headed out for some much needed fresh air and a cigarette.

He left his scutty bedsit, his apartment as he'd often refer to it, pulled up his collar and lit up. His tenancy agreement said 'no smoking' which was why there was always a pile of fag ends on the kerbside. Not all his, he'd often protest to his landlord as he tried to explain that there were other tenants who smoked.

The white flat-roofed converted buildings of the 'apartments' looked out of place with all the semi-detached houses on Hervey Road. Gary often imagined how the buildings would have looked when they were built… with nothing else around. Now the only patch of greenery was the sports field across the road with its once-loved tennis courts and precision-marked white lines. Even the car park was locked up both night and day. Still, at least the local druggies had moved on in recent years, bringing some much-needed peace and quiet to the area.

He walked past his 'home' – the house that should have been his. It was different now. New drive. Blue panelled front door. New car – well it looked new – on the driveway. If only – perhaps one day he'd be able to buy it back – but then would he want to?

Within a few minutes he found himself walking along Shooters Hill Road. Media vans, satellite dishes at the ready, zipped by – BBC – SKY News – ITV – all of them poised to beam despair onto the screens of the news-hungry millions. Each van brought the memories of last night flooding back – the boy – the screams – and the trees. Gary shook the thoughts out of his mind.

It was far too early. For Christ's sake he should still have been in bed. He wandered into the top end of Greenwich Park and sat on a bench overlooking the park's deer.

The scene looked stunning. The early morning mist was rising from the deer enclosure; cervidae enveloped with an eerie dawn-lit afterglow. They didn't care that Gary was there, they'd become used to the human sideshow long ago.

Gary's thoughts turned back to what he was carrying – the evidence. Would they find it? If they did – then what? All that careful planning – for nothing.

As time drifted by, the park came to life. Joggers with a personal best to beat, some who puffed and panted their way along and others who took to the pathways with ease grunted a 'morning' or 'hello' as they passed one another.

Dog walkers, idly flicking tennis balls for Fido to chase, carried little black bags at arm's length hoping that a bin stood waiting around the next bend.

And next – the school kids. Some passing around a cigarette – others passing around a football… all of them passing through the park on their way to a comprehensive paradise.

Gary got up and followed one group of schoolboys along the path and out through the opening in the wall and onto Maze Hill.

"Excuse me," he called out to one of them – a skinny kid wearing a blazer and grey-knee length shorts, carrying a battered brown school satchel over his shoulder. "Have you got a light?"

"Have you got a spare?" asked the boy, delving into his satchel and handing Gary his green clipper.

Gary lit his cigarette and inhaled the smoke deep inside. At the point where he received the satisfying kick that the nicotine fix gave him, he slowly released the smoke. "Yeah... sure."

"Thanks," said the boy, taking both cigarette and lighter from Gary.

The boy – Ethan, as one of his pals had called out – caught the others up, and then as expected, gave them a drag of his fag.

Gary couldn't help but look at him, compare him to the photograph of the schoolboy on his table. Virtually identical. Same tie, same blazer, same stag's head breast insignia... but no prefect's badge.

He followed the boys alongside the park wall as they walked to school. He quite liked the look of Ethan – reminded him of what it was like to be young... to be carefree. But then it reminded him of last night... young Alex Norman... the screams... the dark. Gary shuddered.

He watched as the boys crossed the road and entered the school grounds through the ornate arched gateway. Once Ethan was out of sight Gary picked up his pace and continued the walk down Maze Hill. At the next opportunity he entered the park and headed in the direction of Greenwich. He needed to hurry now, time was of the essence – he'd spent far too much time dawdling about watching the milky young legs going into school.

With a much hastened pace Gary finally left the park and headed down Feathers Place. With a minute to spare, he reached his destination. Number Five Flamsteed Way. The Time Store.

CHAPTER 32

Paperclip

Gary stood at the foot of the steps leading up to The Time Store, took a deep breath, and then...

"Morning." He heard a breathless voice behind him.

Gary turned. There was a red-faced woman leaning against the railings, stretching out her calves. She looked in her early thirties, with an attractive smile and longish brown hair tied back in a ponytail. She'd been running, jogging, probably around the park, he guessed.

"Good morning. Nice way to start the day," he answered.

"Yes. I'll be alright in a second," she wheezed, looking at her watch. "Damn. Still not beaten his time."

"His time?" asked Gary, now at the top step.

"Yes. My brother's. One day though... One day." The woman climbed the steps and took out a key from her pocket. "Here, let me get that. It's probably still locked."

"Thank you," replied Gary.

She unlocked the door and led him through into The Time Store. "You must be..."

"Gary Lockett." He reached into his pocket and took out the invitation card which had arrived in last Monday's post. "I'm here to see Jason Bradbeer."

291

"Ah, yes. Cars, if I remember rightly." She took the card, and turned on some lights. "I'm Sarah Bradbeer... Jason's sister. He shouldn't be too long. Can I get you anything? Tea? Coffee?"

"No... No, I'm fine," replied Gary, looking at the gold line inlaid into the floor. "Is that the meridian?"

"Yes. It runs slap bang through the middle of the house."

Gary followed the line until it vanished under a wall. "Pretty cool."

The front door opened.

"Ah. Morning, Jase. Just in time." Sarah turned towards Gary, "I'll leave you with my brother, if you don't mind. Enjoy your day, Mr Lockett."

"Thanks," replied Gary, as he watched her disappear through an arch at the rear of the store.

"Morning. Sorry, I'm running a bit late," apologised Jason. "Greenwich seems to be a media circus this morning... Film crews and cameras everywhere."

"Yes, it's a shame isn't it?" Gary's thoughts were drawn back to last night; he felt a chill run through him.

"Not really," replied Jason. "I think it's excellent for the borough. Idris Elba was here earlier in the week."

"Sorry?" Gary was lost.

"Idris Elba. You know... *Luther*. They've been filming a movie over at the college. Turned everything French for the week. I think it's called *Bastille*."

"Ah," replied Gary, the penny having dropped. "I'm with you. Yes, that is good for the area."

"Very. Shall we?"

Gary followed Jason to the rear of the store, through the same archway Sarah had passed through. There was an ornate spiral staircase with clocks, dials and numerals twisting their way upwards within the wrought iron. The hand rail was a smooth, light oak which matched the polished floor. Gary was impressed – the staircase alone was worth a bob or two.

Jason led him through the upstairs sales room. Gary stared with amazement, as he realised that The Time Store held a huge number of very expensive watches and clocks.

"This is the Watch Room, where our customers can make their decision in relaxed surroundings," commented Jason, allowing Gary to take a few minutes perusing some of the displays.

"Bloody hell, I used to have one of those," said Gary, pointing at a *Star Wars* watch.

"Yes. But was it a 1977 Texas Instruments watch?" laughed Jason.

"Not sure," acknowledged Gary. "Possibly."

"Oh – let me introduce you to Dan, my brother," Jason said, as he saw him approaching from the other side of the large room.

"Pleased to meet you, Gary," said Dan as he shook his hand. "I hope your experience at The Time Store is all you want it to be."

"Thank you," replied Gary. "I hope so too."

"Has Jason shown you the Globe Room?" asked Dan.

"I'm taking him there now," interrupted Jason, before Gary had a chance to reply.

Gary stood agog, amazed at the collection before him. A museum inside a shop on the outskirts of Greenwich, who'd have thought?

"Awesome. I mean… Wow. Look at that." Gary pointed to a gnomon. "Is that real?"

"Yes," confirmed Jason. "Persian. Third century. To be truthful, it's not really displayed properly. By the time we had the window taken out and the wall removed, that's the only place it would fit."

Jason led Gary past water clocks, compasses, pendulums – some swinging, others not – and globes, some of which depicted the world of today and others which clearly had continents missing.

"Isn't that the clock from the observatory?" asked Gary, looking at a large, round, twenty-four hour clock.

"Similar. This was Shepherd's first attempt."

Jason stopped outside a large door, pressed his thumb against a keypad and showed Gary through. They descended two flights of stairs and entered a room.

"Please, take a seat. We need to wait for Sarah. Coffee?"

"Er… Yes… Yes please." Gary had started to feel a little claustrophobic. The room he was in had no windows, no daylight. He'd felt claustrophobic last night – in the park, but he wasn't in the park now, obviously. He'd been up one flight and down two – the cellar, he guessed.

"Milk? Sugar?"

"Yes, please. Milk and one," he replied, shaking himself out of his daydream.

"Bet you're wondering what's going on? What I've invited you here for?"

"Erm... A classic car show? I've looked on the internet... but there's none local." Gary tried to sound keen, but it wasn't happening.

"What about the Motor Show?" smiled Jason, handing Gary his coffee.

"Is that on this year?"

"It is now," laughed Jason.

Gary thought that Jason was making an attempt at being cryptic, that he was trying to excite him. But it wasn't working – he really didn't feel in the mood. His mind was on children – well, one child in particular – not cars. He was focused on his plan, and up to now, all was going well. He didn't want any distractions. He made himself go along with Jason's enthusiasm.

"Awesome..." said Gary, now displaying more animation. "Did you manage to find any footage of the seventy-four show?"

"We can do better than that."

"Better...? Unless you have a Panther De Ville out back, ready to fire up... I'd love to see what's better." Gary kept up his spirited response.

"Are you two ready to go?" asked Sarah, as she entered the room. She'd changed. Gone was the sweaty, out of breath, flush-faced jogger – she'd been replaced by a smart, sexy, well-presented woman, hair down and wearing an amazing low-cut top. Gary tried not to look – or at least tried not make it too obvious.

"Yes... I did the bracelet yesterday. Just need to get

changed and we can be off."

Gary finished his coffee, put his mug down and followed Jason out of the room.

"This is our Costume Room," said Jason, opening up another door. "If we're going to experience the seventies, we have to dress for the part."

"Dress…? As in a re-enactment?" asked Gary, staring in wonder at the rails upon rails of garments. He had a vague idea of what a costume room would look like, but he'd never expected this.

"Sort of. You'll see," replied Jason, handing Gary a pair of battered black baseball boots, Deep Purple t-shirt and a khaki green parka to wear. Thankfully, Jason was happy with the flared jeans that Gary already had on.

Jason ushered Gary into the changing room and then selected his own clothes to wear.

"You guys ready?" asked Sarah, knocking on the door and entering.

"Yeah, sis. Come on in, we're decent," replied Jason, putting on what looked like a Christmas jumper. "You in a hurry to be somewhere?"

"Auxerre… French lessons."

"Ah… très bien. Do you speak any French, Gary?"

"Please and thank you… that's about it. Oh... and voulez-vous."

"Ah-ha," laughed Jason.

Sarah groaned at Jason's feeble attempt at an Abba impersonation. "Argent, clés et un clip pour le papier."

"Last thing," said Jason, holding out a large brown jiffy bag. "Do you have anything in your pockets? Money, keys, penknife, bottle tops... paperclips, anything like that?"

Gary emptied the pockets of his jeans and handed over his mobile phone, some coins, and the keys to his flat. As he dropped his money into the jiffy bag he could see Jason giving his sister a confused look, as though something was wrong. Gary, holding his keys by the loop of a paperclip, dangled them over the bag. "Anything wrong?"

"No. Nothing at all," replied Jason, allowing the keys to drop.

"See... told you," muttered a gleeful Sarah.

A few minutes later, Gary found himself in an underground passageway with Jason. The never-faltering meridian line, inlaid into the floor, ran down the centre towards the South Pole. Every so often as they walked, they'd trip a hidden motion sensor and another section of the passageway would light up before them – behind them a section would return to darkness.

"You don't seem to be as thrilled as I thought you'd be," commented Jason, breaking the silence.

"I'm sorry. I had a long night."

"Work?"

"Yes. Well, you could call it that," replied Gary, his thoughts drawn back to the events of last night – back to the park.

"Well, once you've seen what I've got planned I'm sure you'll get excited... I know I will," said Jason, as he picked up the pace a little.

Gary had mixed feelings... he knew he should be looking forward to this... *would* be in different circumstances. The Motor Show had been a fascination of his since his childhood, since he'd clapped eyes on the Lotus Esprit for the very first time. But... he had his plan, and the prospect of getting found out was at the forefront of his mind, constantly nagging at him. What would happen if he was busted, caught? It was this doubt which dowsed his anticipation.

Gary smiled. "I'm sure I will soon, as well. I mean – let's face it – it's hard to get excited when all I can see is a bloody tunnel!"

Jason laughed. They both did.

"So... What's your favourite Bond car then?" asked Gary, deciding to lighten the conversation.

"Easy, the DB5 in Skyfall," replied Jason, as they now entered the Round Room.

CHAPTER 33

Earls Court Motor Show, London
Thursday, October 17th ~ 1974

"But how does it work?" asked Gary, who still hadn't calmed down from the excitement of being back in 1974.

"Shall I let you into a little secret?" said Jason, turning back his ring and trying to relax him. "I don't really know."

"What do you mean… you don't know? You must know… you control it, don't you?"

"Control it! I wish I did," laughed Jason. "Come on, let's go and see some cars shall we?"

They'd arrived in a small office to the rear of Earls Court. Thankfully, other than a couple of grey filing cabinets, a wilting yucca plant, and a desk with a telephone, Rolodex and typewriter, the room was empty. Announcements, muffled by the movement of the crowds outside, could be heard faintly over the Tannoy. Jason and Gary slipped out of the office and straight onto stand 99. The Moskvich 1500.

Jason had never heard of a Moskvich, let alone seen one before. As far as he was concerned, Russia didn't make cars – or at least that's what he thought.

"One came up on eBay a while back," said Gary, beaming

with pleasure.

"eBay? You can buy these things on eBay?"

"Yeah. Went for ten times that price though."

With a price tag of £785, the navy blue Moskvich 1500 resembled a shoe box on wheels. Jason couldn't help but feel drawn to the deluxe saloon which was apparently well-equipped for its time, boasting laminated windscreen, radio, seatbelts and halogen auxiliary lights.

Of course, Jason had time travelled to the seventies before, mainly for music – Zeppelin, ELO, Genesis, Hendrix's jam session at Ronnie Scott's – but he'd never paid much attention to the vehicles. Taxis were black, buses were red – that's all he really needed to know.

The huge arena was lined with row upon row of eye-catching, bunting-draped stands, all eager to attract. Swarms of people, guided by massive 'here we are' signage, gathered around the various displays which proudly peacocked the world of motoring. From Alfa to Wolseley, Buick to Simca, all the famous marques, and others not so, were there.

Manufacturers proudly displayed their range of highly-polished cars. Paintwork with countless shades of reds, greens, blues, greys, tans, taupes, whites, off-whites, charcoals, blacks, gold and silver attracted the crowds; and if the double overhead cam, twin carb'd, four-star gobbling monsters failed to grab the attention of Joe Public... then the hot-pants and long legs certainly did.

Although he could drive, Jason didn't own a car. Living in London, and more often than not travelling by jewellery, he had little need for one – however, some of these 'classics' were beginning to pull at him.

"How about one of those?" laughed Gary, pointing at an Austin Allegro. "I could just see you in one of those."

"Would you care for a brochure, sir?" asked one of the grey-suited traders as he handed Jason a small glossy booklet. "This is the new Allegro Sport... a lively little beauty, don't you think?"

"Erm... Thank you," replied Jason, accepting the booklet. "Yes, I suppose it is."

"Have a sit inside," suggested Gary, opening the driver's door. "You don't mind do you?"

"No, not at all," replied the trader.

"Only my friend here is after a nippy little run-around, and I think this would suit him down to the ground."

"Well, sir. The Sport does benefit from the Maxi's 1750 engine so I'm sure..."

"What makes it a Sport model?" interrupted Jason, running the rather large steering wheel through his hands. "Acceleration? Top speed?"

"Mainly the styling, sir."

"Styling?" Jason couldn't help but think that the only thing he knew with less style than this Allegro was his old mate Neil Jones.

"Yes, sir. It can be distinguished from other models within the Allegro range by its special badges, matt wiper arms and perfectly round leather-bound steering wheel."

"Perfectly round?" questioned Jason.

"Yes, sir. Not the quartic design as you'll notice on the

other models."

"I see," said Jason, quickly removing his hands from the *special* steering wheel. "And the music?"

"Music?"

"Yes, you know," said Gary, who was now sitting in the passenger seat. "Radio, 8-track, CD player, MP3, those types of things."

Jason coughed and shook his head.

"Not as standard, sir. But I'm sure your local dealership could perhaps install a top of the range push button radio should you desire."

For the next two hours they wandered from stand to stand, absorbing the atmosphere and enjoying the best in both automotive heritage and mini-skirts. The Lotus Esprit, Jensen Interceptor and Triumph Dolomite Sprint were all on Gary's must-see list.

At first, he didn't mind having Jason as his shadow; it felt kind of nice having someone with whom he could enjoy the motor show experience. But, as time passed by, it started to become uncomfortable and restrictive. Gary couldn't buy a souvenir programme without Jason looking over his shoulder. He couldn't get a drink, or a bowl of chips without Jason standing by his side. Worse still, when Jason needed the toilet he insisted that Gary waited just behind him while he peed.

Gary accepted that there had to be rules, and that Jason was his chaperone, but the toilet – that was going a bit too far, he argued.

"Not at all," insisted Jason, thinking about the time John

had given Dan the slip out of a pub toilet window. "We have to be careful on how we interact with people in the past – what we tell them – what we bring back in time with us. What we take into the future with us."

"Have you ever had it go wrong? I mean, has anyone tried to change things?"

"A few…"

"And?" Gary interrupted.

"We do a clean-up."

"A clean-up! Well, we don't want that." Gary sensed that Jason was becoming defensive and decided to change the subject. "Lamborghini?"

When they arrived at the Italian supercar stand there was a large group of schoolboys milling around, enjoying a motor show field trip. "Kids," commented Jason, not being able to get up close to the V12 wedge-shaped Countach. "They're everywhere… Anyone would think that they were following us."

"Probably are," laughed Gary, hesitantly. He'd been eyeing up one of the shorts-clad boys since the Aston Martin stand, and smiled inwardly at how innocent the child looked.

"Mmm," said Jason, who didn't appreciate the racket which twenty-plus schoolboys could make. "Actually, I don't really fancy this queue. Do you?"

"No, not really. Shall we come back in a bit?" suggested Gary, turning his head for another look at the youngster. "Let's head over to the Vauxhall display and catch a look at the Magnum."

Jason agreed.

They meandered around the Vauxhalls, which, other than the Firenza, all looked pretty much the same – box-shaped. Jason, attracted by the bright yellow paint finish and chrome wing mirrors, was quite taken by the Viva. Gary, having once owned a clapped out Astra, wasn't that keen on Vauxhalls, but even he was impressed by the Magnum's luxury cloth-faced seats, large electric clock and mean looking rev-counter.

"Where next?" asked Jason.

"Over there," replied Gary, pointing towards what looked like a thirties-styled Chicago superhero's car. "The Panther De Ville."

The Jankel designed De Ville with its Jaguar borrowed engine, Bugatti-styled flowing wing lines and big headlights, was created to appeal to the taste of the nouveau riche customer. For the seventies, the cockpit of the De Ville was quite modern and complemented the car's pre-war styled exterior. Jason was gobsmacked – he loved it.

The queue for the pre-production car was massive – far longer than the Countach's, but neither Jason nor Gary cared; they wanted to sit behind the wheel to sense the power and touch the beauty.

Within five minutes, the group of schoolchildren they'd seen earlier joined the waiting line. Some were pushing and shoving others so they could have prime place in their group, to be the first to smile for the teacher's camera as they sat in the car.

The fair-haired youngster standing in the middle of the group grabbed Gary's attention once again, an attention which made the palms of his hands sweat.

Over by the wall, no more than twenty feet away, were the

304

toilets. Gary wondered what would happen if one of the boys wandered off for five minutes – would the teacher follow – stand by the door as if on sentry duty? Then Gary wondered how he'd escape from Jason – could he detach himself from his personal guard?

Then it happened. Gary watched as the young boy approached one of the group's adults – they talked, only briefly – then the boy, with a purposeful stride walked over to the toilet. If Gary was going to do it – it had to be now – there was not going to be another chance.

He tapped Jason on the shoulder. "I need the toilet."

"Toilet? Now?" answered Jason, disbelievingly. "But we're only a few minutes from the front."

"I know – I'm sorry – must be the excitement." Gary tried to sound apologetic. "Look… the toilets, they're only there. You can see the door from here. I'm buttock clenching… I won't be long."

Jason looked over to where Gary was pointing – he was right – they were only a few feet away. "Okay. But please, don't be long."

Gary strode off.

As Gary entered the toilets, he held the door open for two men who were exiting. Then, closing the door behind him, he latched it – no one could follow – not without kicking down the door. There was a vacant stainless steel urinal trough, three sinks and three cubicles – only the furthest of which was in use – it had to be the boy.

The outer door rattled – someone tried to enter – Gary felt

disturbed, his heart pounded faster, he could hear voices – but then they faded, disappeared back into the crowd again.

Gary 'hid' in one of the empty cubicles – waited for the boy to finish – he needed to make his move – needed to be quick – the toilet flushed – the door un-bolted.

Grabbing the boy from behind Gary placed his hand over the youngster's mouth – muted the screams. Gary pushed him to the wall – fear covered the child's face.

"Don't scream." Gary demanded, trying to sound authoritative but not threatening. "I have something for you."

Gary unbuckled his belt and lowered his jeans.

CHAPTER 34

Special Helper

"I was about to come looking for you," said Jason, as he walked towards the toilet and the exiting Gary. "You missed... Shit! What happened?"

Gary's shirt, along with his hands, was covered in deep red spots of blood. "Damn nose bleed," he replied, pointing to the pieces of tissue stuffed up each of his nostrils. "Clouted it on the edge of the toilet door."

"Ouch," laughed Jason. "Do you want to go back in there and clean up a bit?"

"No... No... I'll be alright." The gents toilet was the last place Gary wanted Jason anywhere near. "How about we check out the Triumph stand?"

The Triumph stand, as Gary well knew, was at the far side of Earls Court Arena; he wanted to put as much space as possible between the toilets and himself – just in case.

Jason recounted his Panther De Ville experience, over-embellishing its grandeur with as much gusto as possible. Gary just nodded and grunted, his thoughts were well and truly elsewhere – the toilets.

What would the kid do? Would he tell? He'd have to – how

else could he explain the blood? He could hardly keep something as dramatic as this to himself. Then they'd come looking for him – him and Jason. And then it would be over – caught red-handed. But then what would they do with him – the police – the Bradbeers? Would he go to jail? Imprisoned – but when – the 1970s – could they do that?

"You sure you're alright?"

"Yeah, sorry," replied Gary, snapping out of his prison-related thoughts. "A little concussed, I think."

"Do you want to sit down for a while? Water?" offered Jason, clearly concerned.

"No… I'll be fine," answered Gary. "Do you mind if we give the Triumphs a miss and head off home?"

"No, not at all." Jason scanned their immediate surroundings, looking for a discreet place they could travel from.

"Thanks," replied Gary, feeling a weight lift from him.

"Over there… let's try those." Jason pointed to a doorway with a sign above. STAIRS. "We only need to be out of sight for a few seconds."

Even before Jason had unlinked arms, Gary felt a sense of relief – relief that it was over – in the past. He felt different now that he was back in his own time. His mind was filled with fresh memories – memories of success – memories of change. His heart felt happy.

Gary and Jason discussed their motor show highlights as they walked back along the limestone passage towards the rest room. The Moskvich 1500, Vauxhall's Viva and Magnum, and the Panther, of course. Jason laughed as Gary joked about how quick he'd seen Jason take his hands off the Allegro's luxury leather-bound circular steering wheel.

"Coffee?" asked Jason, as he closed the Costume Room door behind them.

"No, thanks," replied Gary, stuffing his keys and money into the pockets of his jeans. "It must be getting on a bit."

"Not really – it's not even ten-thirty yet." Jason briefly explained to Gary that, in true time, their trip had only taken fifteen minutes or so.

"In that case… Yeah, why not."

Jason opened the door to the rest room and was surprised to see Sarah and Alice in there. Unusually, Sarah was sitting on the table with her feet on a chair. Alice was standing in front of her applying some cream to the scars on Sarah's left forearm; the rest room radio was on low volume – just loud enough to be heard without drowning out any conversation. "Hope we're not interrupting anything."

"No," replied Sarah, throwing a small white tube to her brother. "Don't be silly, Alice reckons this silicone ointment is good for scarring. Might as well give it a go."

"Yeah, why not…" replied Jason, quickly reading the front of the tube. "Take a seat, Gary. Coffee, Sarah? Alice?"

Jason filled the kettle and proceeded to make drinks for everyone. Sarah introduced Alice to Gary, who'd thankfully removed the toilet tissue from his nostrils before entering the rest room.

"So how was it then? Did you two petrol-heads have a good time?" asked Sarah.

"Yeah. It was amazing," replied Gary.

"Had to cut it short though. Didn't we?" commented Jason.

"Short? Why?" Sarah was concerned.

"Oh, nothing. Gary had a bit of a nose bleed."

"It's alright now though," smiled Gary, wanting to move the conversation away from his nose. "Could you turn that up a bit, please?" Gary pointed to the radio, the ten-thirty news was on.

- Twelve year old schoolboy Alex Norman was reunited with his parents this morning after it was discovered that he'd been staying overnight at a friend's house. Lack of communication between both sets of parents and an uncharged mobile phone caused the confusion which resulted in...

"Thank God for that," said Gary.

"Do you know him?" asked Alice, wiping her hands clean on some kitchen roll.

"No... But I was on call-out last night, up at the common... part of the search team."

"Call-out? What is it you do?" asked Sarah.

"Oh... I work up at Lewisham Hospital..."

"Maintenance if I remember rightly?" interrupted Jason, as he recalled their original meeting a couple of weeks ago.

"Yes. But I'm a Special as well," replied Gary, accepting his drink.

"Special what?" queried Alice.

"Constable. I'm a Special Constable with the Met."

"I guess that can be interesting at times?" commented

Jason, passing Sarah and Alice their mugs.

"It has its moments," sighed Gary. "I was with the family last night, the Normans. You can't help it – you become swept along with the emotion of it all. With the tears and what have you."

"I bet," said Jason, sitting beside Gary.

Gary revisited the previous night. He recounted how he'd had the message to report for duty, and was initially assigned duties next to the incident vehicle, and then – along with colleagues – given an area of Eltham Common to search.

Mrs Norman had been hysterical, shrouded with dread; Gary's initial role was to keep the media at arm's length – for the Normans' own protection and sanity. He was actually relieved to be moved – to be part of the search team, scrambling through the dwindling undergrowth – better that than the constant, uncontrollable and agonisingly emotional tears of the Normans. Gary was pleased to be talking about last night – it was actually quite a relief – now he knew his scheme had worked.

After a short while, Sarah, who was now taking Alice along with her, headed for the Round Room and a six month time trip to Auxerre, France. This gave Gary the opportunity to say a massive 'thank you' to Jason and to head off home.

As he descended the six stone steps leading to Flamsteed Way's footpath Gary could feel an excitement coursing through his body, almost like a bolt of electricity. He felt refreshed, invigorated – for the first time in years Gary Lockett felt alive.

With a bounce in his stride he turned the corner into Feathers Place, took out his mobile, scanned his contact list and dialled.

After a few seconds of ringing his call was answered. *"Gary?"*

"It's worked," laughed Gary, loudly. "Our plan... It's bloody worked."

CHAPTER 35

Second Family Meeting
Friday, December 12th ~ 2014

Unlike last week's meeting, everyone was there… and everyone was on time. As the Patrick Kelly incident was on the agenda, John had, once again, been invited.

"Right, shall we start?" said David, taking his place at the top of the rest room table. "Daniel… Put that bloody phone away, will you. You know the rules."

"Dad." Dan slipped his phone – text unsent – into his pocket.

"Seems we've had a busy week. Sales have been good… Very good in fact. Those Submariners you and Emma brought back from New York were a massive help." David paid his youngest son a compliment.

"Thanks." Dan smiled, happy with the praise.

"Yes," commented Jason, laughing. "Can you get a few more?"

"No problem… I'm sure Emma would love to go back."

"And here's me thinking you hated shopping," said Sarah, with a hint of irony.

Jason then gave a recap on all the time travel ventures of the past week, starting with Dan and Emma's trips to see the

313

Eiffel Tower during construction and opening. Next up was their trip to New York for the Rolex Submariners – with a bit of Christmas shopping thrown in.

Jason moved briefly on to Dan's Jolly Roger jaunt with Stuart Ramos, before going on to his father and John's recent trip to witness the events of Patrick Kelly's horrific death – murder. The rest room fell silent for a brief moment – a small sign of respect for John's friend. Jason then touched very briefly on his dad's 'Fox Project' trip.

"Foxes?" questioned Sarah.

"Yes," replied David, almost managing a slight grin. "It's quite fascinating – the life of an urban fox."

"And the retribution plan?" asked Dan, sensing that he wasn't the only one who didn't quite understand what his father was on about.

"Well..."

"There won't be one." John hesitantly interrupted David's response. "Paddy was a man of many words... though most of them were feck – feck – and feckin'!"

Tears welled up in his eyes. John had found it hard to re-live the death of his friend – his best friend. The last week had been difficult to say the least. Five years ago he'd carried Paddy's coffin, lowered it into the ground. He'd read a verse – about forgiveness – about passion – about life. He'd put it behind him now. John had moved on.

Oh... he'd often thought of revenge – retribution as the Bradbeers called it – making them pay. He'd never gone as far as electrodes on their testicles... and flicking the switch. He'd never gone as far as drilling their teeth out... supergluing their mouths and nostrils up… those types of things. The best he came up with, and that with some prompting from a builder he knew, was squirting expanding builders foam in their mouths and up their arses at the same time… then sitting back and watching the fun. But when it came down to it…

He continued. "Paddy Kelly was also a man of peace. He'd not say a feckin' 'thank you' to any of us if he knew we were going to hurt someone in his name… so please, no revenge. Let the police do their work."

Sarah passed John a tissue, smiled and nodded an agreement to his request. The others followed.

"We'll go back in time on Monday to present the evidence," said David. "Come Monday night, in true time that is, they'll have already been locked away for five years."

"Good work," smiled Jason, pleased that his idea of a change in The Time Store direction was paying dividends… not at all monetary… more the instant karma type. "Other than Sarah's trip to Auxerre yesterday, the only other time trip this week was mine… to the car show… with Gary Lockett… which went as expected."

"Did it?" asked David, looking over at Sarah. "What's this I'm hearing about a nose bleed?"

"Oh, it was nothing. Apparently Gary walked into a toilet door," answered Jason, making light of the incident.

"Apparently?" questioned David.

"It was nothing, Dad. Really," replied Jason, feeling as though he was being interrogated.

"How's eBay going?" laughed Dan, interrupting.

Since his return yesterday morning Jason had been

scouring eBay for an old Vauxhall Viva to 'do up', and he'd been talking about his and Gary Lockett's motor show experience at every opportunity. Although, it had to be said, what Jason knew about cars left everyone pondering on his actual intentions for a 1970s rust bucket – unless he was planning on going back in time and completing a five year motor mechanics course. Even then, Sarah had commented that five years may not be enough, judging by the condition of some of the cars he was looking at.

"So what do we have for this week?" asked David.

"I'm taking one of Dan's clients up to Scotland on Tuesday," said Sarah.

"Wasn't that supposed to have been last Tuesday?" questioned David.

"Sorry, that was my fault." Dan's face reddened. "Crossed wires on the dates."

"Mm." It was clear to see by the look on his face, that David wasn't impressed. "So, Sarah. This trip to Scotland, hunting monsters?"

"Yes," she replied. "The surgeon's granddaughter wants some answers."

"Surgeon?" asked John.

"Robert Wilson allegedly took this Nessie pic back in 1934." Sarah slid a copy of the surgeon's famous photograph across the table.

"Okay. Yes, I know that one," said John, immediately recognising the picture.

"His friend…" Sarah fumbled through Dan's notes and found what she was after. "Christian Spurling confessed on his deathbed in 1993 that the photograph was a fake."

"Fake?" asked Jason.

"So it seems," replied Sarah. "According to Spurling, Nessie was little more than a Woolies' toy submarine and some creative modelling."

"And the surgeon's granddaughter?" asked David.

"She just wants to know if what Spurling said was true."

"Okay… No cameras though," said David, granting his approval for the trip. "Anything else?"

"Just the Dorrington cottage thing which I told you about. I'm out all day Wednesday looking into that."

Jason went next. He spent the first five minutes trying to convince his father that the Vauxhall Viva 'barn find' he was going to see in Derbyshire on Thursday wasn't anything he'd put there in the first place. After he batted off a few moans and groans, he changed the subject to Christmas.

"I know it's a bit late in the day… and that some of you might already have made plans… But I'm suggesting that we shut up shop for the year at close of business on the 20th… reopening in the New Year, on the second, which is a Friday. Christmas dinner will be courtesy of Dan this year." Jason didn't wait to see if this prompted any objections from his brother. "It's his turn… Nan and Granddad Lane have already confirmed… John, you and Alice are invited. No doubt Emma will already be here… Anyone else you can think of?"

John declined, he'd already volunteered to help out his friend, Winnie Holroyd, at St. Michael's Hostel. He felt it was his duty every now and then to repay a little of the kindness which he'd been shown. David commended him, and then offered the services of the entire Bradbeer family to the hostel for Boxing Day. No one objected.

"Daniel? What about you? What are you up to this week?" asked David.

"Nothing really. Might go back to Queenscliff... check on the treasure... other than that I'm at the behest of you guys."

"Right then, if that's everything," said Jason, pushing his chair back. "Can I suggest...?"

"Not quite," interrupted David, beckoning his son to sit back down.

"Dad?"

"Not one of you has mentioned Oliver Bradbeer." He looked across at his children. "A week has gone by and you're all trying to tell me that there's no news. Nothing."

Jason looked down at the table, he knew he'd been avoiding discussing anything to do with Oliver – perhaps intentionally. Dan just looked at his father – speechless. Sarah shifted her gaze from father to brothers, then back to father.

David stood up and leaned towards his sons. "Worse still, I'm hearing more about trips for Vauxhall Vivas and pirate treasure than I am about the idiot who attacked your sister."

"But..."

"No buts, Jason. I want you to find Oliver Bradbeer and stop him – stop him before he causes us any more bloody problems." David turned to his daughter. "And Sarah, I need you to do something for me."

CHAPTER 36

The Death of Patrick Kelly
October ~ 2009

He was an old man now, old before his time. Pissed up and useless. All the feckin' roads had been built, all the drives paved. No more work for him. The once-strong Irishman who'd come over to England to seek his fortune had spent his fortune on beer and good times. He'd never bought a house, never settled, and never had a woman longer than a few months. Stayed in lodgings and digs and kipped on people's sofas, slept in the on-site work huts. That was until alcohol tempered his strength, his reliability, his employability.

Now he dossed down in a hostel. He didn't receive a wage, but he still managed to afford cheap whisky. He still worked the roads, the streets. No longer laying tarmac or block-paving, just sitting on it, with a cardboard sign, feeling sorry for himself, and begging for coins. On a good day he still had a sense of humour, time for jokes with the hostel staff and his mate John. Johnny he called him 'cause he knew it riled him a bit.

Paddy Kelly already had a few quid in his pocket. It was October, and although the sun was shining, there was a bit of a chill in the air, so he was well wrapped up in several layers of ill-fitting clothes, tatty gloves and a frayed flat cap. He stood

319

outside St. Michael's Hostel in Camden waiting for John. They were going down the tube station to try and tap a few people for their loose change. Paddy had his blanket and a sign.

KISS THE BLARNEY STONE
ONLY £1

It sometimes worked. Especially if he remembered to take a stone with him.

Where was feckin' Johnny now? Give me a minute or two he'd said. Feck's sake… he'd been waiting fifteen minutes already. Maybe twenty. Valuable earning time, and it was cold standing around. Impatient, Paddy went back into the hostel.

"Ey, Ben," he said. "You seen Johnny?"

Ben was the young lad helping out on the front reception desk as part of his Duke of Edinburgh silver award. He looked up. "Yes, but it was a while ago now."

Paddy tutted in exasperation. "Well, tell him I haven't got all feckin' day. I'm off to the station. I'll see him later at The World's End. If he can be arsed."

"Okay," said Ben.

Paddy left the hostel for the second time that morning and trudged down the road towards Camden Town tube station, looking every bit like the down and out tramp that he was. He found a suitable place to sit and scrounge the day away, it was a spot he favoured – right next to the tube station.

He liked to lean against the join between the pale sandstone of the bank on the corner and the shiny red brick of the station. That way, if anyone from the bank tried to move him on, he could shift along a bit to lean on the red station wall, and if he spotted anyone who worked on the tube, he could shunt himself along the other way and lean on the bank. He could see the side entrance to the pub from here, maybe he would spot Johnny. He draped his blanket over his scrawny hunched up legs, set his sign at the side of him and his begging cap in front of him. He threw his few coins in the cap and waited.

Today was a good day. A bit of sunshine and people developed a sense of humour. They were happy to give 20p, or 50p or even a pound coin to a poor old beggar with a jokey sign. If this was America, Chicago for instance, he'd make a fortune. He'd read somewhere that half the people begging were not homeless or destitute – they had funny signs, they interacted with the tourists, they only came out on sunny days, and then they went back to their studio apartments, cooked themselves a nice dinner and caught a movie on cable TV.

But still, it was alright in Camden today. He'd already had some money before he'd started, a miracle in itself, and now he had a right good wedge. Enough for a Maccies and a few beers, plus a couple of whiskies to round off the night. No sign of Johnny all day, the tosser. And now civil dusk was taking over. Civil dusk, nautical dusk, astronomical dusk, pub. Years ago some clever dick on the tarmac wagon had told him that – thought he was a twat at the time, but he remembered it anyway.

He packed up his blanket into a roll, picked up the successful sign and sauntered to the nearest McDonald's, on Camden High Street. They always served him there, knew he was harmless. He didn't eat in though. He timed his pace back towards the pub with finishing his burger, and deposited the wrapper and bag in the nearest bin.

The World's End pub was not far from the tube station, on the corner of Greenland Road and the main road. It was a weird junction set-up actually – whoever designed the layout here must have been pissed. He wasn't actually sure what the main road was called. Was it still the High Street, or had it merged into something else? He only knew Greenland Road because his school back home in Ireland was on a road of the same name.

He liked this pub. The World's End. He liked the name. He always thought as he entered that it set him in mind of a strange indoor street from Victorian times, with little shop windows at the side of the road. It was not really much like that of course, it was just his imagination. His mind making up stories. He used to get in trouble as a kid, concocting far-fetched tales to explain why he was late back from school covered in mud with his trousers torn up and his new shoes scuffed.

On the roads, in the early days, his stories of back home would be well-received, causing much laughter and gentle piss-taking. But his mates would tell their mates until word got twisted and took on a different tone. Then he was, for a while, branded a liar. Once, someone new onto the site repeated one of his made-up tales back to him. It was so different, he only recognised it as one of his own because of the reference to the one thing that was true. He'd had a brief fling (and lodgings for a week) with the woman who lived in the house of the drive he was tarmacing. And she'd made him pancakes in her pink kitchen.

Paddy ordered a pint of one of the guest ales… one he'd not had before. No Guinness for him – he didn't really like it much. He scoured around the pub for John, but couldn't see him, in the usual place or anywhere else, so he sat down, plonked his blanket and sign next to him, and began to read a Daily Express newspaper which had been left on the table.

There was an article about the International Olympic Committee. They'd just awarded the 2016 Summer Olympics to Rio de Janeiro. So far ahead with all that planning. For Paddy, whose days were all pretty much the same, this seemed ridiculous. Mind you, he did like the Olympics, and he was definitely looking forward to 2012 when it was going to be in London. And more exciting news in today's paper… paleontologists had recently announced the discovery of what they said was an ardipithecus ramidus fossil skeleton. The oldest remains of a human ancestor ever found. Fascinating, Paddy thought, but boring at the same time.

He stood up to get another drink, but as he approached the now crowded bar he inadvertently brushed the arm of someone carrying two drinks.

"Sorry mate," he said, although it wasn't really his fault, and only a few drops of beer had splashed from one of the pint glasses.

"Watch yer fuckin' step." The man glared at him. "Fucking hobo."

Paddy was used to insults, but seriously, that man needed to chill out a bit, else that throbbing vein on his head could very well burst.

After a bit more jostling Paddy reached the bar, and bought

his second pint. The barman, who despite the rush had noticed the altercation between Paddy and the man, spoke briefly to him.

"He had a go at me an' all – dunno who he is – never seen him before – don't think he's from round here."

"Okay pal," said Paddy.

He hadn't got the heart for this tonight. He'd been looking forward to having a bit of banter with Johnny – it reminded him of the old days when he was a decent working man having a few pints in the pub with his mates. Just finish this pint and then off home, he thought. Home, hostel, whatever.

As he turned to go back to his seat across the other side of the pub, Paddy noticed two smartly dressed men standing just inside the entrance door. Both about his own age give or take, wearing suits, one with a cravat for feck's sake, looking like they didn't belong here. They stood briefly, scanning the crowded room, probably trying to decide whether it was worth staying. One of them, the one without the cravat, had something of a similarity to Johnny. Paddy was amused – Johnny would love that, he had a smart twin. They hurriedly left the pub. Good choice, thought Paddy.

Approaching his table, Paddy noticed it was occupied by the shaven-headed temper-fuelled man he'd encountered a few minutes ago, and his drinking partner, who had a full head of hair, but looked just as menacing.

"Back for more are ya?" the first man sneered. He nudged the other one. "Look who we have here, Kev – it's that dirty tramp I was just telling you about."

"Whaddya want?" Kev said.

"Nothing. It's just..." Paddy trailed off. It was pointless even mentioning he'd been sitting there. He wouldn't have expected even the most pleasant of people to give up their seat for him. He retreated, took a few gulps of his beer and left the three-quarters full glass on a small shelf fixed to a pillar. Time to get out.

He felt the cool evening air on his face, refreshing after the claustrophobic atmosphere of the pub. He turned left, pulled his threadbare coat right around him and began to walk down Greenland Road, in the direction of the hostel.

It wasn't long before he changed his mind though. He did an about turn, crossed the road and went left down Bayham Street. Better give the park a once-over – see if Johnny's there. Gotta look out fer yer mates.

St. Martin's Gardens in Camden had originally been a burial ground for many decades in the 1800s, until the bodies were cleared to make way for refurbishment into a park, a quiet haven from busy city life, still enjoyed now by sunbathers, drinkers and the occasional fox. It looked empty as Paddy entered to check if John was there. He walked slowly around, feeling strangely at peace. No sign of Johnny. No sign of any other vagrants actually, not even sitting on one of the few remaining headstones with their worn unreadable, weather-beaten inscriptions. No, Johnny was not sipping coarse whisky and raising a toast to the dead this evening.

Paddy didn't even feel like drinking anymore tonight. "B'Jayzus I'm feckin' cured!" he announced to Cyrus Jones, died 1841 aged 39 years, the only gravestone he'd been able to read properly since he'd been frequenting this place.

He thought he heard a voice. Old Cyrus pouring scorn on his alcohol reform? Two voices. Paddy saw two dark figures walking across the grass towards him.

"Oi, hobo. I got something for you."

"O feck." It was those two angry ones from the pub.

Before Paddy had a chance to react, they rushed at him, one of them slammed a gristly fist in his stomach, thumping his breath away, sending him crashing unceremoniously to the ground.

"That's for splashing my drink."

Bit extreme for a few drops of spilt drink. What was their accent? Was it West Country? Southern? Northern? He was confused – it was one of those English accents where all the words blended into one another but didn't actually belong anywhere. As he lay crumpled on his side on the grass Paddy imagined himself staggering to the hostel and relating his story in his own inimitable way.

But… a sharp kick to his abdomen.

"That's for being a fucking tramp."

Paddy writhed on the ground, curling into a ball of agony.

"Please," he gasped. "I done nothin' to you."

All he could see was the dark shapes of four steel toe cap boots.

"Tramp. Hobo." Another kick.

Hospitalised by two idiots who didn't even know any other more interesting words for his feckin' destitute state. He laughed inwardly. Alcoholic he might be, but at least he had more grasp of the English language than these two brainless thugs. With every kick the same insults.

"Fucking tramp."

Vagrant.

"Tramp."

Beggar.

"Tramp"

Scrounger.

"Hobo."

Vagabond. Bum. Dosser. Clochard.

"Fucking hobo."

Mendicant. Paddy passed out.

He came round to the sound of harsh grating laughter, and realised that he'd only been unconscious for a couple of minutes. They were still there. He tried to get up. He couldn't move. He thought he was broken inside somehow. *Help me.* He wasn't sure if he'd said it out loud.

"Finish the bastard off."

And in the dark, through the haze of suffering, Paddy realised they had a knife. *O feck.*

A sharp pain, a new pain, in his chest... bleeding now. He tried to clutch at where the pain was, to stem the blood. It felt sticky. The grass smelled fresh. He loved the smell of newly cut grass. He was moving.

"Shove him over there, don't want 'im littering the place up."

Not moving now. Those flowers were beautiful, a little meadow of posies right here in the park. His blood would taint them. He closed his eyes.

All silent now, all alone, waiting. But not for long. All those roads he'd worked on… had they led to this? He thought he heard, or more like felt, a tread beside him. A gentle step. Come to collect him, take him to a better place. He opened his eyes briefly. And saw a vision. From the pub. Johnny Brewer's feckin' smart looking twin.

CHAPTER 37

Fox Watch

Wednesday, October 28th ~ 2009

Kevin Taylor, dressed in his customary denim jeans, faded green t-shirt and leather jacket, knocked at his girlfriend's door. She hadn't given him a key – it wasn't that kind of relationship.

He stood shivering in the late October chill.

"Angie!" He knocked again. "Hurry up, it's me."

The door opened. "You're late." Angie, pulling her cardigan around her, moved aside to let him into the small hallway.

"Need a piss." Kev ran up the stairs.

"Nice to see you too," Angie muttered. She went into the living room, switched on the TV and sat down on the tatty green sofa. *Crimewatch* was about to start.

Kev clattered into the room, still doing up the zip on his jeans. He sat next to Angie. He heard the compelling theme music and looked up to see the programme titles. "Do we have to have this crap on?"

"Oh. So you turn up late. Two hours late. Not even a peck on the cheek or an apology. And then you think you can dictate what I watch on my own TV?"

"I had stuff to do." Kev moved to kiss Angie.

She turned away. "Stuff… with Malc, no doubt. It's too late now. I've got work first thing. I'm gonna watch this and go to bed. Without you."

"But I thought…?"

"Yeh, you thought you could come round for a bit of cursory sex." Angie turned up the volume. "This is that woman found by the side of the motorway. Shh."

Kev sat through a detailed behind the scenes report on the detectives who were hunting the killer of a woman whose remains were found by the M5 motorway. He wished he'd stayed out with Malc now. Maybe he could go back to the pub. Angie was obviously not in the mood for anything.

The presenter was just rounding off with the customary 'contact us if you have any information'. Kev decided to have one last try. "I've missed you."

Angie looked at him. Her eyes softened a bit.

- And now, in an extra item tonight, we turn to the brutal murder of Patrick Kelly in Camden three weeks ago. We have obtained taped evidence from the local urban fox watch group, showing the actual killing taking place. Some viewers may find these images disturbing.

Kev and Angie looked up at the TV, like many people drawn to the promise of dramatic footage.

The voiceover ran in tandem-sync with the action. First a few foxes to set the scene.

- Patrick Kelly was a local vagrant, but he didn't deserve to die in such brutal circumstances.

Then the tramp, on the floor, being kicked by one man, watched by another. The faces weren't really clear, but it was enough for Kev. He felt his insides go rotten.

- Thanks to this footage, we have been able to recheck the local CCTV cameras, and we've come up with these images of the suspects.

Angie was glued to the screen. How could he stop her? She loved all this stuff.

"Oh God, Kev. That's you! It looks like you!"

"Don't be stupid." Kev was panicking. "How could it be me?"

"It *is* you." Angie stood up. She had a look of complete horror on her face. "It's you and fucking Malc. You were in London a few weeks ago. What have you done?"

"It wasn't me." But it was.

- Now obviously we will not be showing the stabbing which caused the death of Mr Kelly, but we can inform you that it was administered by the second man.

"Get out, get out, get out. GET OUT!" Angie backed away.

- We are now looking for these two men in connection with this crime. Anyone with any information, please contact us.

Kev's phone rang. He picked up. It was Malc.

"Don't say a thing. Don't say a fucking thing. Okay?" The phone went dead.

Kev opened his eyes. He'd been awake for a while, lying on his side on the hard bed. He focused on the wall in front of him, and touched the pale green flaking paint. He needed a piss. Badly. He sat up on the bed. His head hurt. Behind the small headboard he knew there was a toilet. He'd used it last night. He stood up off the bed and padded round the few paces. The metal toilet didn't have a lid, or a seat. He undid the zip on his jeans and relieved himself, the rancid morning liquid echoing on the cold metal.

They'd taken him in late last night. He'd run in the direction of the pub where he'd been with Malc, but decided against it. He couldn't go home. They had his name. *Crimewatch* had said so. Malc had laughed it off at the time, but he would, he was the one doing all the goading – it was all his idea.

There was a noise from the cell door. The little metal flap went up. Don't say a thing. Don't say a fucking thing.

He'd been sitting in the interview room for twenty minutes. He hadn't given anything away. "It wasn't me. You've got the wrong man."

The officers had been called away. Left him alone. He sipped his water. They had nothing on him. Who the hell films foxes anyway?

They came back. "We've got your friend," one of them

said. "Malcolm Tizzard. Said he's ready to talk."

Kev thought he was about to vomit. Don't say a thing? That bastard.

"So it was Malcolm, Malc, who did the kicking?"

"I don't know what you're talking about."

"Your mate, Malc, and yourself followed your victim, Mr Kelly, out of the pub. You planned it all. You planned to kill. It was premeditated murder. Wasn't it, Kev?"

He closed his eyes. Three faces. Malc's evil eyes and grinding teeth, saliva running down his chin. Angie, horror and terror in equal measure. And the tramp, wrinkled from life, wrinkled from pain, but finally accepting his fate. Honourably.

He opened his eyes. "I don't know. What are you talking about?"

"But it was you, Kevin. It was you who stabbed him. Wasn't it? You plunged the knife into his chest. You committed a vicious and pointless murder. It was you."

"No," he lied weakly. He didn't know what to do. He hated Malc. Hated himself for knowing him. He just wanted to go back to that time in the pub and stay there. Sit there alone with his pint while Malc went out after the tramp in search of a bit of sport.

The officer banged his fist on the table. "Your mate's as good as told us what happened."

Kev's head was spinning. He tried to stand, but sank back in his chair. "He made me do it! Malc. He made me do it!"

They led him along the corridor. Aided him, as he was having difficulty walking. There was Malc, coming in the opposite direction with two other policemen.

"What have you said?" Kev shouted, but as he did so he realised he was incriminating himself further, if that was possible. He then also realised, with a sickening lurch, that Malc was heading towards the interview room. It was Kev himself who'd been interviewed first. Oh God, what had he done?

"You twat," sneered Malc. His face was the epitome of anger, teeth bared, saliva emerging. Malc precision-aimed a ball of spit into the centre of Kev's face.

CHAPTER 38

The Envelope

After leaving The Time Store yesterday, Gary Lockett had made it home from Greenwich in record time. He'd hopped, he'd skipped, he'd run forwards and he'd even run a few paces backwards. In fact, if it hadn't been for an oncoming lamppost he'd have managed a few more steps. Buoyed on by the success of his scheme, he had a new inner feeling, a new self-confidence. Gary Lockett now had a new future… or did he? One way to find out, he thought, as he turned his key in the outer door of the Hervey Road apartment block.

In the hallway, above an old heavily painted cast iron radiator, bolted to the wall for security, were the tenants' individual mailboxes. With his heart palpitating, Gary slowly unlocked and lifted the lid to his box.

Of course, like most people these days, Gary didn't receive much in the way of mail. With utility bills, bank statements and car tax all issued online, it left plenty of space in the mail boxes for junk and circulars to accumulate.

Today however, the postman hadn't left much. The latest *Craghoppers* winter offer catalogue and a UPVC windows brochure were all Gary managed to pull from the box. His heart sank. He ran his hand around the sides of the box, perhaps there was one of those 'whilst you were out' cards, perhaps he had to go and collect something… but there wasn't.

He opened the door to his bedsit. Nothing had changed… everything was as he'd left it. But then he'd not expected anything different – after all, he'd meticulously followed all the instructions he'd been given.

On the table were the three photographs he'd looked at earlier. Young Gary – the footballer. Young Gary – the actor. Finally, the one which had been his father's favourite, the one which had made him most proud… young Gary – the school prefect. Taking his family photo album from a shelf he replaced the pictures back under the clear plastic protection covers.

Doubts were filling his mind, doubts about the plan, doubts about its success… doubts about himself. His phone rang. "Frank…"

Frank Helleken was one of Gary's best friends, if not his best. Originally from Mainz, Germany, Frank had moved over to England some twenty years ago to follow the love of his life, Rena when she'd crossed the North Sea with her work. That relationship had fallen apart some time ago when Rena was relocated back to her home town of Bremen. Gary had first met Frank a few years ago, on a beautiful summer's day at a Bruce Springsteen concert in Hyde Park, they'd been pretty much inseparable since then.

"Just got back."

Frank had been the catalyst for the plan. He'd visited The Time Store over a year ago. Time travelled, with Sarah, for a night of culture with Ludwig van Beethoven. An experience he couldn't help but share with Gary.

"The post's been… Nothing at all."

Ever since that night, Gary and Frank had shared ideas, discussed pitfalls, formulated plan after plan after plan and finally, following an invitation for Gary to visit The Time Store, put into action their get rich quick scheme. A scheme which would take some forty years to mature.

"Yes…. Yes, it definitely won. *Smart Freddy*, twelve to one."

The plan, although intricate in the delivery, was simple. A list of bets – winners of course – mainly horses, tennis and football. Starting with a pre-season pound on Manchester United to lift the 1985 FA Cup. With Norman Whiteside scoring the extra-time winner against Everton, that pound became nine, and by the end of that year it had become £100. A list of successive short odd wins followed, and by the end of the eighties it was touching £200,000.

"Yes… In the toilets… like we'd planned."

It was during his own time trip with Jason that Gary had given his younger self the list, the detailed instructions, and the initial one pound note to start the ball rolling.

"They should've been here today." Gary was sounding frustrated.

For the first couple of years, whilst the pot grew, the bets were placed by Gary, and then, over the following years, they were placed using several solicitors, numerous bookmakers and, initially, three bank accounts. The idea being the more they spread the action around the less likelihood they had of drawing any attention to their wins. It was far better to have wins of a few thousand pounds or so, than to have a one off multi-million pound lottery jackpot.

In the nineties many small, only one or two-thousand pound, losing bets were placed here and there, but these were soon followed up with a couple of nice larger staked, high-odds winners to swell the accounts. The bet on the winner at last Friday's Doncaster meeting was the final flutter on the list, today was the day that Gary should have received the final account details from the last of the solicitors.

"Bank... This afternoon... Two o'clock." Gary was pacing around.

He'd made an afternoon appointment to discuss his own account at the bank in Greenwich – an account which was severely overdrawn. He'd been looking forward to, smugly, producing the account number, necessary identification and the passwords which would unlock an account worth tens of millions of pounds.

"Do they do...? Hang on Frank. Someone's at the door... I'll call you back." Gary, who was about to ask if they still did a second post, was interrupted by a knock on his apartment door.

"Hi, Gary."

"Hi, Natalia." It was Natalia Kaminski, or at least that's what it'd sounded like when she'd introduced herself a few months back after she'd moved in across the hall.

"I see they found that boy you went out looking for?"

"Boy? Boy? Oh, yes," replied Gary, remembering that he'd bumped into Natalia yesterday as he was leaving to join the search for missing schoolboy, Alex Norman. "Thankfully."

Ordinarily Gary would have all the time in the world for Natalia, he'd even been late for work on the odd occasion following a doorstep encounter with her. He found her very attractive. Gary was drawn in by Natalia's deep blue eyes... her shy, yet alluring smile. And if that wasn't enough, then there was her sexy Polish accent, which fascinated him. However, today Gary wasn't pulled in towards Natalia's smile or her eyes... it was her hands... more so, it was the large, somewhat bulky, white envelope she was holding in her hands.

"Is that for me?" he asked.

"Yes... It needed to be signed for... I hope you don't mind... But the postman..."

"No... No, that's quite alright," smiled Gary, outstretching his hand. "I'm pleased you did."

"Is it important?" asked Natalia inquisitively, as she handed the envelope over to Gary. Thankfully he managed to accept it without snatching.

"Sort of." Gary, guessing that Natalia had read the franking label address, tried to look downbeat. "I think it's from my mother's solicitors. "Last lot of papers and what have you."

"Oh... I'm sorry," said Natalia, apologetically. "I'll leave you to..."

"Thank you," smiled Gary, not wanting to sound too eager for Natalia to leave.

Gary felt an upsurge of adrenalin course through his entire body as he closed the door of his bedsit. Clutching the envelope tightly against his chest, he could feel his heart racing, filled with an indescribable excitement, as he tightly closed his eyes. This was it. This was what he'd been expecting. This was his future – his new life.

He now had access to millions – tens of millions in fact. Oh, how he'd lain in bed night after night thinking what to do with it all. Spending the money... saving the money. Using it for good... using it for pleasure. The Lockett and Helleken foundation for people pissed off by their bitter and twisted dead mothers was one idea which briefly gained some support... but then the funds were diverted to 'using for pleasure' once again.

Gary looked at the envelope... at the solicitor's bright red flouncy franking stamp. *K & S Stanton, Solicitors. Headrow House, The Headrow, Leeds, West Yorkshire...* It was real, it was very real.

From the cupboard under his kitchen sink Gary grabbed a bottle of cheap blended whisky, poured himself a shot – then another. Drink in one hand, envelope in the other, Gary entered his lounge and sat down on his tatty bed settee.

Cars filled his mind – fast, of course. Houses – one here, one there, one in the sun, one in the city – big, obviously... well, big enough to have a swimming pool and a snooker table. A posh watch or two – maybe from The Time Store, he thought, laughing inwardly.

Balancing his drink on the arm of the settee, Gary carefully peeled open the end of the envelope, emptied the contents onto the sofa and discarded the envelope on the floor.

Beside him were eleven A5 sized envelopes, some brown, some white, one of which was so thick it had started to split along one of the seams. He knew that this one contained the original paperwork, the instructions which he'd passed to his younger self at the Motor Show. The other ten were from various solicitors' offices, those which Gary and Frank had chosen to carry out small parts of their scheme.

Along with these envelopes there was another, standard

business-sized, white envelope which had an accompanying letter paper-clipped to one corner. Gary placed the envelope to one side and unfolded the letter.

"Dear Sir. Please find enclosed…" Gary scanned the letter, reading aloud key words as he went along. "Envelopes… Following your instructions… Pleased to… Statement… Bank account… Appointment… Following identification… I hope… Yours sincerely."

Gary re-read the appointment details, reshuffled himself on the sofa, took a swig of whisky and then picked up the smaller white envelope. The bank statement, thought Gary.

Of course, he knew it was from the bank. It was obvious from their logo embossed into the envelope. It had been addressed to a Mrs K Stanton – the solicitor who'd been following his directions for the final part of the scheme. Handwritten across the front and highlighted in green – F.A.O. Client Ref: 041367 DO NOT OPEN.

Gary phoned Frank. "It's here."

He turned the envelope over. Just the usual 'if undelivered' message… He ran it through his fingers – there was a lump in one of the corners. A staple, he guessed.

"Natalia from across the hall had signed for it."

Gary could hear Frank whooping with joy on the other end of the line, an infectious excitement they both now shared.

"No, not yet. Hang on, I'll put the phone on speaker and open it." Gary put the phone onto speaker mode and placed it on the sofa. "Can you hear me?"

"*Yes,*" replied Frank, in his German-English accent. "*Open it.*"

"Okay…" Gary carefully peeled the envelope's adhesive sealing flap open and pulled out the contents.

"Gary… Gary…?" It had gone quiet, Frank couldn't hear anything. *"How much…? Come on. How much?"*

"A pound… it's just a friggin' pound," replied Gary, accidentally knocking his drink to the floor. "One fucking pound."

"Is that it? That can't be right," shouted Frank, distressed.

"There's a note."

"Saying what? What's it fucking say?"

"'With compliments from The Time Store. A damn good try – one of the best. Please find enclosed a cheque for your initial pound. I'd hate to think that you'd be out of pocket after all your hard work. Kind regards… Sarah Bradbeer.'"

CHAPTER 39

Flamsteed Way Revisited
Friday, July 30th ~ 1751

Following their father's rebuke Jason and Dan decided against the usual post family meeting at the Plume and, after a quick change of clothes, opted for a time trip back to July 1751, the night Jason Bradbeer hacked off Oliver Bradbeer's left hand.

Dan, using an iron jemmy bar, had forced open one of the rear ground floor windows of No.6 Flamsteed Way. From there he made his way up to the third floor of the unfinished Georgian terrace, an excellent vantage point to take in the evening's events, and waited for his brother.

"Sorted?"

"Yeah," replied Jason, joining Dan, who was now crouching by the window.

"What took you so long?" Dan could tell by the smirk on Jason's face that he'd been up to something – scheming.

"I'll explain later. When this is over." Jason wanted to find out what had happened back in 2009 after he and the South Africans had left. Did Oliver just vanish to Tec-Spa? Or was there someone else lurking in the shadows? Someone else watching?

"Where are you?" asked Dan, looking over at the front of

343

No.5. "Can you see yourself?"

"Second floor, right hand window," replied Jason.

Dan eased up the window slightly, shifted his stare, and focused on the position Jason had given him, "Got you, I think."

"Think?"

"Well, there's some movement over there, so I'm guessing it's you."

Jason didn't bother to look, instead he checked his pocket watch. "It's nearly time – they'll be here soon."

It was just after eight when Dan and Jason noticed movement outside. Three men had suddenly appeared in the street below – time travelled. Two of the men, shaven-headed, both wearing sunglasses and long black trench coats, were standing tall, supporting the third. They released their hold – the third man, 'the corpse' – who they now knew was Oliver Bradbeer – slumped to the ground. Jason looked across at No.5 – he could see himself easing the window open a little.

"We can't leave him here," growled one of the men in a South African accent, as he crouched over the figure on the ground.

"Yes, we can. I've got his ring. Just get the bracelet off him. By the time anyone finds him – he'll be dead."

"Oh, shit! You're right… he wasn't dead!" Dan was shocked. "We could've sworn he was dead. Sarah checked."

"Shush!" snapped Jason. "Listen."

"It's not coming off."

"Turn it tighter."

The first time – back in 2009 – Jason couldn't make out was

happening – but from his new vantage point he could clearly see that the man who was crouched over Oliver was turning a tourniquet.

"It's as tight as it'll go – we'll have to cut it off."

"No – it won't work again if it's damaged."

"I meant the hand – we'll have to cut the fucking hand off. Pass me that axe."

"Shh, voices. Someone's coming." Both men looked towards the park.

"That's us," whispered Jason. "Coming down from the observatory." The voices drew closer, they could make out one quite clearly – Dan's.

Dan and Jason watched as the two South Africans vanished. Seconds later they watched as Sarah, along with younger versions of themselves, walked into Flamsteed Way.

Dan was the first to approach Oliver – but he stopped about three feet away. Then Jason – he was next. Then Sarah pushed by – she held Oliver's left wrist, checking for a pulse – nothing. She shook her head. Jason showed Dan the bracelet. They looked up – they'd heard voices – Jason took the axe.

"Fuck – he's still alive," said Dan. "And you're down there like some friggin' psycho, hacking at the poor guy's arm. No wonder he's pissed off with us."

The voices – the people – they changed direction – they didn't enter Flamsteed Way.

Dan and Jason could see Sarah as she walked away, clearly disgusted. Then they could see Jason picking up the hand – arguing with Dan – touching the bracelet. It glowed – they all disappeared.

"Not quite as I remembered it," remarked Dan, expecting more blood than there actually was. "What's next?"

"Wait and see."

About thirty seconds later Jason (the 2009 version) could be seen darting up the stone steps from the basement and pushing his way through the gate in the railings of No.5 and out on to Flamsteed Way.

The Bradbeer brothers watched as the younger Jason knelt down and pulled back Oliver's coat, revealing the tourniquet on his upper left arm.

Then the South Africans returned. "Leave him to die."

"No. That wouldn't be right, would it? I can't just leave him to die."

One stepped out of the moonlight, walked forward and removed his dark shades. "Trust me, you can."

"Why did you bring him here?" Jason was asking.

"We didn't. It was his bracelet," said the South African, shaking his head. "It brought us here."

"From where? The future?"

"From one future."

"But whose? When?"

"I can't tell you that. You should know – there are many futures if true time isn't maintained."

"Or if the past is altered."

"It hasn't been... You've done what was needed – chopped off his hand." The South African pointed to the axe Jason was holding. "Great minds run in the same gutters."

"Gutters?"

"Never mind. You've got his bracelet now – may as well destroy it. So let's all leave here – and let him die."

"Do you need it? The bracelet…?" asked Jason, allowing the axe to fall to the floor.

"No, not now." The man shook his head. "We know it's in safe hands – you have as much to lose as we do. But he mustn't get it back – ever!"

"Who is he?"

"That doesn't matter now – it's over – at last." The South African walked across to his companion, they spoke for a short while in Afrikaans to one another, turned to face Jason, smiled – and then disappeared.

From their third floor gallery position in No.6, Dan and Jason watched as the younger Jason down on the street below vanished back to his own time – 2009.

No one came to Oliver Bradbeer's aid, no one saved him – resurrected him. It was less than two minutes after everyone else had left that Dan and Jason watched as an all too familiar ethereal glow radiated from Oliver's ankle. A split second later the power of his hidden bracelet spirited his lifeless body away.

"Come on," said Jason. "Let's go."

"Home?" asked Dan, twisting his signet ring palm side.

"No… I need to collect something first."

"What?" Dan was confused.

"You'll see." Jason, with Dan following close by, made his way downstairs and out onto Flamsteed Way. Crossing the road Jason headed over to No.3, and pushed back the wrought iron gate leading down to the basement.

"What the hell are you doing?"

"Just before they left – the South Africans – they stood there… and chatted." Jason pointed roughly at the area from where the shaded duo had departed.

"Yeah," replied Dan, nodding in agreement. "Couldn't understand it though."

"No – me neither. But I know a woman who can," said Jason, waving a small Mp3 voice recorder which he'd just retrieved from under the lip of the top stone step.

"Ah! So that's what you were doing while I was facing a three to five stretch for breaking and entering." Dan had to admit he was impressed with Jason's plan.

"Come on, we need to get back into the house. The night's not over yet. There's still a murder to watch."

It was just after midnight before anyone else ventured into Flamsteed Way. The moonlight, which had earlier lit up the street, had now diminished – obscured by the night clouds.

"Jase," called Dan, nudging his resting brother. "Someone's down there."

"Is it Oliver?" asked Jason, snapping out of his sleep and moving over to the window.

"Dunno, can't tell. Whoever it is seems to be looking for something."

"Certainly seems that way," agreed Jason.

The brothers watched as the figure, shrouded by the darkness, skulked about on the street below.

"What's he looking for?"

"How the hell do I know?" Jason shook his head in exasperation at his brother's question. "Stupid."

"Definitely Oliver though." Dan ignored Jason's comment.

"Eh? How can you tell?"

"He's had to put the lantern down to pick something up. If he had two hands he wouldn't have had to do that."

"Fair point," said Jason, impressed with his brother's perception.

"Now who's fucking stupid?" mumbled Dan, rolling his eyes.

Dan was right, it was a one-handed Oliver Bradbeer down on Flamsteed Way, and he'd just found what he'd been searching for. The brothers watched from their third floor viewpoint as Oliver tucked his bounty into his right pocket and picked up his lantern.

They couldn't tell for sure what happened next – an altercation of some sorts. A man had entered Flamsteed Way – he started to push and shove Oliver around. The lantern fell to the floor – its flame extinguished.

Through the slight opening in the window the brothers could hear grunts, shouts and screams beneath them – chaos was in the ascendancy. There was a vaguely familiar sound, a crack – followed by an immediate flash of light – a gunshot – the pandemonium below ceased.

Moonlight gradually began to seep through a fracture in the cloud cover. A silhouetted Oliver could be seen – axe raised above his head – he swung – the axe fell.

Dan winced, he couldn't look any more. But it didn't matter, his mind fused together the myriad sounds into a vivid

349

image of gore. The sound of the axe repeatedly swooshing through the air as it fell, the sound of bone splintering and the sound of Oliver's crazed laugh would be ingrained on Dan's mind for some time to come.

"What the hell is he doing now?"

The brothers watched as Oliver knelt by the side of the man he'd just killed.

"I think Oliver's just put something in the dead guy's pocket," said Dan.

Seconds later Oliver vanished.

"Sick bastard," said Jason, shaking his head in disgust.

"Do you know who the poor sod is?"

"No. Constable Firth – the local copper – reckoned he was a sailor. Someone who got lost. Maybe he wanted whatever Oliver had picked up."

"The gun he just used?"

"Possibly… Come on, let's go home. We have some Afrikaans to get translated."

CHAPTER 40

Elsie Dorrington
Wednesday, December 17th ~ 2014

Other than having to deal with the hysterical, hyperventilating woman, yesterday's Loch Ness Monster hunt had been a bit of an anti-climax. Sarah had been hoping for a lot more excitement than she actually got – sitting in the freezing cold on the side of a damp hill wasn't her idea of fun. Still, at least once she'd calmed down and accepted that she'd time travelled, the surgeon's granddaughter got her answers, and dinner at the Loch Ness Lodge Hotel was exceptional.

So, at last, Wednesday was here, and although it was Sarah's day off, she had a hectic schedule planned out ahead of her.

She'd already been for her morning run, though this time she'd kept it to once around the park and not the usual three. She'd showered, dressed in some skinny jeans and a white long-sleeved top, tied her hair back with a bobble, eaten a poached egg on toast for breakfast, and was now, finally, speeding around the M25 motorway – northbound.

She needed to get round to the M40 junction before rush hour started, before the M25 became a congested snail-paced car park – and she succeeded. Sarah pulled up at her grandparents' cottage a good half hour before she'd anticipated, just in time for second breakfast.

Her grandmother had already, during a recent phone call, told her everything she knew about Elsie and Norman Dorrington, but Sarah listened patiently as her gran went over the story again. Occasionally her grandfather would chip in with what he could add to the story.

Norman Dorrington and Elsie Blackwell had met and married in 1961. She'd been twenty-four at the time and was well and truly smitten by Norman's good looks and charm, along with his brand new Ford Anglia. Or at least that's what they'd tell people who'd stopped off at Apple Tree Cottage for some of their WI award winning honey.

Sarah's grandparents had first met them in Malta on a Mediterranean cruise in 1987. Norman had treated Elsie to the trip for her fiftieth birthday, and she loved every minute of it. Poor old Norman, on the other hand, was definitely a landlubber.

Living only a few villages apart, they kept in touch, and would quite often have lunch together. But when Helen, Sarah's mother, passed away, there wasn't that much spare time anymore. Funny how a family that spent their lives dealing with time as a commodity, suddenly didn't have enough hours in the day for everyday living.

"Did they not have children of their own?" asked Sarah, keen to move the conversation forward thirty years.

"No, dear," replied her grandmother. "Don't think they could. Or at least, don't think Elsie could."

"Oh!"

"Medical grounds. I don't think she was right… you know… down there. Although she never told me. Well… not in so many words."

Sarah's grandmother finished off the story. Norman passed away in 2011, days before their golden wedding anniversary. Bowel cancer. Within three months Elsie was in a care home – she'd had a fall. She couldn't have coped with Apple Tree – not by herself.

"Do you know which care home she's in?"

"Parkside, I think," replied Sarah's grandmother.

"Where? Where's that?"

"Parkside. It's just this side of Thame."

After another cup of coffee and a slice of homemade fruit cake Sarah, with her grandmother along for the ride, set off for Parkside Nursing Home.

"Gran… Do you ever miss travelling? Through time?" asked Sarah, as she pulled up on Parkside's car park.

"How old are you, Sarah? Thirty-three, thirty four?"

"Gran! I'm thirty-two!"

"And yet how many lives have you lived?"

"Lives?"

"If it wasn't for our friends at Tec-Spa… knocking the years off you… how old would you be?

"Haven't got a clue. Why?"

"Well I'd guess that you'd be over a hundred years old. And I'd hate to think how old your father and grandfather would be."

Sarah looked surprised, shocked. But she knew what her grandmother was saying. A year here – a couple of years there... all done in a true time morning, a blink of an eye. Even in the last week Sarah had been to live in Auxerre for six months, just to polish up on her French.

The entrance into Parkside was through a large conservatory. Sarah rang the doorbell, and within seconds it was answered by a young spotty-faced girl.

"Hello. Can I help?"

"Hello. Yes... we're here to see Mrs Dorrington. Elsie," replied Sarah.

The girl opened up the door and invited them into the conservatory. "If you could just wait here a moment, please." She then scuttled off.

The conservatory was large, spacious and had several high-backed chairs along each side. Some had chocks under, to raise them a little. One chair had been bolted to wooden boards, ensuring that it couldn't tip over. Three of them had residents, heads tilted forwards, snoring away in them. One of the chairs had a black and white cat, curled up in a ball, purring along to the snores.

In the background, the calming voice of Karen Carpenter could be heard *Calling Occupants.* Sarah thought this was a bit ironic, and yet her gran hummed along – almost fitting into the surroundings.

"Hello. I'm Lizzie, the duty manager. Can I help you?" asked a very pleasant looking older lady, her voice almost singing out in time with Karen's.

"Yes. We're here to visit Elsie Dorrington. She still does live

354

here, doesn't she?" asked Sarah's grandmother, concerned all of a sudden that they'd come to the wrong care home.

"Yes, Mrs Dorrington does live here," confirmed Lizzie. "Only... Well, Elsie has been with us for three years now. And I don't think, in all that time, she's ever had a visitor. So you will forgive me if – for Elsie's sake – I'm a little guarded."

"Of course." Sarah's grandmother reached into her handbag and drew out a photograph. "This is me and Elsie by the Leaning Tower – in Pisa – Italy. We were on a cruise. That's where we met..."

"Gran," interrupted Sarah. "I'm sure Lizzie has far more important things to do than look at your thirty-year old holiday snaps."

"That's no problem. If you follow me, I'll take you to her. Can I ask who's visiting?"

"Yes. I'm Victoria Bradbeer, and this is my granddaughter, Sarah."

Lizzie led the two visitors along a corridor. Sarah crinkled her nose at the smell – a blend of Lily of the Valley mixed with the Glastonbury toilet blocks. They were shown into a huge dining room. At one of the tables sat a carer with a mountain of folders; paperwork and charts to fill in and file. The TV was on, but there was no one watching it. On one of the walls, the week's menu, displayed in pictures. Chicken casserole for lunch, cottage pie for dinner. In the corner, facing the window, sitting alone in a wheelchair – Elsie Dorrington.

"Elsie... Elsie. You've got a couple of visitors. Elsie... Victoria's here to see you," said Lizzie, as they approached. "Do you remember Victoria, Elsie? You went on a cruise with her."

"Of course I bloody do," snapped Elsie. "It's my body what's buggered… not my memory."

"Shall I get some tea?" suggested Lizzie, ignoring Elsie's bluntness.

"That would be lovely," replied Sarah, pulling up a chair for her grandmother to sit on, and then another for herself.

Sarah listened as the two old ladies caught up, reminisced about days gone by and how life had changed. Growing old wasn't anything to look forward to. She couldn't help but look at Elsie's feet. Although slippered and bandaged it was plain to see that they were blue and swollen.

Elsie, noticing Sarah's gaze, made an attempt to lift her leg. "They give me water tablets… but they don't work. Getting worse if you ask me."

"Oh," said Sarah. "Are they from the doctor?"

Elsie didn't answer. Lizzie, arriving with the tea, had overheard the tail end of their conversation. "Come on, Elsie. You know what Doctor Mulligan said… once the swelling has gone down and you can walk again, you can go home. You know how much you want to go home now. Don't you?"

"But I can walk," protested Elsie. "I'm up and down all the time, and you know it."

"Well, you know the deal. All you need to do is get up and walk to the door, and I'll gladly open it for you," replied Lizzie, walking off. It was plain that she knew Elsie couldn't stand without any help, let alone walk.

"She'd like that… She'd like to get rid of me. But I won't make it that easy for her," said Elsie, scoffing.

"Do you want to go home? To Apple Tree Cottage?" asked

Sarah, pleased that the conversation had veered to what she'd come for.

"Yes... yes," Elsie replied. "But I know that I couldn't manage. I'd have no one – not even to talk to." Elsie had changed. Gone was the harsh tone – the aggressiveness – which she reserved for Lizzie and her troops. It had been replaced by the tone of a seventy-seven year old widow, one who was lonely, one who needed a little bit more than institutionalised care and attention, however well meant.

"Would you like to go back?" asked Sarah. "Not forever. Just to see it – to see home – perhaps for one more time?"

Elsie's face radiated with the most stunning of smiles as she answered. "Yes."

Two hours later, and with Lizzie's hard-fought consent, Sarah and her grandmother, along with Elsie Dorrington, pulled up on the drive of Apple Tree Cottage.

"We always loved to stop off here..." said Sarah, tucking Elsie's blanket down, into the sides of her wheelchair. "For cake and lemonade."

Elsie had become used to the constant warmth of the care home. Spring, summer, autumn, winter – the heating was always on. She'd almost forgotten what the freshness of a winter's day felt like.

The garden, the Dorrington's pride and joy, had been taken over. Invaded by weeds. The bindweed, ground elder and creeping thistle gave no quarter. Above ground, a harsher winter would have killed them off, although their deep roots would have certainly survived to flourish another day. As it was, with a winter so mild, they weren't going anywhere.

"Shall we go around the back?" suggested Victoria. "I hope that bench is still out there. I can pour us all a nice cup of tea. I know I'm just about ready for one."

The staff at Parkside had been kind enough to make a mini picnic for them to take – a couple of flasks of hot tea, a few fig biscuits and a lemon curd tart each.

Eventually, after a lot of pushing and shoving, Sarah managed to steer the wheelchair around the uneven path to her waiting grandmother, who'd already poured the tea.

"That's where Norman would plant his leeks," said Elsie. She couldn't point, it was far too much effort to lift her arm, especially given the cold. Instead she nodded in the general direction of what was once a vegetable patch. Some of the bamboo canes which had once supported the runner beans lay scattered around, trapped within the nettles and weeds.

"Bet they tasted nice," said Sarah, loud and animated.

"They did. So did the carrots… everything Norman grew tasted nice. Far better than the supermarkets. Nothing on them you see."

"On them?"

"Pesticides," Victoria informed her granddaughter.

"Of course. He grew far too much for the two of us… So the daft old bugger ended up giving most of it away." Elsie sighed. "Still, it kept him busy… out of mischief."

Sarah helped Elsie with her tea. "Was there always just the two of you? I mean… I suppose your children had grown up and left home when you moved here?"

"Norman and me..." Elsie lowered her head. "See, that's the problem. That's why Apple Tree's like this. We never had children."

"Oh! I'm sorry," said Sarah, leaning forward from the bench. "I didn't know."

"We wanted children. Norman wanted two..." Elsie's mouth turned up at the sides as she remembered her more youthful days. "A girl and a boy, one for each of us he'd say... One for each of us. But it never happened."

"Did you ever find out why?" asked Sarah, encouraging Elsie to continue.

"Norman thought it was him... Thought that he couldn't... and I let him." A delicate tear ran from Elsie's eye and trickled over the creases which time had bestowed on her cheek. Using a napkin, Sarah gently wiped it away for her.

"What about the doctors? Couldn't they help at all?" asked Victoria.

"He wouldn't go. I wanted him to go... kept urging him. But he wouldn't."

"Why?" asked Sarah, holding Elsie's frail hand for comfort.

"He was scared."

"Scared?"

"Scared of being told he wasn't a man... Or at least that's what I thought. And in the end... Well, in the end we just never... well, you know. We just never got close anymore. Norman had his garden... his vegetables to look after. And I had... well, I had Norman to look after."

"So is there no one else who could take care of this place

for you? Brothers, sisters... anyone?" asked Sarah, moving the conversation away from children.

"I don't think so," replied Elsie, shaking her head. "I was an only child. Dad went away, not that he wanted to. But I don't suppose many did. Mum never re-married... you know, after the war. She brought me up by herself. It wasn't like today... all the handouts from the government and what have you."

"And Norman? Did he have any brothers, sisters?"

"An older brother, Dennis. A right funny bugger by all accounts."

"Funny? In what way?"

"We'll need to be going soon," interrupted Sarah's grandmother. "Only... I'm going to be needing the toilet and..."

"Okay." Sarah's reply was curt.

"I don't know... never met the man. Except at his funeral," continued Elsie. "Think he wasn't quite right upstairs."

"Funeral?"

"Of course, there were no family there. He didn't have one. Only Norman... and me... And I wasn't really family, not then."

"So what about this place? You know, when you..."

"Sarah," snapped her grandmother.

"No, it's alright," said Elsie, rebuffing Victoria's interruption. "When I die... I suppose it will go to the Crown."

"It will," sighed Sarah, despondently. She'd already done her homework, Elsie was right. If there were no surviving relatives who could inherit, then under the rules of intestacy, Apple Tree Cottage would go to the Crown. Bona vacantia – ownerless goods, as it was known in law.

"Could you imagine the Queen sitting here? Watching the leeks grow… Or Prince Charles and old what's her name. If only, eh? If only."

"More tea, vicar?" laughed Sarah.

"Come on, take me home," said Elsie. "It's cottage pie and bingo tonight, I think. Don't want to be missing that…"

The drive back to Parkside was uneventful. No road works to slow things down, and not too much traffic either. They'd taken Elsie back just in time for her to be wheeled to the dining table.

Sarah thanked Lizzie for the flasks and gave Elsie a goodbye hug. Her grandmother, all toileted, gave Elsie a kiss.

"You should go and visit Elsie more often. She'd love the company," suggested Sarah, about to pull away from Parkside. "Take Granddad while you're at it."

"He wouldn't go… even if I wanted him to."

"But would you? Would you want him to go?"

"Not really… but I'd suggest it anyway. Let him think I wanted him to go with me."

Sarah looked at her grandmother, turned off the engine, unbuckled her seatbelt and ran back into the nursing home.

"Forgotten something?" asked Lizzie.

"Just need to ask Elsie one more thing."

"Come on through," said Lizzie, showing Sarah back into the dining room.

"Elsie?" Sarah called. "Why did you let him? Why did you let Norman think it was him?"

Elsie turned to one of the carers, asked if she could keep her food warm for her, and then asked if she could be wheeled to somewhere a bit more private.

"I was twenty-two when it happened. It was the summer of '59, June fourteenth. Well, it had just gone midnight… so it was the fourteenth. Me… and my best friend, Ann-Marie, danced the night away… Bobby Darin, Buddy Holly… all the greats. I was dancing to *La Bamba*… Richie Valens. Now, he was cute." Elsie smiled. "That's when I met him, John Greger… the man of my dreams. The best dancer I've ever known. 'Course, you know how it is. One thing leads to another… and another."

"Go on," urged Sarah, giving Elsie an encouraging smile.

"He danced me to the sliding door of his Bedford van. It was cream, I think… or a mouldy-looking yellow colour, hard to tell late at night. Then he danced me through the night. It wasn't my first time. Lord, no. But it was my first… and only…" Elsie stopped, she perhaps felt some shame.

"John… He was a one night stand?" prompted Sarah.

"Yes… and to think. In the back of a yellow van of all places," she replied, clutching Sarah's hand. "I didn't want it that way… We'd made plans to see each other the next night, by the clock tower. We were going to share a fish and tatties in the park… and then… and then…"

"Back to the van?"

"Well… we had nowhere else to go," cried Elsie. "But it didn't matter… he didn't show up. Apparently it was Ann-Marie's turn for a 'little bit of John'. I'd had my go."

"What a bastard."

"I've called him worse… and her. She was much more than

362

a one night stand for him, though. They got married, moved to Warwick... haven't seen either of them since that weekend."

"Where does Norman fit into all this?" asked Sarah.

"Nine months later, at the Sorrento. I had a boy. Eight pounds, four ounces."

"Sorrento? A boy... But..."

"When mum found out I was pregnant she packed me off to Birmingham. She knew people there who'd help 'sort me out'... she didn't want the shame. They let me hold him... just for a minute. He was beautiful. His eyes... were beautiful. I can see them now... so blue."

"What happened?"

"I had problems, complications. They told me that they couldn't stop the bleeding. They took him, took my child away... and then took my insides away. I screamed the place down... for days afterwards, so they sedated me. They kicked me out... said I was well enough to leave. But I wasn't... I was causing too much distress to the other patients... probably scaring them. It was mother – she collected me."

"What happened to your son?"

"I don't know... There was a nurse. A young Irish girl, Teresa. She'd bring me my food, clean me up and what have you. She told me that my son had gone to Dr Barnardos... that they collected him straight away, that afternoon. Apparently my mother had arranged it all, least that's what Teresa told me."

"And Norman?"

"When I met him, my Norman. Well that was my chance to escape from my *evil* mother. The day I walked out was the last day I saw her. I'd lost a son... she'd lost a daughter."

Sarah gave Elsie a comforting hug. "Did you ever tell anyone?"

"Just you," answered Elsie. "I lied every month... about... about, you know. Even bought some towels and things... went through the motions... even the moods. So Norman would never find out... As long as he had hope. That's why he never went to the doctor's... he never wanted to lose that hope."

CHAPTER 41

The Sorrento. Moseley, Birmingham,
Tuesday, March 1st ~ 1960
Thursday, December 18th ~ 2014 (True time)

It was Sarah's first day at work. Well, to put it more accurately, her first day in her new job. She should have started yesterday, but there'd been a problem with the lodgings – a water leak of some sorts. So at the last minute Miss Hallam had found Sarah some alternative accommodation.

According to Sarah's research, the Sorrento was a very large Edwardian house built on Wake Green Road by William Adams. He'd named it after his favourite resort in Italy, where he and his wife Ginny had spent their honeymoon. In the past fifty years the Sorrento had been an institution for the poor and the needy, a home for disabled soldiers and a maternity home for women on low income. More recently it had become world famous for its premature baby unit and successful milk bank.

"Here goes," said Sarah, opening the front door and stepping inside.

The first thing she noticed was the smell – the hospital smell. Hospitals had their own unique scent, clinical disinfectant; a disguise for all the other odours – nappies, sick and sluice. It would only take a few minutes – then she would no longer notice it.

Directly in front of her stood a sweeping staircase leading to the first floor – a nurse, escorting a man and a young child were just at the top. They seemed excited by the sound of things – maybe a new addition to the family had arrived. Another nurse came scurrying down, she smiled at Sarah, then disappeared through a doorway on the left.

There were two large rooms, one to either side of the entrance hall. Sarah poked her head inside the one to the right – a waiting room. It smelled like a stale ashtray. Christ, what were they thinking? Smoking in a hospital! Sarah shook her head in disgust.

"Hello. Are you the new girl? I was told to look out for you, I'm Teresa... But you can call me Terri. Everyone else does." Terri had a soft Irish accent, mellow and yet magnetic.

"Hi, Terri. Yes, I'm Sarah. Where do I need to go?"

"Just to the back... follow it around and you'll soon come to the office. You're not due on for another half hour, so why not grab a cuppa... and I'll come and collect you."

Sarah soon found the nurses' office. Nothing much in there, a few filing cabinets, a couple of desks, a sink... and a kettle. She took off her coat and hung it, along with her handbag, on one of the coat pegs by the door. Sarah was wearing a navy blue nurse's dress, belted at the waist, a white cotton apron, neatly tied back, and a heavily starched nurse's cap. She hadn't worn stockings for a couple of years, not since living with Roberto – and they'd been nice lace-topped stockings with delicate bows running up the seams. Not these bloody things,

366

she thought, fighting to adjust her suspender belt.

Nursing wasn't new to her. This was the second time in recent years that she'd joined the profession, the last being in the 1800s, Crimea. Sarah's way of getting over 'that Italian pillock with the inadequate penis', as she now referred to Roberto.

For Sarah, to become a nurse at the Sorrento had taken some planning. Letters here, letters there, training, placement – eight bracelets in all – seven months of living in the fifties.

She was there under the guise of being a senior nurse, and according to her reference letter 'her nursing career would benefit immensely from spending time in maternity'. It was signed by Professor John Brewer, and had most of the letters of the alphabet following his name – some twice.

But she wasn't there to nurse. She was there for information, she was there to find out what happened to Elsie Blackwell's little boy. Taking a small Agfa Isollete camera from her handbag Sarah snapped a couple of photographs of the staffing rotas pinned to the office wall. She then opened the top drawer of the first filing cabinet, the one marked A – J, thumbed through to the B's, and then looked to see if there was a file for Elsie – there wasn't.

She poured herself a cup of tea and stared out of the window. There was a dark green lawn with a series of flower beds cut neatly into it, nothing growing in them yet... save for a few early daffodils. The grass was slightly patchy in places and probably just another two or three weeks away from its first cut of the year.

"You've not got time for drinking tea, nurse," shouted a stout woman with a thick Black Country accent, as she entered the room. "We've got babies to deliver, and they won't hang around until your shift starts."

"Yes, Matron," replied Sarah, putting her cup on the drainer.

"And another thing. Take that ring off… No jewellery, none at all!"

"Yes, Matron." Sarah, inwardly reluctant, complied without hesitation. "Do you mind if I bring my camera?"

"Yes, I do," replied Matron, sharply. "This is a hospital, not some ruddy playground. Why on earth would you want to use a camera?"

"It's for my studies." Sarah dropped her shoulders and lowered her head. "Only, I have difficulty picturing things… in my mind… when I write up my essays."

"Very well," sighed Matron. "But just be mindful where – and at who – you point that thing."

A few minutes later, and wearing a white cotton face mask which covered her mouth and nose, Sarah found herself in one of the Sorrento's delivery rooms.

"Now, you stand there and watch… Learn what happens," instructed Matron. "Right. Here we go everyone… ambulance has pulled up… Mrs Prentice is here."

Both Sarah and Matron took a step back. It was time for the doctors and midwives to take over. Although Sarah was present in the room, she wasn't involved, she was still in her training. It was quite surreal. It felt as though she was floating above it all – watching from afar.

The delivery room was spotless – immaculate. It had a flecked linoleum floor – easy to clean. Lots of radiators, no wonder it was warm in here, thought Sarah. The walls were grey – hospital grey – if ever the colour existed. Trolleys everywhere. Clamps, trusses, straps, towels, bottles, forceps, scissors, bowls, buckets and trays – all within an arm's reach of the narrow delivery bed.

There was a stool at one end of the bed, and a massive spotlight which hung from the ceiling above. Did they really need one that big? A bit overkill, she thought as she clicked down on her camera shutter.

Then it happened. Mrs Laura Prentice was rushed in. Her contractions had become more frequent than every five minutes. The midwife who'd travelled with her had timed them, forty-seven seconds for the last one. Mrs Prentice was in pain, and no bloody wonder. Sarah had just watched her receive a rectal examination to ascertain her cervical dilation. How barbaric.

Gas was called for – scopolamine. Sarah had read that it was standard operating procedure back then – to create the twilight sleep. It didn't take long before Mrs Prentice had a nasty reaction, started hallucinating, started kicking and struggling. Out came the restraints.

As birth became imminent one of the doctors administered a pudendal block, and then the forceps were whipped out. Time seemed to flick by rapidly in that room. It was as though everything… as though life itself was on fast-forward.

Baby Alison Prentice was delivered into the world with a dented head and forceps bruises, her poor mother didn't remember a thing.

There were three more deliveries during Sarah's shift, all pretty much followed the same pattern, although none of them were in and out as quick as Mrs Prentice.

Between births Sarah followed Terri. She was to forget what she'd learned at King's College, learn the 'Sorrento way' she was told. She couldn't argue really, this place was good at what they did.

The next six days rolled into a routine. Feeding, cleaning, bed making, nappy changing, taking photographs and tea drinking. Sarah enjoyed everything about the Sorrento. Everything except for the restraining. Everything except for the crying. Everything except the stillborn. Everything except for the screaming. Every day she could add another 'everything except for' to the list. But in the end, watching the gift of life succeeded in wiping away all the exceptions.

Matron was suitably impressed when Sarah offered to work her two days off. Commitment to her training would go down well on her report, Matron commented. Sarah didn't want time off. She'd spent the first week getting her feet under the table, getting to know how the Sorrento operated. Getting to know how the people operated.

It was on what would've been Sarah's second day off, Wednesday 9th March, when a tearful, heavily expectant Elsie Blackwell was admitted, by her mother, to the Sorrento.

"I've got a bit of an upset tummy," feigned Sarah. "I'm going to sit down for a bit, write up some notes… see if it eases."

The ward sister didn't mind, Sarah was an extra pair of hands for the day. She'd grafted well that morning already, so a rest would probably do her good.

"Hi, Terri," said Sarah, entering the office. Terri was preparing a new file for Ms Blackwell. "Who've you got there?"

"Elsie Blackwell... Who've you got?"

"Tess Coe," replied Sarah, pretending to read some details from a blank piece of paper. "She came in by herself, last night... From Kings Heath, one of Dr Grainger's."

"Lucky girl. I wouldn't mind his hands on me... If you know what I mean?"

"Isn't he a bit too old for you?" asked Sarah, sitting down at one of the desks with a cup of tea.

"Nooo..." laughed Terri. "At least yours is a local girl... Mine's from Bristol."

"Bristol," gasped Sarah, almost spluttering her tea everywhere. "Bit far away. Anything else?"

"No... Nothing. Just her mother for next of kin."

"Oo!! Bit of a mystery girl, our Ms Blackwell," joked Sarah. "Have to keep an eye on her."

"Could you imagine... her child? It could belong to someone famous... Cliff Richard or... or..."

"Quiet please," shouted Matron, entering the office. "What's all this chitter-chatter going on in here? We can hear you out in theatre."

"Sorry, Matron," said Sarah and Terri in unison.

"I should think so... Now what's all the noise about?"

"It's the new arrival. The one Nurse Donnelly is doing the paperwork for," answered Sarah. "Seems we don't have a lot of information about her... not even a doctor."

"I gather you're referring to the Blackwell girl? Her mother is a very old friend of Sister Foyle... It's a shame what's happened to that poor girl, a crying shame. No one should ever have to go through that." Matron gave them both a stern look. "You pair should be ashamed of yourselves. Laughing at that poor girl's misfortunes. Now out of here... the pair of you. Haven't you got sluices to do?"

Two days later, at 8.27am, on Friday 11th March 1960, Elsie Blackwell gave birth to a baby boy. It wasn't quite like Elsie had remembered – the scopolamine saw to that. Yes, her child was taken from her once the cord had been cut, but then so was everyone's back then. Elsie wasn't any different to any other mother at the Sorrento... or any other hospital in the sixties.

Severe haemorrhaging followed the birth, the doctors had fought to stop it, but in the end the removal of Elsie's uterus was their only option. It was no comfort for Sarah to think that, during her time as a nurse at the Sorrento, Elsie wasn't the only one who'd had to undergo a hysterectomy. And even one... that was one too many.

It was Terri, following Sister Foyle's instructions, who'd told Elsie that someone from Dr Barnardos had taken her son. Night and day Elsie screamed the place down, demanding her child back... crying just to hold him one more time.

In the early hours of Sunday morning a large black Austin pulled up on the drive. Sarah, upstairs on the second floor, tweaked the curtain to one side – she wanted to see what all the commotion was about. That's when she saw an obviously sedated Elsie Blackwell being shoved into the back of the car.

Another woman – older – got out of the front. Sister Foyle approached her – hugged her – they exchanged words – Sister Foyle handed over some papers – the woman signed them. Two minutes later the car pulled away. Sarah went downstairs to the nursery.

She went over to the far wall – cot four. The baby's identity tag read: Baby: Gates. Mother. Kathleen Gates. D.O.B 11/03/1960. Sarah took a pen from out of her pocket, twisted off the top and then pressed the clip – it was a torch – an ultra-violet torch. She shone the light on the baby's forehead – there it was, nice and clear – in UV pen – written by Sarah, moments after his birth… EB.

CHAPTER 42

Philomena
Greenwich Park, London
Friday, December 19th ~2014

They set off, at a steady pace, from the refreshment van parked outside the observatory. Down the hill, right at the pond, past the swings, up to the deer and then back along Blackheath Avenue, returning to the van. Hopefully, by the time they returned, their bacon sandwiches and coffee would be ready.

It wasn't very often they had the chance to go out for a run together – the three of them. So Sarah, who'd have rather stayed tucked up under her duvet that morning, especially as she had a late night out planned with Alice, reluctantly agreed.

Although there was another hour before the observatory opened, before the tourist rush, there were still quite a few people milling around – mainly those who hadn't bothered to check the opening times.

"Thanks," said Jason, taking his coffee from Dan.

Jason was sitting underneath the statue of General James Wolfe, the Conqueror of Canada, a man who'd achieved so much, carved a nation, fought in many wars – and yet died at the youthful age of 32.

"Don't!" said Dan.

"Don't what?" Jason smirked.

"You know damn well what," said Sarah, handing round the sandwiches.

"Oh! Look at James up there. A hero if ever there was," mocked Dan.

"And to think, half the people out there... his age," Sarah continued the mocking, pointing in the general direction of the city. "Are still in their beds."

Dan and Sarah both had a good laugh – at Jason's expense, of course.

"But it's true," mumbled Jason. "Lazy bastards. Should get off their arses and do something."

They had one of the best views in London from where they were sitting, if not the best. To their left, the Royal Observatory, home of time itself. Below them Greenwich Park, a Royal Park at that. Straight ahead, the Queen's House with its amazing colonnades, commissioned in 1616 by Anne of Denmark, wife of King James I of England. Beyond that the Greenwich jewel – Wren's twin-domed masterpiece, the Old Royal Naval College. The distant skyline boasted The Dome, Canary Wharf, St Paul's, The Gherkin, The Shard and the Eye. Yep! It certainly was a good view.

"So, what you gonna do?" asked Dan, biting into his bacon and egg.

"I don't really know," munched Sarah, runny egg dripping down her chin. "I've changed it all... I stopped Elsie meeting Mr Greger. She never got pregnant... baby never existed... Greger still married old what's her name... so no change there. But then... Elsie didn't give Norman a second glance. She married someone else, settled down, had two kids, and dies in three years."

"Job's a good 'un then," said Jason, who'd already finished his breakfast.

"It is… until you add into the equation that Norman Dorrington accidentally has a collision with one John Winston Lennon as he's leaving for Hamburg."

"So, what you're saying is that no Norman and Elsie… no Beatles?" Dan sounded distraught.

"Pretty much. We spent…"

"We?" asked Jason.

"Dad… Dad and I. We spent most of yesterday afternoon hopping through the sixties and seventies. No matter what we changed, no matter what we did… if Elsie and Norman don't get together…"

"Chaos?"

"Yes, Dan," replied Sarah, her voice echoing with despondency. "Pretty much."

"Then just walk away. Leave things as they are," suggested Jason, throwing his rubbish into a nearby bin.

"I can't do that." Sarah gave her brother a look of contempt, she hated his cold-heartedness. "Elsie needs some closure on all of this… Especially after losing her baby."

"But that was decades ago. What difference would it make now?"

"Difference?!" snapped Sarah, throwing her half-eaten sandwich in the bin. "You heartless bastard! It would make a world of difference to that little old lady sitting all alone. In a friggin' care home… with no one. With no family."

"So what you gonna do then?" Jason snapped back. "Elsie… this is your son. He's fifty-five years old now… I hope you don't mind… But can you sign your house over to him, please?"

"Jase, that's a bit harsh." Dan reprimanded his brother.

"No, Dan. No, it's fucking not." Jason steamed on. "Hello, Billy Gates. Do you know those kind people who brought you up? Your mum? Your dad? Well… have I got news for you, Billy Gates…? They lied. You were fucking adopted."

"Brian," said Sarah sheepishly, knowing her brother had a point. "His name's Brian Gates… not Billy."

"What did happen to Elsie's child, this Brian?" asked Dan, sensing that things needed to calm down.

"He was taken from the Sorrento later that morning. Handed over to his *new* parents, Mr and Mrs Gates – Allan and Kathleen – by none other than Sister Foyle."

"But what about Barnardos? Where do they fit in?"

"They don't, Dan. That was just a red herring," explained Sarah. "Once Elsie was strong enough to travel, she went to the Dr Barnardos home – Hallow Park, in Worcester, where Terri had told her they'd taken her son."

"What happened?" asked Jason, his interest now aroused.

"Nothing… the place had closed down in '59. Didn't re-open again until '61."

Dan had bought three more coffees. "But what I don't understand is why? I mean, why? Why go to all this bother?" he asked, handing out the drinks.

"It was Elsie's mother who wanted the child adopted – 'got rid of'. She thought she was doing the best for her daughter."

"Best?"

"I met her… Two weeks before she died. Asked her straight out… Asked her why she did it."

"And?"

"Jase, what you have to remember is that she brought Elsie up by herself. It hadn't been easy for her, relying on handouts and hand-me-downs, on her knees scrubbing, or whatever, just to scrape by each week. Elsie's mother wanted better for her. She told me that back then no man would take on a single mother – take on another man's child. It was Elsie's mum who signed all the papers, signed her own grandchild away."

Three camera-laden tourists sat on the bench next to the Bradbeers, one asked Dan to take a picture of them with the observatory in the background – he obliged.

"Come on. It's getting busy up here, let's go home," suggested Jason, heading off.

Dan and Sarah finished their coffees and then caught up with Jason.

"So… I understand the mother's motives. But what about the hospital? Are you trying to tell us that they were involved?" asked Dan, still trying to piece together the puzzle.

"No… Yes… Sort of. Sister Foyle had connections in the church, she knew who to talk to. Forced adoption was rife in the sixties. Did you know that more than 16,000 babies were adopted? Many against their mother's will."

"How many?" said Jason, almost disbelieving.

"Watch *Philomena*."

"Phil-o-what?"

"*Philomena*, Dan. It's a film. Steve Coogan and Judi Dench.

Watch that… then you might understand."

Dan nodded. "So, what next then?"

"Dunno… Don't know what to do now. Perhaps Jase is right. Who am I to mess about with their lives? Jase?" Sarah prompted her brother for a suggestion.

"Well, you know my opinion already," he replied. "But… Go and see him… This Brian. He might already know he's adopted… at least if he does you're halfway there. I'm assuming you know where to find him?"

"Of course," smiled Sarah.

CHAPTER 43

Kathleen Gates
Sunday, December 21st ~ 2014

"Thanks for letting me come with you," said Alice, getting into the passenger seat of Sarah's car.

"No problem. I'm glad of the company," replied Sarah, turning down the CD player to a more sociable level.

Sarah had asked Alice on Friday night, whilst they were out, hitting the town, if she wanted to take the ride up to Birmingham to meet Brian Gates.

Alice leaned over and gave Sarah a 'hello' kiss… on the cheek. Sarah smiled.

Since being born in the Sorrento almost fifty-five years ago Brian Gates had spent all his life living in Birmingham. Other than the summer package holidays to the Costas his 'parents' had taken him on, and his occasional trips into Wolverhampton, Brian had never ventured out of the city's boundaries.

With Kathleen and Allan Gates he'd been given the best start in life any child could have wished for – they doted on him.

Brian sailed through his school years with ease. He had support, love, encouragement and an academic mind – which he applied. All in all, he had a very good education, O levels, A levels and then onto a degree in Manufacturing Engineering.

"So what does he do now?" asked Alice, replacing Brian's dossier into a folder with his name on. "There seems to be nothing about him since the collapse of Rover and that was…"

"About ten years ago," interrupted Sarah. "I can find a few bits and pieces on him up until 2005… but nothing after that."

"Oh well. At least you've got an address. That's a start."

That's about all Sarah did have. According to the Register Office records Brian Gates had never married and never had any children. He was on the electoral register up until 2005 – it showed him as still living with his parents. And 2013's list only showed his mother at the address – Allan Gates had passed away the previous year.

"Pretty sad isn't it? I mean, not married… no kids… and still living at home with your parents. Christ, gotta be something wrong with him… if you know what I mean," commented Alice. "Mind you… thank God I have my own place."

Sarah didn't respond. As things were, she didn't want to get married or move out of Flamsteed Way – perhaps she should get herself pregnant, save herself from being tarnished as 'sad'.

Driving out of London seemed easy, Sarah thought, traffic was quiet. Perhaps it was always like this on Sundays, perhaps it was with Christmas being just a few days away, kids not at school and what have you.

Their conversation was somewhat limited during the drive and seemed to focus on sibling relationships. Dan and Emma's infatuation for each other saw the journey through to coffee and toast at the Oxford services, after which it was Jason and Rhiannon's turn to be under the spotlight. However, given that neither Sarah nor Alice had met Rhiannon, that topic was short-lived.

They made good time on their drive to Birmingham, pulling into the Hopwood services for another caffeine intake just after 10.30am. However, what should have been a brief watering hole stop was dragged out to over an hour by Sarah looking for a new book to read. Eventually, and prompted by Alice's need to be back home for late afternoon, Sarah gave up her search for a book and the two of them headed back out to the car park.

"Closer than I thought," said Sarah, who'd just tentatively entered Kathleen Gates' postcode into her satnav.

"Are you okay?" asked Alice, noticing Sarah had become jittery.

"No… not really. It's just…" Sarah sighed and turned towards Alice. "It's just… Well, it's just become real."

"Real?" Alice held Sarah's hand in hers and lightly clutched it in a comforting way. "You don't have to do this, you know. We could always just go shopping or something."

Deep in thought, Sarah gazed out of her car window. It had just started to rain, not a heavy downpour, more that light drizzly stuff her mother had called indecisive rain. *'Coat or no coat? Brolly or not? Why can't it just chuck it down and be done?'*

Alice continued to talk, offering pastel words of encouragement and understanding – but to Sarah each word seemed muffled and incoherent. Outside, people hurried but didn't rush – or did they rush but not hurry? It didn't really matter either way – they moved steadily, with a purpose – their decisions made.

Sarah thought her decision had been made – it had. Drive

to Birmingham – meet Kathleen Gates – meet Brian Gates – discuss Elsie – hey presto Brian inherits a house worth nearly a million quid – and more importantly, Elsie gets to meet her little boy, at last. But what if it all went wrong? This wasn't *Long Lost Family*. What if Brian's adoption was Kathleen's secret – one she'd much rather keep?

Sarah could feel her eyes watering up as she pondered on the rights and wrongs of it all. Then she felt a tissue brush across her cheek as Alice wiped away a fallen tear.

"Who are you doing this for?" asked Alice, breaking Sarah's daze. "I mean, from what you tell me Elsie doesn't know anything about Kathleen or Brian, and they certainly don't know about Elsie."

Sarah lowered the side window, she needed some air. Alice had a point. Who *was* she doing this for? Elsie? Brian? Herself? Christ, how she wished she'd never turned down Apple Tree's drive, if only those frigging traffic lights hadn't been there. "I don't know… I really don't know."

Alice gently brushed Sarah's hair to one side. "Come on, let's go and see Kathleen."

Sarah nodded through a brave smile; she liked Alice, she liked her brashness, her strength and her sensitivity. There was something about her, an attractiveness in her eyes which Sarah was drawn towards – she leaned forward and lightly kissed her cheek. "Thank you."

Including stopping off at a lay-by for some flowers, it took Sarah's satnav eight minutes to guide them from the services to Mrs Gates' house in Rednal, Birmingham.

Kathleen lived in a post-war semi which overlooked Cofton Park, her home since the day it had been built. Holding the flowers, and with Alice by her side, Sarah hesitantly rang the doorbell.

"Well, she's in then," said Alice, as she offered a 'hello' wave to a face staring at them through a twitched net curtain.

A few moments later the front door slowly creaked open and Sarah and Alice were greeted by an elderly lady who was clutching a yellow cotton duster.

"Mrs Gates?" asked Sarah. "Kathleen Gates?"

"Yes," smiled Kathleen. "Can I help?"

"Mrs Gates. My name is Sarah Bradbeer and this is my research assistant Alice. We're…"

"Oh, do come in," interrupted Kathleen, turning her back on Sarah and Alice and walking off down the hallway. "I've got some really nice fruit cake if you'd like to try some… Come in, come in… I'll put the kettle on."

Sarah shook her head and laughed inwardly, how sweet. Kathleen would have happily grabbed anyone off the doorstep, just for the chance to have some company.

The house had a homely smell, one which reminded Sarah of weekends at her grandmother's. It wasn't any fragrance or flowers, it wasn't any potted plant or potpourri, it was the good old-fashioned smell of home cooking – Sunday dinner, to be precise.

Kathleen's lounge befitted her age, with furniture which was built to last, built to serve a purpose rather than to match any anaglyptic swirl or sideboard ornamentation.

"Would you like any help, Mrs Gates?" shouted Sarah, as

she motioned for Alice to go into the kitchen to give a hand.

It felt weird to be this close to the answers, all those shifts at the Sorrento – the delivery rooms, the nursery, the nappies. Then there was Apple Tree – Elsie and Norman's life of lies, deceit and yet unconditional love. Sarah looked at an aged Gates family photograph hanging proudly over the dark wood sideboard – proud father, loving mother and cherished son. If only, thought Sarah.

"That was taken over forty years ago," declared Kathleen, who had followed a tray-bearing Alice into the lounge. "Just put it down there, my dear. Allan – God rest his soul – had it taken for our wedding anniversary. Tea?"

"Is that your son?" asked Alice, now looking at the picture.

"Yes, that's Brian," replied Kathleen, sitting down in a chair opposite her guests. "Just about to start his last year at King Edward's."

Sarah and Alice watched as Kathleen removed a knitted tea cosy from a round ceramic pot and poured out three cups of tea. "Thank you." Sarah took one of the cups.

"Now what can I help you with?" asked Kathleen eagerly.

"We work for Meridian Television," answered Sarah, taking a card out of her handbag and handing it over to Kathleen. "They've been commissioned to make some documentaries about maternity and fostering."

"And adoption," Alice interrupted.

"Yes, and adoption. The programmes are about how much things – practices and what have you – have changed since the sixties. One of the hospitals they've chosen to research is the Sorrento…"

385

Almost in mid-stir, Kathleen stopped stirring her tea and sat back in the chair, her dark hair emphasised the sudden pallor of her face. She'd not heard the name Sorrento mentioned for over twenty years.

"That's where Brian was born, wasn't it?" continued Sarah. "Do you remember much about the hospital at all? Any stories? People?"

"No, not really," croaked Kathleen. "It was so long ago."

"Not even Sister Foyle? Apparently she was quite a character, surely you must remember her? Or Matron… with her thick Black Country accent?"

"No… sorry," replied Kathleen, shaking her head. "I do remember a nice young Irish girl though. She'd bring me tea and biscuits… Teresa… I think she was called Teresa."

"Teresa Donnelly," smiled Sarah, her mind jumping to a raucous night of cheap wine and cheese they'd had in Terri's lodgings. "I have a photograph of her… Would you like to see it?"

Alice gave Sarah two pictures from the Brian Gates folder.

"Here you go." Sarah handed Kathleen the first of the photos. "Teresa is on the left."

It was an old black and white group photograph which had a touch of newness about it… old in the sense of it had been taken well over fifty years ago, but new, as in the film was processed and developed a couple of days ago. Sarah had taken it in the nursery before she'd left the Sorrento – a little reminder of the people she'd worked with. Terri, Matron, the nursery girls… Sally and Rose, and then, begrudgingly standing on the right, Sister Foyle.

"That's Sister Foyle... on the end there," pointed Sarah, as she watched Kathleen, vaulted memories rekindled, give a little smile.

"Then there's this one," continued Sarah, hesitantly passing Kathleen the second photograph. "I think you might recognise a few people on here."

Kathleen, lost for words, stared in disbelief at the picture. A few seconds later, with her eyes welling, Kathleen gave the photograph a hug.

Alice, noticing an emotional shift, spoke softly. "We'll clear these cups away for you, Mrs Gates. Could you give me a hand please, Sarah?"

"Well, I never expected that," sighed Sarah, placing the tray on the kitchen worktop. "I mean... did you see her reaction?"

"You're having second thoughts again, aren't you?"

"Second, third... tenth. Truth is, I really don't know anymore," Sarah wailed. "I can't help thinking that Jason was right. Maybe I should've just walked away... just left the damn cottage to rot."

"Cottage? And what cottage would that be, my dear?" asked Kathleen, standing in her kitchen doorway and drying her eyes.

Over a fresh brew Sarah told Kathleen all about the day she pulled into Apple Tree cottage. She talked, in depth, about her own childhood memories – lashings of lemonade and wedges of buttercream sponge cake. Sarah explained how, on a cruise, her grandparents had befriended Elsie and Norman Dorrington... and then she emotionally recounted the Parklands conversation she'd had with Elsie. She told it all – John Greger, Elsie's own mother, the Sorrento... baby Blackwell... the lies.

"I met Teresa – it was her who told me about the forced adoption," Sarah lied. "About Sister Foyle. That's her, by your side in the photograph, isn't it? At Brian's confirmation."

"Yes, that's Bridget. She used to live next door... her and her husband. That's him there, Kenneth Foyle." Kathleen pointed to a stocky chap standing with a group of men in the left of the second picture. "They were supposed to be Brian's godparents, the Foyles... But Bridget said it wouldn't be right... what with the adoption, the hospital... and what have you."

Sarah and Alice were fascinated. They listened as Kathleen told them about everyone in the picture. It emerged that there were no photographs of the confirmation – well, until today, no known photographs. There should've been two of Allan's work friends snapping the day, but a forgotten camera was one excuse... a dropped camera and spoilt film the other.

"And the adoption?" asked Alice, sensing the right time to move Kathleen back to the reason they were there.

"Well, it wasn't for the want of trying... but I suppose it just wasn't meant to be..."

Kathleen told how she'd *caught* on a couple of occasions in the late fifties, but both had ended in miscarriages, both had ended in tears. It was Sister Foyle, an advocate of the work done by The Sisters of the Sacred Heart of Jesus and Mary over in Ireland, who'd suggested adoption. She'd told Kathleen all about how it worked... it was in the best interests for both an unmarried mother and her child... it opened a pathway to a healthy future for them both.

Bridget had said that, for a small donation, she could arrange an adoption, through the church of course. Allan had been doubtful, he'd had his reservations, but Kathleen, distraught with disappointment, had readily agreed. Sarah, her feelings burning with rage at this point, excused herself and visited the bathroom.

Sister Foyle – who did this fucking woman think she was? What gave her the God damn right to do this to people… to Elsie? Sarah's emotions flicked back to Apple Tree cottage. To a fragile, weathered old lady, one who'd long given up on any hope of seeing her child, despite always keeping a candle lit for him. Sarah swilled her face with cold water to conceal her tears.

"Does Brian know he's adopted?" asked Alice, prompted by Sarah's return. "Have you told him?"

"He's known for some while," sighed Kathleen. "I suppose they know in the end. I think that they sense it… feel it."

"Feel?"

"It was as though part of him knew something wasn't right… that he knew he didn't belong. So in the end we told him."

"How did he take it?" asked Sarah.

"Very well. He was sort of…" Kathleen sought for a word, one which would suit. "Excited."

"Excited," gasped Sarah, unable to comprehend.

"Yes… He'd guessed right. I suppose he was just over the moon with that."

"And how did you feel?" asked Alice.

"Relieved at first. You know? Cat out of the bag and what have you." Kathleen looked at Alice and Sarah for a sign of understanding. "No more lies... No more secrets."

"Does he know who...?" Sarah stopped to rethink her question.

"Who they are? Who his real parents are?" said Kathleen, giving Sarah a helping hand.

Kathleen's answer was no. She never knew that her son, her Brian, was Elsie Blackwell's little boy... more so, she never knew Elsie even existed. By the time Brian was asking questions Bridget Foyle, the only person who could answer them, had moved... back to Ireland.

"How would you feel if we told him?" asked Sarah. "Would you mind? Only I wouldn't want it to..."

"No, of course not," interrupted Kathleen. "I think he has a right to know. Don't you?"

Sarah agreed. "Does he live far?"

"No. They live by the railway station."

"They?" Alice was surprised.

Kathleen walked over to a montage of family photographs hanging in one of the alcoves. "That's Brian... in the middle. With his... with his..."

"Girlfriend?"

"Yes... that's Lisa. They used to work together, up at the Austin. She's a lovely girl. The one underneath... that's little Charlie, their son," Kathleen proudly smiled. "My grandson."

"Aw. He's lovely," said Alice. "He's got gorgeous eyes."

"I've not seen them since summer. They were supposed to be coming to dinner today... but Lisa's been off work all week. She's full of flu, bless her. I don't suppose you two fancy a bite to eat, do you?"

390

CHAPTER 44

Lost in Translation

"I'm the guest," said Emma, pushing Dan away. "You get out and make the coffee, cheeky bugger."

"Oh! Okay," said Dan, smirking. He knew he'd been chancing his luck. He gave Emma a kiss, pulled back the duvet and then hauled himself out of bed.

"Nice arse," commented Emma, as she watched Dan slip into a pair of pyjama shorts.

Emma was lying on the bed playing with her phone. Dan admired her shapely figure, especially the curve of her lower back and the roundness of her nice – firm – bum.

"Yours isn't bad either," he said, as he slapped her left butt cheek and ran out of the bedroom.

Dan and Emma hadn't seen each for over a week, Emma's work commitments and office parties, along with a promise to spend last weekend with Alice and their father meant Dan had been put on the back boiler for a week.

They had a lazy day planned for today. Coffee and croissants in bed, a fumble through the newspapers – Dan hoped for another fumble through the sheets – lunch with Jason and his new girlfriend, Rhiannon, at the Clarendon Hotel down in Blackheath village. A gentle saunter through the park to work the pudding off, and then a few beers in the Plume to round off the day. Perfect.

"It's a pity we couldn't hook up Jase and your Alice together... That would be a laugh," said Dan, as he re-entered his bedroom carrying a tray with their breakfasts and a couple of 'Sundays'.

"You'd stand more chance of hooking your Sarah up with Alice," replied Emma, taking the tray and one of the newspapers.

"Noo!!" Dan laughed. "They went out together, Friday... for dinner."

"I know... Alice told me. They had a nice night."

"And?" quizzed Dan, pushing for more.

"Nothing, silly. They're going to Birmingham today, something about an apple tree... Oh, and..."

"Yes?"

"She'd love to come here for Christmas... if that's okay."

"Sure," smiled Dan, sliding back into bed. "Sarah can pull her cracker."

They laughed.

"Is anyone time travelling today?" asked Emma.

"I don't think so," replied Dan, who then changed his mind. "Oh, hang on. Dad is, why?"

"Nothing." Emma had a playful smirk on her face, she was obviously scheming something. "Where's he going?"

"South America... He loves it there. Why, what are you thinking?"

"Oh… I don't know. Perhaps a trip to see the Northern Lights… Or somewhere nice and hot."

"Yeah… I'd like to see you explain how you got a sexy suntan when you go to work tomorrow. Anyway, we can't… Jason's already booked the table."

"What's Rhianna like? Have you met her yet?"

"Rhiannon," corrected Dan. "As in the song. You know, Fleetwood Mac?"

"Sorry?" Emma was lost.

"Never mind. She's nice," he paused. "Well, she looks nice… I've only seen a photograph, so it's hard to tell."

They whiled away the next hour or so, eating, drinking, reading, commenting and then fumbling. It was the fumbling that eventually put them in the position of… running late.

Although it was quite mild for a December Sunday, the weather forecast suggested wrapping up well, and perhaps taking a raincoat, just in case there were some light mid-afternoon showers.

During their brisk walk across the park Dan brought Emma up to date with what he'd witnessed back in 1751. He sort of sympathised with Oliver a little. After all, who wouldn't be a tad peeved about having a limb hacked off?

Apparently, he told Emma, Jason had a friend who was fluent in Afrikaans, someone who could translate the voice recording for them. Hopefully there'd be some news on that over lunch, mentioned Dan, who was eager to find out what had been said.

They exited the park, crossed the road, and continued their walk across the heathland's open pathways. Ahead of them, to the left of the church, in a row of Georgian fronted buildings, The Clarendon Hotel.

They made their way through the glass reception porch, a more recent addition to the 18th century buildings, and headed for the Meridian Restaurant to sample the Clarendon's popular Sunday carvery.

"Nice," commented Emma, as she looked past the busy tables, beyond the Christmas décor, straight through the pianist and focused on the Clarendon's gardens.

"Jason's suggestion," replied Dan. "He wanted to bring Rhiannon to somewhere a little more upmarket than the Plume."

"Good choice."

"Speak of the devil… there's Jason. By the window." Dan led the way to their table.

"Emma. You're looking lovely," commented Jason, standing up and giving Emma a kiss on the cheek. "Dan."

"Jase."

"Rhiannon's just popped to the ladies room. She won't be a moment. Drinks?"

Jason ordered an Argentinian Malbec, a pint of pale ale for himself, after much indecision another for Dan, and some mineral water.

The table talk, for the next few minutes, centred on the tunes being rattled out by the Clarendon's pianist – 'tidings of comfort and joy… comfort and joy' followed by 'hanging up your stocking on the wall' – accompanied by the Bradbeer male voice choir.

Jason, announcing that Rhiannon was on her way over, stood up to do the introductions. Unfortunately, Dan was in mid-drink cycle, that awkward moment when the glass has been raised but not quite reached the mouth, the point where you have to decide whether to continue and drink… or put down the glass. Dan continued.

Rhiannon was medium height, a few inches shorter than Jason. Her hair was black, short and styled in one of those modern asymmetric cuts, over-styled as Emma would later comment to Alice. She wore heavy make-up, dark eye shadow with side flicks, and a dark red lipstick.

She was wearing a chic swirl patterned black chiffon halter neck dress with a beaded neckline, a pair of black evening heels and was carrying a black clutch bag. All in all Jason had done well.

"Rhiannon – Emma. Emma – Rhiannon." Jason began the introductions.

"Pleased to meet you," smiled Emma, feeling slightly underdressed.

"Pleased to meet you too. I really like your…"

Rhiannon was abruptly stopped mid-sentence by Dan, who was coughing and spluttering a mouthful of pale ale all over the table.

"You alright there, Dan?" asked Emma, concerned about his sudden crimson complexion.

"Oh… and this is my brother, Dan. As you can see, he's not quite mastered the art of drinking without slobbering everywhere yet," laughed Jason.

Rhiannon smiled and nodded.

"Sorry about that," apologised Dan, picking up a napkin and wiping some beer from the back of his hand. "Must have gone down the wrong hole."

"And here was me thinking it was my hypnotic charm," laughed Rhiannon, accepting Dan's apology.

"Your accent...? South African isn't it?" asked Dan, regaining his composure.

"Well done," replied Rhiannon, taking her seat at the table. "I'm impressed. Most people go straight for Australian."

The general introductions continued over starters. Rhiannon, enjoying her cocktail of crayfish and avocado, listened intently as Dan and Emma, unable to tell the truth, recited their well-rehearsed 'how they met' scene almost word perfect. Jason encouraged Rhiannon to talk about her role in her family's business, a conversation she admitted she often preferred to avoid. After all, she informed them, being an undertaker's daughter wasn't the most glamorous vocation in life.

Emma went for the Clarendon's roast leg of lamb, the others, swayed by the Yorkshire pudding, opted for the topside of beef for their main courses.

After seeing a lady at the next table being served with her dessert, the four of them were unanimous in their decision to follow suit and have the strawberry cheesecake. They weren't disappointed.

It was during coffee that the subject turned to South Africa. Emma and Rhiannon exchanged schoolgirl stories with one another, each having boarded in Dubai and Cape Town respectively. This allowed Jason to surreptitiously bring up the subject of languages, which led straight into Rhiannon's fluency in Afrikaans.

"By the way, did you find time to listen to the recording I gave you?" asked Jason, trying not to sound too eager.

Rhiannon opened her clutch bag and removed a folded piece of A4 paper. "Yes. I think you've got some explaining to do though," replied Rhiannon, running the paper through her fingers.

"I will, later," said Jason.

"That would be fun to watch," muttered Dan, watching his brother unfold the paper.

Jason's eyes scanned the sheet, left to right, slowly moving down the page as he read to himself. When he'd finished reading he took a picture of the sheet, and then emailed the photograph to his father, along with a short message. 'Do some digging pls. CU in pof, later, Jase'. Seeing that the message had been delivered, Jason handed the paper over for Dan to read.

I never expected that.

I know. Who'd have thought that we'd be meeting Jason Bradbeer?

No, not that, stupid. Oliver shouldn't die until Christmas Eve… quarter past seven…. remember? After he leaves the Earl … When he goes home.

Well it's done… I've got his ring… they've got his bracelet. So dead or alive, Oliver stays here… which, my dear brother, means our work is done.

Done?

Yes... surely. If Oliver's here our future, their future must be stable. Now, can we go?

Okay. What about Ben Abbott? Do we need to put him back in true time?

Father said to leave him. He only created small ripples. Time's already healed as much as it needs to.

"But…" Dan looked puzzled.

"I know." Jason took the paper and re-read it, once again concentrating on every word which Rhiannon had written.

"Come on, will you? What's it say?" asked Emma, eager to see.

Jason passed Emma the paper. "Get the bill please, Dan. I need to call Dad. He needs to check his email."

After a couple of minutes Rhiannon went in search of Jason and soon found him, phone to ear, pacing around the Clarendon's glass porch.

"Is everything okay?" she mouthed silently, as she approached.

"Listen Dad, I've got to go…" Jason paused. "Yes… No… Yes, I agree. Probably best if we don't."

"You okay?" This time, concern clearly showing, Rhiannon spoke.

"Yes… Just give me a few seconds," replied Jason, covering the mouthpiece. "Sorry, Dad. What was that?" Jason, sensing that Rhiannon was uneasy, gave her a reassuring smile.

"Okay… We'll come straight to yours…"

Another pause – more instructions.

"Yes, you're right. I'll bring her with me. We're on our way." Jason let out a long sigh.

"Jason? Something's wrong, isn't it?"

Jason tapped out a quick message to Sarah, slipped his phone into his pocket and turned to Rhiannon. "Come on. Get your coat… it's time you met my father."

CHAPTER 45

Creaking Door

Brian Gates hadn't flown far from the nest. He'd moved in with his girlfriend, Lisa, who rented a place on the fourth floor of Morris Tower, an eleven-storey block of flats across from the old car factory.

Except for an area now owned by the Chinese, Longbridge had thrown in the automotive towel years ago. The mega-acre site, once Europe's largest car assembly plant, was now home to a state-of-the-art college, multi-coloured youth club, affordable shoebox-sized housing and a vibrant new town centre.

Following Kathleen's advice, Sarah and Alice had parked in the town centre's multi-storey. Apparently it would be 'much easier' to park there, and walk across to the tower block.

Along with a twin, aptly named Austin, Morris Tower was situated on the corner of a housing estate just off Longbridge Lane. The local authority residence had seen many tenants come and go during its forty-plus years. Amongst them – proud Mini makers with families to feed, city commuters with trains to catch and social scroungers with Oprah to watch. Many of today's residents were sat either waiting for God… or waiting for welfare.

Whilst their siblings were tucking into Sunday lunch at the

Clarendon, Sarah and Alice, excited at the prospect of finally meeting Brian Gates, reuniting him with Elsie and restoring Apple Tree to its former glory, approached the outer door to Morris Tower.

"Are you sure this is the right place?" asked Alice, having her doubts.

"That's what she's written down, look." Sarah showed Alice the brown paper bag given to her by Kathleen. It was packed with sweets, crayons and a colouring book for Charlie... and on the outside of it was scrawled Brian's address.

"Okay then, here goes." Alice pressed the buzzer for Flat 12.

A minute passed – no answer.

"Press it again," said Sarah, not one for standing around in the cold.

Alice didn't need to. The solid blue door, with its wired glass panels, swung open towards them, followed by a rather 'glam' pram-pushing mother with an accompanying toddler dawdling behind.

"Here... Let me hold that," said Sarah, grabbing the door and preventing it from closing.

"Thanks," said the mother, grateful for the help. "Come on, Kanye. Hurry up, will you... and say thank you to the nice lady for holding the door."

Kanye, struggling to put his mitts on, just looked up at Sarah and smiled.

The entrance foyer to the flats was just as shabby as the outside. Directly in front of them was the lift, which sported a pair of hand-painted grey doors – on top of which, using a sparkly red spray paint, someone called Jamel had publicised his undying love for Chantelle.

On the wall a communal noticeboard displayed the block's cleaning schedule, a list of contact numbers for repairs, the local service providers and drug advice centres. Alongside these were 'For Sale' notices for razor blades, Dolce & Gabbana handbags and Ray-Ban sunglasses (several designs available).

"Got a bit of a niff to it, hasn't it?"

"Must be the toilet," replied Sarah, pointing to a puddle in one of the corners.

"Mm… nice!" Alice pressed the lift call button.

The inside of the lift wasn't much better. It was nothing more than a pressed-aluminium box adorned with misspelt graffiti messages and a collection of empty cider cans. There were, however, several business cards touting such essentials as minicab hire, 24Hr pizza delivery, the services of Eastern European escort ladies, Shroom sellers and an STD clinic; all of which ironically vied for space along the edges of the obligatory 'What to do in the case of an emergency' sign.

"Fourth floor?" asked Alice, finger poised to button-press.

"Yes," replied Sarah, who, seconds later, was thankful that the lift worked.

The fourth floor hallway was pretty much the same as the ground floor entrance, same graffiti, same smell, same love and attention. Still, at least the distant hills gave the residents a glimpse of life beyond their own doorsteps, commented Sarah, as she pointed out the view to Alice. As with the other floors, not that Sarah and Alice had paid any attention, the fourth floor had three flats.

The door to the first, the one on their left, No.10, looked as though it would have been more at home in Beirut – not Birmingham. It was almost vault-like, hinged bars crossed the solid steel door embedding themselves tightly into the walls at intervals around the door frame. If the cell-style peephole didn't give the residents a clear view of any callers, the two cage-mounted CCTV cameras bolted to the ceiling certainly did.

In stark contrast to No.10, the door to No.11 was completely different. It had a normal, Georgian-panelled red composite door, with brass furnishings, a well-worn welcome mat and a polite message from the local Neighbourhood Watch team, informing any cold-callers to sling their hooks.

"Well, this is it then," said Alice, pointing at No.12.

The door to Brian and Lisa's flat wasn't too dissimilar to No.11's – same style, similar colour, same furnishings. The only noticeable differences were around the lock, latch and hinges – they'd been repaired – several times by the look of things.

"I know… I know," whispered Sarah, not letting her butterflies get the better of her. "It feels weird… changing lives with the push of a finger. Here goes."

She took a deep breath and pressed the bell.

"Well someone's in, then." Alice was referring to the sound of a child shouting on the other side of the door, probably Charlie, she deduced. This was quickly followed by the sound of a door slamming – and then nothing – silence. Alice rang the bell again.

After another minute had passed, Sarah, usually a fairly patient soul, decided to be a bit more forward. She banged a clenched fist on the door several times, then lifted the letterbox flap.

"Mr Gates… Brian Gates? Could we have a moment please, Mr Gates?" Sarah banged again.

"You can knock all you want, but they'll not come out… they never do." There was a woman, maybe in her late fifties or early sixties, standing in the half-open doorway of No.11.

"Never?" said Sarah, crossing the hallway to talk to her.

"Well, not if you're from the social," replied the woman, giving Sarah the onceover. "Or the housing."

Sarah, gathering that the woman was fishing, plying for gossip, didn't throw any bait. "Oh, we're not from…"

"Aren't you? That's a shame… I was hoping you were. Might get some peace and quiet, then."

"Peace?"

"Yes, we've not had much around here. Not since…" The woman didn't continue. She'd heard the latch being removed from No.12, and she stepped back inside her flat and gently closed the door.

Sarah, her attention now on the opening door, walked back to join Alice.

"Hello… Brian? Brian Gates?" asked Alice, talking to a door which had only been opened a fraction. "Do you mind if we come in?"

"He's not here."

"Is that Lisa?" asked Sarah. "We're not from the social."

"Or the housing," added Alice.

"Mommy, Mommy. I can see Daddy coming… Who are you talking to, Mommy?" After a bit of pushing and pulling, a small boy managed to squeeze himself into the doorway, opening the gap a bit further.

"Hello," smiled Sarah, crouching down. "And you must be Charlie."

Charlie, turning shy, didn't answer.

"I've brought you some presents," said Sarah, offering Charlie the brown paper bag. "They're not from me... Your Grandma Kathleen sent them."

Charlie, suddenly losing his shyness, turned to his mother for permission to accept them. A slight nod of approval was all he needed; seconds later, Charlie was scooting off to his room... the bagful of goodies tightly gripped in his small hands.

"Kathleen? How is she?" mumbled Lisa from behind the door; a sadness in her voice.

"She's good," replied Sarah. "Little lonely, but good. She tells me you've got flu. She made out that you're bedridden with it."

"Erm... Well I can't..." Lisa stopped. The lift shaft mechanism had started. "You'd better go. He'll be back soon... He won't be happy."

"Lisa? What's wrong?" Alice pushed at the door in an attempt to open it – Lisa didn't have the strength to stop her.

"Oh, my God!" Both Alice and Sarah were startled by what they saw.

Lisa, head down, stood trembling in the open doorway, clutching a navy bathrobe across her chest. Her forearms were covered in bruises. Varying colours, from the blackest of blacks to the faintest of yellows, swathed both arms, only the slightest hint of pinkness remained.

The sudden noise of the lift moving upwards made Lisa

raise her head. Sarah's eyes were drawn directly to a pendant Lisa was wearing, she herself had one similar. A tree of life – a dreaming tree, as she called it. Lisa's was slightly different though, there was a word engraved under hers – Sarah couldn't read it. The pendant had been Sarah's excuse not to look higher – not to look at Lisa's face. But it hadn't worked.

Lisa had a small, cute, dimple in her chin and rounded lips – although one side of her top lip looked a lot fuller than the other side... *a punch*, thought Sarah. Other than a touch more purple, the colouring on Lisa's left cheek mirrored the colouring of her arms... *a boot*, perhaps. Sarah couldn't see Lisa's eyes, but guessed from the rather large sunglasses and steri-strips above her left brow that they wouldn't look nice.

The lift door creaked open, seconds later Brian Gates stepped out into a scene he hadn't expected.

Instantly foaming at the mouth, hackles raised, Brian darted across the fourth floor landing, brushed past Alice and Sarah, and pushed Lisa back through the doorway where she crumpled in a dishevelled heap on the floor.

"Mommy... Mommy," screamed a chocolate-faced Charlie, running to offer what little protection he could to his mother.

Sarah put herself between Brian and Lisa. If he was going to lay another finger on that poor woman, he'd have to get past her first.

"Come on... come on... You pathetic bully. Hit me, why don't you? Let's see what sort of a fucking man you really are." Standing her ground, Sarah goaded Brian. "It'll be the last thing you ever do."

Brian, clearly seeing the fury in Sarah's eyes, stood back. "How many times have I told you people to mind your own fucking business?" he ranted. "Leave us alone."

"Alice..." Sarah indicated for Alice to go inside the flat. "Call the police. Let's get this piece of shit locked up."

"No... No," pleaded Lisa. "Please don't. Not the police... His mother, Kathleen... it'll break her heart."

"Have you got somewhere you can go? Where we can take you?" asked Alice, closing the flat door behind her.

"She's not going any fucking where," shouted Brian, pacing the landing. "I'll fucking find her... and when I do. When I do..."

"Oh, shut up." Sarah had had enough. Palm facing upwards she pulled back her fist to the side of her rib cage, lunged forwards and, twisting her fist upwards at the last second, struck Brian Gates in his solar plexus.

She walked over to where he landed and looked down with disgust. Was this really Brian Gates? Elsie Blackwell's little boy? The baby that Sarah had cared for in the Sorrento? The family man, portrayed by Kathleen? Sarah's heart sank. All that hard work – for nothing. All the hopes she had of reuniting a mother with her long lost child – gone.

"Shall I tell you who I am, Brian? And why I'm here?" asked Sarah, looking through the window at the distant hills.

Brian, the wind knocked from his sails, the anger dissipating, dragged himself to his feet. "I don't care who you are... or what you want."

Sarah turned and looked at Brian. "Well... I know you're adopted."

"And?" Brian suddenly looked confused.

"I know who your mother is… your real mother," continued Sarah. "You see… my friend, Alice, and I have come up from London."

"London? For what?"

"Well… We were going to tell you about your possible inheritance."

"Inheritance? What? Who? How much is it?" asked Brian, his voice now mellow.

The door to No.12 reopened. Alice, carrying a hurriedly-packed suitcase in one hand and a Thomas the Tank Engine backpack stuffed with toys in the other, led a tearful Charlie and a brave-faced Lisa to the lift, and pressed the call button.

"How much?" asked Brian. "The inheritance… How much?"

The lift door once again creaked open. Alice carefully ushered both Lisa and Charlie inside and, finger hovering over the ground floor button, waited for Sarah to join her.

Sarah walked past Brian Gates, stepped into the lift, and once again turned to face him. "Millions," she said. The lift door closed.

Following a very brief stop at Kathleen's, Sarah soon had the car heading southwards on the motorway, heading home.

Lisa's bruising had come as no surprise to Kathleen; she'd had her suspicions something wasn't quite right for some time, but could never quite put her finger on what it was. It'd been her, concerned for her grandson's well-being, who'd pestered the local social services to make repeat visits.

Before they'd left for London, Sarah had given her phone number to Kathleen, and promised that they'd come back to visit in the New Year. Sarah even promised to take her out for lunch, a treat Kathleen hadn't had for quite a while.

Alice, who'd wanted to be back for a late afternoon movie with friends, decided it would be best to give her apologies, and spend the evening with Sarah, *unwinding*, as she'd put it. Sarah, not wanting to hit the wine bottle alone, accepted her company.

An intended brief stop for coffee was made even briefer, after Sarah had received a text message from Jason. It read, *'Hurry back, meeting at dads. Jx'*.

It was just before 4pm when Sarah, feeling exhausted, pulled up outside No.5 Flamsteed Way.

They were greeted by David, who seemed to be pacing around the Clock Room like an expectant father. "Hi, Sarah."

"Dad...? Anything wrong?"

"No," replied David, noticing his daughter had got company. "You're back just in time. Jason and Dan are upstairs waiting for you."

"Good," smiled Sarah, guessing that this probably had something to do with Oliver. "As you can see, Dad. I've brought some guests... Lisa... Charlie... This is my father, David."

CHAPTER 46

Too Many Bens

The family sat patiently as David, a stickler for common courtesy, went to brew some fresh coffee. The two Bradbeer brothers, along with Emma and Rhiannon, sat in complete silence, an awkward moment if ever there was one.

Of course, if Rhiannon had been aware that her new boyfriend came from a family of time travellers, then everyone would have struggled to get a word in edgeways.

It was Sarah, who'd left Lisa and Charlie in Alice's capable hands, whose arrival broke the silence. "Have I missed anything?"

"Only this," replied Jason, handing Sarah the sheet of paper with the South Africans' translated conversation.

"What's that mean?" asked Sarah, looking at her watch. "Quarter past seven?"

Jason shrugged as Sarah continued reading. "'Dead or alive… future stable'. Well, that's good to know, but I wonder what it all means. And who is this Ben Abbott? Do we know him?"

"No," replied Jason. "Haven't a clue."

"Sarah." Emma quickly inclined her head towards

410

Rhiannon.

"Oh, I'm sorry. I'm not usually this rude… I'm…"

"Sarah?" Rhiannon stood up and offered Sarah her hand. "It's okay. I can see that I've stumbled into a family… erm, crisis."

"I wouldn't say stumbled, my dear," said David, entering his lounge with a tray of coffee. "If it wasn't for you we'd still be running around, none the wiser. Sarah, could you fetch the cream and sugar through, please?"

"Dad."

"So, Ben or Benjamin Abbott, anyone?" asked David, pouring the coffee. No one answered. "Come now. You all have those internet phones, surely one of you has taken the time to look him up."

Both Jason and Dan sat speechless, as did Emma who was conscious that her smartphone was on the arm of the chair, right next to her.

"There's one… a Methodist evangelist," answered Rhiannon. "Born in Pennsylvania… America… way back in 1732."

The Bradbeers were impressed.

"I… I looked it up… I hope you don't mind. Only, I was…"

"Intrigued," interrupted David. "And who could blame you, my dear. I'm guessing that you'll have several questions of your own by now."

"Yes, quite a few."

"Well, hopefully we'll all have some answers soon," said David, who could clearly see that Rhiannon was anxious about the whole situation. "This Ben Abbott… a priest you say?"

"Yes. There are others though… Ben Abbotts that is." Rhiannon, calming down a little, opened her clutch bag and took out another sheet of paper. "Benjamin Vaughan Abbott… another American… famous lawyer… wrote loads of books. But he died in 1890."

"Jason, you get the priest. Eighteenth century, he's favourite. Sarah, the lawyer," instructed David, without hesitation.

"That's not all," Rhiannon continued. "There are also 121 professional Ben Abbotts listed on Linkedin as well… Plus a few Ben Abbatts."

"Okay… this may take longer than we thought," sighed David, accepting the enormity of the task before them. "Are there any others?"

"Not really," answered Rhiannon, passing her Ben Abbott notes over to David.

"Not really? That generally means there is," prompted David, who'd heard enough *not really* excuses over the years to know that there was more to come.

"There's this local man. Well, local to you that is… Lewisham. A real rags to riches story…" Rhiannon, her mouth becoming dry, paused to drink some coffee. "Used to be a tramp…"

"Tramp?" interrupted Emma, brusquely. "Do you mean he was homeless?"

"Yes, well… erm. He came into quite a lot of money… not too long ago."

"Money?" asked Dan.

"Yes… not too sure where from though. But he donated most of it to places like Shelter and what have you."

"Okay, very good work indeed. Thank you," smiled David, delighted at Rhiannon's input. "Daniel, he's yours."

"Is there anything that I could be doing to help, Mr Bradbeer?" asked Emma, eager to assist.

"Yes, my dear. You can pop round to Sarah's… see how your sister is getting on with our new guests."

"Guests?" Jason and Dan both looked at their sister for answers.

"Yes, guests," smiled David, taking some enjoyment from the looks of surprise on his sons' faces. He then turned to Rhiannon. "I can sit here and answer some of this young lady's burning questions… And perhaps then we could take her on a little trip somewhere… It's the least we can do."

Sarah, happy with the plans and not wanting to wait for her brothers, headed off for the Costume Room to change into something more befitting nineteenth century America. Before following their sister, Dan and Jason gave brief hugs and kisses to their respective girlfriends.

"Oh, Daniel. Perhaps, if he's not too busy, it might be prudent to take John along with you."

"Yes, Dad." Dan, very Sarah-like, rolled his eyes.

"Oh, and Dan…"

"Dad?"

"Try not to lose him this time."

CHAPTER 47

Windfall

"This is gonna be a complete waste of time," moaned Jason, entering the Costume Room.

"What is?" asked Sarah, who'd already changed clothes and was now wearing a rather drab olive green dress.

"Going to America, what's the point?"

"Mm," said Sarah, trying to tie her hair back with a cotton ribbon. "Do you mind?"

Jason took the ribbon. "I mean, a Methodist priest and a sodding lawyer – Dan's is favourite if you ask me."

"Where is he?"

"He doesn't need to get changed, does he? He's bringing the bracelets. There," said Jason, pulling the ribbon tight.

"Thanks." Sarah approved. "Is John coming?"

"No – I couldn't reach him. Dan can go on his own."

"Bloody hell, Sarah," laughed Dan, entering the Costume Room. "You look like a bag of spuds."

Sarah gave her younger brother a look of contempt.

"Here you go." Dan handed his brother and sister a shimmering bracelet each.

With Jason dressed more like Maverick than Methodist, the three siblings headed for the Round Room. As they walked along the limestone passageway, the motion sensors tripped into action – light on – light off.

Sarah paused at the edge of the Round Room, just by her father's battered old armchair. "This place gives me the shakes."

"Shakes?"

"Look at me…" Sarah was trembling. "I can't do it."

She was scared, she'd felt it a little last week – the Auxerre trip – and then Loch Ness. But she wasn't alone then – Alice – the surgeon's granddaughter – they'd been there. The thought of two against one had offered her anxiety some sort of a compromise – it had relaxed her.

But then, there was the trip she'd done for her father – the one to undo Gary Lockett's audacious plan. She'd taken a carving knife with her – waved it frantically on her return – stabbing and slashing the emptiness.

Now, travelling alone – she'd have to come back – on her own. What if *he* was here – waiting? Sarah shared her anxiety with her brothers.

"Go with Dan."

"But…"

"No buts," insisted Jason. "We need you to be focused for this, and if you're quivering like a leaf… then there's no way you're going to be able to concentrate."

"Jason's right," said Dan, echoing the sentiments of his brother. "We don't want you doing anything stupid – just because you're not in the right frame…"

"Okay… Okay." Sarah removed her travel bracelet. "You're right… You're both right."

Dan and Sarah only travelled back as far as summer. Dan had chosen Greenwich Park, the Royal Observatory, early July – it would certainly be warmer – and lighter. Sarah was impressed.

"Bloody hell!" snapped Sarah. "I mean. Shit, I forgot!"

"Sis?" Dan turned, concerned for his sister, but then laughed uncontrollably.

"It's not funny." Sarah was fuming.

"Yes, it is…"

"I look awful… What if we see someone we know?"

"Who…? Who are we gonna see in the park, this late…?"

"Jonesy – what about him? You're always on about him taking the dog out at night."

"Jonesy doesn't have a dog – and even if he did, you'd have to go some to dress worse than him."

"Fair point," laughed Sarah, seeing the funny side. "You sure he doesn't have a dog though?"

The two Bradbeers walked through the park, heading in the general direction of Blackheath railway station.

"Don't you think it's strange?" asked Dan.

"Strange… What?"

"That, out there…" Dan pointed randomly into the night. "There's another you – another me. Probably in the Plume."

Sarah thought about the glass of wine she'd promised herself – a nice, hot relaxing bath – an evening of nothingness – she suddenly felt envious of the other Sarah.

"I wouldn't have met Emma yet – and John would still be lost."

"And my arm wouldn't have these ugly scars."

"True…"

Sarah, having pretty much killed that conversation, moved on to talking about her day, about Brian – about Lisa.

"Good on you, sis." Dan commented on Sarah's dramatic re-enactment of the punch she'd used to knock Brian Gates flying. "So what of them now… this Lisa and…"

"Charlie."

"Yes. What's your plan?"

"Don't really know. I'll give Lisa a few days to adjust – to feel safe. Then talk to Gran, see what she suggests."

"Pity Mum isn't here. She'd know what to do," sighed Dan.

Their arrival into Blackheath diverted the topic of conversation back to the matter in hand – they now had to concentrate on finding Ben Abbott.

Rhiannon had told them that, since coming into money, Ben had funded a late evening drop-in centre, for the local homeless, in a shop he rented across from Blackheath's station.

It had become very popular in recent months, so much so, that even local retailers and delicatessens would leave odds and sods, leftovers and such like, for Ben and his small team of helpers to distribute.

Sarah suggested, and Lord did she need one, a drink at the Railway, a pub a few doors down from the station. They'd be able to sit at the benches under one of the windows, and make the best of both worlds – drink and duty.

From their vantage point, Dan and Sarah watched as Ben, who appeared to know everyone, interacted with those who his set-up attracted. It wasn't just the older people, those who carried the same weather-beaten ingrained look upon their faces, it was the younger ones as well, those who perhaps had different tales to tell – drugs – the need to escape – pressure at home. But, whichever way, Ben welcomed and helped them all.

Dan and Sarah had a second drink, and watched for another hour. When it seemed as though Ben's night was easing, they went over to see him.

"Ben, isn't it?" asked Dan, stepping inside the small shop. "Can you spare a minute?"

"If you help us pack away and clean up a little – then, yes," replied Ben, who was busy stuffing a load of blankets into an industrial washing machine.

"Erm…" Dan looked around for what needed to be done.

"There's a sink in the back… roll your sleeves up and get stuck in." Ben nodded in the general direction of the small back room. "You're a bit late, love. We might be able to scrape you a sandwich together, if that's okay?"

"Pardon?" replied Sarah, looking confused. "I'm with him."

Ben stood up and apologised. "I'm sorry. I thought… you know… looking at your dress… that…"

"No… she works up at the observatory," shouted Dan, as he smirked to himself in the back room. "They've been doing a re-enactment of sorts."

"Ah! Yes… yes. I remember those well," smiled Ben, his facial creases disappearing slightly, as he did so. "Now, how can I help you?"

Sarah, accepting Ben's apology, did the introductions. "I'm Sarah Bradbeer, and your dishwasher… that's my brother, Dan."

"Did you say...? Bradbeer?" asked Ben, somewhat surprised.

"Yes... is the name familiar to you?"

"No... well... yes," stuttered Ben. "An old friend... someone I've not seen for... for a while... T-tell you the truth... I'm not even sure that was his name."

"Do you mind if we ask where your money came from?" asked Dan, drying his hands and joining his sister. "Only... sorry to be abrupt, but... from what we can tell... one minute you're destitute... next minute... well, all this."

"Is everything alright, Ben?" asked the last of his volunteers, who was about to head off home. "Do you want me to wait a..."

"No..." interrupted Ben. "You get yourself off home. I'll lock up."

"The money?" asked Sarah, reiterating her brother's question.

"A gift," replied Ben. "From a friend... well, someone I did some work for."

"Quite a gift if you ask me," said Dan, trying not to sound too sarcastic. "Must be one hell of a friend."

"No... no... it wasn't like that. My friend... he gave me a lottery ticket."

"Don't tell me, it won?" asked Sarah.

"Well..."

Dan decided to press Ben a little further. "Was it from Oliver?"

"Oliver? Oliver who?"

Dan's phone rang. As though on auto-response he slipped

his hand inside his jacket and pulled it out to answer.

"Dan! No," snapped Sarah, reminding him that he shouldn't answer. "Not now."

"It was you, anyway," mumbled Dan, slipping his phone back in his pocket.

"You've seen one of those before, haven't you? A bracelet... like my brother's?" Sarah had seen the way Ben looked at Dan – at his wrist – when he took out his phone.

"Look – I need to be going. I have some people to see... some things to drop off." Ben walked to the door, opened it, and gestured for his visitors to leave. "It's getting late."

Sarah waited for Dan to step outside, and then, with Ben and herself alone in the shop, whispered insistently to him. "No problem. I'll get my brother to go back in time – you know – time travel."

"But..."

"It'll be like all this – all this *good* you're doing – it'll be as though it never happened."

"What? You'd... you'd... do that?" Ben gave Sarah a look of horror. "You'd take that little comfort away..."

"If it stops him... if it stops Oliver, then yes."

Ben, purposely leaving Dan outside, closed the shop door. "You'd better come through, then."

"Thank you," said Sarah, relaxing.

"I don't an Oliver. But I think I know who you mean. He called himself Phelix... Phelix Bradbeer." Ben explained how he'd met Phelix, and how his new friend had paid him to be his guide. "I thought there was something funny about him, though. He kept asking questions about cars – parking – traffic lights – Christ, he'd never even heard of rocket science," laughed Ben.

"What was he after? I mean… what did he want?"

"The jewellers… the one down the road. He was waiting for it to open."

"Any idea why?"

"No – none at all."

"And the bracelet? Was he wearing one?"

"Two," sighed Ben, who was now getting tired.

"Two?" Sarah hadn't expected that. "Are you sure?"

"Yes, well I think so. One was definitely on his wrist… like your brother's… and…"

"Yes?"

"When we were on the bench… when we were being *honest*… he'd crossed his legs… and, well… I never actually saw a second bracelet… but I saw its glow."

"And the money? That was him as well, wasn't it?"

"Yes – I never believed him – you know, the time travelling stuff. Thought he was just full of bullshit – a dreamer."

"So what happened? What changed your mind?"

"It was when I went to sleep that night… well, tried to. It's not much fun sleeping outside when it rains. That's why we wash their blankets…" Ben looked over at the whirring washing machine.

"Ben? Ben… what happened? When you went to sleep? What had he done?"

"A ticket," sighed Ben, his thoughts returning to the questions. "There was a lottery ticket… pinned to my blanket… and a note… he left a note."

"What did it say? The note... can you remember?"

"A gift from..." he shrugged, then grinned. "A gift from another time."

Sarah, having the information she needed, beckoned for Dan to rejoin her.

"All sorted?"

"Yes, Dan," replied Sarah. "All sorted."

"And the money?" asked Ben. "Will it be...? I mean, our drop in... can we keep it?"

"What money?" smiled Sarah, linking arms with her brother. "I don't know about any money."

Sarah, along with her brother, disappeared.

CHAPTER 48

Time, or Time?

"I never expected that."

"So, it's obvious he was surprised."

"I know. Who'd have thought that we'd be meeting Jason Bradbeer?"

"And they know – either will know, or already know – Jason." David sighed. He couldn't think about the future – the past. What really concerned him was the present. More importantly, how it affected those he cared about – his children.

"No, not that, stupid. Oliver shouldn't die until... Christmas Eve."

"Stop."

David had intended to take Jason's new girlfriend, Rhiannon, on a 'thank you' time trip... but David, being David, had decided that he needed to tie up some loose ends first. And so, being extremely apologetic, he'd now asked Rhiannon to translate the Afrikaans for a fourth time.

"So he shouldn't die until Christmas Eve? That doesn't make sense. Christmas Eve... when?"

"Quarter past seven... according to the recording. *After he leaves the Earl... When he goes home.* That's what he says next."

"Quarter past seven... that just doesn't make any sense. Are you sure?"

"Well, that's what he said. Negentien vyftien – nineteen fifteen." Rhiannon looked at her watch. "Yep. Quarter past seven."

David laughed... then laughed some more.

"Mr Bradbeer?" Rhiannon had a look of surprise upon her face.

"All will be revealed, my dear. All will be revealed," said David, his face returning to its usual deadpan expression. "What's next? Something to do with an Earl, didn't you say?"

"*After he leaves the Earl...*"

"So, for Earl we could have... nobility, a name perhaps, or even some tea. Anything else?"

"There's a couple of American towns and the Edinburgh Airport Rail Link... but that's about it," replied Rhiannon, who was scanning down some listings on her smartphone. "Oh... and a pub or two."

"Pub?"

"The Earl of Camden, the Earl Ferrers, Spencer, Essex, Mercia... there's loads of them."

"Is there an Earl in Greenwich?"

"There was one, down Churchfields. The Earl Grey. Look." Passing her phone over, Rhiannon showed David a picture of a tall, narrow redbrick building.

"Of course, yes," said David, recognising the building. "It's by the church. My father used to drop in for a quick one after Sunday service."

"Did he ever take you in with him?"

"No…" replied David, shaking his head. "It wasn't a very family friendly pub. More barrack room than ballroom."

"Ah! A bit on the coarse side?"

"Yes, very. Right. Shall we move on? Something about home next, wasn't it?"

Rhiannon turned back to her notes. "Yes. *When he goes home*… Do you know where this Oliver lives?"

"That's the easiest part… he lives here, of course," replied David, immediately realising that his answer would add to Rhiannon's confusion. "Well… he used to. What's next?"

"*Well, it's done… I've got his ring… they've got his bracelet.*" Rhiannon, as though expecting some input from David, briefly paused.

"Carry on."

"*So, dead or alive, Oliver stays here. Which, my dear brother, means our work is done. If Oliver's here, our future, their future, must be stable.*"

"So it would appear that our fates are intertwined with theirs." David sighed heavily. "Worse… they now think that the future's stable."

"Isn't it?"

"Not any more. Whatever Oliver's up to… we need to stop him before it's too late." David pointed to Rhiannon's notes. "Is there anything else?"

"No… they go on to talking about Ben Abbott next," said Rhiannon, putting her notes down. "You already know about him."

"Well done, my dear. Very good work." David praised Rhiannon for her input, then picked up the coffee cups. "I'd better do a fresh pot, they'll be back soon."

"Soon? But they've only..." Rhiannon didn't continue. David had already left the room.

"I wonder what he wanted with the jeweller's?" said Jason, fastening his bootlaces. "It's not as though he's got much use for a wristwatch, is it?"

"No, I suppose not," laughed Sarah, walking out from one of the changing cubicles. "Dan's in the office... he's going to see what he can find out."

Leaving their brother to investigate the jeweller's, Jason and Sarah swiftly made their way up to the apartments.

"You go on ahead... I just want to look in on Lisa and Charlie," said Sarah, heading to her own apartment. "I'll only be a minute or two."

"Hi. Where's Dad?" asked Jason, walking into his father's apartment and giving Rhiannon a kiss.

"Making *more* coffee," replied Rhiannon, who was looking at a framed photograph on David's fireplace. "Amazing likeness, don't you think?"

"What's that?"

"The man in the picture... standing with your father. He looks just like Churchill, don't you think?"

"Yes," smiled Jason, feigning a closer look. "I can see what you mean."

"You're back then?" David, carrying a fresh pot of coffee,

entered his lounge. "Where's…?"

"Dan's still out, following up a lead. Sarah's just popped next door… she'll be back soon."

"Jolly good, and John? Did Daniel manage to get hold of him?

"No… I tried, but there was no answer."

Once Sarah had joined them, and coffee had been poured, the Bradbeers shared their findings with one another. Sarah went first, updating her father on what Ben had told her – about Oliver calling himself Phelix – about the lottery ticket – about the bracelet – and about the jeweller's.

"So, that's where Daniel's gone then?" said David. "Do we know if it was specifically this jeweller's that Oliver came to visit… or was it the first he happened to stumble on?"

"Don't know. Hopefully Dan will be able to tell us more when he gets back," replied Sarah.

"Okay… well, thanks to Rhiannon we know a lot more now. According to our two South African friends, Oliver was supposed to die in 1915… not at quarter past seven."

"That makes more sense," acknowledged Jason, smiling at Rhiannon.

"Does it?" asked Rhiannon.

"I'll explain later."

"That's what everyone keeps saying," muttered Rhiannon.

"And what about the earl?" asked Jason.

"The Earl Grey… used to be a pub… opposite the church… down Roan Street," said David.

Jason shook his head, he hadn't got the foggiest. "I'll check it out when Dan gets back."

"Anyway," David continued. "Oliver was supposed to die on Christmas Eve, 1915… after he leaves the pub."

"Well that's good then, isn't it?" smiled Sarah, feeling somewhat relieved. "Our work is done."

"Not quite," sighed David, dousing his daughter's moment. "If only it was that easy."

"If only *what* was that easy?" asked Rhiannon, with a confused frown. "I'm not following any of this. Jason?"

"Erm… me neither."

The conversation was interrupted by Alice, who, following a light knock on the door, stood at the entrance to David's lounge. "Sarah, do you have a minute?"

"Yeah, sure. Is everything okay?"

"Yes, well sort of. The heating's come on… and, well… we can't figure it out, and it's roasting in there. Plus, Charlie's fast asleep on the carpet… and although Lisa says he's fine, do you mind if I put him in your spare bedroom? And – more importantly – we can't find your corkscrew."

"Now that *is* an emergency," laughed Sarah, standing up. "Come on, I could do with a glass of wine."

"Me too," said Rhiannon, following. "It might help me understand a bit more of what's going on."

Once the three women had left his apartment, David continued. "Okay, let's work backwards. Oliver was supposed to die in 1915."

"The South Africans?"

"Possibly. But, I'm guessing that he should've died in 1751, probably killed by the South African duo… the bracelet then would've spirited him off to Tec-Spa… they'd have patched him up… and from there he'd have ended up in 1915."

"All good, until we interfered. When we met James Bradley," interrupted Jason. "The arm."

"Yes, exactly. And on that day, according to the translation, the South Africans said that everything was sorted, they'd got Oliver's ring – we'd got his bracelet – and the future was stable. However, they said it was stable because they thought that Oliver, without his bracelet, was going to die… as in no Tec-Spa intervention."

"But he didn't."

"No, Jason, he didn't. Your sister's arm is proof enough of that, isn't it?"

"Erm, I suppose so." Jason felt suitably reprimanded. "But hang on, if I had his arm – his bracelet? How could he…?"

"Listen," David interrupted. "Oliver must be going to 1915 for a reason. You need to get to the Earl Grey and find out why… stop him."

"Stop who?" asked Dan, entering the room. "Oliver?"

"Yes," replied Jason. "I'll tell you all about it on the way to the pub."

"Pub! Looks like I'm back just in time."

"What about the jeweller's? Anything?" asked David.

"It closed down a few years back," replied Dan, who then handed his father two sheets of paper. "Found this on the internet though… Looks like Oliver went in for a brooch, and ended up doing a bit of armed robbery."

"Robbery?"

"Yes, Jase. Not his first time either. He held up the local pharmacy in October, 2013."

"Any idea what he took?" asked David.

"Penicillin from the chemist... and filler wire from the jeweller's."

"Filler wire?"

"Platinum filler wire... they use it in..."

"Yes... I know what it's used for," interrupted David. "I just wondered why Oliver wanted it."

"The clasp... on his bracelet... maybe that's what he used to alter it," suggested Jason.

"Possibly..." David sighed. Yet another piece to fit in the ever expanding jigsaw, he thought. "Alright... you two get off to the Earl. When Sarah gets back she can go and talk to the jeweller... see if there's anything else... something that might not have made the papers."

It only took Dan and Jason fifteen minutes to cover the short distance to Roan Street.

The narrow side road ran just off Greenwich's main high street. It was one of many local roads where, every so often, Victorian cobblestones melded with the concrete and slabbed footpaths of more recent years.

There was an odd quaintness about Roan; a mix of Georgian, Victorian and Edwardian housing interspersed with 1970s modern family houses... the latter probably complete with Formica worktops and frightening turquoise bathroom suites.

On the corner of Churchfields and Roan, standing taller than its more contemporary neighbours, the Earl Grey. Built in 1913, just before the onset of the Great War, this one-time local was now just another of Roan's many 'houses of character'.

"So this is where it's supposed to happen then," said Dan. "On Fiona's doorstep."

"Fiona? Who the hell is Fiona?"

"Oh… just some girl I used to fancy at school. She used to live with her gran, down here… No.8 Churchfields. Fiona Cartwright… she'd do anything for a liquorice allsort… if you know what I mean," replied Dan, adrift in his schoolboy memories. "Think she ended up marrying one of your old mates… Chris Cowan."

"Really!" Jason was surprised. "Come on. Let's go to the Mitre… get a beer. You can tell me all about this Fiona."

After buying a round of drinks each, and slightly later than they'd planned, Dan and Jason arrived back at their father's apartment.

"Where's Sarah?" asked Jason, slumping down onto the sofa.

"Getting some much needed sleep," replied David, somewhat abruptly. "I suggest that you two get some as well, you'll need it."

At 11pm, with Lisa and Charlie fast asleep in her spare room, and the Brewer sisters and Rhiannon sharing stories and wine in her lounge, Sarah Bradbeer left her apartment and joined her father and two brothers in The Time Store's rest room.

"Right," said David, leaning forward towards his sons. "The translation is quite clear... Oliver should die after leaving the Earl. That means you two need to be there before it opens."

"Do we know what his intentions are?" asked Dan. "I mean... do we know why he's in 1915?"

"No... that's the problem. We don't," replied David. "All we know for sure is that, according to the South Africans, the future – both ours and theirs – will only be stable once Oliver dies."

"So you're saying that you want us to kill him?"

"No, Jason... how can you possibly kill someone who's already 116 years old? Surely, as far as we're all concerned, he's long since dead."

"So you're suggesting that we verify that?"

"Exactly." David's reply and expression were devoid of feeling.

"And me?" asked Sarah, wondering what her role in all this was.

"The jeweller's... I want you to go there."

"It had closed down when I got there," added Dan. "All we know is that Oliver pinched some filler wire."

"Right," said David, his sternness disappearing. "I've prepped some bracelets and laid some uniforms out for you two in the Costume Room. Sarah, go to the jeweller's first, then join your brothers. Who knows, they might need you."

CHAPTER 49

Showdown
The Earl Grey, Greenwich.
Christmas Eve, 1915

Jason and Dan, both wearing navy blue naval officer's uniforms, had clasped palms to bracelets and arrived back in 1915 – Christmas Eve. Their point of arrival – the guest room of No.5 Flamsteed Way.

"Have you been here before?" asked Dan, checking out his new surroundings.

"1915? Not what I can remember," replied Jason, shrugging his shoulders. "You?"

"Yes… but not London," answered Dan, who was now gently tapping against the wall that he would, one day, have to fix and re-plaster. "Do you think our great-granddad Philip could be on the other side – in the rest room?"

"Possibly," said Jason, shrugging his shoulders once again. "Come on, we need to get going."

The two brothers left The Time Store's guest room, and, using the gardener's gates, skirted across the rear gardens of Flamsteed Way to the basement yard of No.1.

"Oops," said Jason, rounding the corner, and almost

colliding into a coalscuttle-carrying footman as he did. "Sorry."

Not waiting for a reply, he and Dan bounded their way up the steps, through the iron gates, and out on to Flamsteed Way.

It was just after 11am, and although they'd an hour until the Earl Grey opened, they still walked at a brisk pace.

"I can't see him being there this early, waiting for the pub to open. Can you?"

"I honestly don't know," replied Jason. "We might have to spend all day in there."

"Really!" Dan smiled.

Walking alongside the herbaceous borders which separated Greenwich Park from the Queen's House, they began to make their way towards St. Alfege's Church. Behind the gleaming white colonnades of the house, the Royal Naval College flicked by; as the two brothers hurried past, Dan thought it was almost like a silent movie in his peripheral vision – or perhaps a zoetrope.

Thankfully, with the Royal Medical School closed for the Christmas holidays, there were no students milling around outside the school's buildings for them to have to avoid.

"Not seen that building before," said Dan, pointing to a rather ornate redbrick building on their left.

"Me neither." Jason read the sign above one of the entrance doors. "Public Baths. Wonder when they pulled it down?"

They were just about to step out of the park's grounds, when Dan, noticing something wasn't quite right, stopped and turned around. "Something's missing."

"Erm..." Jason, thinking aloud, agreed. "The statue? King... what's his... shit? What's his name?"

"William."

"That's the fellow… what made you remember him?"

"Dunno," replied Dan, crossing King William Walk. "Just came to me."

At first glance other than a road name or two, nothing much had changed in this area of Greenwich. The Tavern still looked the same – better, if anything, mocked Jason, who was not a fan of their ales. He recounted to Dan that he'd actually once considered buying an apartment down Nevada Street… but decided against it when he'd noticed which pub would've been his local. Dan didn't blame him.

It was their walk down Stockwell Street that yielded the biggest shock to the two brothers. Of course it didn't come as any surprise that the all too familiar, yellow brick Hotel Ibis wasn't there… after all, that wouldn't be built for another ninety years or so. It was the building in its place that caused Dan and Jason's heads to turn – Greenwich Park Railway Station.

"Greenwich Park! Did you know about that?" asked Dan, who couldn't believe that Greenwich used to have two railway stations.

"Erm, no. But I vaguely recognise the building," replied Jason. "It used to be a timber merchant… and before that… I think it was a billiard hall."

Leaving the hustle and bustle of southbound commuters behind, Dan and Jason continued on their way to the Earl.

Considering it was Christmas Eve, the mood on the streets seemed very sombre, not as festive as they were used to – but with the country in the grip of war, that was to be expected. Still, even though they were in 1915 – a hundred years in the past –

the roads were busy with traffic; there were more than enough buses, trucks, horses and cars out there... all of them battling against one another in a bid to navigate the capital's streets.

As Jason and Dan neared the church, the footpaths were becoming busier, and even though they were in mid-war, England's shopkeepers – the haberdashers, chemists, tailors and dressmakers, butchers and bakers – all did their utmost in peacocking their window displays, with the aim of relieving the local Londoners of the pennies in their pockets.

"Carry on," said Jason, returning a salute to a couple of passing bag-laden naval ratings.

"You love it, don't you?" said Dan, shaking his head at his brother.

"If you dress the part – you have to play the part," laughed Jason.

Dan agreed.

The brothers stood on the kerb of Church Road; across from them, behind the black iron railings, stood another of the Greenwich stalwarts, Hawksmoor's St. Alfege's Church. And it looked somewhat different to what the brothers were used to; much cleaner, much whiter, and less blackened by emissions. Ordinarily, when Jason and Dan needed to cross Church Road, they would have used the traffic lights, but as city planners hadn't considered them necessary here yet, they resorted to dodging the traffic.

As they walked down Roan Street, Dan pointed out the cobbled road surface and boxed gas-fuelled lanterns, a retro look which would fit perfectly in their own time, he suggested. Halfway down the street there was a smartly dressed congregation of people heading into the church; festive prayers to deliver in their hopes of keeping entrenched loved ones safe, thought Jason.

As they had done, only hours earlier, the two brothers stood on the corner of St. Alfege's Passage and Roan, and looked across at the Earl Grey. Although only recently built, it had been sited between two rows of Victorian terraces, and – in its proper time – no longer looked out of place. On the corner of the passageway was what they knew as the quirky boutique bed and breakfast, with its leafy garden and topiary horse – here in 1915, it was a local grocer's/sweet shop.

"Let's go in there," suggested Jason, pointing at the shop. "We've still got another thirty minutes to wait until the pub opens."

"Good morning." There was a man, shoulders back… almost standing to attention… behind the counter. "How can I help, sir?"

"Good morning," replied Jason, removing his cap. "At ease, my good man… At ease."

"Sir." The shopkeeper relaxed.

"We're from the Ministry." Jason looked around, then peered over the counter. "Are we alone?"

"Yes," whispered the shopkeeper.

"Good-ho! I'm Commander Bond… This here is Captain Sparrow…" Jason leaned across the counter and whispered. "Have you heard of the Secret Service?"

"No… Should I have?"

"Absolutely not… Hardly be a bloody secret if you had, would it?" replied Jason, tapping the side of his nose. "Hush…

hush, and what have you."

Jason went on, explaining to the shopkeeper that they needed to use the room above – they had it on good authority that a man – code named 'Harmless Harry' – was passing on state secrets, to the Austrians. The Earl Grey was, as far as they knew, Harry's drop point.

"I was that close to peeing myself," said Dan, who'd struggled like hell not to laugh. "I mean, Commander Bond!"

"No need for formalities in here," laughed Jason. "Feel free to call me James."

The shop's upstairs window offered them a perfect view of Roan Street. Nothing and nobody could enter the narrow cobbled side street without them noticing. At a little after midday, the landlord of The Earl Grey unbolted the front doors, picked up a few pieces of windswept litter which had settled on the pub's doorstep, then returned inside and waited for the crowds to arrive.

The first hour or so saw a steady stream of customers come and go through the pub's double doors. Workers, on an early holiday finish, stopped off for a swift one on their way home. Shoppers with last minute gifts – or last minute sprouts to buy, ambled through the doors. Squaddies and seamen – miles from home – with ladies to court – dropped in for a little Dutch courage.

"Here we go." Jason had seen someone.

"Is it him?"

"Possibly… in that doorway." Jason pointed to a house, one where he'd seen a movement. "On the left."

"Got him," said Dan. "Are you sure it's Oliver?"

"Not yet." Jason needed the man to step out into the open... He needed to see his arm.

Two soldiers walked in through the pub's open door, seconds later, the man Jason was watching stepped away from the house, out onto the footpath.

"Bingo! It's him."

Jason was right, it was Oliver Bradbeer down there, on Roan Street. It was their distant cousin, and he was following the two war-weary servicemen into the Earl.

"Why now?" Jason was unsure how long Oliver had been there. "What's he up to, I wonder?"

"Dunno... But I bet he's freezing out there, without a coat on."

"Dan! You're a fucking star," smiled Jason, patting his brother on the shoulder.

"What?"

"He wants a coat – an army greatcoat. FUCK!"

"Why does he need a greatcoat? I don't get it, I mean... I know it's cold, but..."

"It's so he can go home."

"Home?"

"Yes – if he's dressed like a hero – they'll accept him as a hero – especially with that arm."

"But..."

"No buts, Dan. We have to stop him getting home... simple as that. I think it's time you had a beer."

"At last."

Dan walked through the entrance door of the Earl and into a

dimly lit, tiled corridor. To his right, there was a heavy wooden door with a smoked glass upper panel. Etched in the centre of the panel was the brewery's triangular insignia, and under the panel was a brass plate which read, BAR. Dan pushed open the door.

There were about twenty people in the bar, some laughing and joking, others sitting in silence – but no Oliver, thought Dan, scanning the room. At one of the tables under the window sat four men, sipping at pints and playing dominoes. Dan thought it was quite surreal; them drinking beer and playing games whilst their *brothers,* ankle deep in rat-infested trench water, fought the Jerry only an hour's easyJet flight away.

With flames dancing, a roaring fire cracked and spat as it kept the winter's chill at bay and gave the bar a homely feel. Above the fireplace hung a portrait of Charles Grey, the second Earl Grey – the man the tea is named after, realised Dan.

Paintings of ships adorned the Earl Grey's walls – tall-mast clippers racing the wind and funnelled steamers ploughing through the Atlantic swell hung alongside Armada-beating ships of the line. Behind the dark-wood bar a portrait of the King – George V – hung for all to bless.

"At ease, gents… Please don't." Two sailors had noticed Dan's arrival and were about to make way for him. "I'm just a guy… dropping in for a drink. Please, carry on."

"Yes, sir." The men saluted.

To the left of the bar there was another door – same brewery insignia – same brass plate – only this time it read, TOILETS. Next to the door, screwed to the wall, were several coat hooks. Dan was just about to order a drink from the bar when he noticed the door creak slightly open. Not enough for anyone to walk through – but certainly enough for an arm to slip through and lift a coat from one of the hooks. Oliver, out in the corridor, it had to be, figured Dan.

"There goes my pint," muttered Dan, slamming the door against Oliver's arm. "No, you don't."

Dropping the coat to the floor, arm throbbing with a dull, but already fading pain, Oliver, retreating, fled the Earl.

Run, urged Phelix.

"I am fucking running," snapped Oliver, pushing his way past a couple of people entering the pub, and heading straight for the passageway.

With his heart pounding, Oliver ran – like he'd never run before – he ran as though his very existence depended on it – for it did.

Behind him, he could hear the Earl Grey's door clattering on its hinges, as his pursuer burst out of the pub, giving chase.

"That way… I'll head him off."

Two of them.

Phelix was right, Oliver could hear them. One of them was trying to cut him off – by the sound of it he'd gone down Roan. Oliver could hear his footsteps fading into the distance. But the other's – Oliver could feel them echo in his mind, as their sound bounced from the brickwork of the narrow passageway.

It didn't matter now if Oliver had a coat or not – it didn't matter what anyone thought of him. He just had to get home – get through that door.

Another deep breath, another foot forwards – mouth

already dry, lungs already bursting – Oliver hastened his stride, but his nemesis didn't falter.

Rounding the passageway's dogleg, Oliver was nearly brought crashing down as he charged headlong into a group of people exiting St. Alfege's churchyard – his rhythm stuttered as he jolted forwards.

"STOP HIM."

It was that Jason – the bastard who hacked off my arm, thought Oliver, recognising the voice behind him.

Come on, move it!

With renewed vigour, picking up his gait again, Oliver turned the corner, and ran out onto Church Road.

He hesitated at the kerb... cars, lorries, horses... everywhere. For once the traffic was moving quickly – but he had no choice – there was to be no stopping – he had to continue. With a blind leap of faith – a hope in his heart that the traffic would stop – that cars would brake – Oliver ran out into the road.

He knew he had no choice. Get caught – then what? What would they do? Whoever *they* were. Prison? Surely not.

Blasting horns, screaming wheels, abusive shouts... the sounds behind him broke his train of thought. He needed to stay focused... focused on his goal. But what was happening?

Oliver chanced a hasty look backwards, and saw Jason – his hunter – hands splayed on the paintwork of an abruptly halted sedan. But Oliver could see the other one, Daniel, crossing by the church, he was the closest now. The pursuit was continuing – the threat was real.

In the market – lose yourself.

Oliver, thankful for the breather, allowed himself to be engulfed into the slow-paced shuffle of last minute market shoppers.

"Let me through... LET ME THROUGH."

Shit! He could hear Daniel pushing his way through the throng. Oliver allowed himself another brief look behind – a cursory glance over the shoulder. It was almost biblical... how the crowd were parting for his uniform-clad chaser.

With his adrenalin racing, Oliver grabbed a propped-up bicycle and pushed it to the ground as he ran. That'll slow him down, he thought – but it didn't. If anything, his one-handed feeble attempt had cost him time.

To his left – the market stalls – more people. It felt as though – almost lemming-like – they were being drawn towards him. Oliver, his senses now overloading, felt suffocated – but he knew for certain that he needed to keep going – he needed to press on.

Moving forwards, he saw a chink within the bustling horde. The bag-carrying mass had started to thin, and with a sudden deftness, Oliver took full advantage – and once again, fuelled by pulsating desire, he gained momentum.

And if it wasn't prison, would *they* kill him? If he was caught... would his own family kill him?

Don't be stupid, Oliver. You fucking idiot.

But was he? Was he being stupid to think that he faced a life of incarceration? Was he being a fucking idiot for fearing the noose? The unknown was taunting him – he felt trapped.

He was now on Turnpin Lane, passing what would eventually become the Copperpot shop – he knew that at best he was four, maybe five minutes from home – from sanctuary. Then the bastards would pay – it would be their turn to suffer. Yes, he'd have to say sorry – yes, he'd have to live with his father's scorn – but Isaac would never be custodian – and these fucking Bradbeers would never exist. Oliver had made it through the market.

"Ale please, Joseph…" Passing the Ship Tavern, Oliver thought about the deaths – Payne's, Wells' – Fletcher's. There was no longer any remorse – he didn't have time for that – he didn't have time for weakness.

Into the college grounds. Although there were no crowds to slow him down – there were no crowds to slow *them* down either. He knew they weren't far behind – he could hear the iron segs on their shoes, sparking on the stone pathway, he could hear the deep panting as their lungs demanded more air – they were getting louder, getting faster – worse still, they were getting closer.

Oliver, digging deep, drew on his last reserves – this was his domain – his time. Knowledge must surely give him the upper hand, he thought. As he ran past the Pepys Building, home of the racket courts, he looked round again. They were still there – still on his tail.

And if he made it home – made it through the door – would *they* follow? *Could* they? What about the rules? What about the God-damned friggin' rules?

As he darted along the Thames footpath, flashbacks were playing in his mind – of the night he'd been chased by the so-called press gang. If only he had the Bulldog now, if only he could pull its trigger one more time – bang, you're fucking dead.

Oliver, laughing wildly, played out the scene as he headed for the King Charles Court.

Shit! Look…to the right.

One of them was cutting across the college parade grounds. If he got there first – to Flamsteed – then all would be lost. Oliver felt drained – his legs suddenly felt heavy. His purpose began to fade.

"Stop, Oliver." It was Jason… shouting at him. "Stop this, now."

What the hell are you doing?

Oliver had stopped – but so had Jason.

The two antagonists – rivals in time – were both gasping for air; standing no more than fifteen feet apart, they faced one another. Oliver took one pace backwards – Jason took one forwards.

"Stop this?" cried Oliver, taking another step back. "And do what? Hang?"

"But you wouldn't, would you?" Jason spoke calmly. "This is your time, Oliver… you've done nothing wrong here, have you?"

Jason was right, he hadn't. But what if he handed himself over… what if he let *them* take him? Would he have to face life on a prison hulk or would a date with some 18th century gallows await him? Or worse – Australia?

"Then, just leave me alone… let me go home," shouted Oliver, this time taking two steps back.

"If only it was that easy… You could always use your bracelet… and go back to whenever you came from."

"It *is* that easy… Haven't you done enough damage

445

already?" Oliver waved his stump. "This is your doing."

"I know," sighed Jason. "I know… and don't you think I'm sorry? Don't you think I regret it?"

He's lying, Oliver. Look at his eyes… he's lying. You've got to run, Oliver. RUN.

He did. Having already lined up his escape route – Oliver bolted through the archway to his left. Jason followed.

Oliver shot through the second arch and entered the central courtyard. "For fuck's sake…" It was Daniel – he was running towards him now.

To Oliver's right there were three options. Steps up – offices, he'd be trapped. Steps down – if his memory was right, the laundry. Oliver, choosing the third option, barged open a pair of doors and entered the King Charles lecture rooms – with Daniel Bradbeer two seconds behind, Oliver slammed and locked the door. Disturbing desks and chairs as he passed, Oliver hurtled to the far door, and exited onto the parade ground. Albeit temporarily, he'd escaped from his pursuers.

"Impressed?"

A little – but which way now? They'll come round both sides again.

"I know… that's why we're going this way."

Not only had Oliver used his brief respite to cool down and rest – he'd also used it to plan. To the right of the door he'd just come through, behind some waist-height black railings was another set of steps which led down to the laundry. Bounding down them two at a time, Oliver made his way to the King Charles Court basement, entered and then latched the door securely behind him.

Brilliant plan. Phelix was being sarcastic. *What are you gonna do now, though? Sit here until you die?*

"Shh, will you! Voices - they're outside."

"Anything?"

That's Jason.

"No. But the door... he's definitely come out."

That's Daniel. They're both panting – you can't have closed that door, moaned Phelix.

"Have you tried the basement?"

Oliver could hear the iron segs clicking on the steps as one of the Bradbeer brothers descended. With each step taken, the noise grew louder. Oliver's heartbeat quickened as the sound from the sole-protectors grated at him. Had he latched the door properly? Had he missed something? He couldn't help but think he had. The door moved – Oliver flashed back to The Ship – room seven – Marlow – it had been the same – only this time he was the one being hunted.

"Locked."

Exhaling the deep breath he'd held, Oliver calmed, the door had stood firm. He could hear the footsteps once again – but thankfully, this time, fading.

He'd got no time to relax – he had to keep moving. Oliver knew that time wasn't on his side – but then it never had been.

Grabbing a cadet's tunic from one of the laundry rails, he made his way through the King Charles basement rooms. Of course he'd been here before – the school had brought him a few years back. Apparently, he needed to learn about vaulted ceilings and what have you... not such a waste of time after all, thought Oliver, passing from one room to another.

Oliver… Oliver? Can't you just use the bracelet… go back and start again?

"They want us to do that, don't they? Didn't you hear him? That Jason… he suggested it."

A trap?

"Possibly," sighed Oliver, fastening one of the tunic's many brass buttons. "Home – Flamsteed Way – it's the only option."

Oliver had reached his exit door – go any further and he'd have to turn back. Again there was a set of steps which led up to the King Charles central courtyard – Oliver took them slowly. Save for a couple of cadets who'd chosen not to return home for Christmas – the courtyard was empty.

Hesitantly, Oliver stepped out into the road which ran between the college's courts. He could see one of them – one of his chasers – Daniel – standing at the top end of the Grand Square. Turning up the tunic's collar, Oliver, head down, casually walked in the opposite direction, towards the West Gate.

Rounding the corner of the King William Court, he started to pick up his pace – just as well, he thought – Jason, who was standing on the parade ground, had seen him.

Oliver ran for one of the doors and grabbed the handle; the door was locked. Shit, he thought – that had cost him precious seconds – Jason was almost upon him. Oliver ran for the next door – if this was locked *they* would have him.

He was less than three minutes from home – three minutes from safety. It didn't matter what his father did to him – belt – birch. He'd get over that – perhaps he deserved it anyway – far

448

better than hanging – far better than prison. Then one day, perhaps in ten years or twenty… who would care… he'd be custodian… Oliver Bradbeer would make the rules… Oliver Bradbeer would control time.

The door was open – Oliver ran into the busy kitchens. The clattering behind was a sign that Jason had followed.

"Grab him! Someone stop him," shouted Jason.

Oliver picked up a knife and lashed out wildly. "Come on, then. COME ON." But, faced with a flashing blade, wielded with such fierce venom, none of the kitchen staff moved – none of them interfered.

Jason – palms held up, empty hands on show – stepped closer. "Don't be stupid, Oliver – don't do anything you'll regret."

"You're not going to stop me," ranted Oliver. "I'm gonna make it, you know. Make it home."

"Let me take you – let *us* take you home. I'm sure that, together, *we* can explain things to your father – make him understand."

"NO." Lashing out violently, Oliver launched himself at Jason.

Cut him… make the bastard suffer. Make him feel Death's Sting.

Repeatedly, Oliver slashed at Jason's left arm, cutting through the coat he was wearing, slicing through the shirt. Oliver had one intention – to maim Jason Bradbeer.

Jason was on the back foot – hemmed in by a hot kitchen range, he couldn't go anywhere. Oliver lunged forwards, and as he did so, the knife slid effortlessly into Jason's undefended chest. Watching the fear of death shine in Jason's eyes, Oliver twisted the blade.

"JASON... NO." Daniel had burst through the door.

Run.

In one corner of the kitchen was a large wooden door. Releasing the knife, his hand covered in Jason's blood, Oliver ran for it.

One set of stairs and another door later, he was at the back of Thornhill's masterpiece – the Painted Hall. Officers were seated at the benches enjoying lunch; candles and Christmas for the privileged, scoffed Oliver, fleeing across the black and white tiled floor.

He had barely made it down the three steps to the lower level, when the clash of silver and porcelain hit the floor behind – Daniel. Swiftly passing the herringboned dining tables, Oliver, heart rate quickening, felt that he had the advantage.

The *Cat* – Daniel – having witnessed the death of his brother, was fuelled by his rage. The *Mouse* – Oliver – having gained his revenge, was fuelled by his euphoria. The chase continued.

Sending a valet flying, Oliver jumped down the steps at the end of the dining hall, turned left at the bottom and then headed for the lower level. Even over his trail of petty chaos, Oliver could hear the metal segs in Daniel's shoes rattling across the tiles – he was gradually closing the distance.

Oliver knew what he had to do. Stairs – Ripley's tunnel – spiral – out through the chapel entrance – through the colonnades – negotiate the Romney Road – Park Row – home. If only it was that easy.

Careful.

Phelix's warning came too late. Oliver, descending the stairs too quickly, had slipped and was now in a crumpled heap at the foot of the stairs. Daniel, now at the top, was almost on his shirttails.

Get up and run, you idiot… run!

He did. Oliver, leaving a bloody handprint behind, pushed himself to his feet, and quickly headed down the Chalk Walk corridor – the Ripley tunnel.

The tunnel, with its flaking paint and musty smell, had an off-putting air of dankness about it. Oliver didn't like it down here, the pungent odour was bad enough – but the constant echo of his every movement was worse. The close walls and vaulted ceiling, along with the arched bricked-up windows and stone slabs caused the sound of Oliver's every move to ricochet. His boots, his breathing, his panic, Phelix's interjections – everything – created an unnerving cacophony of tight reverberation. It wasn't long before Daniel, pressing hard at his heels, entered the tunnel and added to the discord.

Once through the last of the tunnel's archways, Oliver took an immediate right, pushed open a door and swiftly started to ascend the narrow spiral staircase – then stopped.

"Excuse me… Excuse me," shouted a man, coming down the stairs.

For fuck's sake! That's all you need.

The voice belonged to a rather portly man, who was carrying a large stack of plates. Oliver pressed himself tight to the spiral's outer wall, whilst the man carefully negotiated its stone steps.

"STOP HIM."

451

Oliver's politeness had cost him dearly – Daniel was upon him – and now, it was only the plate carrier who separated the *Mouse* from the *Cat*.

"CAN'T YOU JUST LEAVE ME ALONE?" Oliver, grabbing hold of the iron handrail for support, ferociously kicked out.

With the sole of his boot well placed, Oliver sent the large man, the plates, and Daniel crashing to the stone floor below. He then swung round, and ran upwards.

Oliver could hear the choir singing in the Queen Mary Court chapel – Christmas carols, he thought, as he pulled open a heavy exit door and ran out onto the colonnade pathway.

Hark how all the Welkin rings,

Glory to the King of Kings…

"I think you'll find it's 'Hark the Herald Angels sing'," panted Oliver, whose running pace now resembled a slow trot.

Think you'll find I'm singing the original – not that bloody cover version those witches were wailing.

It was plain sailing now, thought Oliver, dropping his speed down to that of a fast walk. Through the gap between the pillars, over the lawns, across the road and home.

Once on the lawn, Oliver removed the cadet's tunic and headed for the Romney Road. Given that the country was at war, and given that the Romney Road was the most direct route to the Cinque Ports, it was understandable that the traffic flow would not only be constant – it would also be heavy. Troop carriers, horse-drawn artillery units and motorcycle despatch riders all blended in with local buses, trucks, cars and drays. Oliver had nearly made it – or had he?

There was movement – fast movement – hurtling towards him from the right. It was Daniel, he was running – at high speed – along the colonnade's pathway. Oliver threw the tunic to ground and ran. The chase had resumed once more.

The road was what – perhaps a hundred yards away? If Donaldson could cover that in under ten seconds, surely Oliver could do it in twenty.

At eighty yards – Oliver's heart was racing.

At seventy – his mouth had dried. Through the corner of his eye the *Mouse* could see the *Cat* leaping rapidly towards him.

Sixty yards to the road – Oliver's lungs, stretched to the max, felt like they wanted to burst open. Even though he was crossing the grass, Oliver could hear Daniel's feet pounding in pursuit.

Fifty yards – midpoint – ten seconds to the road. Drained of stamina, Oliver was being propelled by nothing more than a desire to win.

Forty yards – and with his sides about to split – Oliver could hear Daniel's erratic breathing – it was as though he was right by him – bellowing into his ear.

Thirty yards – an image of Annie, standing in the enclosure, flashed before him – how lovely she looked.

Twenty yards – the footpath was in sight. Oliver – head left, head right – looked for a gap within the traffic, one he could aim for. One which, at the very least, would see him safely to halfway across.

Fifteen yards – another image of Annie, slumped before him – covered in her own blood – how much he loved that woman – how much he missed her.

Ten yards to the road – Daniel was what? Five, perhaps six feet behind him. There were to be no second chances, Oliver had seen his gap.

Five yards – Oliver, swerving through pedestrians, was on the footpath. His timing was perfect – after the omnibus – before the horse carriage – Daniel would have no choice, he'd have to stop. Oliver had decided that, once home, he was going to tell his father everything... perhaps his father might be able to save Annie.

Oliver put his head down as he ran out into the road. He could hear the carriage driver hurling abuse at him as he struggled to regain control of his startled horses.

Now, pausing in the centre of the road, all Oliver had to do was allow an approaching wagon to pass, then he'd be virtually home and dry.

"Come on," muttered Oliver, walking against the flow of traffic. "Get out of the fucking way."

With the wagon now clear, Oliver looked up.

Fuck... I never expected to see him again.

On the opposite side of the Romney Road, fresh from a trip to Tec-Spa – Jason-friggin'-Bradbeer. Standing next to him, with a cricket bat resting on one shoulder and a look of revenge in her eye, was... "Sarah Bradbeer."

Sarah, taking a step forwards, swung the cricket bat over her head – she was taunting him.

Run back – the way you came.

The omnibus had moved on, but as Oliver turned, in his panic to escape, he fell heavily in front of the carriage.

Within seconds, and with Oliver Bradbeer lying face down

underneath the hooves of two Clydesdale horses, the whole of the Romney Road was brought to a chaotic standstill.

With the carriage driver cursing for the second time and carefully steering the horses away, both Jason and Dan ran over to where Oliver had been trampled.

"Get his bracelet before he dies," instructed Jason, pulling frantically at the ring on Oliver's finger. "We can't have him sodding off to Tec-Spa."

Dan, not very sympathetically, ripped at Oliver's shirt sleeve. "He's not wearing one."

"He's got to have one somewhere," snapped Jason, who was clearly agitated. "Check his pockets."

Sarah, barging her way through the melee of people who'd gathered around the scene, joined her brothers. "Here, let me," she said, kneeling beside Oliver.

"Wouldn't bother... I've found it," declared Dan, who was holding a platinum travel bracelet, which he'd removed from Oliver's pocket. "He won't be going anywhere."

"Well done, Dan," smiled Sarah, removing Oliver's left boot. "But I think you've missed this one."

Sarah, using a pair of side cutters, removed the glowing bracelet from around Oliver's left ankle. "Now, he's definitely not going anywhere," she proclaimed, with a voice of authority.

"Sarah?" Dan looked puzzled.

"Oh. Just something Ben Abbott told me about," bragged Sarah, putting both cutters and bracelet in her pocket.

Several minutes later a white LCC ambulance arrived to take Oliver to the South-Eastern, Deptford. As Jason and Dan helped place Oliver's inert body onto a stretcher, Sarah, for one last time, checked him for a pulse – she didn't find one.

Gently, Sarah placed Oliver's arm under the blanket he'd been covered with, and, shaking her head slowly from side to side, lifted the blanket to cover Oliver's face.

"I'll go with him," said Jason, climbing into the back of the ambulance. "You two get off home... it's been a long day."

As the ambulance disappeared and the Romney Road returned to a modicum of normality, a solitary man, standing on the lawn of the Queen's House, raised his collar against the chill.

Edward Bradbeer, heavy of heart, lowered his head and whispered a small prayer for his lost son. Then, with the closing 'Amen' still echoing in his mind, Edward resolutely turned away, and began the short walk home to his wife, Jane.

CHAPTER 50

Abide with Me
St. Alfege's, Greenwich

Isaac hadn't lied when he'd told Oliver that he'd been to his memorial – or when he'd told him there was no body. He had – and there wasn't.

As soon as Sarah had removed Oliver Bradbeer's bracelet, that was it – he'd become just another fragile human being. It had been Jason who'd whisked him away – taken Oliver to where he would eventually exhale his last breath – to where he'd die.

Edward hadn't objected. His son – his own flesh and blood for God's sake – had not only failed *him* – he'd also failed the Bradbeer heritage. It was Edward's own failure – the simple fact of being Oliver's father – for which he fell on his sword, and for which he would, in a few years time, hand custodianship of The Time Store to Philip, his brother.

During his sermon, Reverend Tackley spoke highly of Oliver, of his achievements in both education and theology. Of his love of history and his passion for Greenwich – of a future which might have been.

The priest spoke at great length about the strength in the

bond between father and son, about the bond between God, the Father… and God, the Son. He concluded the service by committing the memory of Greenwich's lost son, Oliver Bradbeer, into the trust of the Lord. Then finally, with spirits raised, Reverend Tackley led a packed congregation as they raised the roof of St. Alfege's with their rendition of Lyte's *Abide with Me*.

Edward, requesting some time alone, knelt at the altar. As the congregation cleared, his thoughts drifted to where he'd gone wrong – to the mistakes he'd made. Had he been too hard on his son? Too soft? What would he do differently, if he could have the time again?

An anguished Edward walked down the aisle towards the exit, towards his Jane. He noticed that he hadn't been alone in confessing his grief. There was a man, on the final pew, head bowed in prayer – Edward joined him.

"Thank you for coming."

The man responded with the faintest of nods.

"And thank you for stopping him."

"You must understand… We had no choice."

"I do… Trust me, I do." Edward, a tear rolling down his cheek, sounded lost. He gazed around the church – perhaps in search of a sign of sorts – none came. "But what next?"

"In your diary… your journal. You write of moving to Menston."

"Yorkshire?"

"Yes… apparently you and Jane are happy there. So I'm guessing that's as a good a place as any to start."

"Perhaps you're right…"

458

There was no reply – David Bradbeer, having paid his respects, had placed his palm to bracelet and returned to his own time.

CHAPTER 51

Hope

Christmas at The Time Store had been far noisier than in recent years, far more festive as well. Once again Jason and Dan, much to the disgruntlement of their neighbours at No.9, had strapped their enormous inflatable snowman to the wall of No.7 – which, according to the complaints, lowered the appeal of Flamsteed Way.

With his sons busy annoying the neighbours, David, with a little help from young Charlie, decorated the family Christmas tree and then emptied two large sacks of presents under its boughs. Lisa, who'd been given firm instructions that she was to do nothing but rest, was brought to tears when she noticed that several of the gifts had Charlie's name on the tags.

"But, how? I mean…" she sobbed. "When did you get these?"

"Twenty-four hour shopping is amazing, isn't it?" was David's reply, at which both Sarah and Alice laughed.

The big day itself was as expected – the music blasted, the alcohol flowed and the turkey was troughed.

Emma was more than impressed with Dan's culinary skills – cooking for twelve wasn't a task she'd have enjoyed doing. Although, when it came to the dessert, she did help with the brandy sauce.

"Look at him," said Lisa, happily watching her son on Grandpa Lane's lap. "All those blinking gadgets and gizmos and his favourite present is a Mickey Mouse watch."

"Ah," laughed Victoria. "It might be a Mickey Mouse watch… but trust me, it's no ordinary Mickey Mouse watch."

When dinner was over David, along with his parents and in-laws, disappeared to his apartment for some much-needed peace and quiet. "Any excuse to get out of the pots," moaned Jason.

Boxing Day saw the Lanes leave and Rhiannon arrive. Lisa's bruising had all but cleared, and what little remained was easily concealed with some strategically applied foundation. For the first time since her arrival in London, Lisa felt confident in her appearance, and was able to leave Flamsteed Way. So whilst Dan, Jason, Sarah and Emma were helping out over at St. Michael's hostel, Alice and Rhiannon took Lisa and Charlie out for a day visiting Greenwich's delights.

A late dinner at the Plume meant there was to be no cooking in the Bradbeer household that day. Instead, both family and friends laughed and joked well into the night – except for a tired Charlie, who was sparked out by 8pm and had to be carried off to bed.

After breakfast on the Saturday it was time for the Bradbeer siblings to say goodbye to their grandparents.

"So we'll see you about ten, then?" said Victoria, getting into David's car. "If you change your mind though, and want to come another day… you will let me know, won't you?"

"Yes, Gran," replied Sarah. "New Year's Day is good…

Hopefully there'll be less traffic about. Don't forget to call the home and sort it out."

"I already have, my dear. I spoke to them a few days ago."

Sarah, ever-impressed with how well organised her grandmother was, gave her a kiss goodbye and then joined her brothers in waving the car off.

"How did it go then?" called Sarah, walking into her apartment.

"As expected," sighed Lisa, trembling.

"Oh, that good, eh?!" Sarah gave Lisa a reassuring smile.

"He didn't care about us... he never asked how Charlie was – whether he missed him," cried Lisa. "All he did was rant about money... his money."

"I'm sure he cared... he might not have said so... but I'm sure he did," lied Sarah. She didn't have the faintest idea whether Brian cared or not – but her words offered some calmness – and that's what mattered.

"Money... God... he's obsessed by it. Truth is..." said Lisa, tears flowing again. "I... I really don't know what he's going on about."

Sarah closed her eyes and sighed. She thought about her secret for a moment, about Elsie. Yes, she'd told Lisa that they'd been to Birmingham to discuss Brian's adoption, but Sarah hadn't told Lisa about Apple Tree, about the possible inheritance – it wasn't her place to do that. "And Kathleen? Did you manage to call her?"

"Yes." Lisa perked up. "And Charlie did... He told her all about our Christmas... about his watch from Santa... Nannie was so pleased."

"That's good… I was thinking… do you mind if I kidnap him for the day? Take him to see the Queen and perhaps a ride on the Eye."

"I think that's a brilliant idea," said Emma, coming in from the kitchen with a packet of biscuits. "Lisa can come shopping with me and Alice. A bit of retail therapy would do you the world of good… don't you think?"

But, a couple of days later, Brian had succeeded in making Lisa very scared. Not scared for her own safety, not even scared for Charlie's – she was scared for Kathleen's. Brian, hell bent on claiming what was 'rightfully his' had, that morning, resorted to using threats against his *mother*. Sarah was convinced – she had to act.

By the time New Year's Day had arrived, thanks to Sarah's reassurance, Lisa had relaxed.

"Come on, Charlie. Put Dan down and get in the car will you… Sarah's waiting," shouted Lisa, laughing at her son trying to cling onto Dan's shoulder. "We don't want to be late, do we?"

"You know what to do?"

"Yes, sis. Don't worry… He'll be in good company," replied Jason. "Enjoy your day… and give 'Philomena' our love."

Sarah, allowing herself an 'I told you so' smile, pulled away.

It was just before noon when Sarah, who'd stopped off at Copthorne to pick up her grandmother, pulled into the car park at Parkside Nursing Home.

"Morning." They were greeted at the home's conservatory entrance door by a very cheerful Lizzie. "Come on in. Elsie's expecting you."

"Thank you," smiled Victoria.

They were shown into one of Parkside's more private residential lounges, one which the home normally reserved for more sombre occasions. "Do make yourselves at home," said Lizzie. "Now, can I get you some tea? And biscuits of course," she said, tipping a wink at young Charlie.

A few minutes had gone by (according to Charlie it was actually two minutes and forty-three seconds) when a young care assistant entered and held the lounge door open.

Sarah leaned toward Lisa. "They must be bringing Elsie in now."

"Nobody's bringing me in..." said Elsie, shuffling into the room under her own steam.

"Wow!" Sarah couldn't believe it. "Look at you."

It had been the phone call that Victoria had made before Christmas which had made the difference. News of a grandson had given Elsie good reason – good reason to eat, good reason to take her medication, good reason to try, and a very good reason to live.

The afternoon passed by quickly, lots of talking, laughing and reminiscing – Grandma Elsie even read Charlie a story from his favourite book – something she'd been longing to do.

Elsie didn't ask about her son, and no one talked about him. What wasn't talked about... couldn't be lied about. Having her grandson was more than she ever could have wished for.

When it was time to leave, Lisa and Charlie presented Elsie

with some parting gifts. Charlie's gift, as selected by Victoria, was a silver photo frame – all he needed to do now was to give his Grandma Elsie a big hug and smile for the camera – Sarah would take care of the rest.

In return, Elsie gave Charlie two gifts. The first – a neatly wrapped parcel, no longer than a shoebox. The second – a small envelope.

Lisa didn't have much to give, what little money she'd escaped with was all but spent, and there was no way she was going to allow Sarah to buy the gift for her.

"I want you to have this," said Lisa, removing her tree of life necklace and clasping it around Elsie's neck. "Other than Charlie it's the most precious thing I own. It was a gift from my mother… and in some way I'd like to think of it as being a link – a link to Charlie's two grandmothers."

"That's so sweet," said Victoria. "What a beautiful thought."

Sarah recognised the necklace. The first time she'd seen it was at the flats… when Lisa was covered in bruises. "The word at the bottom? What does it say?" asked Sarah.

"Hope," answered Lisa.

"Well, you've certainly given me that," smiled Elsie.

"And a grandson," added Victoria.

Elsie then turned to Sarah, as though seeking her approval for what she was about to do – Sarah smiled and nodded that all was okay.

"Now, Lisa. Open up your hand, I've got a gift for you." Elsie opened her purse and removed two keys. "These are for my cottage – for Apple Tree – I want you to have them. It's yours now, yours and Charlie's – I want Apple Tree to be your new home."

Lisa, after some moments of disbelief, reassurance, amazement, acceptance, and gratitude, gave Elsie a hug – a huge hug. For the first time in recent memory, the tears that flowed in Parkside's small private lounge were tears of joy.

Charlie hadn't seen his mother and grandmother exchanging gifts, he'd been far too busy opening his own. "Mommy… Look what I've got… It's a digging stick."

Lisa laughed. "Silly sausage… It's a trowel, and what have you got there?"

"Some flowers…"

"They're leeks, Charlie," said Elsie. "And when you're in your new home… I'll come and show you where to plant them… If you don't mind, that is."

"And Grandma Kathleen?" asked Charlie, all excited.

"Yes… and Grandma Kathleen," smiled Elsie.

CHAPTER 52

Asylum

Night had drawn in quickly, or so it had seemed. The heavy rain, howling wind and violent sky had prematurely darkened the winter's evening. Without warning, a torrential storm had turned civil dusk into a thunderous night.

A dark blue Vauxhall Velox, which had trundled slowly down the hospital's gravelled driveway, pulled up outside the entrance to the gothic-styled lunatic asylum. With umbrella pulling hard to break free, a young nurse descended the five stone steps and waited for the Velox's passenger to emerge.

"Doctor Parker. Welcome to High Royds... I'm sorry that the weather couldn't be a bit more welcoming, though," shouted the nurse, fighting to be heard against the wind.

Dr Colin Parker had recently been appointed Head of the West Riding Pauper Lunatic Asylums. Today, he was making his first visit to High Royds, a modern asylum capable of holding 1300 patients in the leafy green village of Menston, West Yorkshire.

Dr Parker had previously held an experimental post at Colchester's Severalls Mental Hospital where he was a much celebrated pioneer of electro-convulsive therapy and the use of frontal lobotomy. He was now seen as a highly regarded trophy in asylum circles, a prize the West Riding committee members were pleased to have.

After spending two hours in the company of Dr Stephen Cherry, High Royd's manager, dutifully inspecting the various facilities – kitchens, wards, recreational and rehabilitation units – Dr Parker turned his attention to the patients.

"Are you sure you'd rather not return when the weather is more favourable?" asked Dr Cherry, as forked lightning cracked against the night.

"I'm fine," replied Dr Parker. "A bit of rain never hurt anyone."

"Shall we start with the incurables?" There was no answer. "I mean… Shall we start with…"

"I know what you mean," interrupted Dr Parker. "And, yes. It's as good a place to start as any."

The two men entered a long basement corridor. On a bench, half reading – half dozing, sat the area's night warden, a man who was obviously more interested in counting sheep than counting those in his care. A man who, come tomorrow, would be after a new job.

"And who do we have here?" asked Dr Parker, staring through the peephole of the first room.

"Jean," replied Dr Cherry. "Jean Stead."

Jean sat tucked away in the far corner of her green padded room, thumb in mouth, rocking herself slowly from side to side. At first glance she looked as though she was in her fifties… but if anyone had the chance to pass her on the street, when she was *dressed* for church perhaps, then they'd have said she looked in her twenties.

Dr Parker quickly flicked through Jean's notes, and made a suggestion. "Lobotomy – we'll do it next Tuesday."

Leaving Jean, the two men swiftly moved on down the corridor. Dr Cherry handed Dr Parker the next patient's notes.

"And who do we have here?"

"Gates, sir. Brian Gates."

"What's his story?" asked Dr Parker, looking into the room.

"Tried to kill his own mother," replied Dr Cherry. "Keeps rambling on about money… Reckons she's hiding millions from him. Poor old woman hasn't got two pennies to her name."

"Lobotomy it is, then… Might calm him down, don't you think?"

Dr Cherry nodded in agreement. "Next, we have a strange one. Bit of a war hero… France."

"France?"

"Yes. There's a couple… living in the village. Seem to have taken a shine to him… he reminds them of their son apparently."

"And his diagnosis?" asked Dr Parker.

"Multiple personality disorder."

"Let's take a look at him, then," Dr Parker suggested.

Dr Cherry unlocked the door and the two men walked into the room. "Good evening… and who do we have today?"

The man turned and looked Dr Cherry in the eye, and smiled. "Oliver… Oliver Bradbeer."

Ask him if he's seen the bracelet… tell him we need it… Go on, ask him.

"Patience… I will."

Ask him, NOW.

"SHUT UP, PHELIX… Can't you see I'm talking to these nice men?"

END

For news and updates about the forthcoming adventures of the Bradbeer family, follow The Time Store on Facebook.

https://www.facebook.com/The.Time.Store

Greenwich Maps

A selection of maps highlighting the ever changing face of Greenwich.

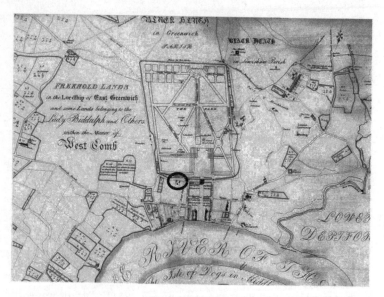

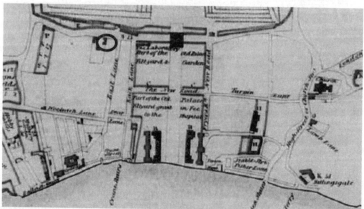

Samuel Travers map c1695   Circled ~ The Plume of Feathers (1691)

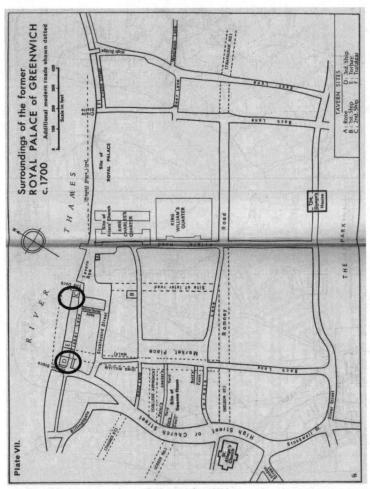

Greenwich c1700
Circled (top) ~ 18th Century Ship Tavern
Circled (bottom) ~ 19th Century Ship Tavern
Compare the development of the Greenwich Hospital on the Travers
map ~ could possibly cast doubts on which map was produced first.
(Note: The word "hospital" was used in its original sense of a place
providing hospitality for those in need of it, and did not refer to
medical care, although the buildings included an infirmary.)

Greenwich 1746
Circled ~ St Alfege's Church
(Note: No development on north bank of river).

Darton's map of Greenwich c1817
Circled ~ Flamsteed Way
(Note: Deptford development in the bottom right... still no visible
development across river or to the right of Greenwich Park)

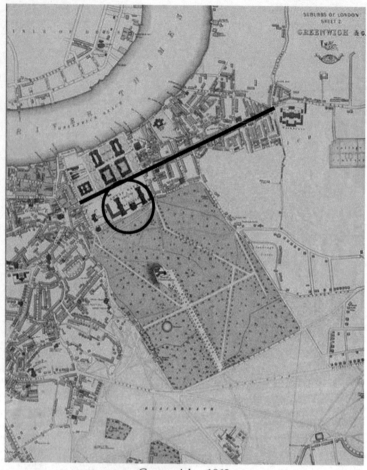

Greenwich ~ 1862
Much has changed since the 1817 Darton map.
The Romney Road (black line) now cuts through both East Street and
Park Row. Greenwich has vastly developed on either side of the park.
The Royal Navel Asylum (circled) a school for orphans of naval
personnel killed in action whilst defending Britain's interests has been
built. This will later go on to be the Royal Hospital School and
eventually The National Maritime Museum.

476

By now Dutch engineers have drained the marshlands on The Isle of Dogs, and although out of map both the West and East India docks are now over fifty years old.

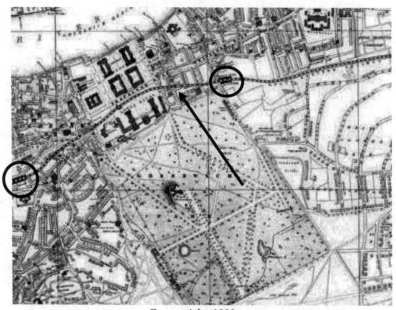

Greenwich ~1888

Greenwich now boasts a railway line, which built using the cut and cover construction method, mainly runs under the borough. Greenwich (L) and Maze Hill (R) stations are both circled. The Greenwich Park line hasn't as yet been built. The arrow points to the location of Flamsteed Way.

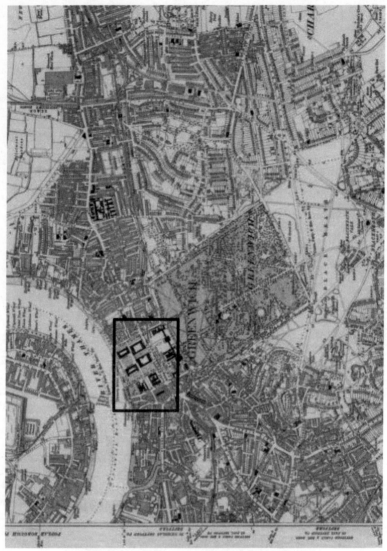

Ordinance Survey Map, Greenwich ~ 1915
Highlighted section on next page shows the route taken by
Oliver/Phelix whilst being chased by Dan and Jason.